"WHAT'S THE MATTER?" SHE TEASED. "CAN'T STAND MY COMPANY?"

"I've got troubles, Rachel. Things I've done. People I've…disappointed."

"You haven't disappointed me," she said gently.
A rueful feeling shot through him. "Not yet, anyway."

Rachel peered at him, wondering about the secrets he was hiding. "Everyone sins, Nick. You ask for forgiveness, you make peace with yourself, you move on."

"There is no forgiveness for some things."

"Then you learn to live with them."

"I'm trying." He gave a short, mocking laugh. "I just can't seem to get the hang of it."

She touched the back of his hand, her common sense gone in a rush of sympathy. "Maybe you need help. A friend."

He looked down at her hand. Her slim fingers rested lightly on top of his, and he was tempted. God, he was so tempted…

Please turn to the back of this book for a preview of Annie Solomon's upcoming novel, *Dead Ringer*.

LIKE A KNIFE

ANNIE SOLOMON

WARNER BOOKS

An AOL Time Warner Company

Cover design and art by Tom Iafuri

Warner Books, Inc.
1271 Avenue of the Americas
New York, NY 10020

 An AOL Time Warner Company

ISBN 0-7394-3369-5

Printed in the United States of America

To the Tuesday Night Club—Beth, Trish and GayNelle—and to my cyberfriends Linda and Jo. I couldn't have done this without your friendship and support, not to mention the red ink.

To Becca, for all the lunches and dinners with my many imaginary friends. Finally, you'll get to read about them.

And to Larry, who brainstormed even when he was brain-dead. My rock, my shelter, my love.

Acknowledgments

I'd like to thank everyone who read the manuscript in its early stages—online and off—particularly Jean Brashear, who offered gracious and continuous encouragement.

Thanks also to all who helped make this book as accurate as possible. To Patricia Hamblin of the Wilson County Sheriff's Department and to Cassondra Murray and Steve Allen Doyle for the help with guns and weaponry. To Mike Rosen of Kroll Background America for talking to me about background checks. And, finally, to Drs. David Allen and David Schmidt for their medical knowledge and willingness to help with information on wounds and their aftermath. Any mistakes are my own.

When will redemption come?
When we master the violence that fills our world.

New Union Prayer Book

LIKE
A KNIFE

Chapter 1

The duplex stood bald and cramped in the gray morning light. It was barely six, and Rachel Goodman watched the building through the windshield of her car. Her glance swept over the place, taking in the black iron security door that sagged on its hinges and the peeling green paint on the shutters. She sighed a short, determined breath, swung the end of her French braid off her shoulder, and got out of her father's battered VW Beetle.

How would you have handled the Murphys, Dad?

Stupid question. The late, great David Goodman would have made a speech and picketed the place.

Pressing the doorbell, she waited for an answer; when none came, she knocked. She knew they were home. Mr. Murphy worked the night shift and should have only just returned. And there were all those kids. She rapped on the door again and kept it up until she heard the sound of a baby crying and Cecile Murphy's irritated voice from inside.

"Awright, awright, I'm coming, for crissakes. Jesus, who the—" The door opened. The woman in front of Rachel wore a faded nightgown and a shabby bathrobe that didn't quite meet around her swelling middle. She shifted a baby in her arms, not seeming to notice its screams. Another small face peered at Rachel from behind the woman's leg. In the background, the blare of cartoons blended with the sound of children fighting.

"Who are you? It's six in the morning, f' God's sake."

"I'm sorry, Mrs. Murphy. I know it's early, but you haven't returned my phone calls—"

"Shut up!" Cecile shouted over her shoulder. "The both of you! And turn that thing down, Eddie. You wanna wake your father?" She swung back to Rachel and gave her a narrow look. "You're that teacher, aren't you?"

"Yes, I'm Rachel Goodman. Look, could I . . . could I come in for a moment? I'd like to talk to you."

Cecile blocked the doorway. "I don't think it would be such a good idea. Mike—that's Mr. Murphy—he don't want little Carla going to no Catholic school."

"You know it's not a Catholic school. It's in a Catholic church, but I run the school, there are no nuns. It's a special program for children who have been victims of violence, like Carla. Look, your niece has been happy at St. Anthony's. She'd just started playing again."

"Well, she's still as dumb as a lamppost."

Rachel reined in her temper. Carla's mother had been stabbed to death in front of the child. How could Rachel explain to this woman what that experience was like? How the white ice of terror froze you up inside? Rachel's own memories surged to the surface, but she pushed them away. "Sometimes it takes a while for kids to speak again. No one knows exactly what happened that night. She doesn't feel safe yet."

Cecile's chin jutted out defiantly. "I got kids of my own who don't go to no fancy school. I don't have money enough for them, why should we spend it on her?"

Of all the selfish, ignorant—Rachel bit down on the words before they could escape. "I can get a grant or a donation. If I can get the fees paid, would you change your mind?"

"We don't take charity. Besides, I got four kids and another on the way. I don't have time to be carting Her Majesty off to some private day care." Without another word, she slammed the door in Rachel's face.

Rachel stared at the door, stunned into immobility. Then she turned to go, shoulders drooping in defeat. *You can't save everyone.* But knowing it in her head and knowing it in her heart were two different things.

She trudged back to her car, fumbled for the keys, and let herself inside. Hands on the steering wheel, she waited a beat to restore her equilibrium before pulling away. Although it was still early, traffic was already thickening. She inched along, reliving the scene with Carla's aunt.

You haven't failed.

Yeah, tell that to Carla.

When she got to Astoria, she shoehorned the ancient Beetle into a parking space a few blocks from St. Anthony's. Reaching for her tote bag and purse, she tried to put the morning fiasco behind her. She'd wait a few days, try the Murphys again. Besides, she had other things to think about. Like the letter she'd received yesterday. *Thank you for your grant application, but due to budget cuts we have been forced to turn down some very worthy projects.*

God, she was tired of begging. Hadn't she had enough to last a lifetime? First, she'd begged St. Anthony's for free space to house her special preschool, then she'd begged a hodgepodge of charities for grants, next she'd be begging on the street.

She slammed the car door and faced the gritty streets of New York's largest borough. In front of her, a neon sign idiotically blinked OPEN over and over again, even though the gyros place was closed until later in the afternoon. Just like her. Closed but not shut down. Not yet.

She marched the few blocks to the church, past the tiny Greek butcher shop and the discount shoe store on the corner. Mentally, she ticked off all the things she needed. Decent art supplies, a new playground, a staff psychologist so she wouldn't have to depend on piecemeal volunteers, and most important of all, another home. That was what the grant application had been for—to buy a run-down house she could turn into a permanent home for her preschool. She had six weeks left on her agreement with the church. She tried not to panic, but time was running out.

She thought of one place to go for the money, then quickly dismissed it. Though they were wealthy enough, her aunt and uncle were not exactly supportive of her work with children. Of course, there was always Chris. But even her cousin had never been good at getting his parents to see how important her school was.

She ran around the back of the church and through the gate in the sagging metal fence that enclosed the ramshackle playground. Someday the begging would end. She'd find the money to turn her school into a real institute, a place where every child who experienced violence would have a soothing place to heal.

But right now, all they had was this place. She scanned the woebegone yard, the wobbly picnic bench and half-bald sandbox, the single rusty swing left hanging in the set. She let out a long, slow breath. *One problem at a time. You can't do everything.*

Trudging to the yard door, she twisted the knob. Surprisingly, it didn't give. She checked her watch. Sixthirty. She was early, but she'd been early before, and Nick had always been there ahead of her. Ever since he'd replaced the old church handyman six months ago, Nick had been reliable as the sun. A mystery, but reliable. With a grunt of irritation, she dug in her purse for the key, found it eventually, and opened the door.

She inhaled the smell as she stepped inside. Paste and finger paint and the peculiar smell that signaled children. The tight ball in her stomach relaxed a bit. Maybe Father Pat would have some emergency fund-raising ideas. Rachel wasn't Catholic, and her children came from many religious backgrounds, but if Father Pat spoke for her and her program, his voice might be loud enough to drown out Bill Hughes and the other members of the Parish Council who would be glad to see the back of her and her kids. If she could extend their agreement, she'd have time to find another grant.

As she strode down the hall to her office, she noticed the open classroom doors, chairs down from the desks and ready for the day. If Nick wasn't there, who had set up the chairs?

She got her answer when she reached her office and saw him asleep behind her desk. *Terrific, now I'm running a homeless shelter.* But if he needed a place to stay, surely the couch in the church kitchen was far more comfortable than that old, tippy chair.

She leaned against the doorjamb and crossed her arms, watching him sleep. His big, rangy body overwhelmed the rickety executive chair, and for once his face looked serene. The heavy black brows and tough, craggy lines were almost smooth. If Felice and the other teachers could see him now, they'd stop calling him Mr. Hermit. Or the other names they called him behind his back. Creature from the Black Lagoon. Alley Oop. That was because during the first few weeks Nick used any excuse to stay in the basement. If you needed him, you stood at the top of the steps and called down. Up he'd trudge, like a tired dog.

Yet gradually Rachel had come to realize that Nick's one-word replies, the way he looked through, not at you; the way he finished a job quickly and retreated to the basement—it was all part of a calculated strategy to keep his distance. Like a wind-up toy that was never released, everything about him was an expression of tension—his dark unsmiling eyes, the somber set to his mouth. Even his work shirts were always buttoned up tight to the neck.

A dozen times a day she caught him staring at her. Caught herself staring back. She'd had kids like that. Kids who'd had so much trouble in their lives that anything normal seemed strange. Frozen little lumps of ice, they moved only when prodded and spoke only when spoken to. Like Nick, they looked at her as if she wasn't quite real. Underneath, she saw the same longing in Nick she saw in them. Make it real. Make it stay. Make everything all right again.

She sighed. Whatever his troubles, he wasn't a kid, and she didn't need another project. She had enough to worry about without taking on one more needy soul. Setting down her purse, she walked to the desk and saw what hadn't been obvious from the doorway. A thin film of sweat on his forehead, hands that clutched the chair arms in a death grip, eyes that raced back and forth beneath closed lids.

He was dreaming.

And from his body language, it wasn't a pleasant dream.

Gently, she touched his shoulder. "Nick," she whispered, "Nick, wake up."

The instant her hand touched him, his eyes flew open and he leaped from the chair, knees bent, fists clenched in a fighting stance. Only his rapid breathing broke her stunned silence.

"You . . . were asleep," she said at last.

He blinked, straightened slowly. She stared at him in astonishment. He swallowed and looked around at the chair as if amazed to find it there. "I'm . . . God, I'm sorry," he said helplessly.

Rachel waved away the apology. "It's okay, really. I just thought—" She cleared her throat and peered at him. "Are you all right? Do you need a place to stay? I can arrange—" She caught herself, off to the rescue again.

"No, no." He began to inch his way toward the door.

"No, I'm fine. I'm just . . . I had a bad night, and when I couldn't sleep, I . . . I thought I'd get a jump on things."

"If something is bothering you . . . if you want to talk or anything . . ."

He wiped his mouth with the back of his hand; uneasiness flooded his dark eyes. Clearly he was aching to leave. "I'm fine, really. There's nothing. . . . I'll just"—he gestured over his shoulder with his thumb—"go downstairs."

"If you change your mind—"

He nodded and slid out the door.

In the corridor, Nick banged the back of his head against the wall in an agony of embarrassment. Stupid, stupid, stupid. How could he have fallen asleep like that? And the look on her face. As if it mattered. As if *he* mattered.

He shuddered and tried not to think about the dream images still shrouding his head: the shadowed Panamanian street, the knife, the small dark eyes that begged for nothing.

He knew why the dream was back. Because she was back. Shelley Spier. Like a ghost, she'd appeared on his doorstep last night, just as he remembered her. Legs incredibly long, skirt short and tight, hair thickly wild. He hadn't asked why she'd come or what she wanted. It was all over her swollen, bloody face.

"I left him," she said. "Just like you always told me to."

His chest tightened at the memory. Her beautiful face, bruised and battered, her voice pleading with him. *Let me stay here. With you. Just tonight, Nicky. Please.*

And he'd said yes. He'd let her wrap her arms around his neck as she'd once wrapped herself around his heart.

"I've got something," she said in his ear. "I've got something Rennie wants real bad."

He didn't ask her what. He didn't want to know. He'd tucked her into his bed and stayed until she fell asleep. Then he left.

Once, he would have headed for the first bar he saw. Last night, he just headed into the street, that nightmare name vibrating inside his head.

Rennie Spier.

Merchant of death and saver of wayward children. Purveyor of guns and plastique. Friend to all the little places with names no one could spell and ancient grievances to war over. Friend to him.

But Nick didn't want to think about Rennie. Instead, he concentrated on the lifeless storefronts, dead in the dark. The Guyana Bakery, L'Abelle Salon, Key Foods. When the stores gave out, he counted parked cars. Duplexes turned into apartments and apartments turned into supports for cloverleafs and overpasses. The highway gave way again to liquor stores, drugstores, and used car lots.

Somehow he'd ended up at St. Anthony's. In Rachel's office. He remembered curling his hands over the arms of her chair, closing his eyes. Her calm, comforting presence had stolen over him, and he'd let it come. But he'd only meant to stay a few minutes. A few dreamless minutes.

"Nick?"

He whirled at the sound of Rachel's voice. She stood in the office doorway, a grown-up tomboy in jeans and a loose, white shirt with the sleeves rolled back at the wrists. Her eyes, the color of new pennies, gazed at him with great kindness.

"There's watermelon for ten o'clock snack. Could you bring it outside and give us a hand cutting it up?"

As always, she'd pulled her honey brown hair into a braid that was already starting to fray. Wisps of hair floated around her neck and face, and he longed to touch them. Instead he shoved his hands into the pockets of his work pants. "Sure." He backed down the hallway toward the basement steps. "Ten o'clock. I'll be there."

He hid in the basement, working on a bench for the picnic table in the yard. He was glad to have something to occupy his hands and mind. Something besides his late-night visitor, or the concern in Rachel's face.

A few minutes before ten he brought the melon out to the playground. Children gathered to watch him cut it up. Every pair of eyes seemed to accuse him. Yesterday he would have said he was over that. But today the guilty sickness had reappeared, like the dream. Like Shelley. Last night, his old life had swooped down out of the darkness, and he had opened the door and said, Come in. Was he crazy? It had taken him six years to get free. To numb himself enough to forget. Now, in the space of one night, it had all flooded back.

Which meant no one was safe.

As if his thoughts had sprung from his head and become real, a small hand edged toward the blade he'd just put down.

"Don't touch that!" He smacked away the little fingers.

Snatching the knife, he cut himself in the process.

But now, watching her through the window as she played with Joselito, wistfulness seeped through him.

Stop it.

But he couldn't. Six years ago, a huge iceberg had frozen in his chest, and now it suddenly cracked and split as it thawed inside him.

By six-thirty Nick was shoving a dry mop down the hallway outside Rachel's office, reaching for any excuse to linger.

"No, I can't wait," he heard her say. "I've got twenty kids, and they get snack twice a day. I know you're shorthanded, but I can't explain a work slowdown to a five-year-old."

He leaned against the wall, his arm wrapped around the long handle. He could push that mop all weekend. He didn't want to go home. He didn't know what he would find there. Shelley, maybe. The dream, probably.

He could go to the gym. The punishing physical workout was a refuge—the only time his mind turned off completely. But he didn't go to the gym. Instead, he walked to Rachel's office and stood in the doorway as she impatiently flicked the braid off her shoulder.

"Look, Mr. Ganetti, I'm grateful that Grand Union is making a donation, but if I can't get it delivered, what good is it?" She closed her eyes and rubbed her forehead. "Just tell me how to get there, and I'll pick it up myself. Yes, I understand the cases are heavy, but—"

"I'll go with you."

Rachel glanced up and saw him standing in the doorway. "What? What did you—"

"I'll help you pick it up."

"Wait, Mr. Ganetti, just a minute—" She covered the receiver with her hand and studied him. "We'll have to go tonight. If I don't pick it up tonight, he's going to dump it."

Nick let out a slow, tense breath—what was he doing?—and nodded.

"Problem solved, Mr. Ganetti. Just tell me how to get there." She put her thumb and forefinger together and signed okay to Nick. "Thank you, Mr. Ganetti—from me and the children." She slammed down the phone and fell back into the ancient swivel chair behind her desk. "God, what a pain! But beggars can't be choosers."

She gathered up her keys and wallet. The office was a tiny cubicle, just big enough for a scarred wooden desk and the wobbly executive chair Nick had fallen asleep in. A door led to a larger supply closet, but Nick knew it was mostly filled with recycled greenbar paper. Looking around, he had to admit supplies were thin.

"I'll meet you out front in ten minutes," Rachel said. "Oh, and Nick—" She stopped him with another golden smile before he could turn away. "Thanks."

Shelley Spier scurried down a deserted street in Long Island City, her heart beating fast enough to fly. On either side of her empty warehouses reached up to the sky, blocking out the moon. Broken windows and boarded-up doors stared down like huge faces with blind eyes. A shiver slithered down her back.

Why in God's name had they decided to meet here?
So Rennie won't find you.

But Rennie was everywhere. She could feel him peering down from the warehouses, following her every step.

Suddenly a car zoomed by, and Shelley jumped as if it were Rennie himself. Flattening herself against the side of a building, she watched the car disappear into the shadows.

You're being ridiculous.

She knew it but couldn't help herself. Goose bumps pricked her arms. If Rennie caught her now, a beating was the least of her worries.

Don't let him catch you, then.

No, she wouldn't. She was almost home, almost free. Rennie would never hurt her again. He'd never hurt anyone she loved again.

But first she had to get to the meeting place.

Heart still pounding, eyes searching every empty window, she continued up the street, the click of her high heels echoing on the pavement.

At last she saw what she'd been looking for. On the other side of the road and half a block up, the building with the huge *H* painted on its side. *H* for *haven.* For *hello,* for *help.* She remembered joking about it days ago when they'd finalized their plans. Now, as she stood in the darkness smelling the rank odor of the East River that lurked beyond the decaying warehouses, the letter shouted simply "here." A liquid feeling of relief washed over her.

She was here. She was safe.

She stepped off the curb, looking over her shoulder. What was that? Was someone following her? Crossing the street, she peered into the shadows behind her, ears intent on the slightest sound. But all she heard was a cat in the garbage can. Laughing at her skittishness, she faced the welcoming building and heard the sudden squeal of tires behind her.

Her heart leaped in her chest. She twisted around to pinpoint the car's direction but headlights blinded her.

She didn't even have time to scream.

Chapter 2

It took Nick and Rachel three hours and four trips in Rachel's VW Beetle before they finished transporting the cases of graham crackers and fruit punch from Grand Union's warehouse to St. Anthony's. Afterward, she grabbed a pizza and drove to the marina in Bayside, where she parked beneath a streetlight close to the dock.

In the distance, glittering lights outlined the Throgs Neck Bridge, which dominated the night sky. A few feet away, tethered boats rustled in the water of Little Neck Bay. Nick got out and stretched; he'd be sore tomorrow, but the physical activity had been as good as any workout. And as mindless.

Rachel opened the pizza box on top of the VW's front end. The aroma of tomatoes and garlic wafted out and mingled with the smell of water from the bay and exhaust from the highway nearby.

Nick eyed the dull red hump of the late sixties Beetle,

now faded to the color of a much-washed flannel shirt. Where had she gotten this heap?

Once, he could have picked her up in a limousine and taken her anywhere. Le Cirque, Tavern on the Green. If she wanted pizza, there was Sam's in Brooklyn, where the sauce was made with fresh tomatoes and the cheese homemade. He'd never had pizza like that anywhere else except Italy.

Regret faded when she bit into a slice of pizza and, laughing, pushed the melted strands of cheese off her chin and into her mouth. *Such a pretty mouth.* Brown eyes sparkled mischief, and another shard of ice melted inside him. What would she do in a limousine anyway?

"What's so funny?"

"Nothing."

"Nothing? Must have been pretty good to set you off, Mister Nicholas-Never-Smiles Raine. Look at you—you look like the cat who just swallowed the canary."

Was it true? Was he smiling? God, he was.

He leaned toward her. For a single, startling instant she was close enough to kiss.

Go ahead. You want to, and you haven't wanted to in a long time.

She blushed, and their eyes met.

Starlight mingled with lamplight, and the whole of it bathed Rachel's face in a warm glow. The light made it seem as if her skin were lit from within.

His heart stopped. *Beautiful. So beautiful.*

A breath away, the laughter died in her eyes.

As if in a trance, he saw his hand move to cup her face. In a moment he'd be kissing her.

What are you doing, Nick?

"You have cheese on your chin." He wiped it off, trying not to like the feel of her too much. He glanced away, toward the half-eaten pizza. Toward the water, where the boats glimmered in the bay. Anything but her.

"Thanks," she said softly. "And for helping me out tonight."

He nodded, still not looking at her. "Do you do this kind of thing often?"

"What kind of thing? Pizza in the moonlight?"

A flash of embarrassment went through him, but he turned to find a teasing expression on her face. "I meant Ganetti, donations . . ."

She laughed wryly. "Oh, all the time. You're looking at the beggar queen of St. Anthony's preschool. Donations, grants, loose change . . ."

"Doesn't the church help out?"

"Some." She nibbled at the slice of pizza. "The space comes rent-free, but parish resources are stretched. There's a group on the Parish Council that would like to shut us down so they could rent out the space—rent I can't afford right now." She chomped thoughtfully. "Can't really blame them. Too much to do and not enough to do it with."

"That's because you won't settle for what you can get. You care too much," Nick said.

She smiled ruefully. "Now you sound like Felice. Rachel to the rescue, like I run around in tights and a cape." She shook her head. "Believe me, I'm no superhero. If I was, I would've already figured out a way to rescue the preschool. Caring just comes with the territory. It's what I do. My job."

Her job. He'd crossed paths with lots of do-gooders—

social workers, counselors, cops—but he'd never met the real thing . . . until Rachel. "Begging for handouts, home visits, late nights. I don't see anyone else doing those things."

She shrugged. "Kids are so helpless. Someone has to look out for them until they're old enough to do it themselves."

"And that someone is you?"

"Why not?"

He watched her out of the corner of his eye. She looked like a Sunday-school teacher with her open face and guileless eyes. What was she doing struggling with the world's bruised and battered?

"The better question," he asked quietly, "is why?"

Rachel hesitated. Along the dock, black water cradled the boats, making them thump and swish under the sly wedge of moon. She listened in silence, knowing she was being evasive. But it was always hard to tell people who she was. "Look, my mother was . . . my mother was killed in front of me," she said at last. "Shot. In a robbery." She took a breath and plunged into the rest. "Perhaps you heard about it. Her name was Paula Goodman."

He turned to her in surprise. "*The* Paula Goodman? You're David Goodman's daughter?"

Rachel said dryly, "I guess that means you know all the particulars." She wasn't surprised. After all, who didn't know the details of her mother's murder and the subsequent founding of the Safer America movement by Rachel's father? The story was public legend.

"I didn't realize he had a child," Nick said.

Rachel threw him a pale smile. "Neither did he most of the time. Too busy selling that new world order." The old bitterness began to engulf her, but she wasn't about to get into a long sob story about her father. She changed the subject. "You know that boy today, Joselito . . . it was really great the way you spoke to him."

He shrugged, and she could tell the praise made him uncomfortable.

"I didn't do much."

"Yeah, but you did it in Spanish." She tore into another slice of pizza and peered at him, wondering how far to push. "He's Peruvian, so that's all he understands right now. His parents were anthropologists. They were living in the highlands, studying Andean culture, when they ran into the Shining Path. Ever heard of them?"

Something happened to Nick; a subtle kind of withdrawal she'd seen him do before. One minute he was there, and the next he'd drifted away, this time gazing out over the night as if he could see through it. "Yeah, I've heard of them," he said softly.

"They gunned down his parents like animals and left Joselito to watch them bleed to death. His only relative was an aunt who lives here."

An icy misery bit into Nick, and with it came flashes of memory. The improvised airstrip hacked out of the jungle. The ground meeting his feet as he swung down from the belly of the plane. He heard the thickset mestizo shouting rapid orders, the crack of a crate pried open, the first testing rattle of machine-gun fire.

All at once, he was opening his apartment door again, letting the dark thing that was his past inside. Hands suddenly clammy, he looked around for signs of Rennie. They were out in the open, easy targets. Instantly he scanned the cars parked nearby, looking for tails, for anything and anyone that shouldn't be there.

"It's been very hard for Joselito," Rachel was saying. "He lost everything. His parents, his country, even his language."

Her voice brought him back to the present, and to her bright eyes, which were turned so expectantly on him.

"He needs a friend," she said.

He understood what she was asking. But friends like him were the last thing that little boy needed. He wiped his hand on a paper napkin and forced calm into his voice. "Are you finished? We should go."

She sent a shrewd glance his way, a look that saw more than he cared to show, but in the end she only smiled. "I guess it is late." She finished the last of her slice and began gathering up the remains of their meal.

Uneasiness flickered low in his gut as he took the trash to the can. Irrational as it was, he couldn't escape the notion that Rennie was out there, watching. And the last thing Nick wanted his old boss to see was Rachel beside him.

While Nick cleaned up, Rachel slid behind the wheel of her car, watching him through the windshield. Something had happened a moment ago, something that brought wariness back to his face. She was tempted to ask about it but stifled her natural impulses. He wasn't one of her kids, and she wasn't his confessor. Besides, she knew from experience that wounded creatures heal in their own time. But she couldn't resist one tiny piece of information, so when he got in the car and she pulled away, she risked a direct question.

"Your Spanish sounded good. Where did you learn?"

She sensed another withdrawal, but when he spoke, his voice was offhand, almost indifferent. "Traveling. Spain, South America."

"You were raised here, weren't you—in New York?"

"I grew up all over the city. I never knew my parents. When I was thirteen, I met someone. He . . . he kind of adopted me."

"That was nice of him. You were lucky."

He smiled, and it was tinged with something. Irony? Chagrin?

"Yeah," he said, "real lucky."

Ten minutes of directions led her to the front of his house. A streetlight caught the home in its soft beam and surprised her. Somehow she had imagined Nick in much more meager surroundings.

"Do you rent it?" she asked.

"I've got a room around back. In the basement."

She nodded. The basement. Of course. "Well—thanks for the help. Snack for another few months."

She glanced over and caught him looking at her. Shadows of moonlight drifted through the windshield, dappling him, and she drew in a sudden breath. How striking he was, all lines and angles like a sculpture. The skin stretched tight over his jaw, cheekbones high and taut. Her gaze traveled down to his neck and throat, to that place where his skin disappeared into the cloth of his tightly buttoned shirt. She had an almost uncontrollable urge to undo the button at his throat and free him. She fastened her hands on the steering wheel, afraid they might fly off and do something without her.

"Well . . . guess I'll . . . see you tomorrow."

"Thanks for dinner."

She nodded. "You earned it. Anytime you want to help out, dinner's on me."

Nick looked away, the tight coil inside his chest twisting tighter.

"What's the matter?" she teased. "Can't stand my company?"

Shelley's battered face rose up, and he hoped to God neither she nor Rennie were waiting for him. "I've got troubles, Rachel. Things inside that won't let go. Things I've done. People I've . . . disappointed."

"You haven't disappointed me," she said gently.

A rueful feeling shot through him. "Not yet, anyway."

Rachel peered at him from across the gearshift, wondering about the secrets he was hiding. "Everyone sins, Nick. You ask for forgiveness, you make peace with yourself, you move on."

"There is no forgiveness for some things."

"Then you learn to live with them."

"I'm trying." He gave a short, mocking laugh. "Christ, I've *been* trying. I just can't seem to get the hang of it."

She touched the back of his hand, her common sense gone in a rush of sympathy. "Maybe you need help. A friend."

He looked down at her hand. Her slim fingers rested lightly on top of his, and he was tempted. God, he was so tempted.

But the prickle at the back of his neck told him Rennie was near, hovering like the dream, a black vulture, waiting, watching. Nick got out of the car. "I'll see you tomorrow."

Loping down the drive, he rounded the corner and

waited out of sight until the sound of her engine faded. Then and only then did he slowly unlock his door and brace himself for what was inside.

Nothing. No one. His place was as quiet and sparse as it always was, as if Shelley's visit had been a mirage. The bed was tucked into the sofa, his coffee cup dry in the dish rack, the towel he'd packed with ice for her bruises folded neatly over the edge of the sink.

Relief flooded him, leaving his knees a little wobbly. He plopped down on the couch without bothering to open it into the bed and slept dreamless.

In the morning, he woke with a strange sense of hopefulness. *Maybe you need help. A friend.* Rachel's words made his pulse race, his ears buzz. His body ached from lifting the cases at the warehouse, but as he rubbed his chest, it felt as though his heart was waking up, the tired blood circulating once more.

By the time he got to St. Anthony's, the sky was high and blue, and he decided to finish fixing the hole in the fence. Joselito and a group of kids stood around and watched, but for once, their closeness didn't bother him. Maybe Rachel was right, maybe things would work out. The past was over, he had a new life ahead of him, if only he could reach out, learn to feel once more.

"Nick." His heart thumped at the sound of her voice, as though he were sixteen again. Before he could stop himself, his mouth curved into a wide grin. He looked up.

She stood over him, tense and unsmiling. "The police are looking for you." Behind her, two uniforms walked toward him.

He went cold, the sight of the cops like frost in spring.

Rachel asked, "Do you know a Shelley Spier?"

Tongue stuck in his mouth, he couldn't answer. The police eyed him. "Nicholas Raine? Would you come with us, sir?"

It took only a few minutes to cross the ground, but it seemed like hours. Kids froze, teachers stared. The whole world slowed. He passed Rachel, her face pale, heard the blur of Shelley's name from the cops. They took him right up to the police car, put a hand on his head to push him in, and closed the car door behind him.

He was polite and cooperated fully. First lessons die hard, and he'd been Rennie Spier's best student.

Never upset the authorities, but never tell them anything.

So Nick told the police nothing about Shelley's visit. Even after they showed him the pictures.

"Couldn't find any identification on her. No prints on file. We had to use the ring to ID her." Detective Pat May pointed to the picture of Shelley's blood-smeared diamond ring. "Recognize it?"

Nick nodded, not trusting himself to speak.

"Any idea what she was doing in that part of Long Island City? She was a long way from Gramercy Park."

Running from Rennie. "I don't know why she was there."

The cop eyed him suspiciously, and Nick took the look without flinching.

"Where were you last night, Raine?"

"Home."

"Anyone vouch for that?"

"Only my empty coffee cups."

When they finally let him go, he took the first bus he

saw and rode for hours. He tried to block out the photographs, but he saw the pictures anyway, even with his
eyes closed. The bloody street. The mangled body.

The next morning his name was all over the television
and radio. He was in the basement, already packing,
when Rachel found him. His face felt stiff, his insides
frozen. He focused on shoving things into a grocery bag.
A cracked coffee cup, an old shirt. He didn't want to talk
to her; he didn't even want to see her. He just wanted to
go.

She waved a newspaper in front of him, but he didn't
look at it. He'd already seen the headline in the dis-
pensers at the bus stop and in the hands of the bus riders:
ARMS KING'S QUEEN IN HIT-AND-RUN HOMICIDE. Inset in
the column was his own picture and a caption: "Spier as-
sociate Nicholas Raine leaves precinct after talking with
police." The article even mentioned that he now worked
for Rachel's preschool at St. Anthony's Church.

"The mop and pail are upstairs." His voice sounded
wooden, but it only matched the way he felt. "I bought
the fluorescent bulbs for the office but haven't had a
chance to replace them. The fence isn't finished yet either. You better get someone in to do it soon."

Rachel looked at the paper; the answer to the puzzle
that was Nick stared up at her from the page. She'd never
seen him in anything but faded work clothes, but in the
picture he was wearing a suit. An expensive suit. He was
smiling; the photograph caught him in a cocky wave.

"You should have told me, Nick."

He laughed. "Told you what? That I used to peddle
guns and bombs and other assorted what-have-yous to

any little tyrant with a buck? Yeah, I'm sure that would have been a real strong character reference."

Too angry for words, she said nothing as he gathered his things. When she'd hired him, the church had run a routine background check on him, but all it had turned up were two arrests for public drunkenness, and that had been years ago. Nothing about his connection to Rennie Spier and his arms-dealing empire. Knowing Nick had earned money from the very violence that made her school necessary—that had robbed her of parents and childhood—outraged her. He'd hurt her, hurt the school. How could he matter anymore?

But then he took down a finger painting he'd rescued from the trash, carefully rolling and packing it as if the childish picture were a precious work of art. A wave of compassion for him washed over her, liquid and warm, as unwelcome as it was keen.

"I called you yesterday," she said. "What happened? Where were you?"

"You know where I was."

"All day?"

But he didn't reply. Suddenly, Rachel was furious again. Her head ached. She'd spent all day worrying about him, and he stood there like an automaton, giving her monosyllabic answers.

"You're going to have to speak to me sometime, Nick, I'm not going to let you walk out of here like this."

"I don't see how you can stop me."

"I know where you live. I can camp out until you talk to me." Their gazes collided. His was like ice.

She got right to the point. "How long has it been since you worked for Spier?"

"Years."

"How many years? One, ten, fifteen?"

"Six." He crossed his arms and confronted her. "All right? Six years."

"And did you have anything to do with his wife's death?" There was a tiny beat of silence, a frigid impasse where they just looked at each other. "Did you?"

Nick turned away and ran a hand over his tired face. "No." He said the word as if he'd been saying it all day. "I didn't have anything to do with it."

"How could you—you were with me that night."

"That's right."

"You told the police that, didn't you?"

He rolled up another finger painting. "Sure I did. I'd be stupid not to."

"So they no longer suspect you of anything?"

"I'm clean as a whistle." But he didn't look at her.

"Nick," she scolded gently, "I'll just tell them myself."

With an angry snap, he flicked the bag away. "Didn't you almost get shut down last year? You told me the Parish Council is just looking for an excuse. My picture was in the paper. The *school* was in the paper. Leave it alone. Let me finish packing. Fifteen minutes, and I'm gone."

The vehemence of his response made her step back. He was right; keeping the school out of the police report and out of the media were all that mattered. The next six weeks were crucial, and the last thing she needed was to get mixed up with him.

But he hadn't done anything, a tiny voice protested, and she could prove it. She swallowed, knowing what was right and what was practical weren't always the same.

A sudden glow illuminated the top of the steps, and a boy spoke. "*Allí.* There—Nick." For a moment the outline of an adult holding a child was silhouetted against the light. Then footsteps crunched over the steps and descended.

Joselito looked like a toy in the man's arms. Wide and massive, the man was built like a linebacker, but his casual air and easy grin rendered him harmless—a big teddy bear with an unruly mop of sandy hair. Yet in spite of his apparent friendliness, hostility shot across Nick's face when he saw who it was. Rachel's welcoming smile froze on her lips.

"Put the kid down," Nick said.

Uneasy, Rachel looked between the two men. "Nick, who is—"

"Put the kid down!"

The man flashed Joselito an easy smile. "I'm not hurting you pal, am I?" Joselito grinned back at him, and the man turned to Nick. "See?"

"Put him down. Rachel, take him upstairs." And when she didn't move fast enough, "Now, Rachel—move!"

It was more emotion than Rachel had seen from Nick in all the months he'd worked there. It propelled her like nothing else would have.

When she got to the top of the stairs, Felice was barreling toward her. The other teacher was a large, square woman, almost as wide as she was tall. Today, her love of bright colors had her swathed in a loose, swirling dress that hung from her massive bust in yards of hot red and orange.

"Bill Hughes is on the phone," she said, panting from exertion, her face flushed almost as red as her dress.

God, not now. "Take a message." Rachel put Joselito down and sent him out to the yard. "I'm not up to fencing with the Parish Council."

"Okay. Oh—and here." She handed Rachel a message slip. "A reporter from the *Post* wants to talk to you about your friendly neighborhood killer. Where is Nick, by the way?"

Rachel gritted her teeth, holding onto her patience. Felice may have been her friend, but she had a wicked tongue and wasn't always careful about using it. "He's not a killer, Felice. Don't repeat that. And he's downstairs, packing."

"You fired him?"

"He resigned."

Felice quirked an eyebrow, obviously surprised. "That was nice of him. Now if we can get the reporters to keep our name out of the paper, maybe Bill Hughes will leave us alone."

Rachel sighed, her mind on the man in the basement with Nick. "Don't count on it."

As soon as the door closed behind Rachel, Martin Ferris flashed a tired grin and ruffled Nick's hair.

"Hey, Nicky. Nick. It's me." He pulled Nick into a big bear hug. "God, you look terrible, you know that?" Holding Nick at arm's length, Martin examined him. "Who does your clothes? Man, whoever it is, they're choking you to death." He tugged at Nick's tightly buttoned collar, and Nick swatted his hand away.

"What do you want, Marty?"

Martin sighed. "What's wrong with you? Can't I look up the guy who's practically my brother?"

"What do you want? Or should I say, what does Rennie want?"

"Okay, so maybe he does want to see you." For a minute, a bone-weary look crossed Martin's face, etching deep lines into what Nick remembered as a normally placid facade. Six years was a long time between visits, but still, Martin looked old, as old as Nick felt. But then, killing the boss's wife could do that.

"Forget it."

"Come on—five minutes for an old friend." Martin roamed around the room, poking at the shelves.

"Don't touch anything."

The big man picked up a drawing from Nick's paper bag and unfurled it. Nick pulled it out of his hand.

"I told you not to touch anything."

"Jesus. Okay, okay."

"Now, are you going to tell me what Rennie wants?"

Martin sighed. "Better let him tell you himself, Nicky. Otherwise, he'll have my balls for breakfast."

Nick clamped his jaw shut and indicated the stairs with a curt nod. Christ, if he had to put up with one more piece of crap today . . .

Careful to make sure Martin left the building, Nick escorted the large man back up the stairs. Nick trudged behind, carrying the paper bag like a sack of groceries. The rolled-up drawings stuck out from the top like celery stalks. On the way out, Rachel stopped him.

"Are you okay?" She eyed Martin suspiciously.

"Sure," Nick said, "fine."

Martin winked. "Look, why don't I wait for you outside?" He sauntered out, and that was when Nick saw the limousine, parked like a fat, black insect at the yard gate.

A crowd of children pressed against the fence, staring at it. Something deadly snaked through Nick, and all the paranoia of his dinner with Rachel came back in a flood. Rennie close enough to see her, to see the kids.

Rachel eyed the car. "Who is it?"

He jumped at the sound of her voice. "No one. Nothing." He pushed her back. "Get away from the door."

Uneasy, she glanced over his shoulder. "Why? What's the matter?"

"Look, I gotta go." He plunged into the yard, knowing the only way to keep Rennie away from them all was to get in that car.

"Wait a minute!" She ran after him, holding out a corner of recycled computer paper. "Here. It's my number at home. Go ahead, take it. In case you need someone to talk to."

Nick stared at her outstretched hand, feeling Rennie's eyes on her. "Go back inside. Take the kids with you."

"Fine, but here." She tucked the scrap of paper into his shirt pocket. "You don't have to use it, but I hope you will. At least let me know you're all right." She looked at him closely, her expression half worried, half exasperated, then went to sweep the kids away from the fence.

His mouth was so dry he couldn't have responded even if he wanted to. Instead he forced himself to walk past her, waded through the sea of kids, and faced the limousine at the curb.

Chapter 3

Martin held the limo door open and bowed in mock servility. "Look who else came to see you," he said. "It's a regular family reunion."

"Hello, Nicky," greeted a familiar husky voice.

"Frank." Nick acknowledged the stocky man behind the steering wheel. A peasant stuffed into a suit, Frank had a round, dark face that showed stubble an hour after he shaved, and even in his sixties showed the outline of his beard. Not a subtle man, but a loyal one, he'd been Rennie's partner for more than thirty years.

Martin started to slide into the passenger section, but a third man spoke from deep inside the car. "Why don't you keep Frank company," Rennie Spier said.

Anger flashed across Martin's face before he could paste on his grin again, but he did what he was told, waiting for Nick to get in and slamming the door behind him before getting in the front with Frank.

The car pulled away, and Nick gazed out the window.

Rachel stood in the yard, still herding the kids inside. He kept his eyes on her until she disappeared, then focused on whatever passed by the window. Anything but Rennie.

As Frank drove, he flicked an uneasy glance in the rearview mirror. The partition between front and back was closed so he couldn't see much, but that didn't stop his agitation. He took a Tums from the roll he kept on the dash and bit into it. Jesus, he wished they could bury Shelley and forget her.

Martin shifted in his seat. "What do you think's going on back there?" His voice was sharp and tense. The man had been on edge for weeks. Ever since Rennie had started talking about Nick again.

Frank shrugged. "They're making peace."

"You didn't see the look on Nick's face when he saw me. If they're making peace, I'm my mother's uncle."

"Look, we all know how you feel about Nicky coming back."

"That's because he'll only make trouble and screw things up again."

"For who?"

A tiny, telltale pause. Then, "Fuck you, Frank."

Frank shook his head and glanced over at Marty, who was slumped in the seat, glowering out the window. Who could blame him for being aggravated? Nick was back. After six long years the prince was back.

On the other side of the partition separating driver from rider, Nick could feel Rennie's eyes on him.

"Let me look at you," Rennie said, his voice gentle.

Nick heard affection, and the encompassing familiarity of Rennie's accent. What was it exactly? Greece. Albania. Spain. He and Marty had countless arguments about it, but they never did find out. "You used to enjoy riding with me, remember?"

Nick's stomach shifted, and he was thirteen again, riding around like a king in the limo with Rennie. Yeah, he remembered. He remembered exactly what went on in Rennie's limousines. Bribes and handshakes. Smiles when the deal went through, threats when it didn't. Death and money were what this car was all about.

"Look at me, Nick." Rennie's voice persuaded, coaxed, and demanded all at the same time. It pulled at Nick like a magnet, separating him from his own will. He raised his eyes.

Six years evaporated in an instant. Rennie was the same. The same. Thick white hair, crinkly blue eyes. Nearly seventy now, and still tough, still vibrant, still that enormous . . . presence. His broad shoulders and massive arms were squeezed into a tweed sports coat, as if he were going to tea at the Plaza and didn't want to scare anyone. He was big. Still so big. Those huge hands. Christ, they had savaged Shelley's face. Choking on fury, Nick squeezed the armrest so hard he felt the outline of the steel frame beneath the leather.

"I've missed you," Spier said.

"Where are we going?" Nick watched the limousine enter the Brooklyn-Queens Expressway.

"Nowhere. For a ride. I just want to see you. Talk to you."

"Stay on this side of the river."

Spier smiled. "Sure, Nicky. Whatever you say." But

Nick didn't say anything. He stared out the window to avoid looking at the other man. "The funeral is tomorrow," Rennie said into the silence. "I hope you will come."

Nick's gaze swiveled to Spier's face. He saw sadness there. Grief. "Seven years we were married, seven years for good luck." Rennie shook his head and smiled sadly. "I have no luck with women, Nicky. No luck at all."

Nick said nothing. A ten-year-old fragment of conversation floated up from his memory.

"Don't get too close to him, Nicky boy," the soft Irish lilt was saying in his head. "You think he's tame, you think he's civilized, but he ain't." Danny Walsh leaned in, whispering low. The smell of his beery breath wafted out with every puffy word. "He's tiger wild, and he don't like being crossed. Don't matter who you are. Ask him about his first wife if you don't believe me—go ahead, ask him. See what he says."

They'd been in a bar in Amsterdam; Danny was chasing the IRA dream: surface-to-air missiles that could take down British helicopters. Nick was in Amsterdam to make an initial assessment and possibly negotiate a deal. It was his first overseas assignment; he was young, just barely twenty-two, and though he'd been working for Rennie since he was sixteen, he still had something to prove to an old salt like Danny who liked to tease.

"Why don't you tell me yourself, Danny?"

"Because I can see by your face you wouldn't believe me." Danny smiled. "That tiger's got you, boy-o, tight and fast. Do you love the old man, Nick? Do you love him like your da?" And Danny had laughed long and hard. But he'd told the story at last, after much coaxing, and a few more pints of Grolsch pilsner. "She was Cuban, Nicky, from the old crowd before Castro. And they take their politics real serious. Spier had a big deal going with one of their fancy brigades in Miami, and she found out he was selling to Fidel, too. So she told her father, and Spier lost the job."

"So you're saying he killed her?" Nick bristled, and Danny had shrugged ironically.

"She killed herself, Nicky, from the shame of it all." He winked. "At least that's the story they gave out." He leaned back in the booth and sighed. "She was lovely, was Mrs. Spier—dark and slender. I heard he did it himself, you know. Didn't they find traces of phenobarbital in her blood? He gave her enough to make her woozy, took her up to the roof, and helped her fly."

The limousine lurched, and Nick's memory jolted to a stop. They were at a traffic light. Frank made a left and another left, and they were back on the expressway again, heading east this time. The gentle rhythm of Spier's voice ticked on, and Nick realized he'd been speaking all along. Tears shone in the older man's eyes. They turned the icy blue into something almost warm. "You don't understand, Nicky. I am trying to tell you, but you do not understand." Spier was half laughing now, and something like joy blazed through the tears. "Shelly—she was like an oasis, full of water, fertile and ripe." He leaned forward and gripped Nick's arm. "It's a miracle, Nicky. A miracle. Like Abraham in the desert."

But Nick hardly listened. Images swam in his head. Shelley's swollen, bloody face as she stood in his doorway. The picture the cop had shown him the day before—her beautiful body twisted and broken, her glorious hair soaked in a blood-stained puddle. Suddenly he couldn't stand breathing the same air as Rennie Spier.

"Stop the car." Nick knocked on the partition, and Martin opened it. "Pull over, stop the car."

Spier gave Martin a curt shake of the head.

"Sorry, Nicky," Martin said.

But Nick had had enough. He lunged through the partition and grabbed Frank around the neck, squeezing his windpipe against the back of the seat. The car careened over the shoulder and back onto the road.

"What the hell's the matter with you?" Martin fought to pry Nick's arm away and also steer the car.

"Pull over. Do it!"

"All right, Nicky, Jesus." Martin steered the wheel so the car skittered to the shoulder. It stopped with an abrupt squeal.

Nick shot out of the car so fast he tripped and had to scramble to keep his balance.

"Hey, Nick, wait a minute!" Martin's feet crunched on the loose gravel as he raced after Nick. "Come on, five more minutes. Can't we talk for five more fucking minutes?"

Martin grabbed Nick's shoulder. Without stopping, Nick pivoted and swung. The blow snapped Martin's head back. Fury flew into his eyes; he glared at Nick, and Nick glared back.

A slow grin surfaced on Martin's wide, fleshy face. He shrugged and held up his hands, signaling he was through. Nick backed up a step. He waited. But Martin didn't attack, he didn't move at all. Nick dropped his fists.

He was half turned around when Martin tackled him.

Nick landed in the gravel of the shoulder, his face inches from the edge of the expressway. Cars raced by, humming speed. Martin pressed Nick deeper into the pebbles, his face closer to the edge. "Do it, Marty. Take my fucking head off. Go ahead, do it."

But Martin only pulled Nick to his feet. "I wish to God I could. It would put you out of your misery."

He shoved Nick back toward the limo. When Spier stepped out, Martin had Nick firmly pinned against it.

Nick met Spier's eyes. The older man's were hard and flat. Without blinking, he slapped Nick, hard enough to knock him down if Martin hadn't been holding him.

The power of it brought tears to Nick's eyes, but he blinked them away. His lip burned, and he tasted blood. But he kept his gaze on Spier. "What the hell do you want?"

Spier touched Nick's face, caressing his cheek and the cut lip. "I don't like to hurt you, Nicky. But I will."

Nick made himself stand still. "Go ahead. You think I give a fuck?"

Spier smiled and patted Nick's cheek. "There are many ways of hurting. Not all of them draw blood." He signaled to Martin to release his hold, then continued in a quiet voice. "We had a son, Shelley and I. A boy. He's disappeared. I want you to find him for me." He took out a pristine white handkerchief and handed it to Nick, indicating the blood on his face. "I need you, Nicky. Don't disappoint me again."

They hustled Nick into the car. This time Martin sat in the back, blocking Nick's access to the door. A thousand questions ran through his head, but he couldn't find his voice to ask a single one.

"I have a meeting," Rennie said. "Martin will tell you the rest."

They unloaded him and Martin in front of a diner, where the two of them sat in edgy truce in a red leatherette booth. Nick ordered coffee and stared at the thin film of grease in the slowly congealing liquid, his thoughts thick and slow as sludge. Across the table, Martin's big frame hunched over a Greek salad. Spearing chunks of feta cheese, he gestured with his fork.

"Three months ago Shelley started disappearing every Sunday. Rennie thought she was getting some on the side, so he sent me after her. She's seeing a guy all right, but he's three feet tall and can't tie his shoes."

"How . . . how old is he?" Nick asked.

"Six," Martin said. "Almost six."

A ripple of silence passed between them. Did Marty know about Nick and Shelley? Nick had never said a word. He could only assume Shelley hadn't either.

Martin kept his gaze on his plate, fishing for a tomato. "She ran away after you left. Nearly drove Rennie out of his mind. First you, then her. Don't think he didn't put two and two together, either, because he did. But you weren't exactly keeping a low profile in the drunk tank, so we knew you weren't together. Shelley . . ." He shrugged. "She just disappeared."

Nick thought about that year, the year after he left Rennie. It was still a blur. An unending nightmare of sleeplessness, of drinking to keep the dream away, of scrounging whatever he could to keep from going back. Stealing, begging, nodding off on park benches until the dream woke him or the police woke him. Shelley had been smart not to tell him she was leaving. He would have sold her back to Rennie for the price of a six-pack.

"When did she come back?"

"A year later. Broke, sorry. And Rennie, you know him, he hits her a few times to remind her, and then all is forgiven. He buys her a new fur, new rings—the stuff she'd been hocking all year to keep her going—and it's like it never happened."

"No one runs away, has a kid, and doesn't tell for six years. It's crazy, why would she do that?"

Martin hesitated. Something almost like sadness flashed in his eyes before he looked back at his plate. "I don't know, Nicky. I don't know why she did half the crazy things she did."

Nick stared over his head, the craziest thing of all still unspoken between them, even after all this time. But if Martin knew about Nick and Shelley, he wasn't admitting it now. "She really hated Rennie," was all he said.

Nick watched a noisy group of women and children settle into a table. "Where's the kid been all this time?"

"With some aunt of hers no one knew about. Way the hell out on the Island. Amagansett, Narragansett, something like that. That's where the kid was born, and that's where she dumped him."

"So what happened? Three months ago Shelley suddenly has a change of heart?"

"Three months ago the aunt died, and Shelley needed someplace else to stash the kid."

"Where?"

"I don't know. If I did, Rennie wouldn't need you, would he?" He shoved his plate away. "I'm not hungry.

Let's get out of here." He peeled some bills from a roll and threw them on the table. "Come on, I'll call a cab."

Nick grabbed his arm. "Who beat her up, Marty? Did you and Rennie take turns working her over?"

Martin stiffened. "You're a sick bastard, you know that?"

"Yeah? Whose idea was it to run her down?"

"Don't do this, Nicky."

Nick slid out of the booth and stood. He leaned close so no one else would hear. "Rennie and I had a deal. I promised I wouldn't hurt him if he let me walk, and he did. I left. I kept my end of the bargain for six years. I'm not coming back, Marty. Not for him, not for his kid, not for anything."

He left Marty and took a bus home, carrying the paper bag he'd packed at St. Anthony's. On the way, he bought a newspaper. He hadn't read the paper in years, but he needed a new job, so he'd start with the classifieds.

It was a pretty spring day, and several stores had tables outside. A dark-haired girl holding a toddler was combing through clothes racks. The child squirmed in her arms, waving his hands as Nick approached. He grabbed at Nick's shirt, and the girl said, "No, no, Sam," and at Nick, "I'm sorry."

The baby babbled happily as Nick passed. He felt the boy's eyes follow him down the street. He didn't want to think about the baby. Or about fathers and sons. It wasn't his problem, he didn't have to get involved. But his mind kept floating back, doing the math, telling himself it was possible. Possible. Possible. The word echoed with every step.

Nick let himself into the basement apartment and put

the bag on the counter near the sink. He threw the newspaper on the table. Ignoring the blaze of headlines about Shelley on the front page, he looked through the classifieds, tearing out whatever looked promising. Janitors, day laborers, anything that required no skill and few references. As long as he was nowhere near children.

That night he fell asleep in his clothes, the newspaper on the floor where he'd dropped it. The phone woke him. Bleary-eyed, he sat up, blinking away sleep. The phone rang again, and he shuffled over to answer it.

"We hear you're looking for a job," a voice on the other end said. "There's one waiting outside." The line went dead.

Nick rubbed his face, trying to wake up. The only window was in the door, but a curtain hid it. Cautiously, he lifted a corner and peered out into the impenetrable night. Nothing.

Easing open the door, he inched his way toward the street, gaze skimming in all directions. Halfway up, the drive curved. From here, Nick could see a Buick parked in front. Without warning the car's back door swung open, and out fell a large, bulky roll, like a carpet.

Instantly, the Buick peeled away, tires squealing.

Dread circling his gut, Nick ran the rest of the way and skidded to his knees in front of the bundle. Hands and feet tied, a cloth sack over the head. Fingers shaking, he ripped off the bag. Rachel's braid, wild and untidy, flopped like a dead fish on her shoulder.

God, no.

His stomach jolted to his feet as he brushed the flyaway hair back from her face. Tape covered her mouth, and her eyes stared terrified and sightless, but she was alive, whimpering tiny distressed squeaks. Relief flooded him, so powerful that for a moment he couldn't move. Then he put his hands against the side of her face, and she jumped.

He said, "No, it's okay. It's me, Nick. You're safe; I've got you. I'm going to pull off the tape. It might hurt, so hold on. Ready?" The eyes continued to stare, so he gathered her in his arms and holding tight, yanked the tape away. "There you go. Shh, it's all right, you're all right. Shh—"

He repeated the comforting sounds, stroking her hair and holding her until she came back from the dark place she'd been. As if she were waking up, sense seeped back into her face.

"Nick?"

"It's me, Rachel, I've got you, you're safe."

Tears pooled in her eyes. "They tied my hands." She sobbed quietly, as if tying her hands was the worst they could have done. "They . . . they tied my hands."

Quickly, he pulled out his penknife and sliced through the ropes digging into her wrist and feet. Chafe marks scraped the skin raw in both places.

I'll kill Rennie for this.

A neighbor pulled aside a curtain to stare at them, then quickly disappeared. Ignoring the intrusion, Nick sat in the driveway, rocking and crooning to Rachel. Cloudy moonlight softened the edges of the drive and drifted over them. He held her tight against him, feeling her body shake and her tears soak his shirt.

When at last only the trembling remained, he spoke. "Are you hurt, Rachel? Can you walk? I want to get you inside." He helped her stand, but her knees buckled when she started to move. In the end, he carried her like a child.

She cried again when he placed her on the couch. He put his arms around her and stroked her hair. Gradually she calmed down and, after a few minutes, pushed herself away.

"Okay." Her voice was thick with tears. "Okay, that's enough. No more crying."

"It's okay, cry all you want, you have every right."

She shook her head and hiccuped. "I can't . . . do it anymore. If I keep going, I'll never stop."

"How about a cup of coffee?"

She nodded. "And a tissue." She gave him a watery smile. "Make that a mountain of tissues."

"Sorry, no tissues. How about a roll of toilet paper?" He grabbed a roll from the bathroom, handed it to her, then crossed to the sink and filled a pot with water for coffee. He held up a jar of Maxwell House. "I've only got instant."

"Mmm, my favorite." She blew her nose.

He took a coffee cup out of the sink and washed it. "Want to talk about it?"

She hiccuped again. "They were waiting for me in the parking garage at my apartment."

"Who was?"

"I . . . I don't know. They grabbed me from behind. Before I even knew what was happening, they taped my mouth and t-tied my—" She started to shake again, and the hysteria mounted in her voice. He was beside her in an instant.

"It's okay. You're safe. I've got you."

She nodded. "I know. It's just hard . . ." Fresh tears

started, but she fought her way through them. "They tied my hands then, too ... when my m-mother ..." She looked down at her hands and whispered, "I can't bear to have anything on my wrists. No bracelets, watches, or anything."

"I'm sorry, Rachel, I'm so sorry." He knelt down in front of her and took the hands she was staring at. Gently, he said, "Did they ... did they touch you ... hurt you?"

She gulped and shook her head. "No, nothing like that."

"What about broken bones, bruises?"

She lowered her head and shook it again. He tipped her face back up to his. Tears swam in her eyes again.

"Are you sure?" He spoke quietly. "I have to know. If they hurt you in any way, I've got to know."

"They ... they were rough, but they never hit me or ... or anything."

The water had boiled by then, and he poured her coffee. As she reached for the cup, she noticed the marks on her wrists for the first time.

"I'll go out and get you something for that," Nick said.

"No." She looked up quickly, panic in her face. "I don't want you to."

"You can come with me if you like."

Relief settled over her face. "All right."

"Do you want me to call someone? Your family maybe?"

"There's only my aunt and uncle, and—"

"What are their names?" He picked up the phone.

"Elliot and Julia Bradshaw, but don't call them."

"You should be with someone who cares about—"

"Please." She shook her head. "Don't. I'll be all right."

"What about Felice, someone from school?"

"No! Don't call anyone. I . . . I can't even call the police. The Parish Council is already in an uproar about—" She flushed.

"About me."

She nodded and looked away. "I can't afford any more bad publicity," she said, and Nick felt sick.

She finished the coffee and sat back against the sofa, eyes closed. Her hair was still a tangle, half in and half out of the braid. She looked exhausted, and the sight twisted his heart.

Don't look, then. Take off. Get that salve. Or a drink. Find a bar. A drink is what you need.

Instead he went into the kitchen for more coffee. But when he got to the sink, his legs gave out. Bracing his elbows against the counter, he put his head in his hands. At least they hadn't hit her. But terror was only the opening move. He raked his fingers through his hair, pulling hard. How many times had he done it himself? Talk first, then warn. Then kidnapping, broken fingers, torn ears . . . He knew the steps by heart. And he still had to face Rachel with it. God, he didn't want to. He'd rather run, fly, anything than tell her this was his fault.

"Nick!"

"I'm right here." He stepped into the light so she could see him.

"Sit with me?"

He sat down and put his arm around her. She sighed,

a huge, fluttery sound. "God, I wish I could stop crying. Talk to me. Tell me something happy."

He couldn't think of anything happy. But he told her about the hotel in Chicago where he'd gotten so drunk, he fell asleep on top of the covers and woke up in the morning with a thick, brown goop all over him. "Know what it was?" He leaned back against the couch and stroked the top of her head.

"Mm-mmm," she said sleepily.

"The chocolates. The chocolates the hotel puts on your pillow when they turn down the bed. I plopped down right on top of them, and they melted all over me during the night."

Her mouth turned up in a smile, and he smiled himself at the sight. He talked half the night. He told her about the best tapas bar in Seville and the best nude beach on the Riviera. She would sleep for a while and jerk awake, panicked. Then Nick would tighten his hold on her and talk some more.

The one thing he didn't tell her was why she'd been terrorized and dropped at his door. While she slept, he called himself coward and swore he would tell her the next time. But the next time he always found himself telling her something else. Vincente's in Buenos Aires. The Only in Vancouver.

Early in the morning he called St. Anthony's, telling them she was ill and wouldn't be in. Then he called a cab. When it came, he knelt in front of the couch and gently brushed the hair away from her face. "Rachel," he whispered, "I'm taking you home." She curled deeper into the sofa, and he had trouble waking her. When he finally got her inside the cab, she snuggled up against him and slept some more.

Nick got her to her apartment, where she shuffled into the bedroom. "I'm so tired," she mumbled.

"Let me call someone to stay with you." He pulled down the bedspread and tucked her in.

She reached for his hand and managed a sleepy, "Stay. Please."

He sat on the edge of the bed. "For a little while, but then I have to go." He didn't even know if she heard him.

He watched her sleep, her face peaceful at last. Rising, he found the phone in the kitchen and called a nearby pharmacy for some salve for the raw spots on her wrists. While he waited for it to be delivered, he wandered back into the bedroom and noticed the photos for the first time. Mostly black-and-white news photographs, they ranged over her dresser in various shapes and sizes, all depicting her father, David Goodman. He stood on a makeshift speakers' stand at an outdoor rally; behind a podium at the National Press Club; in the Oval Office, shaking hands with the president. And one small snapshot, tucked into a back corner against the mirror, of a very young Rachel and both her parents. She smiled at the camera in gap-toothed happiness, nestled between the father who had yet to abandon her and the mother with Rachel's gentle brown eyes.

He glanced over at the bed, trying to feel what she must have felt. To have so much and lose it all. No wonder she was so fierce about the school and the children.

When the salve arrived, he put it on the kitchen table, where she would be sure to see it. A brief note explained

what it was for, and then it was time to go. But instead
of the door, he found himself in her bedroom.

Afternoon sun gilded her half-undone braid. Rene-
gade hair lay like polished copper on the pillow. *So
clean, so good.* On impulse, he eased onto the edge of
the bed and smoothed back the soft wisps. She stirred,
murmured, then turned on her side, one hand by her
cheek. He slid his hand over hers, feeling how small it
was. *So vulnerable.* For one exquisite moment, he fitted
his fingers through hers, his heart thumping. *Don't let
go. Don't ever let me go.* But of course, she wasn't letting go. He was. Slowly he released his hold and stood.
His chest hurt, but he managed to walk out of the room.
Then out of the apartment. By the time he found the subway into Manhattan, he was even breathing again.

Chapter 4

Nick arrived at the Gramercy Park headquarters of SATCO, the Spier Advanced Technology Corporation, while Shelley's funeral reception was in full swing. Descending in the glassed-in elevator that took him from the corporate offices at street level to the lavish living quarters below, Nick had the grim notion that he was falling into hell.

Through the elevator's glass walls, Nick watched the party approach, scanning the crowd for Rennie. Most of the guests were customers, not friends. Representatives from half the developing world swilled Rennie's wine.

The elevator hit bottom, and the door opened. Nick had already spotted Rennie, surrounded by people murmuring words of sympathy. But before Nick could push his way into the circle, he was spun around and enveloped in a fierce bear hug.

"Jesus H. fucking Christ. Nicky!" A wiry man with an Irish lilt and thinning sandy hair pummeled Nick's back.

"I didn't think to ever see your face this side of paradise."

"Or the other." A glance over Nick's shoulder showed Spier disappearing into the crowd. He threw Danny Walsh a quick grin. It had been years since he'd seen the IRA troubleshooter. He must have been close to fifty by now but still looked lean and fit, sharp-eyed as ever. "Hello, Danny. What are you doing here? I'm surprised they let you in the country."

Danny smiled, laugh lines scrunching around astute green eyes. "Oh, I'm real respectable now. A peacekeeper, if you can believe it." He leaned in close. "On the trail of a rumor, in fact. An arms shipment to the Liberation Council."

The council was a loose umbrella for all the groups who didn't support the peace in Northern Ireland. Anyone who traded in arms or plastic explosives knew about it.

"Thought I'd see if anything . . . interesting turns up," Danny said, looking around. "And of course, pay my respects. How about you, lad? Back with Spier again?"

"Not exactly." Nick surveyed the gathering. Where had Spier gone?

"You know, every time I kick back a pint of pilsner, I think of you."

Nick couldn't help a grim smile. "Yeah, getting drunk is my specialty."

Danny's laugh boomed over the noise of the crowd. "Well, boy-o, every man has his special gift."

There he was, across the courtyard.

Danny gave Nick a hearty handshake. "If you need

anything, Nicky, you whistle at me. Grand to see you—"

But Nick was already moving away. He cut through the crowd, gaze on his target. He conjured up the hole in the ground that had just swallowed Shelley, pictured Rachel, wrists bruised, sleeping like an angel.

Then he was face to face with the man who had been his teacher, his mentor, who had defined his life for over twenty years.

"You touch Rachel again, I'll kill you." Someone gasped. Nick ignored it. "You hurt anyone again, I swear I'll rip your fucking heart out."

The people around them melted away until the two of them were alone. Fury flashed across Spier's face, but only for a instant. He smiled. It was a wolf's smile, victorious, satisfied. "I don't think violence will be necessary. Do you?"

A silent message passed between them.

Leave her alone, and I'll do what you tell me.

Do what I want, and there's no reason to bother anyone else.

The deal made, Spier eyed Nick's work clothes, which were matted and wrinkled from the long night of tears with Rachel. "Go find something decent to wear. You're working for me now. Show some respect. I'll send Martin to fill you in." He put a fatherly arm around Nick's shoulders and gave a shout of laughter. "God, it's good to have you back! Welcome home, Nicky. Welcome home." A rough squeeze, and he was gone.

Frank watched the reunion with a burning sensation in the pit of his stomach. The guys had a pool going, the odds running three to one that Nick would stay away. But Frank had bet against the odds. Nicky had a soft streak that got him into trouble, got them all into trouble. And Frank didn't think it would be any different this time. Rennie tumbling down the road to disappointment, and Nicky, well, who knew where Nicky would end up? Frank had a feeling about bringing Nick back, and it wasn't a good feeling.

He thumbed a Tums from the roll in his pocket and sucked it down. Sidling up to Rennie, he drew him aside from a circle of well-wishers. "You think he'll find the kid?"

Rennie didn't ask who Frank referred to. Together they turned to watch Nick weave through the crowd and disappear out a doorway. "He'll find him."

Doubtful, Frank shook his head, and Rennie clapped him on the shoulder. "You're an old woman, Frank. You worry too much."

Frank did worry. But then, he never understood what Rennie saw in Nicky Raine.

Frank still remembered the day he'd caught Nick and Marty in Rennie's yellow Porsche. He'd hauled the two pipsqueak car thieves into the kitchen, pitching them into hard-backed chairs so he and Rennie could have some fun. Frank got out the Luger—a war souvenir, an antique that wasn't even loaded, though the kids didn't know that—and pressed the gun under Marty's chin.

"Why'd you try to steal the car?" Marty was blubbering by then, melting into the chair like a blob of butter in the sun, but Nicky . . . well, Nicky always wanted to be a hero.

"Leave him alone," Nicky had muttered, and when

Frank continued to ram the gun under the other boy's chin, Nick scowled and spoke louder. "Fuck you, man. You want to shoot him? Go ahead, be my guest. But it was my idea, asshole. It was me who did it."

So Frank gave him his chance, cramming the weapon against Nick's throat. "Okay, big shot, you want to tell me what you think you were doing?" He could see the kid was scared enough to crap his pants, what with the gun shoved in there so tight it cut off his wind. But the boy answered fast enough.

"I like yellow," he croaked. "It's my favorite color."

Jesus, Rennie had roared. And repeated what Nicky had said, and roared again. But then, Rennie liked a smart mouth. And he was always crazy weird about having a son.

After that, reeling in the kid wasn't hard. It was like that story of the gingerbread house. All Rennie had to do was give Nicky a whiff, a taste of what he could have, and he was hooked. What was he going to do anyway— say no? He had nothing to look forward to except hustling hot watches on the street.

So it started. A weekend here, a week there, then summers, and suddenly Nicky had his own room, a key. By the time he was sixteen, Rennie had given Nick the Porsche he'd tried to steal.

And now he was back, roaming the halls the way he used to, upsetting everyone, a potential damn pain in the ass.

"And what if he finds the kid," Frank said, "and doesn't hand him back . . . or the rest?"

Rennie smiled, but the expression never reached his

eyes. "Then he'll bleed, Frank, and so will everyone around him."

Cold settled at the base of Nick's spine as he left the reception. He moved surely, the route imprinted on his memory. Left down the hallway, then right, then down three steps. He steeled himself against all the familiar sights. The walls, the furniture . . . they looked the same. God, they smelled the same. White carpets hugged the floors, white silk moiré covered the walls; white wool, leather, or silk swathed the furniture. It churned his stomach to see that deathly frost again.

At the entrance to what had once been his suite of rooms, he balked. He remembered the first time he'd slept there. New clothes on the chair, a TV, a phone. He thought he'd died and gone to heaven; he'd never have to cruise a dirty, noisy street again.

Safe at last.

He'd been seduced once. Could Rennie do it again?

As if in answer, a voice said, "It's just the way you left it."

Nick turned. Martin had a sly, knowing expression on his face. "It's all here. Your suits, your clothes. Rennie wouldn't let us touch any of it." He pushed past Nick and opened closets and dresser drawers. "It's a fucking shrine, Nicky. A shrine to the fallen angel."

Nick took a step into the room. He hadn't realized it, but he'd been holding his breath, waiting for a trap to spring. But no monster jumped out at him. *It's just a room. Your room.*

"Here, Rennie wants you to take a look at this." Martin flipped a manila envelope at Nick, then squeezed his massive body into a leather armchair.

"What is it?"

"Open it up and see for yourself."

Nick's hands slowed when he saw what was inside. He snapped a quick look at Martin, who gazed back with thin-lipped satisfaction. *Bastard.* Clearly, he knew what the contents of that envelope would do to Nick.

Sliding onto a small couch, he pulled out the photographs and spread them on the coffee table. Eight-by-ten black-and-whites, taken with a long lens. Surveillance photos. Each one showed Shelley and a solemn, dark-haired boy in a playground. On the swings. By the monkey bars.

"What's his name?"

"Isaac."

Nick stared into the boy's face. Was Nick's own looking back at him? No, the boy was Shelley all over. He had her heart-shaped face, her mouth, and the curve of her brow. But he was dark. Dark as Rennie, whose hair had been inky before turning white.

Dark as Nick.

But Rennie's eyes were blue, Shelley's green. Whose eyes did the boy have? They looked out at Nick, serious and unsmiling. In the black-and-white photos, they could have been any color.

Nick asked, "Did you take these?"

"Why? Don't you like the play of light and shadow?"

Nick ignored the sarcasm. "What park are they in?" He noticed a gnarled tree in the background of several shots, but few other markers. Given the angle of the pictures, they could have been taken anywhere.

"I don't know. I took a lot of pictures."

"Come on, Marty, give me a little help here. You help me, maybe I can help you."

Martin snorted and rose. "You think I need your help?" He paced away, light on his feet for such a bulky man. "I know what you're up to, Nick. You're here to make trouble for everyone."

"Only if I can."

Martin turned, eyeing him with thinly veiled hostility. "Go ahead and try. We're all in the clear. Or maybe you haven't seen the police report. The night Shelley died, Rennie and Frank were at a Cancer Society fund-raiser. Rennie was on the dais. Two hundred people can give him an alibi."

Nick scoffed. "So what? Rennie's the master puppeteer, pulling the strings behind the scenes. What about his favorite puppet? Where were you?"

Martin cocked his head, gave him a don't-be-stupid look. "Sweden. Checking out a used trawler for SATCO Marine. Got the passport stamp to prove it. I didn't do it, Nicky."

"Someone else, then. Some day man. A freelancer."

"Rennie kills his wife and hires a stranger to do it? Someone he barely knows and trusts less? Come on, you know him better than that."

"Yeah, I know him real well."

"Then stick to the job he wants you to do."

"Or what?"

"Or someone will pay another visit to your teacher friend."

Nick moved so fast, he didn't realize what he was doing until he had Martin's shirt bunched in his fists.

"You touch her, you so much as breathe the same air—"

"Or what—you're going to kill me?" Martin snatched his clothes out of Nick's hold. "I don't think so. You can't. You never could."

"Well, maybe that's why Rennie wants *me* to find the kid. That way he has a chance of staying alive."

Martin stopped straightening his tie and shot Nick a lethal look. "You son of a bitch. You were in that alley in Panama, too. You had a gun—anytime, you could have stopped me."

"You should have let him go."

"He *saw* us, Nicky. No witnesses, that's Rennie's first rule. Jesus Christ, it's been six years. How many times do we have to do this song and dance?"

"You should have let him go."

"Well, 'should have' are two of the most overused words in the dictionary, pal."

That night, Nick slept in Rennie's house for the first time in six years. And just like old times, a dream woke him, as familiar and bloody as ever. He sat up, sweating in terror, heart thudding so fiercely in his chest he thought it would burst through his skin.

But something was different. The face in the dream, the eyes that hoped for nothing. *They* were different. He flipped on the bedside lamp, and the face in the dream appeared with the light, in the photographs he'd left scattered on the night table.

Isaac.

After that, Nick didn't bother going back to sleep. Once there, the dream mutated inside his head anyway, waking him several times a night. Instead he pulled on some clothes and borrowed one of Rennie's cars. By four A.M., he was parked across from Rachel's apartment building.

Would she go to work? After everything she'd been through, he wouldn't blame her if she took some time off. But he wasn't surprised when two hours later her VW drove out of the lot. She was nothing if not dedicated.

Following at a discreet distance, he watched for a tail but didn't spot one. But that didn't mean he'd take Rennie's word for anything either. He'd make sure she was safe, even if he had to secretly escort her to and from work every day for the rest of his life.

He held his breath, knowing she would park the car and get out. How would she look?

He drove past her, turning his head away in case she happened to look up, and double-parked halfway down the block. Standing in the open wedge of the car door, he leaned against the roof to watch. But she had already started to walk away. He saw the braid sway against her back, watched her hike up the church steps and disappear inside. Was she all right? Would she ever be all right again?

Rachel jumped as the phone rang in her office. She took a breath to steady herself, but her hands still shook as she reached for the phone.

"Rachel, dear, how are you?" Julia's voice trilled over the phone and Rachel's heart sank. Her mother's sister, Julia, had taken Rachel in after her mother's death and her father's virtual abandonment of her. Along with her husband, Elliot, and her son, Chris, Julia was the closest thing Rachel had to a family, and right now, she was the last person Rachel wanted to talk to.

"I . . . I'm fine," she lied. If her aunt found out what had happened two nights ago, she'd only say, I told you so.

"Well, I wouldn't blame you if you weren't fine. We saw that man's picture in the paper, the one involved in the Spier hit-and-run. Rachel, I had lunch with Patricia Sydney today, and she's still interested in talking with you about the headmistress job at Bellwood."

Rachel put a shaky hand to her forehead. "I already have a job."

"But why put yourself in this position? Exposing yourself to the dregs of society, to murderers like that man who works for you."

She gripped the phone tighter, holding on to her patience with difficulty. "He's not a murderer. And you can stop worrying. He resigned. But largely because of the publicity, not because he did anything wrong."

"The police seem to think differently."

"Then the police are wrong! Nick had nothing to do with Shelley Spier's murder. I know, because I was with him that night." She groaned inwardly. What she wouldn't give to take those words back! Sinking back into her chair, she braced herself for Julia's reaction.

"Another effort to rescue the starving masses?" Rachel could picture the condescension chilling her aunt's face. "Isn't that school bad enough? Do you have to drag every stray cat to your door?"

"Julia—"

"If your father was here, oh, wouldn't he be laughing

now? You have no idea how it hurts me to see his influence in you. My God, the man's been dead for three years, and you're still his little socialist pawn."

She'd heard this so many times, she should have been deaf to it. But she wasn't. "I don't want to have this fight now."

"He killed your mother, Rachel, as surely as if he pulled the trigger himself."

Rachel gasped. "That's an outrageous thing to say, and you know it."

"I know he dragged my sister to the ends of the earth to live with scum, and they killed her for it."

"The Bronx is not the ends of the earth, and he didn't drag her. She *wanted* to help people."

"I couldn't bear it if the same thing happened—" Tears suddenly choked Julia's voice.

No, she could never tell her aunt what had happened the other night. Rachel rubbed her forehead in an effort to push back her looming headache. "You're upsetting yourself over nothing. Nick is . . . is gone. Look, your mascara is probably starting to run. And I'm . . . I'm busy. I have to go."

Not a good idea, Rachel. But she hung up anyway. Another moment, and she'd have burst into tears.

She closed her eyes, hoping the nightmare would go away. But no matter what she did, she could still feel the hood going over her head. Still feel the darkness, the terror.

And Nick.

God, Nick.

What had happened to him? She'd woke to find him gone, and been unable to reach him ever since.

A knock sounded. What now?

"Come in."

Father Pat stood at the threshold. Tall and gaunt, he had a kind face that, at the moment, wore a stern expression.

"Rachel, I've just received a phone call from Bill Hughes. He's been trying to reach you for days."

"I know. I just haven't had a chance to call him back." Or the desire to.

"He tells me you've been harassing the Murphys about their niece, Carla."

"I didn't harass them. I made a home visit to ask them to reconsider their decision to pull Carla out of the program."

"These incidents can't continue. You must realize that. The council meets next week, and I can't guarantee they'll extend our agreement. At least not now. You can't expect people to support you if you ignore their concerns."

The warning was clear. "I'm sorry. You're right, of course. I'll call him." She held up a hand. "Promise."

"And the Murphys?"

She sighed. "I'll . . . I'll slow down."

"Good." The priest peered at her closely. "Are you all right?"

She made her mouth form a smile. "Yes, of course."

"You were out yesterday. Nothing serious, I hope?"

"Just a summer cold. I'm fine."

The priest nodded and left, closing the door behind him.

A burning sensation wafted through Rachel's consciousness. She looked down; she was rubbing her wrist, right over the bruises. God, she hadn't done that since she was a child. She'd rubbed her wrists raw for years after her mother's murder. The unconscious, obsessive gesture scared her more than anything.

You are not *going to fall apart.*

Separating her hands, she sank back into her armchair. If only she could tell someone what had happened. Vomit up every detail until she was free of them all. But she wouldn't risk hurting the school by telling anyone, not even for her own peace of mind. Nick was the only person she could talk to, and he had disappeared.

Fortunately, everyone assumed the publicity about Nick's connection to Shelley Spier's murder had caused the dark circles under her eyes and the strain in her voice. Rachel let them think what they wanted. She was still hiding the truth a few days later, when Felice poked her head into Rachel's office.

"That good-for-nothing Bill Hughes called me at home." The large woman stepped in. As usual, her massive, square frame was swathed in a swirling mass of bright color—hot pink today. "Said the Parish Council had doubts about your judgment. He wanted some dirt on Nick, but I didn't tell him anything."

Rachel sighed. "There isn't anything to tell."

"That's exactly what I said. He did his job, right? He never did anything else but his job. They can't shut us down for that, can they?"

"They can try."

"But they won't. You've pulled us away from the edge before. You'll see, you'll do it again."

Her confidence put Rachel on the verge of breakdown, unable to handle anything, much less Bill Hughes and the rest of the Parish Council. Misinterpreting, Felice gave Rachel a friendly smile. "Look, I know you're bummed. But this'll all blow over soon. In a week or two, everyone will forget about Nick."

If only *she* could forget him. Why did whoever it was drop her at Nick's door? Who would want to terrorize her? Why? The questions haunted her, making it impossible to put the experience behind her. But the only one who could give her the answers she needed had vanished. God, what had happened to him?

Just then, someone rapped on her door. Rachel looked up to see a small, scrappy man with a hangdog face and sharp, watery blue eyes.

"Miss Goodman? I'm Detective Pat May." He stepped in and shook her hand. "I understand you wanted to talk to someone about Nicky Raine?"

She'd completely forgotten the phone call she'd made to the police a few days ago after wrestling with her conscience about Nick. Now it was as if the universe had heard her cry and sent an answer to it.

Felice slid out the door, and Rachel settled into the chair behind her desk, gesturing the detective into the seat across from her. He opened a notepad.

"Raine says he worked for you."

She nodded. "He was a . . . a handyman. He cleaned up, fixed things, helped with the kids. We needed another teacher, but I couldn't afford one. Nick was a big help."

He eyed her speculatively, as if he didn't believe her. "And what was it you wanted to tell us?"

She sighed, aware this would pull her in further, but committed to the truth by her phone call. "Look, Detective. I wanted to let you know that I was with Nick the night of Shelley Spier's murder."

May's eyebrows rose. "Raine didn't mention it."

She looked down at her hands. She'd been afraid of that. "That's why I called you. Nick didn't want to involve the school any more than it already was."

"A real boy scout," May said dryly. "So where and when were you together?"

"One of the grocery stores had a large donation they couldn't deliver. Nick helped me pick it up. We had a pizza afterward." She gave him the details, including times and addresses.

May wrote everything down in his book. "Nice and convenient, you coming up with an alibi for him."

She bristled. "It may have been . . . convenient, but it's also the truth."

"Is it?"

"Why would I lie about it?"

"I don't know, Miss Goodman. I just know people do from time to time."

"If I were going to lie, I wouldn't have called you. The last thing I need is for this school to have any association with Nick or Shelley Spier's death."

He rose. "Well, the city appreciates you coming forward. We'll check this out." He turned to go.

She rose to see him out, trying to decide whether or not to ask about Nick. This might be her only chance to find out what had happened to him, but it wasn't smart to ask; the less she knew, the better. And yet questions about her kidnapping and his safety gnawed at her, an open sore that wouldn't heal.

Still debating, she walked Detective May to the door,

where he gave her shabby office a sharp-eyed scan. "Hard to imagine Nicky Raine working here."

She remembered Nick's tense dedication and found her mouth tilting up in a small smile. "He did a good job. Never missed a day."

The detective shook his head with a curt laugh. "The conscientious janitor. Well, I guess he's back in more familiar territory now."

Her awareness sharpened. "What do you mean?"

"He won't be hammering nails for Rennie Spier."

"R-Rennie Spier?" She frowned.

"That's right." May tucked his notepad into his pocket. "Swimming with the sharks again."

"Are you sure?"

He shrugged. "As sure as anything in life." He threw her a cynical smile and left.

Rachel closed the door behind him, a sick lump in her stomach. Nick couldn't be working for Spier again.

Her hand tightened on the doorknob. What was it her father used to say? *We may have been victimized, but we don't have to be victims.* Well, she was tired of feeling like a victim.

Setting her jaw, she reached for her purse. The local branch of the public library was only a few blocks away, and she strode down the streets doggedly. When she got there, it didn't take long to find the information she needed; the accident had put Spier and his arms-dealing business on the front page for days.

She copied the articles and spent the night reading them. Compelled to devour every scrap of information, she ignored the rumbling in her stomach that meant dinnertime had come and gone. She didn't stop to check the clock on the wall or stretch her legs. She read the words again and again, each time hoping they would say something different. Something better. But it was always the same.

Spier represented a vast empire that fed on violence, the kind of violence that had killed her mother. How could Nick be a part of that horror?

It must be a mistake. A misunderstanding. She wouldn't believe it. Not until she heard it from Nick's own mouth.

Chapter 5

Nick stood in the center of a neighborhood park on Staten Island and held up the surveillance photographs, comparing them to his surroundings. Around him, kids ran while mothers watched. Wrinkled men played dominoes at a cement table. He counted benches, swings, all the ingredients except one. No gnarled tree. He clamped his jaw down on a howl of frustration.

Every day. Every goddamn day for weeks, he'd tramped through the five boroughs looking for the park with the gnarled tree.

Every day he came up empty.

Marty had been no help. "You want to fuck Rennie," he'd said, "don't expect me to help you pull down his pants."

Marty was off on his own search for the boy, vying for the prize of Rennie's approval. It was a sad, one-man competition; Nick could care less.

Clenching his hands into fists, he walked the two

blocks to his car, searching for the dead zone he'd lived in for the last six years. The numbness was gone. He was furious at Rennie, panicked he wouldn't find Isaac, and Rachel—every day guilt racked him. Was she all right? Was the light back in her eyes? Newly awakened feelings thundered inside him. On his way to the car, he stopped in the middle of the sidewalk and forced himself to breathe normally.

What he wouldn't give for a drink. For the once-familiar whiskey haze. Anything to dull the roar.

He looked down. The photographs were crumpled in his hand. Slowly, he released his taut fingers and smoothed out the boy's image. Two faces haunted him now. The one in the dream and this one. Every day both faces pulled him in deeper and deeper. One was beyond help, but the other . . . Was he happy? Was he safe? And that one final question. The one Nick pushed to the back of his mind, where it churned inside him day after day: Is he mine?

He slid into the car and stared blindly out the windshield. What if he did find the kid? What then? Would he hand him over to Rennie like a new puppy?

He shoved the key into the ignition and jerked the car into gear. He didn't know what he was going to do. And he had to hurry if he was going to make it to St. Anthony's in time to shadow Rachel home.

He braced himself for the ordeal. This was his life. Morning and evening, he made the silent run from Rachel's apartment to the church and back again. A guardian angel two car-lengths behind, anonymous, invisible. Twice a day he faced the one thing he wanted most in the world and couldn't have. And in between, he chased down different kinds of ghosts.

Murdered moms and missing children.

But it was better this way.

The word echoed inside his head all the way to St. Anthony's.

Better. Better. Better.

When he got to Astoria, he cruised the block where he'd seen Rachel park her car that morning.

It wasn't there.

He rechecked the street. No, he was sure this was the right street. He checked the time; she never left this early.

Something was wrong.

Mouth dry, he used the car phone to call the school. Felice answered. He asked for Rachel without identifying himself.

"She left early today. Would you like to leave a message?"

He declined and disconnected.

Where had she gone? *Don't panic.* But knowing she could be anywhere and he couldn't protect her sent waves of alarm rushing through him.

He raced to her apartment, cursing the traffic. He always knew she was home because he could see her windows from the street, and the first thing she did was turn on the lights. They were dark now. Making doubly sure, he searched every corner of the parking lot and the surrounding streets. No sign of her car anywhere.

Damn.

This was exactly the kind of moment Rennie waited for. Get her alone. Unprotected.

A new wave of fear washed over him. Tires squealing, he turned the car around and flew into Manhattan.

He was on the east side of Gramercy Park, speeding for the underground garage, when he saw her.

Clutching a folded piece of paper, she stood in the middle of the sidewalk, looking lost. Her braid was its usual sweet tangle, and she wore a loose sleeveless dress that skimmed her knees, leaving bare legs and sandaled feet.

He slammed on the brakes. Blinked. Was he seeing things?

No, there she was, cool and fresh, her dress a minty green. Just as she'd looked that morning when he'd watched her climb the church steps.

What was she doing here?

He parked the car and got out. His heart was pounding so loud, he was sure the whole block could hear it.

Just then she turned and saw him. Surprise made her stare. She half raised a hand, as if to wave, hesitated, then took a step forward. "Nick?"

Jesus Christ.

He lengthened his stride, almost running, grabbed her arm and pulled her off the sidewalk into the alley between two brownstones. He didn't mean to growl, but panic exploded inside him. "Are you crazy? Why did you come here?"

Rachel stared at him, speechless. What could she say when she didn't even recognize him? The suit and tie, the Italian shoes . . . She could have passed him on the street and not known him. He looked like his picture now. Like the picture in the newspaper after Shelley's death. Slick. Fast.

He shook her. "What are you doing here?"

His anger jolted her out of her dazed confusion. "I'm . . . I was looking for you."

"All right, you found me." Impatient, annoyed. "What do you want?"

To throw her arms around his neck; he was alive, he was all right. But relief warred with outrage. Look at him. She'd been frantic with worry; how could he look so . . . so good? So angry. "I want you to let go of me, for one thing." Her voice came out hard and tight. "You're hurting me."

"Better me than someone else." He released her arm, but his face was still tense and irate. "Look, you have to get out of here. Now."

He was right; she had a bad feeling about this. The clothes, the attitude, none of this was the Nick she knew. "Not until you answer some questions."

"I don't have time for questions."

"Make time."

He muttered a curse under his breath, scanned the alley as if for enemy infiltrators. "Five minutes."

Gee, thanks. "I spoke to the police about where you were the night Shelley died. They told me you're with Rennie Spiers now. Is it true?"

He looked as though he wanted to strangle her. "You spoke to the police? For God's sake, are you *trying* to set yourself up as a target?"

She curbed her impatience. "I'm trying to do what's right. You were with me, Nick. You didn't kill Shelley. But you did disappear. Right off the radar screen. For all I knew you could have been lying in a ditch with your throat slit." She paused to look him over. "But you weren't, were you? You were just getting a makeover."

"Sorry to disappoint you."

She could have bitten off her tongue. "I didn't say I was disappointed." Not yet, anyway. "So . . ." She looked at his face, at his dark eyes sharp with anger, at the rough twist of his mouth, and hoped against hope. "Is it true? Are you working for Spier again?"

She held her breath. His jaw tensed. "Yes."

The word hit her like a fist in the stomach. The man who had held her all night, who'd been sweet and gentle and made her feel safe in her darkest moment, that man would not work for a monster like Spier.

So it must have been some other Nick who checked his watch and said, "Four minutes."

She bit back a nasty reply, but even so her words came out on the edge of sarcasm. "So . . . is this your new uniform?" She waved her hand in front of him, indicating his attire. Somehow, the expensive clothes made his betrayal all the more real. And her own feelings all the more confused. Because much as she wanted to turn her back on him, the truth was, he took her breath away. She hated what he was doing, why couldn't she hate him? Why couldn't she turn around and walk away?

"It's wicked of you to look so good," she said.

His lips thinned into a tight smile. "Rennie demands a certain . . . standard from his associates." He watched her with unfeeling black eyes. "Three minutes."

That was it. She'd had it. She didn't know this man. "Forget it." She stalked off. "I don't need you. It says right here Rennie Spier's headquarters are in Gramercy Park." She'd brought one of the newspaper articles with her, and now she waved it over her shoulder. "I'll find it eventually and ask *him* my questions."

"Wait a minute. Wait a minute!" He captured her arm, spun her around. "You stay away from Rennie."

"Why? What's he got to do with me?" She yanked her arm out of his grasp. "Or is he behind that little unexpected visit your friends paid me?" Did his face blanch? In the dimness of the alley she couldn't be sure. "They were *your* friends, weren't they?"

"That's not the word I'd use."

"Really? What would you call them?"

The wall of steel softened. "Rachel, I—" He took a step toward her. She backed away.

"He used me, didn't he? The . . . kidnapping. Releasing me at your doorstep. He wanted you to do something. Something you didn't want to do." Nick didn't say anything. He didn't have to. The answer was in the stricken look on his face. "What did he want?"

"It doesn't matter."

She pivoted toward the street. God, she was tired of fencing with him.

He ran to block her way. "All right. He wanted *me.*"

"And you went? After six years, he snaps his fingers, and you come running?"

His eyes hardened into two black coals. "He didn't exactly snap his fingers, did he?"

No, he hadn't. Rennie Spier had used *her.* Hurt her. All at once she understood. "You did it for me, didn't you? My God. That's why you disappeared so suddenly, why you haven't contacted me, called . . . You were afraid he'd use me again."

He looked away, as if ashamed. "You don't have to

worry about . . . about anything like that happening again."

"Oh, Nick." Her throat squeezed shut. Her anger dissolved, and suddenly she felt like crying. That he would do that for her. Turn his life upside down to protect her. "I . . . I don't know what to say."

"Don't say anything. Just go."

"No one's put themselves on the line like that for me. Ever. Not even my father."

He grabbed her by the shoulders and pushed her backward toward the street. "You're welcome. Now get out of here."

His hands on her shoulders felt good, but she ignored the little skip her heart took. Instead, she dug in her heels, stopping his backward drive. "What does Spier want you to do?"

"Rachel—"

"The sooner you answer my questions, the sooner I'll go. Spier wanted something from you. What?"

He dropped his hold. Propping one elbow against the side of a building, he sighed and rubbed his forehead. "The usual stuff—rob from the poor, fight for the rich, inspire corruption, and reward greed. Bring death and destruction to one and all."

"I'm serious."

"So am I." He crossed his arms and leaned his back against the wall, eyeing her.

"And are you enjoying your work?"

"Yeah, I love it. Great benefits."

A wave of warmth for him washed over her. He was such a liar. "Nick, I can't let you do this."

"It's not up to you."

"I'll be all right. I'll call the police. I'll tell them what you said."

He laughed, pushing himself off the wall. "The police? You think the police can protect you from Rennie? They couldn't protect his own wife from him."

"His wife? What do you mean?"

"He killed Shelley." Nick said the words with quiet conviction.

A ripple of uneasiness fluttered low in her stomach. "He killed his wife? But Nick, why?"

"Let's just say he had his reasons."

"Are you sure?"

"Oh yeah. So don't think he'd hesitate a second before doing the same to you." The look he threw her said, Do you see now? Do you understand? "Get out of here, and don't come back."

She bit her lip, the reasons for his insistence shimmering inside her. Hanging around him could put herself and her school in danger. Nick was a grown man; he didn't need her help.

But how could she abandon him here, especially after what he'd done for her?

"Come with me," she said, knowing it wasn't smart but saying it anyway.

"You're not listening. I can't see you. Ever."

"Look, if it means getting you away from Rennie Spier, I'll take the risk."

"You will?" But before she could take another breath, he grabbed her from behind, pinned her arms and imprisoned her against him. "Remember what this feels like?" His voice rasped in her ear. "The tape over your mouth, the hood over your head? You struggled, didn't you? Just like you're struggling now."

"Let me go." She twisted, but he only tightened his hold.

"You're locked in darkness, drowning in fear. Will they hurt you? Kill you?"

"Stop it."

"Will the sound of your dying be just like your mother's? Will you scream like she screamed? Bleed like she bled?"

"I said, stop it!" Heart pounding, she fought him, but her efforts were as useless now as they were then. He was too big, too strong. The memory of that night slammed into her. The swift surprise, the helplessness, the bowel-loosening trip in the car. She heard the shot that stopped her mother's life, saw the lifeless look in her eyes as she lay on the ground. The two memories merged into heart-thumping hysteria. "Let me go. Stop it, *stop it!*" But the voice in her ear crooned on.

"Remember, Rachel. Next time you're willing to risk your life, you remember what this feels like." And with that, he flung her away.

Breathing hard, she tried to get the saliva back in her mouth. She rubbed her arms where he'd held her. "You bastard."

"Yeah. And I'm the good guy."

Her heart was beating so fast, it was a wonder it didn't fly out of her body. Legs shaking, she stumbled away from him. Out the alley. Down the street. As far as she could get.

Nick watched her go, forcing back the bile that threatened to spew out of him.

Rennie would have been real proud of him.

He wiped his mouth with the back of his wrist. His hand was shaking. Sweat glued his shirt to his back. What he wouldn't give for a drink.

He peered out the mouth of the alley and saw her get into her car. Forcing his legs to move, he sprinted to his own and managed to turn it around in time to follow her. No matter what she thought, no matter what he said, he would keep her safe.

Between the city traffic and the tie-ups on the expressway, the sun was almost down by the time she made it back to her apartment. Guilt stalked him as he inched forward. He shouldn't have grabbed her, shouldn't have frightened her.

It was for her own good.

Yeah, the way a whipping was for your own good.

From across the street, he watched her park her car. She got out and disappeared inside the building. He timed his watch for a minute, ten seconds, the length it always took her to reach her apartment and turn on the light. Raising his head, he focused on the fifth-floor corner window.

A minute and a half.

Two minutes.

Still the apartment stayed black.

When five minutes had come and gone, and the window remained unlit, he reached underneath the seat and pulled out the Beretta Rennie stashed there.

A hundred scenarios flooded his mind as he slammed the car door and raced across the street. Someone could have been waiting for her inside. Someone who'd put his hands on her, touch her, hurt her. He dodged speeding cars. Braking tires squealed; horns blared. Blood pounded in his ears, drowning them out. He concentrated on one thing only: getting to Rachel as fast as he could.

No time to wait for the elevator. He took the stairs, two at a time.

Faster. Go faster. She could be dead by now.

He burst through the door at the top of the fifth-floor staircase, took half a second to orient himself. *Left. Go left.* He didn't waste time knocking on her door. The sound would only warn whoever was inside. Holding the gun so he could fire it instantly, he kicked in the door.

Nothing. No sound.

The apartment was dim, but light spilled in from the hallway. He spun around, both hands wrapped around the gun, which he held in firing position. From the doorway, his view covered most of the living area and kitchen. Empty. Hugging the walls, he slid down the hallway toward the bedroom and bathroom.

"Rachel?"

No answer. Panic rose. He tried again, louder this time. "Rachel, where are you?"

"What are you doing?" The voice came from behind. He whirled. She was standing in the apartment doorway. "Pushing me around wasn't enough? Now you're going to shoot me?"

His gaze searched the doorway and the area over her shoulder. "Are you . . . are you okay?"

"Not if you keep pointing that thing at me."

He looked down at the weapon trained on her heart, and his gut clenched. The first time. The first time in six years he'd held the cold ice of a gun in his hand. And he hadn't even thought twice about picking it up. *This is what you are, who you are.*

Repulsed, he lowered the Beretta. She stepped into the room, leaving the door partially open so the hallway light could illuminate the apartment.

"What do you want?" Her voice was harsh and unwelcoming.

"Your lights didn't come on." The gun weighed heavy in his hand. He stashed it at the small of his back, beneath his jacket, where neither of them could see it.

"The power is out. And the phone isn't working either. I had to go down to the manager and tell him." Her eyes narrowed. "How did you know about the lights?"

Caught, he couldn't think of an excuse fast enough. "I . . . I followed you." Delayed relief at seeing her whole and alive was making his legs quake. He leaned against the wall until they stopped.

"You followed me? Why? According to you we're not supposed to see each other."

"I . . . I wanted to make sure you got home okay. You were upset . . ." God, that sounded lame. "When the lights didn't come on, I thought—"

"You thought your friend Rennie Spier had gotten to me? Sorry to ruin your day, but it was just a bunch of kids on the first floor."

"Kids?"

"Yeah, a stupid prank."

A prank? Not likely. Senses on alert, he scanned the large living area. "Is it only your apartment?"

"Seems to be. My lucky day. Manhandled by you, then by a couple of twelve-year-olds."

"And the phone is out, too?"

"Perfect ending to a perfect day." She went into the kitchen. He heard her riffling in cupboards and drawers. "I have a flashlight here somewhere."

While she was gone, he calmed himself enough to take a quick look at the phone in the living room. He felt around the wall; the wires were intact. Whoever had done this had done it at the control box, which meant a knowledge of communications beyond most twelve-year-olds. Then again, any twelve-year-old with a good pair of wire cutters could have randomly snipped a few connections. Maybe it *was* just coincidence that Rachel's apartment had been blacked out.

Except he didn't believe in coincidence.

She came out of the kitchen with a couple of plates holding lit candles. "Flashlight batteries are dead. Figures." She placed one of the plates on the coffee table, the other on an end table next to the couch. The flickering lights cast a soft glow on her face. A glow that didn't hide the animosity clouding her normally gentle expression.

"You can go now."

"In a minute. I want to check—"

"No. The last thing I need is some tough guy whose lifestyle can get me hurt, or worse. Get out. Now."

Well, he'd wanted her mad enough to stay away, hadn't he? *Be careful what you wish for.*

"When do they expect to get your power back?"

A flicker of panic flew across her face. She swallowed hard. "Maybe tomorrow."

All night in the dark, no phone, no way to call for help. And idiot that he was, he'd seen to it that the door was half off its hinges, the lock broken. After what Rennie had done to her, she must be terrified.

"Maybe you should stay somewhere else tonight."

"I'm not the one leaving. You are." Sheer bravado, but she had guts, he'd give her that.

"Don't you have family who'll put you up?"

"Not without a lot of questions."

"A motel, then."

She studied him. The candlelight turned the wisps of hair around her face into strands of gold that he itched to touch. But he kept his distance. He had to.

She said, "What's going on here? As long as you do what Spier wants, I'm safe. A hostage for your good behavior, maybe, but safe. Why would your precious Rennie Spier renege on your deal?"

"I don't know. I've been asking myself the same question and haven't come up with an answer." Except who else would want to hurt her?

"There is no answer. Like the manager said, it was a prank."

"Maybe." He shrugged out of his suit jacket. "And maybe not."

"What are you doing?"

"Where's your screwdriver? I'll fix the door."

"No, you won't." Her chin was up, her mouth a grim line.

"You can't stay here with a door that won't lock."

"I can do whatever I damn well please. It's my home, my life. Now get out." She threw his jacket at him and shoved him toward the door. He let her push him out and close the damaged door as best she could. It didn't matter. He wasn't going anywhere.

The minute he was gone, Rachel sank to the floor. Had he seen her hands shaking? Just the thought of staying in the dark apartment sent waves of terror through her. She hadn't slept with the lights out in weeks.

But that didn't mean she wanted Nick to keep her company either.

Liar.

She could go to her aunt and uncle's. Or to Felice. They'd put her up for the night.

But she didn't trust herself. She'd probably blurt out everything about Spier and the kidnapping, and then where would she and her kids be? Without a school, for one.

Besides, she wouldn't let anyone chase her out of her own home.

She stood, planting her feet on the floor. She could do this. It was just a temporary power outage. No one was hiding in the closets. Remember: victimized, but not a victim.

So why was her heart thudding?

A knock. Her body jerked. She sucked in a breath.

Take it easy. It's just the door.

"Who . . . who is it?"

"It's me." Nick again.

God, go away. She swung the unlocked door open. "I thought I told you to—"

"Here." In his outstretched hand he held a cellular phone. "In case you need to talk to someone."

Why did he do this? First he made it seem as though he were the last person on earth she should be around, and now . . .

Why did he have to be so rotten?

Why did he have to be so nice?

"And here's my pager number." He picked up her hand and scrawled a number across her palm with a ball-point. "If anything happens, *anything,* call. I'll be here in five seconds."

Five seconds? She said dryly, "Where you staying these days—outside my door?"

He did that avoidance thing he liked to do—he looked away, looked down, looked back up at her. Then didn't answer her question. "Don't worry about it. I'll get here."

She nodded, too irritated to press him. "Whatever." And closed the door again.

She scraped together a cheese sandwich by candlelight, and drank the last of the milk to keep it from spoiling. Since the air-conditioning had gone with the electricity, she opened all the windows before going to bed, hoping the cross-ventilation would cool down the apartment.

Too hot in the bedroom, she lay on the couch wearing only a tank top and panties. For some reason, she felt safer in the living room, where she could keep her eye on the damaged door.

It was only a prank. Nick was wrong. He had to be. He was trying to scare her. He *liked* scaring her.

The candlelight made monsters of the furniture. She knew she should blow out the flames, but couldn't bring herself to.

I won't let fear control my life. Rennie Spier used me once. I won't let him keep on abusing me.

She focused on the things around her. This is the couch, this the armchair, over there is the basket of magazines. Everything the way it should be, everything in its place, everything safe.

Everything safe.

Her hand strayed to her wrist, but she caught herself.

They won't come back. They won't.

Curling her body around Nick's cell phone, she memorized the number on her hand. It took her a long time to fall asleep.

Chapter 6

It was after two when Nick heard Rachel scream. The sound sailed through the partially opened door and outside into the hallway where he'd stationed himself all night. Gun drawn, he shouldered himself through the door, expecting two men, three, God only knew what . . . and saw her writhing on the couch, eyes closed in sleep, hands fighting off an unseen assailant.

He tucked the Beretta beneath his jacket, in the waistband at his back, and knelt by the couch. What to do?

In the shaft of hallway light that pierced the darkness, she was nearly naked. She wore a shred of cloth that bunched up, so he could see part of one round breast. The sight sent blood straight to his groin. God, he couldn't touch her. Not like this.

But he had no choice. She cried out again, her voice shot through with hysteria. He got between her arms, letting her hands slap at him. "Shh, it's all right. It's just a dream." He shook her, but she became even more agitated. Finally, he did the only thing he could think of. He pulled her toward him, wrapping his arms around her and holding her tight against his chest. "Shh, I got you. You're safe."

He rubbed her back and whispered sounds of comfort. She felt small in his arms, her shoulders round and soft, her bones delicate, fragile. She smelled so good. For a moment, he let himself enjoy the sensation. Her breasts pressed against him, her legs, long and bare, and close enough to touch.

He knew the minute she woke up. The moaning died out. She tensed, and a pang went through him, knowing she would pull away. She did.

"What happened?" She rubbed her eyes, looked at him accusingly. "Why are you back here?"

"I heard you scream."

"You heard me scream?"

"You were dreaming." He stood up. Better get as far away as he could. "Have you been dreaming a lot lately?" He knew a thing or two about nightmares, and it killed him to think of her suffering because of him.

"You *heard* me . . . ?"

He sighed. "Look, I—I've been outside. In the hall-way."

She stared at him.

He shoved his hands in his pockets. "Are you okay now?" No answer, but he didn't need one; he could see she was fine. "Good. I'll just go—" He thumbed over his shoulder, then turned in that direction. Her voice stopped him.

"You've been outside my apartment. All night." Like she was trying to get it straight.

"Hey, don't worry, I'm not gonna make a habit of it."

"Come here, Nick."

He reached for the doorknob.

"I said, come here."

He swore silently and turned.

She sat cross-legged on the couch in her underwear, her hair wild, her eyes demanding. She looked vulnerable as a child, sexy as the most alluring woman. He swallowed. How could he resist? Reluctantly, he stepped over to the couch.

"Sit."

"I better—"

She grabbed his hand and tugged him down next to her.

"Look at me." When he didn't, she took his face in her hands and turned it so he couldn't avoid her. Her eyes were wide and gentle. The eyes he'd missed. The look he thought he'd never see again. "Thank you."

"It's just for tonight." He couldn't breathe. Her hands bracketed his face, her mouth so close.

"Thank you."

"One night. Just in case."

"In case Rennie Spier comes for me again?"

"In case it wasn't a prank."

She smiled. Soft. Kind. "Thank you."

"You're . . . you're welcome."

She let him go, and his heart started beating again. Then she stood, and once again, his lungs clogged up.

"If you've been out there all night, you didn't have dinner. If it hasn't gone moldy yet, I can make you a cheese sandwich."

She lit a candle, and in the flickering light he could

see her nipples outlined against the thin fabric of the sleeveless shirt. Her panties didn't come anywhere close to covering her navel. Between the bottom of the shirt and the top of her panties, a band of skin gleamed smooth and tantalizing.

"Sure. Whatever." Anything to get her out of the room. "And maybe you should—" He cleared his throat. "Maybe you should put on some clothes."

She looked down at herself, then up at him. His face heated. A smile tugged the corners of her mouth, but she said nothing, only disappeared down the hallway toward the bedroom, candle in hand.

God, had he blushed? Had he actually blushed? Christ. He was a grown man. Grown men didn't blush.

Thirty seconds later she was back, wearing the same undershirt thing and a pair of denim shorts. A very tiny, very tight pair of shorts. He groaned inwardly. No way would he be able to choke down a sandwich.

But if she realized the effect she had on him, she didn't say. She glided into the kitchen and lit another candle.

Under cover of gathering ingredients, Rachel watched Nick strip off his jacket, loosen his tie, and roll back his shirtsleeves in an effort to get comfortable in the heat of the un-air-conditioned apartment. She hadn't been blind, she'd seen the hungry look on his face when he'd told her to put on some clothes. Some mischievous sprite had made her reach for the shortest, tightest pair of shorts she owned. Not that it mattered. He raked his fingers through his hair, looking as though he'd rather be anywhere but here. And when he turned, she saw the gun at his back.

The best reminder out there that she shouldn't be trying to entice the guy who carried it.

"When do you have to report in?" She put a couple of cheese slices between two pieces of bread, opened the cupboard for a glass. At least the water would be cold.

"I don't punch a time clock."

"Rennie lets you come and go as you please?"

"As long as I get the job done."

She put the sandwich and the glass of water on the counter that separated the kitchen from the living room. "What job?" And then immediately wished she hadn't asked. She had her own problems to worry about; she didn't need to take on his, especially if they had anything to do with Rennie Spier.

But he plucked his jacket off the couch. From the inside pocket, he took out a battered photograph and slid it on the counter toward her. "Shelley had a son in secret. Rennie wants me to find him."

Shock skittered through her as she picked up the picture. A sober, dark-haired boy stared back at her. "What's his name?"

"Isaac."

She came around to join him. "He looks so serious. I wonder if he knows what happened to his mother." The memory of her own loss created an instant connection with the boy in the picture. "He must be suffering terribly. Do you have any idea where he is?"

He shook his head. "I've been tracking down the playground in the picture, but so far, no luck."

"His mother must have left him with someone she trusted. Friends, family."

"Shelley's only friends were green and had pictures of

presidents on them. As for family, she had an aunt out on the island who took care of the kid until she died a few months ago."

"But why would Shelley hide the boy from Rennie?"

"Who knows? She was crazy." He stared at the sandwich moodily, and like so many times before, she sensed he was holding back painful memories.

"Hard to tell what she was like from the stories and pictures in the paper," she said quietly. "Except that she was beautiful." She shook her head. "So sad. All that potential, wasted."

"Potential?" He snorted in disdain. "The only potential she had was for being manipulative and selfish."

His voice was so vehement it surprised her. "You didn't like her very much, did you?"

He stared over the counter into the darkened kitchen for a long time. Then softly, "I didn't say that." Something crossed his face. Wistfulness? Regret?

"You told me once that someone adopted you when you were a kid. You meant Rennie Spier, didn't you?"

He tensed, almost imperceptibly. "So?"

"So, I wouldn't want Rennie to get his hands on my son, either."

He turned his head, meeting her gaze. A pinprick of hurt flared and died in his dark eyes.

"I'm sorry, I shouldn't have said that."

Face impassive again, he shrugged. "Blast away. I'm sure I deserve it."

Did he? "I just meant she might've had a good reason for what she did. Maybe she was thinking of him." She nodded toward the picture of the dark-haired boy.

"Maybe." But from the tone of his voice, he didn't believe it.

Sliding the candle nearer, she studied the face in the photo. "He doesn't look like Rennie, does he?"

"How would you know?"

"I did some research. Besides, Rennie Spier's picture was all over the paper." She peered at the boy more closely. "There's something about his eyes, though. Something familiar."

Before she could figure out what, Nick swiped up the photograph and tucked it into the inner pocket of his suit jacket.

"What did I say?"

"Nothing. I shouldn't have shown you the picture in the first place. It's not your problem."

She searched his face, but he avoided her gaze. Just as well. He was right; it was none of her business. Or at least, she'd like to think so. Hard to do when a child was at risk.

Picking up the glass, he pressed it to his forehead. "Man, it's hot in here."

Abruptly, he put the gun on the counter and tugged his shirt over his head. Underneath, a sleeveless undershirt sculpted his smooth chest. A thin film of sweat oiled his dark skin. His shoulders rolled broad and powerful, the muscles in his arms firm and well defined.

Her breath caught. Why did he have to be so beautiful?

Desperate for distraction, she worked to keep her gaze on his face and not the muscles that rippled every time he moved. "So is that why you think Rennie killed her? Because she stole his son?"

"He's done it for less."

She could believe it. "Do the police know?"

"The police have wiped Rennie off their suspect list. He has an airtight alibi, and so does Frank."

"Frank?"

"Rennie's partner. His rainmaker."

"What's a rainmaker?"

He leaned toward her to recapture the water glass. The sudden closeness sent her heart swerving. "The guy who drums up business. Twists whatever arms need twisting. Although I don't imagine Frank's much muscle these days. Martin probably handles most of the rough stuff."

"And who's Martin?"

"You met him. At the school." He rubbed the glass with its cool contents over the center of his chest. Her mouth went dry.

"The, uh . . . the linebacker who looks like an over-grown teddy bear?" *Stop that. Stop doing that.*

He smiled grimly. "Yeah, that's him. A real lovable guy. Supposedly, he was in Sweden buying a boat for Rennie's marine division."

"Supposedly?"

"He could have sent someone in his place. Or used a fake passport to sneak back into this country. The only trouble is, his story pans out so far. I checked."

"So you have no proof?"

He shook his head. "Not yet."

"What's your next step?"

"Keep digging." He brought the glass of water to his mouth and swallowed half the contents, his powerful, tanned throat working smooth and strong.

Tearing her gaze away, she escaped into the kitchen. "Did you ever stop to think that maybe Rennie didn't do it? Plenty of people must want to get back at him. You don't get to the top in your line of work without making a few enemies."

"Yeah, that's the theory the police are working up. But I say the answer is closer to home. A lot closer."

She ducked her head, busying herself by pouring water into another glass. When she finished, he was walking into the room.

"I'll admit a hit-and-run isn't Rennie's style," he said, refilling his glass from the sink. "The outcome is too unpredictable. And he likes to work up close and personal. Frank used to tell these stories of what Rennie could do with a stiletto—" He stopped, as if suddenly remembering where he was and who he was talking to. He stared hard at the glass in his hand. "It doesn't matter anyway, Rennie just pays the bills now. He's not too fussy as long as no witnesses turn up and the job gets—"

His head snapped up. Slowly, he placed his glass in the sink.

"What is it?"

He put a finger to his lips and mouthed the words, "Stay here." A fast glance at the gun on the counter that clearly said, No time. He was already moving out of the kitchen and into the living room.

Then she heard it, too. A noise. At the front door. Her heart began to pound. *They won't come back. They won't.*

But they had.

A hulking shape entered the apartment. Backlit from the light in the hall, he had no features, and before she could better define him, Nick dove, knocking the other man off his feet.

She watched in helpless terror as the two men fought. They rolled over the floor, half in and half out of the apartment. In the dark, she couldn't see much, but she could hear everything. The sickening thud of bone meeting flesh, the grunts and muffled cries of pain.

Stop. God, please stop.

But what if they did, and Nick didn't get up?

In answer to her question, the two men crashed into the doorway, slamming the door against the wall once, then twice. She jumped each time, her heart racing.

Finally, Nick had the hulk by the throat, smashed against the doorjamb.

Breathless and still struggling to maintain his hold, Nick called out, "The gun, Rachel, throw me the gun."

She hesitated for half a second. A gun had been the source of her life's greatest wound. Could she pick one up now, even in her own defense?

"Throw me the goddamn gun!"

Not in her defense, maybe, but in Nick's. Swallowing her revulsion, she leaped to retrieve the weapon. Too late. The hulk used Nick's momentary distraction to break his hold and run down the hallway.

A curse, and Nick raced after him.

She followed, running out of the kitchen, through the front door and down the hallway.

Nick disappeared through the stairwell door. Heart in her throat, she ran after him. A flight below, he stopped, turned toward her and then back toward the escaping man.

"Go back!" He pounded halfway down the steps, then

slowed again when she didn't stop. "Dammit!" He raced back up, grabbed her by the wrist and pulled her the rest of the way down the stairs with him.

The man was gone by the time they reached the lobby. Still holding on to her, Nick ran outside. They searched the grounds, but found no sign of him.

Teeth chattering, though the summer night was warm, she asked, "Who . . . who was he?"

He ushered her into the building, stabbed the elevator button with one sharp, furious finger. "I don't know. A day man, probably." His face was turbulent, his voice hard with repressed rage.

"D-day man?" She had to stop this shaking.

"Day man," he practically shouted. "Free agent. Hired hand."

"Hired by who?"

"Who do you think?"

He dragged her back into the apartment, where she wet a washcloth and tried to wipe away the blood dripping from the cut over his eye. He pushed her hand away. "I'm fine."

"You're bleeding."

"I'm fine!" Grabbing the cloth, he threw it against the wall over the couch. She picked it up and threw it back at him. It hit him in the face with a smack and fell to the floor.

"Clean yourself up, then." She stormed down the hallway into the bedroom, slamming the door behind her.

Jerk. She plopped down on the bed, trying to subdue the shakes.

A knock on the door. "Go away."

He opened the door. In the streetlight that filtered

through the window she saw the blood on his face was gone. "Look . . . I'm sorry." He stood in the doorway, shifting the wet washcloth from one hand to the other. "If I had been able to catch him, talk to him . . ."

She glowered at him. "Go ahead, rub it in. If I hadn't hesitated, if I hadn't slowed you down on the stairs . . ."

A kind of bleakness seeped into his face. "It's not your fault, Rachel. None of this is your fault." He swallowed and looked down at the washcloth in his hand.

Her heart twisted. Gently, she said, "It's not your fault either. You didn't send that man tonight. You didn't send anyone to hurt me."

He threw her a sad, bitter smile. "That doesn't change the fact that none of this would have happened if not for me."

There was truth to his words, but she wouldn't acknowledge it. Not when the larger truth lay at someone else's feet. "If not for Rennie Spier," she said quietly.

She took the washcloth from him and laid it over the sink in the bathroom. When she came out, he was sitting on the couch, elbows on knees, head in his hands. The pose accented his strong neck and the smooth expanse of his broad shoulders, making him look both powerful and powerless at the same time. She had a sudden urge to put her arms around him, hold him, comfort him.

But she didn't. She might not blame him for what had happened, but tonight only proved that getting close to him was dangerous.

"Nick, something still doesn't make sense to me. You said Spier brought you back to find his son. Won't threatening me only drive you away?"

He took his hands away from his head and stared out

at the room. "No, he's pulling the chain, forcing me to heel. Making me do what *he* wants. Find the kid and forget the rest."

"What rest?"

"Proving he's a goddamn murderer."

A shiver of fear raced through her. Nick didn't notice. Face grim, he scooped up his shirt and jacket and stood. "Let's go."

A new kind of fear began to percolate. "Go? Go where?"

"Anywhere. Your family. A hotel. Arizona. Mexico."

She swallowed. "I told you, I'm not going anywhere."

"But that was before—"

She shook her head. "I'm not leaving."

He stared at her, black brows drawn in a frown. "Are you crazy? You can't stay here. Not now."

"I'm not leaving."

"Why the hell not? It's hot as an oven."

"That's just for tonight."

His jaw clenched. "What about the door?"

"I'll get it fixed."

"This is ridiculous. You can't stay. I won't let you."

"*You* won't let me?" She glared at him. "What are you going to do—haul me over your shoulder and drag me out?"

"Of course not, but—"

"No one is chasing me out of my own house, Nick. I did that once. I lost my mother, then I lost my father and my home. Every familiar thing, every beloved memory. Never again."

"This is different. It's just for a little while. A few weeks. Until I can prove Rennie—"

"After my mother died, my father dumped me at my aunt and uncle's. He swore it would only be a few weeks, too."

"For God's sake—"

"Those few weeks lasted the rest of my life, Nick. The rest of my life!" She was trembling again, but this time as much in anger as fear. "Well, *I* choose now. Me. Not you or Rennie Spier or anyone else. And I choose to stay. No one is pushing me out of my life again."

"Look at you, you're shaking."

"I'm scared. You think I'm an idiot? I'm scared spitless. But I'm still not leaving."

"Christ." He shot her a black look that was lethal as a bullet. "Then neither am I."

Chapter 7

Nick spent the rest of the night on the floor, leaning against the couch, gun drawn, guarding Rachel and the broken door. Even if he wanted to rest, he wouldn't have been able to. Not with her asleep on the couch behind him.

All night long, her nearness teased him. Her bare legs rested against his back, skin to skin; her breasts lay inches from his hand with only a thin film of material covering them. Once, she rolled over so her arm embraced the width of his shoulders. He swore and moved away.

In the morning, he stood over her while she woke like an angel, smiling and sleepy-eyed. For half a second he imagined watching her wake up like that for the rest of his life.

Dream on, pal.

Arms behind her head, she yawned and stretched, pushing her breasts out. "Morning."

He suppressed a groan. "It's late. Better hurry up."

She opened her eyes and saw him, and he watched the memory of what had happened the night before flit across her face. Her sleepy smile faded, her shoulders tensed.

She sat up, bare legs dangling over the edge of the couch. "Is everything all right?" He eased away, needing distance between them, but she grabbed his wrist. "Nothing else happened last night, did it?"

He looked down at her fingers on his wrist. Every nerve ending lit up. "No," he snapped, pulling his arm away. "We don't have much time. Let's go."

She sat up, worry plain in her face. "What's wrong?"

What wasn't? He hadn't slept, she was practically naked, and he couldn't think for staring at her. And Rennie was still out there. "Nothing's wrong. Except your insane idea to stay here."

Her beautiful mouth frowned at the snarl in his voice, and she looked down at her hands. "Look, I'm grateful for what you did last night, and for keeping me company—especially since you can't possibly understand why I wanted to stay." She lifted her face and her eyes were soft and pleading. "I . . . I don't want to fight about it. Not first thing."

He let out a long, exasperated breath, feeling himself cave. But if he let go of his irritability, he might have to grab onto something he wasn't ready for, and certainly couldn't have. "There's no point hanging around more than we have to," he said flatly.

"I know that." She stood up, and he fixed his gaze on a spot just above her head so he wouldn't gape at her barely clad body. "Look, I'll be ready in twenty minutes." She headed for the bathroom and shut the door behind her, and a moment later he heard the shower turn on.

To keep his mind off what she was doing in there, he made a few phone calls to see if he could arrange a replacement for the broken door, but it was too early to reach anyone.

Fifteen minutes later, she came out of the shower wrapped in a towel and drying her hair.

Was she *trying* to drive him crazy?

"Nick, I . . . I appreciate everything you've done for me," she said softly. "And I don't expect you to baby-sit me. I know you have . . . things to do. Murderers to catch." Her mouth formed a thin smile. "And there's the boy. You have to find him. Can't do that if you're stuck to me like glue."

Her face was flushed, and she smelled like freshly cut flowers. A dewy film made her graceful shoulders and neck glow. He buried his gaze in the phone book. "Get dressed."

"Nick—"

"If you want to get to school before the kids do, you have two minutes."

Silence. Out of the corner of his eye, he saw her pivot and march down the hall to the bedroom.

Thank God.

When she reappeared, she wore another skimpy dress that bared her shoulders and showed her legs. In pale orange, the sundress set off the peachy rose in her cheeks and the highlights in her braid. He smothered a curse and turned toward the front door, ordering her inside while he scouted the hallway. Determining the corridor was safe, he let her advance to the elevator, then checked it before letting her enter.

Rachel watched the James Bond moves with increasing apprehension. "Nick, you're scaring me."

"Good." He bit off the word the way he'd been biting off all his words since she'd woke up. As though he wanted to bite off her head.

But the thing was, she didn't need him to underscore the danger. She was scared enough already.

Outside, he guided her away from the parking garage.

"Where are we going?"

"My car is across the street."

"*Your* car? But—"

"We don't need two, and mine is in better shape."

When he led her to his car, she understood why. The silver Porsche was sleek and shiny in the early morning light. "Better shape is an understatement," she said dryly.

"It's Rennie's," he snapped.

"Uh-huh. Part of that . . . standard he requires of his associates."

She shouldn't have needled him, but she couldn't resist. At least sarcasm might break through the aloof shell he'd grown overnight. She knew her decision to stay in her apartment had been incomprehensible to him, but this morning he was like a bear with a burr up his butt. Was it fear for her, or something else?

She didn't know, and she wasn't going to risk losing a finger or toe, or some other tender part of her, by asking. She laid her head against the seat and bottled up the surge of dread when he took the gun from his waist and stuck it in the glove compartment. He pulled away, and she looked out the window, forcing her breathing into a normal rhythm.

He dropped her at St. Anthony's, pulling up to the front steps instead of the yard. "Go through the church. It's more public. I'll pick you up at six. Stay inside until you see the car."

Despite her best efforts, her heart started thudding. "Do you think he'd do something at the school?"

"If I did, I wouldn't leave you here."

"Then why—"

"Because it makes me feel better." Another biting reply. Her distress must have shown because he cursed softly, clearly struggling with his temper, his patience, or whatever else was bothering him. "I have an errand, and I don't want to worry about you while I run it, okay?"

"Are you going to look for the boy?"

"Maybe. Look, just do me a favor, okay? Keep the kids inside, or let Felice take them to play in the yard. Send out for lunch, and stay away from windows and doors."

She bit the inside of her cheek, anxiety making her skin tight. "All right." She slid out of the car and walked up the steps to the church doors.

Nick watched her disappear into the church. She hadn't asked him to go in with her, and he hadn't offered. Hell, the last thing she needed was him showing up again. But he got out of the car and hung around the street, keeping an eye out until the rest of the teachers arrived.

The irony wasn't lost on him. Yesterday, he would

have done anything in his power to keep her away from him. Now, he was doing everything he could not to let her out of his sight.

And the bridge that went from there to here was Rennie Spier.

Just then, his cell phone rang. It was one of the carpenters he'd called earlier.

"I need a security door installed in an apartment in Forest Hills," Nick told him. "Steel reinforced with an electronic lock and two heavy-duty deadbolts."

"No problem. How about two weeks from Thursday?"

"I need it done today."

The man laughed. "Good luck, pal."

Nick got the same answer at all the other places he'd called.

After six more tries, he asked, "How much does a job like that go for?"

The repairman said, "Depends. I come out, give you an estimate."

"Whatever it costs, I'll triple it. Cash. If you can do it today."

The man whistled. "I don't know. Triple? Geez. Let me see what I can work out." He put the call on hold and returned a few minutes later. "Today is impossible, no matter how much you offer. But I can move things around for tomorrow, first thing."

"Done." He gave the address and hung up. That left only tonight to worry about.

He slid into the car and twisted the ignition key. At the moment Rachel was safe, surrounded by the kids, teachers, and the church staff. Now he had to make sure she stayed safe.

He drove to Manhattan and parked on the street a block from SATCO headquarters. Before he got out, he opened the glove compartment and stared at the Beretta he'd stashed inside. He didn't want to start feeling as though he couldn't go anywhere without the 9mm, but he also didn't want to get caught short. *Fuck it.* He wrapped his hand around the grip and slipped the gun under his jacket.

Entering Spier's compound, Nick took the glassed-in elevator to the top floor. In the weeks since he'd been back, he'd avoided the corporate levels, as if staying away made working for Rennie less real.

Now he headed straight for Spier's office. Memories assaulted Nick as he took the familiar route. He'd been sixteen when he'd completed his first big job for Rennie, smuggling twenty tons of explosives to the airport in Atlanta, where it was shipped to Germany and then on to Libya. A pinch of that stuff could have blown him to hell and beyond, but he sweated the hundreds of miles because he wanted to impress the man who'd been both God and father to him.

His stomach clenched. He'd been so young then. That was long before he understood the connection between what he did and the headlines. Before the booze and Shelley. Before Panama.

Steeling himself, Nick plunged into Spier's office. Quickly, he scanned the spacious room. The bank of television screens banding the walls hung dark. No one sat in the plush conference area with its hidden bar. He walked to the desk, knowing someone in the security office was watching his every move. Well, he wasn't keeping it a secret. He was looking for Rennie; if they alerted him to Nick's presence, he'd see him that much faster.

The curved desk, carved out of a single piece of smooth, white birch, sat empty. Rennie didn't leave papers lying around, but the secure-line button on the phone was lit. Was Rennie using someone else's office? Carefully Nick depressed the line. A voice flooded the room, but it wasn't Rennie's.

". . . tonight," Frank was saying. "Two men." He paused. "I know Martin usually makes the calls. Now I'm making them."

Nick stilled. Frank was putting a crew together. A small crew. Small enough to handle a lone woman?

Anxiety spiked in his chest, but he forced himself to stay calm. Ignoring the whirring cameras that followed his every move, he strode down the hall and slid into Frank's office.

He was still on the phone at his desk, his round, beard-heavy face concentrating on whoever was on the other end. He held up a stubby hand, signaling Nick to wait, but Nick's fingers were already tight with the urge to punch something. He depressed the line button, cutting off the call.

"What the—" Frank jerked upward, but Nick pushed him back into his chair.

"I hear you're setting up a meet," he said, not wasting time. "What's Rennie up to?"

Frank looked as if Nick had lost his mind. "What the hell's got into you? Jesus." Frank tried to retrieve the call, but Nick tugged the cord out of the wall.

"Is Rennie going after Rachel again?"

"Who?"

"You know damn well who, but if you want to play games"—he drew the Beretta from behind his back—"I can play games."

"Whoa, hold on." Frank retreated into the chair and held up his hands. "Slow down. Put the gun away, for chrissakes."

Nick's hand tightened on the weapon; he struggled to keep his voice pleasant as he neared Frank. "Someone cut the power to Rachel Goodman's apartment and tried to attack her last night."

Frank's squinty eyes narrowed in puzzlement. "Goodman. That's your girl, isn't it? The teacher."

Nick almost lost his tight-lipped control. "She's not my girl. She's the director of the school at St. Anthony's."

"And someone tried to get into her apartment?" Frank shook his head. "Wasn't us."

"Who the hell else could it be?"

"On my life, Nicky, it wasn't us. Lose the piece."

"Convince me." He pressed the barrel deep into Frank's head. Beneath the muzzle, a sweaty film slicked the older man's skin. He was breathing hard, and for a long while, he said nothing.

"I could've crushed you, Nicky." His voice was low, the words halting. "I had your life in my hands, and I let you live. I'm asking you to do the same."

Nick remembered that long-ago day in the kitchen, when Frank had held an old, rusted weapon to a boy's throat. "If you're talking about that Luger, you know damn well the thing wasn't loaded and wouldn't have fired even if it was."

"I'm not talking about the Luger. I'm talking about you. I know more about you than you think, Nicky. I know more than anyone, except—" His eyes flicked up to Nick's, then slid away. "Except maybe Shelley."

An icy draft slid up Nick's spine. Was Frank saying he knew about the affair Nick had with Shelley? Dumbfounded, he let his hold waver.

Frank reached up and eased the gun away from his head. "But I believe in peace in the family. I don't like to see hearts broken . . . or heads." Slowly, he rose. "So I keep things to myself. That's why you can trust me when I say we had nothing to do with whatever happened to your girlfriend."

Head high, he stood, pushed past Nick, and walked out of the office. Nick stared after him. If Frank knew, if he even suspected . . . but he couldn't know. He would have told Rennie, and Rennie would have . . . But Nick wasn't dead.

He ran to the doorway. "Frank!" The older man turned, careful and dignified. But Nick couldn't ask, not straight up, not knowing whether or not he'd be revealing something too deadly to say out loud. "Where's Rennie?"

Frank pursed his lips, eyeing Nick with a long, assessing glance. "I should have you whipped for pulling a piece on me. I'm your friend, Nicky, your best friend. And as your friend I'm telling you, you're acting crazy again. Like you did right before you left the last time. And that means no one's going to trust you with nothing. Especially Rennie."

With a last disgusted glance, Frank shuffled down the corridor. Nick watched him go, knowing Rennie could be plotting a thousand things, all of which could have nothing to do with Rachel. But until he heard the denial from Rennie's own mouth, until Nick saw the truth in those ice-blue eyes, he wouldn't count out Spier as the man behind last night's attack.

In the meantime, sweat and sleeplessness had taken their toll. With no desire to linger, he took the elevator down to his suite and headed straight for the shower.

Fifteen minutes later, he was dressed in a fresh shirt and a clean suit. Knotting his tie, he gazed in the mirror. The scarlet set off the sleek white of the starched shirt. The jacket draped his shoulders with elegance and sculpted his waist at exactly the right point.

Nick looked at his reflection, and his skin crawled.

He yanked the tie off his neck, then turned his back on the sight of himself.

At six, Rachel peeked out and saw Nick's car in front of the church, just as he'd promised. The sight of him sent a small wave of warmth through her. He'd been nearby all afternoon. She knew because she checked, disobeying him for a few seconds to peek out the window. His presence eased the fear that had beat at the back of her skull all day, fear for herself, but also worry about the boy in the photograph. Watching the children had been a constant reminder. They were safe; was he?

She slipped out the door. Nick waited at the top of the steps, his gaze moving constantly. Using his body as a shield, he escorted her down the stairs and into the car.

He ran around the front, got behind the wheel, and a second later peeled away from the curb.

At some point he'd managed to change his clothes, but in deference to the heat, his jacket and tie were lying on the backseat. The day had taken his edge off. He looked worn down, face tired and lined. She didn't wonder. If his night had been anything like hers, he hadn't gotten much sleep. And who knew what he'd done to keep himself awake during the day.

"Did you eat today?"

He cut a glance over at her. "I'm fine."

His brusque reply was a repeat of the morning. She tamped down her irritation, leaned back, and closed her eyes, just as happy not to talk either. Three-, four-, and five-year-olds were tough enough on a good night's sleep. They were murder on a bad one.

To add to that, she'd been jumpy as hell all day, gasping at her own shadow. But she'd made it through. No threats from Bill Hughes, no warnings from Father Pat. Her school was alive, her children safe. That was worth a month of sleepless nights.

She yawned. What she wouldn't give for a few hours' peace. But in that dark apartment, by herself . . .

She shuddered and sat up. They were on the expressway, past the exit to her apartment. "Where are you going?"

"Shortcut."

"Shortcut? You missed the exit."

"Did I?" He seemed unconcerned.

"If you get off at the next exit, you can double back around."

"I know where I'm going. Why don't you take a nap? I promise to get you there."

She looked at him suspiciously, then sighed. What did it matter how long it took to get home? According to her manager, the power still hadn't been turned on. Which meant another stifling night in the dark. At least the car was air-conditioned. And safe. She leaned back and closed her eyes again.

She didn't realize she'd fallen asleep until she heard Nick calling her name from a great distance. But when she opened her eyes, he was right next to her in the car, holding out his cell phone.

"Say hello," he whispered. He shoved the phone at her so she had no choice but to take it.

"Hello?"

"Rachel, dear, is that you?"

"Aunt Julia?" She sat up, blinking away sleep, and looked around. The iron gate that blocked the road and the large homes beyond it were all painfully familiar.

"What a nice surprise! Come up, we'd love to see you."

The gate swung open slowly, and Nick drove through.

"What do you think you're doing?" she snapped as she ended the call.

"I couldn't get your door fixed until tomorrow. You need a safe place to stay tonight."

"I told you—"

"I don't give a damn what you told me." He slammed on the brakes and, leaning an elbow against the door, raked a hand through his hair. "Look . . . I've got something to do tonight, and you can't stay alone in that apartment."

Should she strangle him now or later? She glowered out the window as he eased off the brake, but couldn't hold on to the anger. Truth was, she didn't especially want to spend the night alone in the apartment, no matter what she said. But how in holy hell was she ever going to explain to her aunt and uncle without making them hysterical?

"If you had to pull a stunt like this, I'd rather go to a motel."

"You'll be safer surrounded by people. And now that I've seen your family lives in a gated community, staying here is even better."

"I suppose you've been hatching this little plot with them all day."

He gave her a mild look. "Relax. They didn't know you were coming until I called from the gate. I used a phone book and a map of Long Island to find them."

Somewhat mollified, she said, "So they don't know anything?"

"Just that we were passing by, and you thought it would be fun to see them."

"Fun?" She shook her head. "Next time you make plans that include me, I'd like a little advance warning."

"They're your family. They took you in when you needed them before, they'll take you in now."

"Oh, yes, they were kind enough to take me in." She paused, hearing the irony in her voice. "I guess you could say they were kind . . . when they weren't calling my father a damned commie or blaming him for my mother's death."

"Blaming him?" Nick shot her a surprised look. "How could it have been his fault?"

"Trust me, they have it all figured out. Thank God for my cousin Chris. I would never have survived my childhood without him." She sighed. "You know what the sad thing is? As much as I defended my father to my aunt and uncle, they were right about one thing. He always cared more about the 'cause' than he did about me."

Old wounds. She forced herself to shake them off as he drove through the stone pillars at the end of the cul-de-sac and moved up to the house, where the drive curved in a bow around the entrance. Several other cars were already parked when they arrived.

He threw his tie around his neck and got out of the car, using the side-view mirror to knot it. He had to bend down and contort himself to see his reflection in the little mirror. "Is it straight? I can't tell."

She came around the Porsche's front end and examined him. The tie was slightly off center, and as she reached up to adjust it, she made the mistake of raising her gaze to his face. All thought of the past fled, and she was instantly caught in the moment. Nick looked down at her, wistful and hungry. The reflection of the setting sun made his obsidian eyes glimmer with heat and accented the blue highlights in his inky hair. Her heart sped up, a tremor fluttered the fingers at his throat. As if he felt her tremble, his hands covered hers, steadying them. An electric pulse shot through her.

"I . . I don't know why you're bothering with a tie."

His eyes ate her up. "I wouldn't want to embarrass you."

"You won't."

Another silence. Spellbound, she couldn't move, couldn't breathe.

In the distance, a door opened. "Rachel, what a treat!"

Rachel blinked and stepped back. Nick reached for his jacket, shrugging into it as Julia came down the steps toward them.

"I'm so glad to see you. What a great idea this was." She smiled and enveloped Rachel in a perfumed embrace. A petite woman with large, dark eyes, Julia had shoulder-length, gray-swept hair pulled back from her face. Trim and ten years younger-looking than her actual fifty-five, she wore a black linen sheath and chunky silver beads. "Come in, come in. You're just in time for dinner." She walked them up the columned front entrance and into the house.

As always, the sweeping foyer with its two-story-high ceiling and imposing granite walls made Rachel uncomfortable.

Nick leaned in and asked in a low voice, "You okay?"

She nodded. It always took a few minutes to adjust to the splendor of "Castle" Bradshaw.

The sound of voices drifted from farther inside the house. She turned to her aunt. "You have guests."

"A small dinner party. Plenty of room for two more. In fact, there's someone here you should meet. But first, aren't you going to introduce me?"

Before she could reply, Nick did. He extended his hand to Julia. "I'm Nick, a friend of Rachel's."

She slipped her hand into his and looked up at him.

Her initial smile turned to puzzlement. "You know, you look familiar. Have we met before?"

Rachel tensed, remembering his picture plastered all over the newspaper. But Nick only smiled. "I"m sure I would remember meeting such an attractive woman. And in such a beautiful setting."

This was a new Nick. A charmer. And Julia beamed, lapping it up. "Thank you. But you should save that kind of nonsense for my niece."

Nick threw an arm around Rachel as if he did it twenty times a day. "Plenty more left over for her," he said with a squeeze.

Julia noted the embrace with interest, and Rachel repressed a groan. Interest meant questions. Questions Rachel didn't want to answer.

Julia said, "I hope you're hungry."

Rachel had had enough. No matter what Nick said, a motel would definitely be better. "Actually, we're only stopping for a few—"

But Nick tucked her arm through his. "We're starved."

She scowled at him, and he ignored the look, pulling her relentlessly toward the dining room.

"Good. I'm so glad you came. Rachel, you've been . . . well, distant lately. Is everything all right? That man hasn't come back, has he? The one involved in the death of that Spier woman?"

Nick's hand tightened over hers. "No," she lied. "Everything is fine." Just fine.

They reached the dining room. Nine people sat around the dark cherry table. She recognized several lawyers from her uncle's firm, a couple of women from her aunt's charity league, and in the middle, hair longer than was fashionable, wearing a T-shirt under a casual, if expensive, sports coat, sat her cousin Chris. *An ally. Thank God.*

She sent him a silent plea for help, but the rat was in one of his mischievous moods. He grinned and winked at her while his mother made a big production of the introductions, tapping on a water glass to gain everyone's attention and then addressing the entire group.

"For those who haven't met her before, this is my wonderful niece, Rachel Goodman, and this—" She turned to Nick.

"Is Nick." He completed Julia's sentence, and everyone laughed. But Rachel noted that he hadn't divulged his last name.

"Elliot Bradshaw." Her uncle, a burly man with iron-gray hair, rose to shake Nick's hand. "Please, sit down." He gestured to the two empty places that had been quickly laid. "What do you do, Nick?"

The inquisition had begun. Rachel drew in a taut breath, but Nick paused only a moment before saying, "I'm in . . . cleaning and repairs."

"Really," Elliot said, laying down his knife and fork. "Do you know Max Sinclair, New York Sanitation? One of our clients."

"Haven't had the pleasure," Nick replied smoothly.

Elliot's eyebrows rose. "Interesting. He runs the biggest cleaning network in the five boroughs."

A server placed a salad in front of Rachel, and she stared at the food. How could she eat? Every question held a hidden trap, every answer had to be a lie.

Chris piped up, a too-innocent expression on his

face. "So Nick, are you a member of any political"—he wrinkled up his nose as if the word carried an unpleasant odor—"organizations? You don't make speeches, do you?"

Nick looked at him calmly. "No."

"Well, that's a relief." He grinned at Rachel. "Now all you have to do is swear you'll send the poor girl flowers every once in a while. She's a sucker for yellow roses," he confided. "And if you make her cry or break her heart, well . . . I'll have to kill you."

"We'll all have to kill you," Julia said.

Rachel's gaze flew to Nick's, the talk of murder, even in jest, scraping too close to the bone. But he was smiling. "I better watch my step, then."

From the head of the table, her uncle's voice boomed. "Chris, introduce her to Dana."

A look of irritation crossed Chris's face, but he turned to the attractive blond sitting next to him, "Rachel, this is Dana Gershon."

"I'm so glad to meet you at last," Dana said with a warm smile. Slim and polished, she had a keen, blue-eyed gaze and a professional air that belied her soft, feminine looks. Rachel wondered if she was one of Elliot's lawyers.

"At last?"

"Dana wants to do a book on your father," her uncle said.

Not a lawyer. Worse, a writer.

"No one's done a definitive biography yet," the woman said, her voice taking on enthusiasm. "I've already talked to my publisher, and they're very excited."

Rachel frowned. The year after her father's death,

she'd been plagued by writers with ideas for articles, books, and TV interviews. The tumult had faded, but every now and again someone approached her. Reluctant to relive her complicated relationship with her father, she always gave the same answer.

"I'm not interested."

"It wouldn't be all that involved. I'd like to interview you, of course, and the Bradshaws." She nodded at Elliot and Julia. "But I was really hoping for a look at his personal papers, records, diaries, anything like that."

"No."

Dana exchanged a glance with Chris, who said in a low voice, "I told you so."

Turning back to Rachel, the writer said, "May I ask why?"

"Sure." She smiled. "My relationship with my father is none of your business."

An embarrassed silence followed. In the middle of it, a fork clanked loudly onto a plate. Heads turned. Julia sat white-faced, her mouth open. She was staring at Nick.

"I remember where I've seen you." She pointed a finger at him. "You're that . . . that janitor from the school. The one involved in the Spier murder."

If the silence had been embarrassing before, it was deafening now. Everyone turned to look at Nick. Casually, he speared a tomato and brought it to his mouth. His manner suggested he could have cared less what they thought, but sitting next to him Rachel saw the pinched white lines around his mouth that told a different story.

"The police are wrong," Rachel said quickly. "He had nothing to do with—"

"That's okay." He chewed slowly, deliberately, meeting Julia's shocked expression head on. "Yes, you're right."

"Your picture was in the newspaper," one of the lawyers said slowly, as if seeing Rachel's dinner companion for the first time.

"Nick . . . Raine." Dana supplied his last name with a small look of triumph for having remembered.

He bowed his head in acknowledgment.

"What are you doing with my niece?" This stern question from Uncle Elliot. "Haven't you brought her enough trouble?"

Rachel winced, but Nick said calmly, "I think that better wait till after dinner." He looked around the table at the embarrassed guests, his expression clearly saying he'd prefer privacy. "For now"—he scraped back his chair—"if you'll excuse me." And walked out of the room.

Rachel sent her aunt a dagger's look and ran after him.

"Rachel!" her aunt called behind her.

"Let him go," her uncle shouted at the same time.

Ignoring them both, she found Nick outside, hands in his pockets, staring at the bevy of BMWs and Mercedes parked in front of the house.

"Nick, I'm sorry. I know what you've done for me, even if they don't. You've turned your life inside out to keep me safe. Because of me, you're working for people you hate, doing things you hate."

He barked a short, bitter laugh. "I'm just doing what comes natural. What I'm good at."

"Rachel!" Elliot stood in the open doorway, still holding onto his dinner napkin. He hurried out to stand protectively near his niece. "I'm sure Mr. Raine has more important things to do. Come back inside." To Nick he said, "We won't keep you."

"Elliot, don't be an idiot. When you hear what he's done for me, you'll—"

"I know what he's done *to* you," Elliot said. "And possibly to another woman—"

She rounded on him, barely holding on to her temper. "I explained about the hit-and-run to Aunt Julia. Nick wasn't there. He's not responsible for what happened." She turned to Nick. "Tell him. Tell him what you told me about Rennie Spier."

The minute Spier's name left her mouth, she wished she could take it back. Her uncle's face grew even more pinched.

"What does Spier have to do with this?"

"Nothing," Rachel said quickly.

"Is that why you came tonight? Are you in some kind of trouble? Has he gotten you into some kind of trouble?" He looked accusingly at Nick.

"No, it's not like that at all."

"That's exactly what it's like," Nick said. "She needs a place to stay. A safe place."

Her uncle's worried gaze shifted from Nick to her and back again. A silent message passed between the two men. It ended with Nick turning toward the cars in the drive.

"Go with your uncle."

"Why? Where are you going?"

In answer, he strolled to his car, opened the door, and pulled the gun out from under the seat. He did it deliberately, making sure both of them saw him do it.

Elliot drew in a sharp breath.

Shucking his jacket, Nick tucked the weapon at the small of his back. "Get inside. I'm going to take a look around." He slammed the car door and walked into the deepening night.

She started after him, but her uncle pulled her back. "Stay here."

But she couldn't. She jerked away and ran after Nick.

Chapter 8

Rachel caught up to Nick as he was heading toward the back of the Bradshaws' house. Without turning his head or missing a step, he spoke in a flat voice. "I thought I said to—"

"I heard what you said."

He sighed. "She hears, but does not listen." But he made no further protest when she tagged along.

The moon was up, though darkness hadn't settled in completely. They tramped in silence. The house sat in the middle of large, sprawling greens that gave way to dark woods in the distance. Clumps of azalea and rhodo-dendron created islands of shrubbery in the smooth grass sea. Nick's gaze only skimmed the plants and flowers, looking beyond them to the far borders. From time to time he turned, walking backward, as if judging various distances. From the drive to the front door. The edge of the woods to the house. A ripple of disquiet crawled up

Rachel's back and she wanted to pretend this wasn't necessary, but couldn't.

Lights came on as they walked, giving them a clear
path, and Nick noted them with interest. "Your uncle installed motion-sensitive lights. What's the rest of the security system like?"

"The house is wired."

"Good."

Standing at the tiered patio at the back of the house,
they couldn't see the edge of the property, which disappeared into the shadowy woods. A tennis court sat at the
far left. The glittery reflection of a swimming pool took
up the center. Nick gestured with his head over to the
right.

"What's over there?"

She turned to face the direction he pointed out, where
the grounds rose into a small hill. A wave of pleasure
washed over her. "My childhood." Impulsively, she took
his hand. "Come on, I'll show you the best thing about
this place."

She pulled him up the slope, liking the feel of his
hand in hers. By the time they reached the top, though,
he'd managed to disengage his fingers and shove his
hands in his pockets. She missed his warmth but didn't
push; she was too excited to show him what lay on the
other side of the hill. They stood at the crest, looking
down. A small pond surrounded by trees shimmered in
the moonlight.

She said, "Ever hear the Mark Twain story *The Prince
and the Pauper?* In the story, Prince Edward of England
switches places with a street urchin who looks like him,

and both get to see how the other half lives. Well, that story is me. Except I played both parts."

"The princess lived up here?" He nodded over his shoulder to the house.

"Someday I'll show you my throne room. It's all pink and white, with angels and fat cherubs playing on the ceiling. My aunt had it done when I came to live here."

"And your father—he was the pauper?"

"David Goodman didn't believe in the 'cult of the material.' The few times he let me stay with him, I slept on a couch he'd rescued from someone's trash." Fondly, she gazed down at the sheltered enclave. "The only place I truly felt at home was down there."

Tramping down the hill, she recalled the countless times she'd made the journey growing up. Even now, after all these years, it still held a certain mystical appeal.

When they reached the bottom, she had a childish urge to kick off her shoes and wade in the water. But Nick stood still, quietly scanning the scene around them. She could tell he wasn't seeing the moonlit pond or the huge, leafy maples that guarded it. He didn't care that she'd chiseled her name in the old wooden swing hanging from one of the trees. He saw only entrances and exits, hiding places, weak spots in the security system.

"What's on the other side of the trees?"

She eyed him, wishing he could forget danger for a moment. "A wall. It's the eastern boundary of the property."

He disappeared into the trees, and she tensed, grateful for his prudence but resentful at the same time. This was her refuge, the one place she could escape her fears.

Now Nick was bringing them into the heart of her sanctuary.

"Okay, it's not impossible to get over," he said when he returned, "but it would definitely slow someone down."

She gave him a tight smile. "I know. It used to slow me down. Then I figured out how to build steps out of rock, and there was no keeping me. Ran my aunt and uncle ragged until they found out what I was up to and dismantled my staircase."

"And what were you up to?"

"Oh, running after my father mostly. Catching his dust." She eased onto the swing and began to drift. It was darker here than above, lit only by the moon. The glow hovered over the surface of the pond, turning it a misty silver. Encircling the water, maples arched into a leafy haven that was snug and private. Safe.

She closed her eyes, inhaling the scent of leaves and moss, and letting the magic seep into her skin while the tension flowed out. "I love this place."

"You're lucky you had somewhere to go. Some kids—" He leaned against a tree and stared off into the night. "Some kids don't."

Was he talking about himself or someone else? The picture of the boy in the photograph rose in her mind, and with it all her anxiety returned. She looked away, into the comfort of the trees, but knew there was no escape, not even here.

Resigned, she asked him the question that had haunted her all day. "Did you . . . did you look for the boy today?"

Her voice seemed to pull him back from wherever

he'd gone. He threw her a tight smile. "No. I went to see Rennie."

Alarm shot through her. "Are you all right? Is he?"

"He wasn't there."

How could he be so calm about it? "Well, what happened?"

"I talked to Frank. He swore Rennie had nothing to do with what happened at your apartment last night."

She studied him, her own doubt mirrored in the lines of his face. "But you don't believe him."

He lifted his shoulders. "I don't know what to believe." He scooped up a branch from the ground and snapped it in two, as if the bough were Rennie himself. "But if Rennie didn't do it, who did?"

"Who else would want you to stop looking for the boy?"

"Or stop me trying to prove Rennie killed his wife." His tone said *this* was the important issue, not the child. He made a frustrated, growling sound in the back of his throat and walked to the edge of the pond.

Sliding off the swing, she joined him and said gently, "No matter what you do, you can't change the fact that Shelley is dead. You can't do anything to help her."

"What's that supposed to mean?"

She picked her words carefully. "Maybe you should . . . forget about Rennie. Concentrate on finding the boy."

His head snapped around to face her. "I let Rennie get away with a lot. I'm not letting him get away with killing Shelley." He strode back toward the trees, obviously wanting an end to the discussion. But she couldn't let this go. Not yet. Not when a child's safety was at stake.

"He's only a boy, Nick. He's probably scared and alone. Who knows where he is, or if he's safe." She hesitated, then plowed on, knowing she was getting in deeper than she should, but unable to stop herself. "If you're . . . if you're having trouble, I could help. We could look for him together."

He leaned against one of the maples and sent her a black look. "You do have a death wish."

She glided over to him. "No, but I know what it's like to live with strangers, to be frightened."

He gave her a pointed look. "He's not you. He's got a whole different set of problems."

"What about the warehouses near the site of the accident?"

"The police combed the area. They would have found a mouse, let alone a six-year-old."

"And the parks? You said the photographs were taken at a playground. I could—" She bit her lip, compelled to do something, anything, despite the lingering threat, so long as the boy was alone out there. "I could do some scouting."

"No."

"Nick—"

"No!" He grabbed her by the shoulders. "You can't. You just can't."

Suddenly, she was staring up at him. Shadowed by moonlight, his face was partially lit, half light, half dark, like Nick himself.

"Please." His expression softened, eyes pleading. "I couldn't take another—" He looked down. "I can't . . . be responsible," he said in a low, grim voice. "Not again."

"You're not. You had nothing to do with what Spier did to me. I don't blame you."

He raised his head, and the moon caught the misery in his face. "You should. Christ, if you only knew—"

"Knew what?" She searched his face, but all it revealed was his struggle to stay silent. Secrets. Always so many secrets.

After a long while, he dropped his hold and looked away. "Nothing. Forget it."

"I don't want to forget it." Gently cupping his jaw with her hand, she turned him back toward her. "Why are you so hard on yourself?"

He stilled at her touch. She caressed him softly, stroking the bitter lines away. She knew it was unwise, knew being near him was risky, but her fingers moved on their own, scraping his jaw, weaving through his hair.

"Don't," he whispered.

"I won't." But she kept right on touching him, tracing the line of his cheek, his eyes, his lips, as if she'd never heard the word *danger.*

He grabbed her wrist, his chest rising and falling with his rapid breathing. As rapid as her own. For a moment she thought he was going to stop her.

Then he brought her palm to his mouth and kissed it.

She drew in a breath. Heat pooled in her chest and between her thighs. As if in a trance, she sank into the circle of his arms. And now there was only the two of them. No Rennie Spier, no aunts or uncles, no menace. Only her and him in this safe, special place. Only moonlight and Nick's raven eyes, hazy with desire. Moonlight and Nick's mouth, descending toward hers.

A twig cracked.

His head came up, his eyes cleared, and before she knew what was happening, he pushed her behind him and drew his gun.

Her heart was still pounding, but for an entirely different reason now. God, it couldn't be. No one could get in here.

"Rachel?" A whisper in the dark. "Are you there?"

Relief flooded her. "It's okay," she said to Nick. "It's Chris."

Her cousin emerged from the lee of the hill into the center of the circle of trees. He stopped short when he saw the gun.

"I'd shake your hand," Chris drawled, "but it seems otherwise occupied."

Nick lowered the weapon and stepped aside. Chris walked past him and put an arm around Rachel.

"Are you all right?"

"She's fine," Nick said.

Chris whirled on him. "Then what do you need a gun for?"

Rachel put a hand on her cousin's arm. "Don't start."

"Come back to the house," Chris said to her. "The dinner party's breaking up."

She looked at him suspiciously. "Did your parents send you?"

"You know better than that." Playfully, he pulled her braid. "But I admit they're worried about you. *I'm* worried about you. Every time I called for the past few weeks, you sounded comatose." He eyed Nick. "Looks like we were right to be worried. What's going on?"

Nick shoved the gun behind his back. "She needs someplace to stay. Someplace safe."

"Why?"

"It's a long story," Rachel said.

"I've got plenty of time."

"Not here," Nick said. "You can talk all you want back at the house." His tone was harsh, his face hard. Where was the man who'd held her a moment ago?

Softly, she said, "Nick—"

"It's late. I have to go." Beneath the curtness he almost sounded relieved that Chris had interrupted them. He gestured for them to precede him up the hill.

As they walked toward the house, she slowed to let Nick catch up to her. It was full dark by now, but the grounds were well lit. The illumination showed every line in his hard, craggy face.

"Where are you going?" He didn't answer. "Are you coming back?"

"I'll take you to work in the morning."

"Not necessary," Chris said quickly. "I can take her."

Nick stopped and turned toward Chris. "Do you have a piece?"

Chris's brow furrowed. "A piece of what?"

"A gun, a weapon."

Chris gave a short, disbelieving laugh. "Am I going to need one?"

"No," Rachel said quickly.

Nick took the gun from the small of his back. "Here." He shoved the weapon at Chris.

"We don't need that," Rachel said.

Chris handled the gun gingerly. "You don't expect me to shoot anyone?"

Nick's eyes bored into Chris like two pieces of heat-blackened steel. "I expect you to do whatever is necessary to protect her."

He wheeled away, leaving them at the front drive. Slipping into his car without another word, he drove off.

She watched him leave, the way she used to watch her father leave, the red glow of his taillights disappearing into the night.

She was sick of the sight.

"Give me your keys," she said to Chris.

"What?"

"Your keys!"

Nick tightened his hold on the steering wheel to stop his hands shaking. He glanced in the rearview mirror once, then refused to look back. Refused to see the hurt in Rachel's eyes, the disappointment in her face.

Forget her. He had other things to think about.

But he couldn't forget the raw ache in his chest when she'd brought her slim fingers to his face. Or the surge of desire when she'd glided into his arms. He was still shaking from her touch.

And from the knowledge that he'd almost told her about Panama. A wave of nausea washed over him as he remembered how close he'd come to revealing the one thing that was sure to make her turn away from him forever. No matter what happened, no matter how strong the temptation or how hard she pressed, he could never, ever tell her what happened.

He depressed the window buttons and floored the gas pedal, jolting the car into high speed. Night air flew in, engulfing him so he couldn't think. Or feel.

Under normal conditions the trip into Manhattan took

forty-five minutes. Nick made it in thirty. By nine o'clock he'd parked the car in the underground garage below Spier's headquarters. A tunnel led into the compound, but Nick headed for the street. He wanted the extra minutes to review his strategy before confronting Rennie.

He got as far as the mouth of the garage, then stopped short. Rachel stood on the sidewalk, calm and cool, as if they met on a street corner every day. He gaped at her.

"What the . . . what the hell are you doing here?"

"Following you." She nodded with her head in the direction of a small Miata convertible parked to the right of the garage. "It's Chris's car."

As if that explained everything. "Why would you—" He pulled her into the shadow of a wall, out of the line of sight. "I told you to stay with your family. You can't come with me."

"I don't want to come with you," she said quietly. "I want you to come with me."

He raked a hand through his hair, at a loss. "Look, I have to talk to Rennie."

"No, you don't. You've done enough. I want you to come back to Long Island. Elliot's a lawyer; he has a ton of connections. We can work something out. Something that doesn't involve you and Rennie Spier in the same room."

Her eyes were dark and steady on his face, and a pang went through him—how could she care so much?—but he pushed it away and muttered an oath beneath his breath. "This is crazy. I don't need you to protect me. Go home."

"Not without you."

Dragging back some semblance of patience, he said, "I have things to do, Rachel. I'm not going with you, and you can't come with me. We talked about this. I thought you understood that staying away from Rennie was your best insurance policy."

"I don't want to have anything to do with Rennie Spier, okay? But I don't want you to have anything to do with him either." She raised her chin. "I'm not letting you run off to God knows what—risk life and limb most likely—all on account of me. No one fights for me, Nick, no one saves me. And no one leaves me behind anymore."

Anymore. As though she'd been left behind a thousand times before. "Oh, I get it. This is about your father, isn't it? Catching his dust, you said."

"It's about you, Nick. And keeping you safe for once."

"Rachel to the rescue?"

She colored, but didn't back down. "Maybe. Call it whatever you want. But you need protection as much as me."

He shoved his hands in his pockets and turned his back to her, facing the corner. He was oddly touched and royally pissed. He couldn't ditch her, not if he wanted to make sure she was safe. But he couldn't take her inside either.

What he wanted to do was strangle her. But before his hands could reach her throat, he saw a cab pull up to the curb half a block up. Martin ducked inside.

The conversation Nick overheard that morning replayed in his head. Two men, meeting tonight. Was Martin part of the team? And did the job involve Rachel?

Nick looked from the cab to the front of SATCO headquarters. He could go in and confront Rennie, and maybe worm the truth out of him. Dicey at best. Or he could follow Martin and find out for himself. Either way, he couldn't leave Rachel.

"Come on." He grabbed her hand and stepped into the street, whistling shrilly and raising his arm to hail a cab.

Rachel said, "What are we doing?"

"We're taking you home."

He flagged down a taxi and they tumbled inside. Nick pointed out Martin's car to the driver. "Double your fare if you can keep that black-and-yellow in sight."

"This isn't my usual route," Rachel said dryly.

"I overheard Frank planning something this morning, and I want to see what Rennie's up to. I'll check this out, then take you back to your car."

She sighed but didn't argue, and he pulled his attention away from her to concentrate on Martin. He was heading uptown; traffic was brisk but not heavy, and they had no trouble keeping him in sight. Ten minutes later, they pulled up to Penn Station, where Martin's cab had just stopped.

"Shit," Nick said softly. Penn Station housed the Long Island Railroad terminal and the Amtrak hub to Boston, Philadelphia, Miami, Chicago, and who knew where else. Martin could be going anywhere.

Quickly, Nick paid the driver and slid out. "Stay close." He wrapped her hand in his own and jogged after Martin.

It was almost nine-thirty, but the station was full of noise. Announcers bellowed train times and tracks in an indecipherable buzz, people scurried to buy tickets or check schedules. Groups of kids clumped together, laughing and shoving, the girls with bare shoulders and midriffs, the boys with loose, baggy jeans. The smell of grease and ketchup and sweat hung in the air. Nick dodged the milling crowds, the beat-up vending machines, and the overflowing trash cans to follow the path Martin set a few yards ahead.

He ducked into the corridor leading to the Long Island Railroad, and Nick breathed out in relief. At least that narrowed the field.

"He's going to a track," Rachel said. All the tracks were below main level, connected by a set of stairs. "Look, I've done this a million times going out to my aunt and uncle. There are two tracks down there. You won't be able to tell which train he boards from here."

A stream of people were plunging down the stairs. Martin joined them, and Nick and Rachel followed.

"Montauk or Islip?" As they slipped through the entrance, Rachel pointed to the line names posted on either side.

"I don't know. None of this makes sense." Martin always said the subway was for losers and hadn't taken a train since he could afford a car and a driver if he wanted one. But he was taking a damn train now.

Two-thirds of the way down the stairs he saw Martin enter the train on the left track. Montauk. Why the hell was Martin going out to the eastern end of Long Island?

"What's in Montauk?" Rachel asked.

Nick shook his head. "Rennie's got a beach house out there, but—" He shrugged. "Besides, we don't know where he'll end up. He could get out at any stop along the way." If he'd been alone, he might have followed

Martin, but he wasn't going to drag Rachel on what could be a three-hour train ride leading to who knows what at the end. They reached the platform, and the train opposite Martin's started to pull out. Nick shouted over the noise, "Come on, let's get you home."

"Only if you're coming," she said stubbornly.

He couldn't help a small smile. "After that stunt you pulled at Rennie's, you think I'd trust you by yourself?"

Rachel's shoulders relaxed; she hadn't realized how tense she'd been. It wasn't so much the cloak-and-dagger stuff, though that had been intimidating enough, but persuading Nick to leave. Now she grinned at him, profoundly glad he was coming with her, even if it was only to personally escort her. Once they got back to the Bradshaws she'd find a way to bully him into staying, and in the morning they'd talk to Elliot. She had no illusions that it was going to be an easy conversation, but at least Nick would have a chance to get free of Rennie now.

They turned around to head back up the stairs, but Nick stopped so fast, Rachel ran into him.

"What's the matter?"

Instead of answering, he jerked her back, shoved her down the track and up against a signpost. He leaned in as if about to kiss her, and her heart leaped into her throat. But he only whispered in her ear, "One of Rennie's men is on the stairs."

"What?"

"Shh."

God in heaven. "But—but how could Rennie possibly know where I'd be?"

"I don't know. But he did. Christ, he's coming down. We can't stay here."

She looked around wildly, but there was no place to go. A few feet ahead, the track ended in blackness, and with Rennie's thug on the stairs they couldn't escape that way. They were trapped.

An announcer made a last call for the Montauk train. Her eyes met Nick's.

"Okay," he said in a low voice, "on three." He made the count and in one swift move, they made a dash for the doors and dove onto the train. Moments later, the doors closed.

Nick pushed her into a seat and shoved her head down as the train jostled into motion. She smelled dirt and feet and the sharp metallic scent of machinery, and then they entered the tunnel out of Manhattan and plunged into darkness. The hand on her head lifted and she sat back, mouth dry, heart thumping wildly.

"Did he see us?"

Nick's voice came out of the darkness. "I don't think so. He didn't try to get on the train."

She let out a long, quivery breath, and seconds later, the lights came back on. Next to her, Nick sat stone-faced.

"So much for keeping you out of harm's way," he said.

She looked down. One hand was wrapped around the other wrist. She pried them apart and tried to ease the tension. "At least now you can find out where Martin's going," she said lightly.

His mouth thinned. "First stop, we're out of here."

"Fine by me. I didn't bring my bathing suit anyway."

A few minutes later, a conductor came through the car to collect tickets.

"We're getting off at the next stop," Nick said, handing him some cash.

The conductor nodded. "Glad to hear it, but so is everyone else. This is nonstop to Montauk, son. Last train of the night. Nothing coming or going till tomorrow."

Nick stared at him, and Rachel's heart sank. She thought of everything she'd planned to do tomorrow, the continued search for grant money, the kids, the mess if she wasn't there to open up. Cheerfully the conductor collected their money and punched holes into the paper ticket, which he stuck in a slot designed for that purpose in the seatback ahead of them. Then he moved on to do the same with the other passengers in the car.

Rachel's brain stayed on stun. "Now what?"

"Christ," Nick muttered and punched the seat in front of them. "Shit." He slumped backward, his head landing with a thump on the chrome that edged the leather seat. He was staring straight up at the roof. "Well, we're not getting off, but then, neither is Martin. And we left Rossi at the platform. . . ." He sighed, then loosened his tie and unbuttoned his top shirt button. "Probably the safest three hours we're going to get is the next three." He crossed his arms and closed his eyes.

"You're going to sleep?"

"I'm going to try." His voice was already fading.

She watched the lines of his face loosen, tempted to brush the hair back from his forehead and help him relax. She rarely saw him this way, loose-limbed and easy, and she wondered how often he sloughed off the burdens he always seemed to carry.

Suddenly, sleep looked very appealing. She put her

head back and closed her eyes, too. "You know, this trip of Martin's may have nothing to do with Rennie," she murmured. "With the suit and briefcase, he looks like a salesman on his way home from a hard day on Madison Avenue."

"Mmm," he murmured, barely there. "Except he's carrying hollowpoints, not talking points."

The hard reality of his words shuddered through her. Suddenly, she was wide awake.

Chapter 9

When Nick woke, Rachel was finally asleep. She'd stirred beside him for the first hour, restless and owl-eyed every time he checked on her. But now she slumped against him, her head resting on his shoulder, one arm flung possessively across his waist.

He hadn't felt her drift close, but he liked it. He smiled, resting his cheek on top of her head. Her slim legs brushed against his own, her bare shoulders, sleek and smooth in the orangeade sundress, pressed against him. He let himself enjoy the sensation, the sight of her beside him, smaller, feminine, warmed by the shelter of his body. They could have been anyone, a normal couple, off for a few romantic days at the beach. Him and David Goodman's daughter.

The irony ran through him like a hard wind. Goodman had been an advocate for public safety, while Nick was the embodiment of violence and public mayhem. The comparison doused whatever lingering fantasies he had.

She was on that train because of Rennie. It always came back to Rennie.

A few minutes later the train pulled into the station and jostled to a stop.

"Rachel." He shook her awake. "We're here."

The clock in the station read twelve-fifty-seven when they got off at the seaside town. Nick kept them in the middle of the passenger pack, scanning for Martin.

"What are you going to do?" she whispered as they ducked behind a billboard to avoid being spotted.

"We're here. Might as well find out where he's going."

When Martin got into a cab, Nick found one too and guided Rachel into it.

"Keep your head down," he said in a low voice.

Somehow they managed to keep Martin in sight without being spotted. Twenty minutes down the highway, Nick started smelling the ocean.

"You mentioned Rennie's beach house," she said. "Are we heading that way?"

He shook his head. "Opposite direction."

Ten minutes later, Martin's cab slowed and pulled through the battered gates of an abandoned fish plant. Nick's heart sank. Dark and overgrown with weeds, the place was ideal for the kind of illicit work Rennie's business demanded. Something big was going down, something bad. Whatever it was, he was beginning to suspect it had nothing to do with Rachel.

"Keep going," Nick said to the driver, and when the cab had sped past the plant entrance, he ordered it to stop, then paid off the driver. The cab turned around and left, and Nick led Rachel back to the entrance. There, he stationed them behind a scruffy pine tree until Martin's cab came back through the fence gate.

"What now?"

Rachel leaned into him and he grit his teeth as her breasts brushed his arm. He moved away. "I don't know. Whatever happens, I don't have a hell of a lot of persuasion power."

"What do you mean?"

"Your cousin has my gun."

He could have kicked himself for that. But he hadn't had time to run into Rennie's and grab a weapon, not without worrying that she might have followed him inside.

"Maybe you won't need a gun."

He heard the faint note of hope in her voice and flashed her a tight smile. "Maybe. But I sure wouldn't mind having the option." He glanced out toward the plant gates again. "Stay here. I'm going to take a fast peek inside. If anyone shows up, either coming or going, I want to know what direction they take. See if you can get a bead on the car and how many people are inside." He didn't really care who else turned up, but he wanted Rachel safe. And she'd be a hell of a lot safer where he'd stashed her than anywhere near the building.

"Okay."

He scurried across the parking lot, grateful that the lights had long ago burned out or been smashed by vandals. Only the moon broke through the inky darkness. The moon and a small bulb that illuminated a boarded-up door set into the ramshackle wood building ahead of him. A car was parked against the back of the building.

He skirted to the left to avoid it and headed around the side, where he was betting on another entrance.

As he turned the corner, he saw that the plant building opened right onto the ocean. And here, for some reason, light blazed, spotlighting the bay and the crumbled piers that led from three wide doors down to the water. Small waves licked the pilings of the one lone dock that still stood upright. The brine smelled rank and musty, and a faded sign over the central door said "Fisher Sea Products."

The murmur of voices drifted toward him.

"Thanks." Deep and rumbling, Martin maybe.

"No problem." Higher, younger. Female? Squinting into the darkness, he saw a teenage girl exit the fish plant, counting a wad of bills.

He blinked. If he had expected anything, it was not a gangly girl in cutoffs and a midriff-baring T-shirt, chewing gum and bobbing to the rhythm of the Walkman plugged into her ears.

Muscles tense, eyes and ears alert to the girl's every possible movement, he flattened himself against the side of the building. Luckily, she went in the opposite direction. A minute later a car engine chugged to life. *The parked car.* He waited for the sound to fade away, hoping Rachel had kept out of sight. Then he slipped around to the front and entered the building.

Darkness greeted him, and the stale smell of space long unused. The faint odor of fish still lingered beneath the dust and mildew. Keeping low and hugging the walls, he crept down the corridor. The glow of a lit room gave faint illumination to the hallway ahead of him.

He followed the light, and it led to what must have

once been one of the plant offices. It was a compact room, empty of furniture, empty of everything except a small, dark-haired boy sitting cross-legged on the floor playing with a worn-out teddy bear.

Nick froze. His body refused to move, his brain refused to think. The boy looked up, a photograph come to life. When he saw Nick, the child's face filled with fear, but Nick barely noticed the emotion in those eyes. All he cared about was their color. *Black.* As black as Nick's own.

The realization hit him like a tidal wave, but before he could move or speak, someone else did.

"Get away from the boy, Nick."

Nick whirled. Behind him stood Martin, huge and square, his hands wrapped around a gun.

Rachel's heart jumped into her throat when the car drove through the gates and swung into the street. Blinded by the headlights and by the fact that no streetlights lit the area, she couldn't see who was in the car. She bit her lip. Was Rennie inside? Did he have Nick with him? Where was Martin?

She hesitated, unsure what to do. Nick had told her not to move, but what if he was in danger and needed help?

Praying she was doing the right thing, she stepped out from under the tree and ran across the lot. The wide expanse contained no hiding places; if another car drove in, or if anyone stepped outside the building, she'd be caught. Mouth dry, she looked over her shoulder at the gates. They yawned like a black pit, wide and empty and infinitely alarming. Her heart began to beat in triple time.

When she reached the building, she paused to catch her breath. Pressed against the side of the fish plant, she hoped no one could see her. Was Nick inside? Was he all right? She took a deep, calming breath that didn't do much to still her shaky legs, and turned the corner to the ocean side of the building. Inching along the front of the building, she saw three entrances with piers leading to the water. The door closest to her was locked, but the main entrance had been cracked open. She slipped inside.

Almost immediately, she heard two men arguing. She crept toward the voices, sure that one belonged to Nick. A liquid wash of relief made her stop for half a second before stealing closer. A third voice spoke, and her heart began to hammer again. It sounded like . . . like a child.

"Is that a gun? Why do you have a gun? Is he a bad man?"

"Yeah, Isaac, he's a bad man."

Oh, my God. Isaac.

Nick's heart squeezed as the boy looked at him in fear, but he ditched the regret as fast as it came. He couldn't afford to think about that now. He could only think about the gun trained on the center of his chest, an HK SOCOM. Developed for Army Special Ops, it was a heavy, brutal weapon that Martin favored.

Nick eyed the .45 and the big man holding it. "I won't let you take him back to Rennie."

Martin laughed, a low, easy chuckle that didn't quite match the expression in his eyes. "You won't? That's good, Nicky. That's real good. And how the hell are you going to stop me?"

Nick judged the distance between him and Martin, rapidly tallying ways of disarming him, which were slim to none. "I'll figure something out."

Martin laughed again, shaking his head. "I'll bet you will. But before you do something stupid, and knowing you, Nicky, that's a given, first, I'm gonna tell you a little something. I'm not taking him back. I'm taking him away. It's what Shelley wanted, and it's what I promised her."

Nick wasn't sure he understood. "What do you mean? What did you promise her?"

"To get her out. Her and her son."

"You were helping her?"

"That's right, Nicky. The big, dumb dog was helping her."

Nick's brain stuttered; he couldn't process what Martin was saying. "You don't expect me to believe that." Martin shrugged, as if to say he didn't care what Nick believed. "But—Christ, why? Why the hell would you do that? What was in it for you?"

"You have a dark, cynical mind, my friend." Martin shook his head. "But because you used to trust me, I'll tell you. *She* was in it for me." The lopsided grin faded, and Nick saw pain behind his eyes. "I loved her, Nicky. I took care of her, or tried to. And if everything hadn't gotten screwed up, we'd have been out of here weeks ago, and she'd still be alive—" Martin's voice cracked, and for a moment he looked away from Nick, struggling for control.

For a split second, the big man's aim was off, but

Nick only noticed it vaguely, still too stunned to care. "Wait a minute—what got screwed up?"

"I bankrolled everything through a dirty deal with the ILC, but the damn ship broke down." *The Irish Liberation Council.* Someone had mentioned the council recently. "That's why I was in Sweden," he said bitterly. "The trawler was just a cover. I had to check on the boat, which put into Malta for repairs. Then my flight got screwed up, and I was a day late getting back. If I'd been here—" He swallowed. "But I wasn't, and Shelley—" He smiled, but it was more like a grimace of pain. "Well, we both know what happened to Shelley. And that left the kid loose. I'm dead if Rennie finds him, so I have to make sure he doesn't."

Nick stared at the beefy man. Martin, the epitome of the dumb but loyal disciple, the order taker, the shuffler. He had loved Shelley, had helped her, had gone behind Rennie's back to work a black-market arms deal. Every assumption Nick had ever made about the way the world worked was suddenly suspect.

And in the silence of his confusion, Isaac spoke. "Mama went away." His voice was low, his manner grave and somber. For an eerie minute, he looked like a tiny old man. "That's why we're leaving. It's a secret."

Nick stared at the boy. At his dark, serious face, his eyes intense and adult. And black. So black.

"That's enough, Isaac," Martin said. "Go wait outside in the hall and tell me if you see anything coming." The boy hesitated, then picked up his bear and trotted over to the entrance. But he didn't go out. He stood in the doorway and faced the two men in the room.

Nick lowered his voice to keep the kid from hearing. "Where are you taking him?"

Martin replied in the same hissed whisper, waving the gun for emphasis. "I'm not gonna tell you, so don't even bother asking."

"He's my kid, isn't he? Don't I have the right—"

"You haven't earned the right, pal. Where were you when he needed you? Where were you when Shelley had to hide him and keep him safe? Nowhere. Drunk."

Nick felt the weight of the boy's hot eyes. It made him sick to think he might have heard that, sick to admit the words were true. "I've been sober a long time. She could have come to me. We could have worked something out."

"Rennie kept a running tail on you, Nick. Monthly reports and everything. If she had told you, you would have wanted to see the kid, and sooner or later Rennie would have found out."

Nick's stomach turned over. He knew Spier had kept tabs on him, but not to that extent. He should have known Rennie wouldn't really let him go.

As if he'd read Nick's mind, Martin said softly, "Rennie's got you, Nick. He always has, and he always will. Me, he doesn't give a shit about. He never hung his hopes on me, never watched me close enough to care."

So Shelley had made her choice. And Martin was right, it was a smart one. Him, not Nick. A whisper of pain shot through Nick, a pain Martin seemed to understand. "It was for the boy," he said quietly. "She would've stayed if it weren't for the boy. She didn't want Rennie to turn Isaac into another one of us. A thug or a drunk."

That, he understood.

"So, what are you going to do, Nicky?" Martin shifted his weight and hefted the gun again, his large, rubbery face collapsing into a hopeful grin. "We were friends once. I don't want to shoot you."

Nick eyed the weapon and barked a curt laugh. "I don't want to get shot."

"Does that mean you're gonna help or be a pain in the ass?"

"Haven't figured it out yet." But he had, he just wasn't ready to admit it. He'd only set eyes on the boy a few minutes ago; now he'd have to watch him disappear into the sunset. Tough break. But wasn't keeping Isaac from Rennie the thought that had been circling his own head all the time?

Martin took Nick's silence for continued stubbornness. The big man's face hardened. "Look, I tried to keep you out of this. Why the hell couldn't you just take the hint and stay away?"

The hint. Nick's focus narrowed. "What are you talking about?"

The tension must have been plain in Nick's face because Martin backtracked fast. "Nothing. Forget it."

"No—you said hint. Did you send me a message, Marty?" But Martin didn't have to answer. Nick stilled. He'd received a message. The night before in Rachel's apartment. "That was your man at Rachel's, not Rennie's."

An angry thump began in Nick's chest.

"I had to do something," Martin said quickly. "I was afraid you'd find us and mess things up."

The thump sped up, fast and hot. He began to advance

on Martin, not caring that his hand had tightened over the .45.

"Stay there, Nicky. Calm down." The big man backed away. "I don't want to hurt you."

"Yeah, but you didn't mind hurting Rachel."

"It was just to scare her. I thought if you blamed Rennie, you'd walk. Why the fuck didn't you walk?"

His chest was on fire. "You sent a goon into Rachel's home to keep me away? You stupid son of a—" With a shout, he leaped at Martin, knocking away the arm that held the gun, but not before Martin squeezed off a round. The shot went wild and pinged into the wall. Isaac screamed and ran out of the room.

"Isaac! Wait!" Nick leaped toward the boy, but Martin spun him around, knocking Nick's head back with a punch that sent him reeling. He staggered through another left to his jaw. Martin was nothing if not huge and powerful, and he put all that force behind his fist. Before Nick could get his bearings, a third wallop sent him to his knees.

Chapter 10

Rachel froze at the sound of the gunshot, a sound she'd heard once and hoped never to hear again. Crouched in the hallway outside the office when the boy flew out the door, she moved too late to catch him. He didn't even notice her; in his fear, he ran blindly down the hall away from her.

Frantic, she wondered what to do. Had Martin shot Nick? The thought made her knees go weak, but before she could decide, she heard the bone-crunching thud of fist meeting flesh, heard a grunt and then nothing.

Oh, God.

Another grunt, as if someone—Martin? Nick?—had hoisted a heavy load. Then footsteps plodding toward the door. She looked around, desperate for a hiding place, and saw a stack of mildewed crates piled against one wall. Legs still feeble, she stumbled and fell, scrabbling behind cover just as Martin emerged from the room, carrying Nick's body over his shoulder fireman style.

Her stomach lurched, and she covered her mouth with a trembling hand. What had he done to Nick?

Suddenly an airplane droned in the distance, and Martin's head popped up.

"Isaac!" He looked up and down the corridor, cursing. "Isaac, where the hell are you? The plane is here." He stepped into a room across the hall, and she heard the sound of wood splintering. Another moment, and he came back out alone. He ran up the hallway, opening doors and checking rooms, calling for the boy. Heart in her throat, she watched him pass right by her as he went down the hall.

Outside, the plane rumbled closer. The sound seemed to echo the buzz of fear in Rachel's veins. What if Nick was— No, she wouldn't let her brain finish the thought. Nick had to be alive, or else Martin would have left him where he fell.

She eyed Martin's big back, her mouth dry, her hands clammy with sweat. Would she have enough time to run to the room where Martin had taken Nick? Sick with fear, she measured the distance. Two steps. Surely she could make it there before Martin spun around and saw her.

But just as she was about to step into the hallway, Isaac ran out of a room, and Martin scooped him up, jogging back toward Rachel with the boy under his arm like a football. Isaac clutched his teddy bear, and the two of them bounced in the huge man's arms. For the first time she was able to get a good look at the boy. What caught

Rachel's attention was not the almost humorous picture he made, but his small white face, his dark hair.

And Nick's dark eyes.

Shock rippled through her, and she almost gasped before remembering where she was. No wonder the boy in the photograph had reminded her of someone.

Their voices filtered through to her hiding place.

"Where's the bad man?" Fear laced the boy's voice.

"He's gone."

"Are we leaving now?"

"Yeah, we're going. Look, you got everything? Where's your knapsack?"

"I don't know."

Martin stopped and muttered a curse. Glancing up at the ceiling, he seemed to be listening to the growing sound of the plane and calculating what to do. "Doesn't sound like we have time to look for it."

"But my truck's in there."

Rachel slid farther into the pile of crates. From between the slats, she saw the tension in the big man's face. His meaty hands tightened over the boy. A new wave of trembling washed over her. What had those hands done to Nick?

"There's lots of important stuff in there, but I have to signal the plane, or they'll leave. Look, you don't want the bad men to get you, right? So we gotta go now. You got your bear, don't you? We'll just have to make do with that." He hurried toward the door, muttering to himself. "Shit," she thought he said. "We'll just have to make do with that."

That was the last she heard, as the two of them disappeared out the door. The minute they were gone, she dashed from her hiding place and into the room Martin had taken Nick.

Except for a broken chair, it was empty. Was she going crazy? She had seen Martin bring Nick in here. Nerves jittery, she had trouble standing still, but she forced herself to calm down and scan the room again. This time she saw the piece of wood shoved through the handle of the steel door cut into one of the walls. A piece of wood that looked suspiciously like a chair leg. She raced over to it and using the heel of her hand, tried to nudge the chair leg out. It was wedged in tight. She shoved again, the circling plane getting louder as she worked. Finally she bent down and, with a heave, shouldered the wood out and opened the door.

At one time, the room must have been some kind of freezer. Shelves for stacking various types of seafood lined the walls, and the smell of fish was powerful. Nick was just starting to sit up when she came through the door.

Relief at seeing him alive brought tears to her eyes, but she blinked them away in the rush to help him stand. "Are you all right?" She ran her hands over him, searching for wounds over the wide plane of his chest and the broad splay of back and shoulders. "I heard a shot and saw Martin bring you in here. Are you hurt? Bleeding?" Her fingers skimmed over muscled arms, stroked his neck and face.

He grabbed her hands, stopping their frenzied invasion. For a minute their gazes locked, and heat welled into her face as she realized what she'd been doing. Touching him. Caressing him.

He stepped back, dropping her hands. "What are you

doing here?" Clearly he wasn't as happy to see her as she was to see him. "I thought I told you to stay by the gate."

She smothered the fierce electric spark touching him had produced. "I got worried when the car left, so I came in to see if you were all right. I was in the hallway while you were arguing with Martin. I didn't hear all of it, but—"

He grabbed her by the shoulders. "Did anyone see you?"

"No."

A long, relieved breath eased out of him and he raked a hand through his hair. "Okay. Good." He rested a shoulder against the wall and took a breath, gathering himself together. "And, well . . . thanks for the rescue."

"My specialty, remember?" A grin tugged at the corners of her mouth, but she was careful not to let it spread and embarrass him further. "Besides, I owed you one."

He shot her a look of wry acknowledgment, then glanced toward the door as though he had no more time for jokes, not even small ones. "Where's Martin?"

"He took Isaac and left, but I don't think they've gone far."

"Why not?" His head had already drifted upward, his attention caught by the buzz of the plane.

She followed his gaze. "Because I think that's Martin's ride."

Nick took a moment to steady himself, then focused on the drone of the plane. "Which way did they leave?"

She led him to the entrance. Through the crack in the doorway, he saw Martin and the boy standing at the edge of a pier while a seaplane landed in the bay.

"So, that's what the lights back here were for," he murmured.

He could still feel the power of Martin's punch rattling his insides, but the residual effects faded at the sight of the man and boy holding hands, waiting for their ticket out. Searing the picture into his memory, he watched the two shapes—one huge, one tiny—brace themselves against the sudden gust of air. The wind blew back their clothes, making their struggle to stand appear almost heroic.

"They look like soldiers trying to beat the odds," Nick said, his throat tightening with emotion.

"You can still stop them."

He could, but he didn't. Never mind what Rennie would do to him. And Rachel . . . He turned to look at her. Her brown eyes gazed back at him, soft and kind. She understood.

"Martin was behind the attack on your apartment," he said quietly.

She nodded. "I heard."

"What else did you hear?"

"Only that Shelley kept the boy hidden from Rennie."

He turned back to the pier for one last look. "I could make Martin pay if you want me to."

"No, let them go. It's what you want. And it's the right thing to do."

"I want the boy safe from Rennie."

"I know. So do I."

They watched the plane door swing open and Martin step through, holding Isaac's hand. And then . . . something went wrong. Martin backed up onto the pier again. He staggered and jerked and then, like a statue toppling, the huge man clutched his chest, crashed to his knees, and fell face forward on the pier.

Nick froze. Jesus Christ, what the—

Then Rennie stepped out of the plane.

A sound that was half squeak, half gasp came from Rachel. She was dead pale, her gaze riveted on the body lying on the pier, a screaming child standing over it. No one had to tell him what she was seeing. Her mother's death. Herself. She opened her mouth to scream, and he quickly covered her cry with his hand, pressing her face into his chest so she could no longer see the scene on the pier.

Holding her shaking body, he watched Rennie scoop up the hysterical boy. Isaac kicked with savage desperation, but Rennie paid no attention. Without another glance, he disappeared inside the plane while Frank and two men retrieved Martin's body. *Two men.* God, that's what the team had been for. They hosed down the bloodstains and sealed the plane's entryway. Another few seconds, and the aircraft took off.

Fast, efficient, deadly. The whole thing had taken place before Nick's brain could register it.

Now he stood motionless, denying the evidence of his own eyes. His body didn't seem to be working; the arm that held Rachel lost its grip, and released from his hold, she staggered outside and sank to the ground, retching.

The sight of her suffering snapped him out of his stunned lethargy. He slipped off his tie and stumbled down one of the dilapidated piers to dip the strip of cloth in the water so she could wipe out her mouth when she was through. Something lay at the edge of a piling.

Isaac's brown bear.

Nick picked up the toy as if it could help him understand. It couldn't. Nothing could. No words, no explanation, nothing could blot out the picture of the boy's anguish as he stood over Martin's body.

Or the fact that Nick stood by and let it happen.

Rachel was sitting on her knees, staring off into nothing when he returned. He handed her the wet tie and she blotted her mouth dully, then sat back again. Laying the bear on the ground, he knelt beside her. She was still shuddering quietly.

"He'll m-miss his bear," she said sadly.

"Maybe we can get it back to him."

The minute he said the words, his purpose firmed. What he felt, what he wanted, none of that mattered now. If he had to hurt people again, if he had to kill someone again, he'd do it. Nothing mattered but getting Isaac back.

Rachel turned to face him. She didn't ask how or when, she didn't ask anything. She just looked deep into his eyes, and the vow passed between them, silent and resolute. They would get the boy back.

But first they had to get out of there.

"Can you walk?" He put an arm around her shoulders to help her stand and felt the tremors rushing through her.

"Of course. I'm . . . I'm fine."

She wasn't fine; she was rubbing her wrists obsessively and still quivering like a mouse. But she'd walk across the parking lot and hike the miles with him anyway. Grateful, he brushed escaping tendrils of hair away from her face. "You can stay here. I'll find a phone, call a cab, and come back for you."

"No. I want to go."

"I don't know how far we'll have to walk before we can find a phone."

"It doesn't matter."

His throat closed up. Somehow he didn't think he could make it through the rest of this night alone, but he would never have asked it of her. And now, he didn't have to.

He held out his hand, and she took it. But they'd barely turned the corner toward the parking lot when Rachel stopped.

"Look." With a trembling finger, she pointed out a pile of rocks and broken wood pieces just out of sight around the corner. The plant blocked most of the light from the bay, but between the remnants and the moon they could make out the crude, fortlike structure, just big enough to hold a small boy. Nick walked over to the aerie, knowing what small boy had built it.

He stared down at the center of the fort, and a shadow caught his eye. He knelt down and felt around inside.

A knapsack. He held up the blue bag along with a red truck that had been lying next to it, and walked back to Rachel.

"It must be Isaac's," she said, grief creeping into her voice. "He couldn't remember what he'd done with it, and Martin couldn't take time to look for it."

She looked so forlorn, his heart twisted. "Come on, we'll take it with us."

She nodded. "When we f-find him, he'll want his things back."

Not if, when. His respect for her went up another notch.

But still she didn't move. He rose and walked back to her, and she stared at the knapsack as if it were a ghost come to life.

"What's wrong?" *Stupid question. What wasn't wrong?*

He tipped her face up. Tears shimmered in her eyes, tears he would have given anything not to see.

"Tell me he'll be all right. Tell me we'll get him back."

"We will. I promise."

And suddenly she was in his arms, burrowed in the circle of his body. He held her tight, letting her cling to him. *I've got you, baby. I've got you.* They stood that way for endless minutes. Eyes closed, he reveled in the soft feel of her, in the illusion of safety his body provided. If he could, he would have held her forever, but the sound of an approaching speedboat made him pull away.

Rachel rubbed at her teary face. "What is it?"

"I don't know." Motioning her to stay still, he sneaked back to the corner of the building and saw the boat heading for the dock. Two men were inside. He ran back to Rachel.

"We have to get out of here." Stuffing the bear and the truck inside the knapsack, he grabbed her hand and started running, shouldering the bag as he went.

He heard the sound of the engine cutting out and knew the boat had landed.

"Who is it?"

"Two of Rennie's men."

The parking lot swallowed Rachel and Nick in darkness, but he wouldn't feel safe until he'd put the plant well behind them. He pulled Rachel through the gates and turned left onto the road. He didn't stop running until the plant was out of sight.

As he slowed to a fast walk, he glanced over at Rachel. She was out of breath, but alarm had replaced the sadness in her face.

"What do you think they wanted?"

"I don't know. Maybe to search the place."

"Why? What are they looking for?"

"I don't have a clue." And he didn't want to know. He just wanted to get her out of there, on a train and back home safely.

And suddenly he remembered the goon at the train station. No wonder he didn't get on the train; he hadn't been after Rachel. He'd been watching Martin.

A sick little shudder went through Nick and he trudged on in silence, glad of the dark. Somehow it seemed to mirror the darkness inside him. The picture of the boy screaming over the dead body etched itself into his brain. Would he ever forget it? He was responsible for two boys now. Two boys in agony.

"Nick, who was in the car?"

Her voice brought him back to the present. "What car?"

"The car that left the plant a few minutes after we got there."

Nick thought back to what seemed hours ago, when the teenager had bopped out of the plant and into the night.

"I think she was a baby-sitter. Martin must have been shuffling Isaac around, farming him out to various sitters."

"Do you think that's how Rennie tracked him down?"

"I don't know."

"But if Rennie knew where Isaac was, why did he need you?"

He shook his head, thinking back over the day and his conversation earlier with Frank. "Maybe he didn't know. At least not when he recruited me. But he knew this morning. Or Frank did."

She looked at him questioningly.

"The job I overheard Frank planning," he said. "Two men, tonight. Two men helped Frank clean up."

She trembled, and for a moment he thought she was going to be sick again. But she swallowed and pushed on. "If they knew this morning, why didn't Frank say something?"

He smiled grimly but didn't tell her about pulling his gun on Frank. "I wasn't exactly toeing the line. And anyway, Rennie probably knew I'd never—"

"Kill for him?"

"Do that particular job," he corrected gently.

She looked away, clearly disturbed, and a shiver rippled through him, as if the blanket of her good opinion had been removed. He clamped down on his jaw, trying not to care and only half succeeding. It was time she knew the truth about him, wasn't it? Time she knew what he was.

They turned up a street and walked half a mile until they reached a major intersection lined with industrial companies. Nick scanned the area but saw no pay phones. They headed west, and as they walked, he felt the weight of her unasked questions. He wished they would remain unasked, but he could hardly say he was surprised when she broke the quiet with one.

"I saw Isaac's face, Nick. He has your eyes."

He nodded, not trusting himself to speak.

"Did Rennie know about—about you and Shelley?"

A rush of shame fluttered through him. The last thing he wanted to talk to Rachel about was Shelley. "I don't think I'd be here if he did."

"How long did you and she . . . when did you . . . start?"

He wanted to lie and say their affair had been brief. He wanted to make up some story about her seducing him. But Rachel deserved the truth. "It started the minute I laid eyes on her."

"Was she as beautiful as her pictures?"

Oh, yeah. "The first time I saw her, she wore this filmy white dress that floated around her like angel wings." He spoke softly, wistfully, remembering. "I thought she was the most beautiful thing I'd ever seen." He gave a short, hard laugh. "And she knew it. She used it. Teased me, tempted me. And I wanted to be tempted. Badly. I spent a year sniffing around her, watching her watch me. A month after she married Rennie, I'd slept with her."

Rachel looked out into the night. "You took a big risk."

She was right. But at the time . . . "I was young and very, very stupid."

"And Shelley?"

He shook his head. "I don't know. Maybe she just liked living on the edge. At least for a while. Then, out of the blue, she got tired of me. Said she was bored. I bored her." He remembered the shock and the hurt, but it was far away, as if it had happened to someone else.

"You told me you hadn't worked for Rennie in six years. Isaac must be six or almost six. Is that why you left? Because she broke up with you?"

"That, and other things."

"What other things?"

"Things I don't want to talk about."

She didn't press him, and he was grateful.

It took them the better part of an hour before they found a phone and a cab company willing to pick them up at three in the morning in the middle of nowhere. But they did finally find one, and waited twenty minutes for it to pick them up and take them to the train station, where Rachel slept on his shoulder until five-thirty-five, when they caught the first train back to the city.

The trip seemed to last forever, and during it, he re-enacted the scene at the pier over and over. Rachel dozed on and off, but when he shut his scratchy eyes, the pictures cycled inside his head, and he woke with a start. What should he have done? What could he have done?

One of those times, Rachel put a hand on his arm. "It wasn't your fault."

He turned to her. How could she know what he was thinking?

"There was nothing you could do," she said. "They outnumbered you four-to-one. They had weapons, you didn't. If you had tried to stop them, they would have killed you. And me."

True, but galling just the same. One more screwup to add to the long list.

Forty-five minutes outside of Manhattan, he thought

to examine the knapsack. Rachel was sleeping again, and opening the bag gave him something to focus on.

He unfastened the latch, raised the flap, and took out the teddy bear, noting how beat-up it looked. Beneath the bear, shorts and a T-shirt stared up at him along with a pair of miniature sneakers. He began to explore, forming a picture of the boy's life through his things. Buried under the clothes, he found a book, a computer game, and a Mets baseball cap.

And underneath those, an inch-thick wad of papers, rolled up and bound with a rubber band. At first he thought it was a bunch of Isaac's drawings, because it looked like the greenbar paper at the preschool, feeder hole strips and everything. But when he unfurled the roll, he didn't find brightly colored pictures of crude houses and people.

He went utterly still. Even without examining it, he knew what it was. What it had to be.

Spier's assets, every last illicit million. Traceable to all the dummy corporate accounts he set up in every hole-in-the-wall Caribbean bank.

Nick flipped the pages to the middle, and it was all there on his lap. Wire transfers, times, dates, amounts. He stared at the numbers in a stupor of exhaustion, knowing he'd done Rennie's bidding at last. Because in the end, he'd found what the men in the boat must have been looking for. What Spier had wanted all along.

Chapter 11

Rachel woke with a gentle prodding from Nick fifteen minutes outside the city. A dark, empty feeling woke with her, remnants of the long, horrific night. She leaned back against the seat, exhausted. She didn't want to think about what she'd seen, wanted the pictures in her head to stop and her life to go on as if none of it had happened. But try as she might, she couldn't forget the boy or Martin, or what Spier had done to them both.

"We have to go to the police," she said to Nick. "We saw Spier kill Martin. We're eyewitnesses. We'll go to the police, and they'll arrest Spier."

He looked at her patiently, the way a parent looks at a beloved three-year-old. "And what happens to Isaac?"

"Nothing. Why should Spier harm him, he's his—" She was going to say, "his son." But she caught Nick's eye. Would everyone recognize what she had? Would Spier know the boy wasn't his? She shuddered. She didn't want to think about what Spier might do if he did.

"No police," Nick said.

His curtness left anger pooling in her chest. Her mother's killer had never been caught either, and as a child Rachel would wake up screaming that the bad man was coming back, coming for her. She didn't want the same for Isaac, especially since he knew who the bad man was.

"You can't let him get away with this, Nick."

His mouth thinned into a grim line, and something hard came over him; something she didn't want to see or acknowledge. "I won't."

She looked down at her hands. Miraculously, they lay calmly separate in her lap. "And the boy—how do we get him back?"

"With this." He hauled up Isaac's knapsack and lifted out a set of rolled-up papers. Removing the rubber band, he flattened the pages on his lap. They looked like the donated computer paper her kids used for artwork—pale green stripes with columns of numbers, names, and dates.

"What is it?"

"A paper trail. Illegal transactions, wire transfers, shell companies. It lays out Rennie's whole organization."

My God. She stared at Nick, floored by the implications.

"Don't even think about it," he said.

"But we can stop him. This"—she gestured to the printout, excitement rising—"this could stop him."

Nick rolled up the printout with a sharp twist, snapping the rubber band in place. "Forget it. The kid comes first. Nothing else matters. Nothing. I'm going to make a simple trade. I get the boy, Rennie gets his life's work back."

"But—"

"No buts, Rachel. And no screwing around. Rennie is serious business."

After last night, she couldn't deny it. But she also couldn't deny that as much as Rennie was brutal, he was also untrustworthy, and the printout was the only leverage they had against him. "So you hand this back? And what—he lets you walk away free and clear?"

"That's my problem."

She shuddered at his flat tone, and the way it shut her out. "And what are you going to do about it?"

"Get you out of town."

"Out of—" Her world was tilting madly again.

"I can't have you out there like live bait waiting to be stuck on a hook and dangled in front of me. Once I make the call to set up the trade, I no longer work for Rennie, and you're fair game. I'll find a safe place for you and Isaac. We'll leave tonight after we make the trade."

She tried to gather her composure. Ten days ago, her life had been normal crazy, not crazy crazy. A week ago— She drew in a sharp breath. "What day is it?"

"I don't know," Nick said, abstracted. "Wednesday or Thursday."

She counted back. It was Thursday. Her heart sank. "Tomorrow is the Parish Council meeting, Nick. They specifically requested my presence. If I'm not there, they'll vote to end my agreement with the church."

He muttered a curse and ran a hand through his hair. "We have to leave tonight."

"But I have to be at that meeting. I haven't found emergency funding or another place to go."

His eyes reflected the anguish she felt, but he was adamant. "I can't wait, it's too dangerous. Rennie could move the boy where I'd never find him, he could hurt him, twist him, do to him what he did—" He swallowed and looked away, his jaw tightening, but she finished his unspoken thought: *to me.* "I'm not leaving him in that house, surrounded by Rennie's people and Rennie's world, not for one second longer than necessary." His face was tense and pale, almost sick with memory. "I'm sorry, Rachel, but we have no choice."

She wanted to argue, to rail against him, but she couldn't quarrel with the look in his face. And every time she closed her eyes, she saw the boy screaming on the pier. She couldn't turn her back on him, whatever the cost.

But the realization, and the choice it implied, filled her with despair.

From Manhattan, they caught a subway to Astoria. Nick walked her to the foot of the church steps, handing her the knapsack. "Put it in the supply closet and lock it up."

She did what he told her, but it went against her grain, as if locking the evidence away was like closing the door on a trap with themselves inside.

She was two hours late, so she went to find Felice and tell her the story Nick had concocted on the subway.

As she walked down the hall, she admired the way Felice had opened the school and organized the kids without her. Felice could handle everything for a few days. And surely Rachel wouldn't be gone more than that. But the thought was like dust, flimsy and insubstantial. She had no idea how long she'd be gone.

When she got to her classroom, Felice was overseeing a finger-painting project. Dressed in reams of bright yellow, she looked like a huge, hot sun with a smile to match.

"Rach! Wondered when you were going to show up."

"Sorry I'm late." She took her over to a corner for privacy, but her face must have given something away, because Felice immediately asked if she was all right.

"Fine." But Rachel knew she didn't sound fine or look fine. "Look, my . . . my cousin was in a car accident."

Felice was immediately solicitous. "Was it bad?"

Rachel nodded. "They don't—" Her voice shook with the lie and gave it an unintended realism. "They don't know if he'll make it."

"Oh Rach, I'm so sorry."

"I . . . I have to take some time off." Rachel was afraid to look at Felice, afraid her face would give her away.

"Sure, Rach, absolutely, as long as you like. We'll be fine here." Felice gave her a swift hug. "You just do what you have to and don't worry about us."

"Thanks."

Rachel trudged down the hall to her office and pulled out her phone book. Riffling through it, she started a list of every agency she could think of. If she could find even some financial assistance, she could keep the school afloat after the Parish Council shut her down.

As she worked, she tried to blot out all thoughts of murder and retribution, but every few minutes her eyes drifted to the supply closet that hid the knapsack and Spier's printout. Justice, vengeance, and safety were inside, so close, so very close.

She turned away and picked up the phone.

For the next few hours she called everyone she knew, but struck out three times over. Times were tough, and money was tight. A band of worry squeezed her head, making it ache.

At noon, Felice poked her head in to ask if she wanted anything from the deli around the corner.

"No thanks," Rachel told her. She'd never get a bite down. She thought briefly about asking Felice to attend the council meeting in Rachel's place. Felice wasn't always politic, but she did care about the school, and any representation would be better than none.

But Rachel quickly dismissed the idea. She wouldn't be able to explain why she couldn't attend herself. Even if her cousin's condition were real, she should be able to take an hour for the meeting, especially if it was important.

So she said nothing. Felice left, and Rachel gave up searching for miracles. Instead, she sketched out some lesson plans, trying to suggest enough ideas for Felice to run the school in Rachel's absence. If there was a school to run. She threw down her pen and looked around her office, tears prickling her eyelids. The scruffy, familiar space was the start of her dream, and now her plans, her kids, were all in jeopardy.

But so was one little boy.

She cut another glance at the closet and swallowed the taste of fear. Abruptly she got up, the choice she had to make suddenly unbearable. Leaving the office and its

deadly contents, she ran to the yard for a breath of air.
Nick had told her to stay inside, but if she did, she'd suf-
focate.

One of the teachers had brought her class out to play;
five small children romped in the warm sun, each at a
different stage of adjustment—squealing, somber, mischievous, and intent. From across the yard, Joselito's
round face lit up when he saw her, and he ran over, flinging himself at her legs before taking off again. She
watched him, the back of her throat tight. She couldn't
believe she wouldn't be there tomorrow or the tomorrow
after that.

Surely she wouldn't have to stay away more than a
few days. Surely Nick would work something out with
Spier.

But can you work things out with a man like Rennie
Spier? It would be like trying to work something out
with a live grenade. The only way to survive was to run
like hell before it exploded.

So she was running. The thought stuck in her throat
like a lump she couldn't swallow past. She was running,
giving up everything that mattered to her, but Spier was
free to kill and maim, to ruin lives all over again.

Unless . . . a shaft of fear pierced her. Unless Nick
killed him. But even as she recoiled from the thought, it
remained wedged in her mind, a hard, clear nugget of in-
tuition she couldn't escape. Because she suspected that
was Nick's plan. And after last night, after seeing the
way Spier had thwarted Martin's escape, seeing the way
he hadn't hesitated or questioned or stopped for expla-
nations before pulling the trigger, she wasn't sure Nick
would succeed. Beneath the heat of the schoolyard she

shivered again. Kill or be killed. Either way, Nick's life would be over.

The only alternative was locked inside the supply closet.

Dragging in a huge gulp of air, Rachel went back inside. She came through the door of her office, fretful and preoccupied, and an arm snaked around her neck.

Jerked backward, she gave a sharp squeal of terror. Instantly a hand covered her mouth. She clawed at the hand, heard the sound of the door closing, heard her own useless, muffled yips. *Not again. God, please, not again.*

A voice hissed in her ear. "It's okay, calm down. It's me, Nick. I'm going to let you go, so don't scream or anything."

The minute his hold loosened, she wrenched herself away and whirled on him in fury. "What do you think you're doing—"

"Shh." He reached for her again, but she swung away. "I'm sorry. I didn't mean to scare you."

"How did you get in here?"

"I told you to get the fence fixed." Which meant, she supposed, he'd sneaked through the hole in the fence and cut across the yard before the kids came out to play, then slipped inside, unnoticed.

She collapsed into the chair behind the desk, leaned back and closed her eyes. *Breathe. Just breathe.*

He put a hand on her head. "I'm sorry," he said softly, slowly stroking downward.

His touch sent warmth rippling through her. She opened her eyes to find him kneeling in front of her, black brows drawn in a worried frown. *It's Nick. Just Nick.* She'd missed those brows and the rough lines of his face. For a brief moment, a picture rose in her mind. A picture of her life entwined with his. Would it be a life-time of days like this, of worrying about what he would do and if he'd come back?

She gazed into his face, his expression full of concern for her, and wanted to believe that everything would be all right. If only her stomach didn't feel queasy with dread. "You're forgiven." She tried out a smile. "Just don't sneak up on me again."

He held up two hands and rose. "I won't, believe me."

She noticed he'd changed into the once-familiar uni-form of khaki green work pants and shirt, as if an ordi-nary guy had replaced the slick henchman. Only now the shirt was open at the neck. Silently, she congratulated him on that small step toward relaxation, even as her own tension mounted.

He looked around the room. "So, are you ready?"

Ready? How could she be ready to walk away from her life, her dreams? "Guess I don't have much choice. How about you?"

"Except for the phone call to Rennie."

She frowned, puzzled. "I thought that's what you were doing all day. Making the arrangements."

He shook his head. "Not until we're ready to leave. We don't want to give him any more planning time than we have to."

No, we wouldn't want to do that. She shivered, a min-now in an ocean of sharks.

"I went to the bank," he said, perching on the corner of her desk. "We'll need cash."

She straightened the pile of instructions she'd left for

Felice. "What's wrong with good old-fashioned credit cards?"

"No cards. Rennie could trace them."

She inhaled a sharp breath. Another probability that hadn't occurred to her. Would she ever learn?

"And I had your door fixed." He threw her a set of keys and an instruction book.

"What's this?"

"It's for the electronic lock."

"The what?"

He looked sheepish. "All right, so maybe I went a little overboard. But extra security never hurts."

"This must have cost a fortune," she said, flipping through the book.

He threw her a tight smile. "It's on Rennie."

Rennie. She was so sick of that name. "Anything else I should know?"

He hesitated, and she sensed he was debating how much to tell her. Finally, he said, "I went to see a friend."

Before she could press for more details, a knock sounded on her office door. Quickly he stepped behind it, and Rachel opened the door partway.

Felice stood at the threshold. "You've got a visitor." She thumbed over her shoulder at a woman standing in front of the finger-painting display. She turned and smiled.

The writer. The one from the disaster at her aunt and uncle's dinner party. What was she doing here?

"I told her this wasn't a good time," Felice said in a low voice, "but she insisted."

"Thanks, Felice."

"No problem." Felice winked and returned to her classroom.

"Get rid of her," Nick whispered from behind the door. As if she needed to be told. She closed the door behind her as the woman came forward.

"Dana Gershon," she said, extending her hand. "We met at your aunt and uncle's."

How could Rachel forget?

Standing guard over the office door, she said to the writer, "I thought I made my feelings about your project clear."

Dana gave her a conciliatory glance. "Let's forget about the book, okay? Chris told me so much about your school. I'd really like to see it."

"Why don't you call me, and we'll set up an appointment?"

The woman laughed. "Once you get to know me better, you'll find I don't brush off that easily."

"I'm sorry, but this just isn't a good time." Her palms were slick against the doorknob, her mouth dry.

Dana peered at her thoughtfully. *Do I look like a scared rabbit?* Rachel hoped not. But whatever her face gave away, it did the trick.

"Okay, some other time. But I'm not giving up. I know what you're doing here is an intensive process that takes patience and money. You're begging for handouts, and from the looks of things"—she waved her arm, indicating the pathetic state of the classrooms lining the halls—"people aren't tripping over themselves to help you out. I even hear you're on shaky ground with the Parish Council, and your space may be taken away."

No maybe about it. The thought sent a stab of pain

through her. "Thinking about doing a piece on me, now?"

Dana laughed. "It has crossed my mind. But actually, I was hoping to help."

In spite of the secret guest behind her door, Rachel's ears perked up. "Help? Help how?"

A small smile turned up the edges of Dana's mouth. "Chris told me your dream is to start a permanent institute to help victims of violence. I'm pretty sure I can work a deal with the publisher to set aside a portion of the book profits for your seed money."

"You're joking."

Dana's smile widened.

"You're not joking." Rachel's jaw dropped.

"It would be great PR for them, and besides the cash, it would be terrific publicity for you, too. You'll never find permanent funding if people don't know about your work." She paused, then spoke with frank sincerity. "I believe in this book about your father, Rachel. And I know it won't be successful without your help. You don't have to answer right away. Just think it over. Here's my number." She handed Rachel a business card. "In the meantime—" She took a checkbook out of her purse. "Can I make a donation?"

Five minutes later, Rachel ducked back inside her office, Dana's check in hand.

"Sorry," she murmured to Nick as she clipped the check to the notes for Felice. For a second, she yearned to stop and savor Dana Gershon's proposal. It felt like a godsend, a lifeline of hope when she'd been drowning in misery. But she stowed that thought for later because she had other things to worry about now. Like walking away from her school and turning her back on the only thing that could bring Rennie Spier down.

As if he'd read her mind, Nick said, "Where's the knapsack?"

Her heart slammed against her chest. "In the closet."

"Get it out, it's time to go. I called Rennie while you were talking, and we have half an hour." Her stomach fell to her knees. "I picked up your car when I was at your apartment. Bring the knapsack and meet me in front in five minutes."

When he was gone, she ran down the hall to give Felice the lesson plans and to tell her she was leaving. On the way back to the office, Rachel grabbed a canvas tote and stopped in the kitchen to pack a box of graham crackers and some apple juice. Her fingers were stiff, the tips icy. She hadn't even asked where they were going. Bringing the tote with her, she returned to her office and unlocked the closet.

She scrutinized the shelves, pointedly ignoring the knapsack. Except for stacks of used greenbar paper donated by area colleges and corporations, the closet was mostly empty. Mechanically, she pulled off a chunk of paper and tore along a perforation to separate it from the rest of the pile. Pale green stripes filled with indecipherable numbers and equations marred one side of each page. But the back side was unlined and clean, perfect for drawing. She stuffed the hunk of paper into the tote and threw in some crayons, wondering if Isaac liked to draw.

Then she turned to the other items in the closet.

Leaning against Isaac's knapsack, the bear sat spread-eagled on the floor. Lifeless brown eyes stared back at

her, as empty as all the others in the roster of death surrounding Rennie Spier. Her heart began to thud. The tote
dropped from her hand.

She couldn't do nothing, she just couldn't. Not after
the horrors Spier had committed against her and so many
others. The horrors he would continue to commit if he
were free and whole. His specter would haunt Isaac for
years; she knew firsthand what that fear was like. Besides, she knew with absolute clarity that Spier would
never hand back the boy and walk away. Somehow,
someday, he'd make Nick pay. The printout was power,
the only protection he had.

Slowly, she bent to touch the knapsack. Running her
fingers over the edges, she debated one last time. She
took a breath for courage, closed her eyes.

Then she opened the flap.

The printout sat right on top. She removed the rubber
band and unrolled the documents. The first page stared
up at her, striped green with columns and numbers that
burned into her eyes.

What should she do? What could she do?

Too late now to copy it all. The job would take fifteen
minutes, and she only had one or two before she had to
meet Nick. Precious seconds passed before the idea
came to her, and when it did, she rejected it even as her
hands moved to complete it. *Are you crazy?* But the
thought didn't stop her from separating the bulk of
Spier's papers from the first four. *Stark, raving insane?*
Swallowing a huge lump, she replaced the missing pages
with the recycled computer paper in her tote bag. Then
she rolled up the whole thing, wound the rubber band

around it, and put the fake printout in the bag, just as Nick had left it.

Oh, my God. For a scant second, she closed her eyes, clutching the rest of Spier's papers to her tightly. She breathed a small, fierce prayer, then placed the stolen documents below a stack of computer paper on the closet shelf.

Before she could change her mind, she shoved the knapsack out of the closet with her foot and slammed the door shut. *Done. It was done.*

Almost immediately, she began to shake. Pressing hard against the closet door, she clamped her lips together, knowing she could still change her mind, still walk away.

Suddenly her father's voice echoed inside her head. *God, not now. Not one of your speeches, Daddy, please.* But it was as if his hand had touched her.

Victim, but not victimized. Take control. You have the power. Nothing will change unless you and I change it.

The words he'd said over and over strengthened her resolve. She'd taken control, grabbed her power. Switching the printout not only paid Spier back—payment he dearly deserved—but protected Isaac and gave Nick the leverage he needed. And no one had to die for it.

She straightened, willing herself to stop quaking, and in a few moments brought her breathing under control. Refilling her satchel with paper, she shoved the bear on top, gripped the knapsack by its shoulder straps, and left to meet Nick.

He was waiting at the foot of the church steps, leaning an elbow on the humped red back of her VW Beetle and watching the street.

"I staked out the place an hour before coming in," he said as she threw the knapsack in the back. "I don't think Rennie has anyone watching it." But his gaze moved ceaselessly until she'd slid into the passenger seat.

Sitting on her hands so he wouldn't see them shaking, she said, "I want to help, Nick. What can I do?"

"Nothing. The last thing I need is for Rennie to see you with me."

"How are you going to make the trade?"

"At the zoo in Central Park."

A distress signal went off in her head. "You're just going to walk in there blind, carrying the printout? What's to stop them from grabbing it and running?"

He gave her a long, tolerant look. "Me," he said evenly.

"Oh, I forgot. King Kong in human form. Meet Nick Raine, the ultimate badass."

Ignoring that, Nick reached over the seat for the knapsack. A jolt of panic sliced through as he lifted out the printout and brought it into the front with him. He slid off the rubber band and began to unfurl the pages.

"What are you doing?" The yelp burst out of her before she could stop it.

"Take it easy. I just need a little something—" Carefully, he removed the top page and rerolled the rest. He handed the printout to her and stuffed the sheet he'd removed in a pocket. "Let's go." He put the car in gear and took off.

"Nick—"

He looked at her questioningly.

She gripped the printout tighter and took a breath. "I could . . . why don't you let me take it in for you?"

He didn't even think about it. "No. Rennie's sure to have the place covered. It's too dangerous."

"Nick, they're looking for a black-haired man, not a brown-haired woman. They don't even know we're together. No one will notice me."

"That's because you won't be there."

"Have you ever been to the zoo? Do you have any idea how the place is laid out?"

"No, but neither does Rennie. That's why I chose it."

"I've been to the zoo with the kids dozens of times. I could find my way in the dark if I had to. Nick, you're going in there completely unprotected. You need an edge, an advantage. I can give it to you."

He threw her a narrow-eyed look. "You're pushing pretty hard here, Rachel. How come? Why are you so hot to do this?"

Because she couldn't let him near the damn printout, or he might look at it too closely. And because she was tired of being Rennie Spier's pawn.

"I'm human, Nick." She said the first thing that entered her head. "I want my own little piece of revenge."

Nick stopped at a red light and studied her. "All right," he said slowly. "But only because I can understand you wanting to personally pay Rennie back. After what he did to you, he has it coming. I admit it would be smarter not to walk in with the printout in plain sight, but if I don't like the way things look when we get there, you don't go in."

She nodded, her mouth dry. "Fair enough." She hoped he couldn't hear the clattering racket of her heart.

*   *   *

By the time they reached the tunnel that would connect them to Manhattan, Nick was regretting his decision. Rachel sat beside him, rubbing her wrists compulsively, obviously terrified.

"You don't have to do this." His knuckles shone white as he clutched the steering wheel. If anything happened to her . . .

"I want to."

He bit back a growl. The worst part of any operation was waiting for it to begin; the best way to endure was to distract. Right now, they could both use some distraction.

"I overheard part of your conversation with that writer. I didn't know you wanted to start a permanent institute."

Her shoulders lifted in an ironic shrug. "Everyone has pipe dreams."

"Is that all it is?"

"Unless you have a few spare millions floating around."

A shaft of black amusement arrowed through him. He kept his gaze on the road, but in his mind he saw the tiny key he'd used at the bank for the first time in six years. The key that opened the box to all his past misdeeds. By rights he should have burned all the money, but weak, greedy bastard that he was, he couldn't bring himself to. So he'd locked it all away. Tainted money. Blood money. Money he'd vowed never to touch again.

Never say never.

"Are you going to help with the book?"

"I don't know." She sounded irritated, and he suspected she didn't want to talk about it.

"The money must be tempting." She answered with another shrug. "Not tempting enough?"

"I'm not interested in digging up the past."

"Why not? I'd think you'd be proud of your father."

She threw him a cynical glance. "I leave that to his fans."

Arms crossed, the obsessive rubbing now forgotten, she sat in crabby silence, staring out the window. But anger was better than fear.

"Well, for someone who professes no great love for him, you sure collected a lot of stuff about David Goodman. You have enough pictures in your room to start a museum."

Her scowl deepened. "What's your point?"

"No point," he said mildly. "Just making a few observations."

"Well, don't. My relationship with my father is nobody's business but mine. Everyone else may think he was a great man, but to me he was just a lousy dad. I've spent years trying to come to terms with it, and I don't want to explore that territory all over again. Why you and half the world think you can—"

"Look." They had reached the zoo. He cruised past the entrance of Fifth Avenue. "There," he said softly, "the guy in the sports coat leaning against the wall reading the paper. And there." He nodded in the other direction. "That bum on the bench. Rennie's men you'll have to pass."

She wrinkled her nose in distaste. "Are you sure? The guy on the bench doesn't look like he's had a coherent thought in a decade."

"He was coherent enough to stuff Martin into a body bag last night."

She drew in a sharp breath, but said nothing.

The streets were jammed, and the closest he could park was a garage on Sixty-fifth. The attendant's booth was empty when Nick drove in, but the man jogged over as Nick backed the car into a small niche on the lower level, out of sight of the booth and the street. The alcove wasn't a real space, but it accommodated the VW's small size without hemming in the vehicles parked in normal slots, and it gave Nick instant access to their ride out. The attendant wasn't happy, but he accepted Nick's hundred dollars to leave the car there and another fifty to leave it without the keys, which Nick pocketed after turning off the engine.

The attendant left, and Nick and Rachel sat in silence. Her hands lay in her lap, and though an air of sharp awareness hovered about her, he sensed her fear wouldn't get in the way of her mission.

He took off his watch and handed it to her. "Put it in your pocket if you don't want to wear it."

She shook her head. "You keep it. I won't be long."

"Okay, but don't get distracted." They got out of the car and he opened the trunk, retrieving his gym bag, which he'd picked up that afternoon. "Here, put the printout in this." He stuffed the printout into the bag, pushing it down between his sweats and sneakers, and shoved the bag in the bottom of her tote. "Drop off the bag, and I'll pick it up like we planned. It'll take you a good ten to twelve minutes to walk there, and the same amount back, plus a few minutes to stash the bag. Thirty minutes in all to place it and get back here before I leave, so don't get sidetracked. And listen." He took her by the shoulders and turned her to face him. Beneath his fingers her body felt small and vulnerable. "If anything looks off—I mean anything—drop the bag and run." He searched her face, wanting to brush her hair back, stroke her cheek, touch her once before she left. What if something happened? What if she didn't come back? An uneasy foreboding filled him. "Promise me, or I won't let you do this."

She lifted her chin. "And how exactly are you going to stop me?"

"How about a right cross to that chin you're sticking out?" His words were light, but the tone was deadly quiet. He met her eyes and saw the message had gotten through. She gave him a curt nod.

"I promise. I'm not any more eager to get caught in the crossfire than you." She reached up and loosened her braid.

"What are you doing?"

"I look a whole lot different with my hair down."

She shook her head, freeing the hair. Soft and thick, it settled in waves around her shoulders and framed her face. Nick's breath caught at the sudden transformation. Unable to help himself, he touched the honey-brown mass. Not because he reveled in the feel or ached for an excuse to touch her. Not because he worried something would go wrong and wanted one last intimate moment with her. No, he ran his fingers through her hair purely for tactical reasons, to settle it strategically around her face.

At least that's what he told himself.

"Good idea," he said with sudden difficulty. "Your

hair can hide your face." Such a gentle face. A kissable face. With great reluctance, he dropped his hand. How would he ever manage to stand still and let her go? "All right, then. Good luck. And Rachel—"

She turned to look back at him, and the moment froze in his mind for all time.

"Keep your head down."

Chapter 12

*K*eep your head down.

Rachel had no trouble following that order and its unspoken warning.

Keep your head down, let your hair hide your face, don't draw attention to yourself.

Aye, aye, sir.

She walked from the car to the zoo at a brisk pace, eyes glued to the pavement, canvas tote clutched in her hand. Underneath paper, crayons, and all the other things she'd packed, the gym bag with its dangerous contents lay like a ten-ton rock. It bounced against her leg with every step.

They had parked east of the zoo between Madison and Park Avenue, so she had quite a ways to go. From this direction, she would have to pass directly in front of the bench with the derelict Nick had pointed out to her. Heart thudding, she calculated the steps between her position and the far side of the bench, what she had come to think of as her safety zone. Once she'd passed the bench, she would be able to breathe normally again.

Ten more steps to go.

Eight more.

Five.

A hard shove spun her around.

The bag flew out of her hand. She landed with a thump on the pavement.

Behind her, two in-line skaters waved their arms, still trying to stop.

She froze. Paper, crayons, graham crackers, scissors, tape, glue—the entire contents of the tote—scattered over the sidewalk. The gym bag at the bottom was clearly visible, half in and half out of the tote. Someone bent to help her. Rachel's heart stopped.

The man on the bench.

"Are you all right, miss?"

"Y-yes."

She nearly wept with terror as he picked up the tote and gathered her things. From a distance he'd looked dirty and ill-kempt, with greasy hair and shoes with holes. Up close, he was clear-eyed and clean-shaven.

"You're carrying quite a load." He hefted the bag.

"My . . . my gym shoes and stuff." Her voice squeaked. *Calm down. Smile.*

He looked at her closely. "You sure you're all right?"

Before she could respond, the two skaters surrounded her.

"Are you okay? I'm so sorry."

"Did you get hurt or anything? Maybe you should sit down."

They apologized and fussed over her while the man on the bench kept a firm grip on her bag.

"Yes, I'm fine. It's all right. Really." *Go away!*

"Well, if you're sure."

She forced herself to smile. "I'm sure, thank you." Her tongue was a cotton wad.

The skaters waved good-bye, and Rachel turned to go.

"Miss?"

A tap on her shoulder. She almost jumped out of her skin.

The man on the bench held out the tote bag. "Don't forget this."

"Oh," she said with a little gulp of surprise. "No, of course not. Thank you." She took the bag from him and walked off. His eyes burned her back all the way down the Fifth Avenue steps to the zoo.

Legs like rubber, she wanted to race away but couldn't. Forced to a normal pace, she rounded the Administration Building and checked the zoo's carillon clock just outside the entrance. Only a few minutes left to stash the gym bag and get back to the car before her thirty minutes were up. She closed her eyes and took a deep breath.

She couldn't fall apart now. She didn't have time.

High atop the arch just outside the zoo, a ring of steel animals did a mechanical dance as the clock chimed the hour. Nick glanced at it, sick with worry. Rachel was supposed to have returned to the car within half an hour, but over forty-five minutes had passed. He'd sweated out the long minutes, hoping any second to see her come around the corner. Then he'd raced to the zoo as if a demon were after him. Now he plunged through the entrance and stood surrounded by clumps of people, mouth dry, palms damp with fear. What the hell had happened to her?

Ahead of him, the crowd undulated like a living thing, forming, splitting, and forming again. He scanned it closely, but saw no sign of her.

He did spot Rennie's men, though. All strategically placed. Knowing Rennie, he'd probably issued orders to kill once the trade was made. The lucky hitter would probably even get a bonus.

But Nick couldn't think about that now. He could only think about Rachel. Did Rennie have her?

Focus. Don't panic.

But his heart was knocking so hard against his chest, it could have broken a rib. If Rennie had hurt her, if he so much as touched her . . .

In front of him, a throng bunched up around a large pool whose glass walls allowed viewers to see the sea lions undulating below the waterline. He walked toward it, the sound of laughter and applause, of children and families enjoying the animal antics, like a wall of noise he shoved into the background. He saw Frank almost at the same time Frank saw him. Rapidly, Nick panned the area around the other man.

No sign of Rachel.

Damn it to hell, what had happened? Where was she?

He cursed himself a hundred times over. Why had he ever let himself agree to this?

As he strode toward Frank, he ticked off his options. If Rennie had Rachel, he had everything—the boy, the printout—and Nick was walking into a trap. If Rennie didn't have her, where the hell was she?

He reached up into the sleeve of the jacket and felt the knife he'd stolen from the church kitchen. Not much good against a bullet, but he wasn't about to use a gun in the crowded zoo. A blade had its own deadly advantages, though, and Nick would use them to the fullest if he had to.

Neither he nor Frank wasted time on pleasantries.

"Where's the kid?" Though he was tempted to ask about Rachel, Nick didn't dare. The last thing he wanted was to reveal her part in any of this, especially if Rennie didn't have her. Instead, he concentrated on what he'd come to do—get back the boy.

"Where's the document?"

"You get what you want when I get what I want."

Frank gestured to the other side of the wide tank. Something moved, separating from the swarm of people: Rennie, his hand like an iron band on the back of Isaac's neck.

Nick's jaw tightened. With a flick of his still-powerful wrist, Rennie could snap the boy's neck in two. Nick's heart sped up, but he forced himself to stay calm while he searched the boy's face. Was he scared? From a distance it was hard to tell.

"Is he okay?"

"Sure he's okay," Frank said. "What did you think—that Rennie would hurt him? Did he ever hurt you?"

More than you'll ever know.

Frank snorted in disgust. "You should be ashamed of yourself, Nicky. After everything Rennie's done for you,

you should turn those papers over to him, no questions asked."

"You'll get your papers when everything is in place, like we agreed."

"You don't produce those papers, Nicky, you'll never see that kid again."

"You'll get your fucking papers," Nick snarled.

All of a sudden, Spier walked away from the pool toward the exit.

"Where's he going?"

"The limo's on its way. We make the exchange in the car."

Nick shook his head. "We make it in the open, by the cafeteria, like I said over the phone."

"Rennie doesn't want any witnesses."

Too bad. Nick's chances of staying alive dropped considerably if he made the exchange inside Rennie's limo. Besides, he couldn't afford to let Rennie call the shots. "We do this in the open with lots of people around, or we don't do it at all. That was the deal. You want your papers back, we follow through on the arrangements we made. Bring the kid to the cafeteria, like we agreed, and they'll be there."

Frank scowled. "How do I know I can trust you? How about a little good faith on your part?"

Nick reached into his pocket and handed Frank the sheet of greenbar paper he'd removed from the printout. Frank unfolded it and looked up at Nick.

"Look familiar? I don't want any trouble, Frank. I just want to make the trade and get out of here."

Frank nodded. "Let's do it, then."

He left to talk to Rennie, and Nick hung back a moment, watching. Frank touched his ear and spoke, presumably into a hidden microphone. All the men were connected by wireless transmitters; Nick's every move was monitored.

Well, let them watch.

He took off for the cafeteria. He still hadn't spotted Rachel, but Rennie would have used her fast enough if he had her. That certainty lightened a bit of Nick's worry. But if Rennie hadn't found her, what had happened to her?

The answer became clear when he approached the patio outside the restaurant. She sat at a table in the far corner, her head bent over a cup of coffee, her hair a thick curtain hiding her face from view. At the sight of her a huge boulder lifted from his shoulders, but before he could find a way to approach her, Frank and Rennie appeared, the boy between them.

The older man led the boy toward a table in the courtyard, and like a rag doll, Isaac sleepwalked where Rennie pushed him. When Nick slid into the seat beside him, Isaac's gaze barely flickered in acknowledgment.

"Are you all right?" Nick spoke softly to the child, but Isaac didn't respond. Looking over the boy's head at Rennie, Nick said, "Let go of him."

A derisive smile edged around the corners of Spier's mouth. He looked as if he were calculating the cost of not complying. Evidently deciding not to push things, he slowly removed his hand from the boy's neck. "It won't matter. He hasn't said a word all day."

"What do you expect him to say after he saw what you did?"

"That's enough, Nicky," Frank interrupted. "Rennie's

put up with your disloyalty, he doesn't have to put up with your disrespect."

"Since when is it disrespectful to tell the truth?"

"The truth?" Frank rose in anger. "That thick slug got exactly what was coming to him—"

"Sit down, Frank," Rennie said in a low voice. "We don't want to make a scene. Let's not forget why we're here. You have something for me, Nicky?"

But instead of giving Rennie what he wanted, Nick reached into his pocket and took out the small, red dump truck he'd found near the knapsack. Placing it on the table, he gave the toy a push. The truck rolled toward Isaac and stopped.

"Go ahead," Nick said. "It's yours, isn't it? Take it."

But Isaac didn't move.

"You're wasting our time, Nicky," Frank said.

Eyes on the boy, Nick picked up the truck and began to roll it around the table in front of Isaac. "I'd call that giving you a taste of your own medicine. Since you've been wasting mine."

"What are you talking about?" Frank made another angry move upward, and Rennie put a hand out to stop him.

"If you knew where Isaac was all along, what did you need me for?"

Beside him, the boy stiffened at the sound of his name.

"We didn't know," Frank said. "We only just found out a few days ago."

One mystery solved. "You should have told me." Nick took the truck and placed it in Isaac's hand. He could

have strangled the two men with his own. "Frank, why
don't you take Isaac to get a snack?"

"Why don't you go fu—"

Nick grabbed Frank by his tie. "He's six. He's seen
and heard enough. Take him inside until we're finished."

Rennie gave his permission with a curt nod, and Nick
shoved Frank away. When he'd recovered his balance,
he pulled the boy off his seat by the hand and walked
him into the cafeteria.

Nick tore his gaze away from them. Alone with Rennie, he said, "So you knew where the kid was and didn't
tell me."

Spier spread his hands in a gesture of conciliation.
"You must understand, Nicky. I had some difficult deci-
sions to make. I did not think you were up to them."

"You mean, you didn't think I was up to killing Marty
for you."

Spier inclined his head. "To put it bluntly, no."

"Or maybe you just wanted to save that pleasure for
yourself."

Spier acknowledged this with a thin smile. "Revenge
is always a pleasure. I confess, I did enjoy it." He looked
down at his hands as if proud of the work they'd done.

Jesus. A wave of nausea rolled over Nick, but he was
careful to keep his face blank. "How did you find them?"

Spier looked at Nick, blue eyes cold as death. "God is
just, Nicky. Remember that. If you are patient, He will
reward you."

Nick scoffed. "God told you where the boy was?"

Rennie gave a little Gallic shrug. "In the guise of
Harry Woodward. You do remember our friend Woody?"

It had been six years since he'd heard the name, but

Nick remembered it. "The pilot. Not too careful about the cargo he flies."

Rennie nodded. "It seems Woody called to firm up a small detail for the pickup. Martin was not there, and Woody, thinking the job was for me, talked to Frank instead." He shrugged. "It didn't take much to learn the rest."

As instructed, Rachel hid behind her veil of hair, wishing Nick would hurry up and get the printout. What in God's name could he and Spier have to talk about?

Her nerves were back, her fingers like ice in spite of the cup of coffee she had them wrapped around. By the time she'd positioned the gym bag, she'd run out of time. Nick would already have left the car, they'd have missed each other coming and going, and he wouldn't know what had happened or whether she'd fulfilled her mission. So she'd made her way to the cafeteria courtyard, where Nick had set up the trade, hoping he'd see her and realize everything was in place as planned. But she'd been perched on the hard metal chair for what seemed like hours, waiting for him to appear.

Now she risked a glance at the table of men, disconcerted at the sight. Thanks to Nick, this was her first glimpse of the short, squat bull of a man who, along with two others, had "cleaned up" after the shooting. *Frank.* But the other man . . . She could have wished never to see him again.

Up close and in daylight, Rennie Spier loomed large and imposing, a powerfully built man, even at his age. Thick white hair gave him a distinguished, European air, but the face was harsh and square. A tyrant's face. Stony ruthlessness flowed from him like a frigid wind, even at a distance. She sensed it in the cruel way he held onto the boy, the smile he gave Nick. Like a wolf ready to spring.

When Frank stood with the boy, she had a better chance to examine Isaac. Against the wide man, the child looked frail and vulnerable. Suddenly the wrenching choice she'd been forced to make—to protect Isaac from Rennie even if her school suffered for it—seemed like no choice at all.

Just then someone jostled her table. The cup flew out of her hand, and coffee sprayed everywhere. She looked up, and Nick was beside her.

"Sorry," he said in that impersonal way one speaks to a stranger. He bent down to pick up the fallen cup and under the table, spoke in a furious whisper. "What the hell happened? Are you all right?"

"I'm fine. I got delayed and couldn't get back in time."

"You got delayed?" She opened her mouth to explain, but he interrupted. "Never mind. Just get back to the car. Fast."

Then he was gone.

Heart racing, she gathered up the wet napkins and slowly walked to the trash can, choosing one that let her move away from Spier's table.

Had they noticed her? Did they think her anything but a random stranger?

A quick glance told her Nick had disappeared into the nearby building housing the restrooms. She pictured the Out of Order sign she'd taped to the women's restroom. Following Nick's steps in her mind, she saw him push the door and tell anyone who asked that he was there to fix a toilet. Inside, she imagined the restroom quiet and empty. Nick passed the first three stalls, all locked with Out of Order signs taped to them. He slid below the door of the fourth locked stall, as she had done a little while ago. Behind the toilet, the gym bag waited where she'd left it.

She walked toward the outer rim of the patio, intending to do as Nick asked and get back to the car. But her feet slowed, and she found herself moving toward the cafeteria instead. How could she go without knowing if the boy—and Nick—were safe? She watched out of the corner of her eye, and in time with her imaginings, Nick reappeared, gym bag in hand.

While he'd been gone, Frank had returned with the boy. Nick set the bag beside Frank and shoved Isaac's seat away, ostensibly so Nick could get closer to Rennie. But Isaac was now on the outside, as far from Rennie and Frank as possible, and in an easy position to grab if they had to run. The boy glanced at Nick's back, then out toward the zoo.

The next instant, her attention shifted from Isaac. Bending down, Frank picked up the gym bag and placed it on the table in front of him. He unzipped it.

The world stopped as he fished inside for the printout and began to pull it out.

She forgot to keep her head down, forgot to hide behind her hair, forgot, in fact, everything except the fact that this was the crucial moment.

Frank was going to verify the printout's authenticity before letting Nick and Isaac go.

Would the first few pages be enough to fool him? If

Frank flipped through the stack, the fake pages could pass as real with their endless columns of numbers. Only a careful examination would expose her ruse. But what if he looked closely?

She stood like a stone, unable to breathe, every muscle tensed and focused on Frank. If they made it past this moment, if luck was with them . . .

If not . . .

She didn't want to think about that. Her heart thudded sickly, her hands clammy with sweat.

At that moment, when she was blind with terror, Isaac bolted from his seat.

Chapter 13

Nick made an unsuccessful grab for the boy as Frank shot to his feet, overturning the gym bag. The printout fell to the ground.

"Goddamn!" Frank spluttered more curses, tangled in the clothes spilling out from the bag. He looked from them to the disappearing boy, back to the bag, clearly not knowing which to tackle first.

"Be quiet," Rennie said to Frank. "Send the men after him."

But Nick leaped first. He dashed off madly in the direction Isaac had gone and ran smack into a noisy family in the middle of the patio. Cokes, sandwiches, and nachos flew into the air. Fists and voices rose.

"Where are you going?"

"What do you think you're doing?"

Move! Get out of my way!

But an elderly woman dressed in black planted herself in front of him and berated him loudly in Spanish.

"*Lo siento,* I'm sorry. I'm sorry!" He shoved a hand-ful of money at the family and extricated himself.

Racing to the edge of the courtyard, he glanced in all directions.

No sign of either Rachel or Isaac. *Dammit!*

But Rennie's men scrambled everywhere. Frank must have called them in while Nick had been arguing with Grandma.

He was screwed. Now that Rennie had the printout and Isaac was on the loose, Nick was dispensable. An open target, he'd be dodging Rennie's men with every step.

Just then, a tiny black head appeared in the crowd, heading toward the nearest exhibit building. Was that him? Nick hoped so. If he didn't get to Isaac before Rennie, the kid would be lost forever. He'd already lost one kid to Spier; he'd rather die than lose another.

He dove ahead, keenly aware that he was making it easy for one of the cohorts to earn his bonus. Spotting a zoo worker, he spun her around. "What's inside that building?" With a frantic gesture, he indicated the struc-ture ahead.

Startled, she blurted out, "The Tropic Zone. It's got—" But Nick had already dashed off.

Plunging ahead, he ran into the building, stopping for a quick look over his shoulder just before entering.

He'd been spotted by the man in the sports coat. The one who, along with the "derelict," had helped Frank scrape up Martin's body last night.

Sports Coat ran toward the building, too.

Nick cursed and ducked inside. Immediately, hot, steamed air assaulted him, and he broke out into a sweat. Towering trees amid heavy jungle overhung the walkway on either side. Birds and monkeys chattered, combining with the din of the mob inside.

He turned around and saw Sports Coat push his way past several people and head right toward Nick.

Without thinking, Nick vaulted over the waist-high Plexiglas that separated the path from the jungle and plunged into the thick growth, Sports Coat on his tail.

A bird with a lemon-yellow face and a huge black beak flew at him. Nick ducked and almost fell flat on his face. As he broke his fall, the muffled whiz of a silenced bullet shot past where his head would have been.

Jesus, was the man crazy? Did he want all of NYPD down here? Stooping low, Nick darted toward a tree with a trunk wide enough to provide cover. Another bullet zipped past where he'd just been. Damn, that must be some bonus Rennie promised.

Throwing himself on the ground, Nick rolled toward the end of the rain forest. With a dull thud, another bullet landed near his shoulder.

He leaped over the glass partition.

Hit the walkway.

Someone gasped in surprise, but Nick scurried away before the person could say more and lost himself in the crowd.

Breathing hard, he sped toward the exit and barely paused to give the area outside a quick pan. For the moment he'd lost Sports Coat, but the boy was gone too. Racing, Nick darted up the hill that held the next exhibits, saw otters and water fowl, but no sign of Isaac. Running on, Nick came to the penguin house and dashed inside.

Sweat cooled on his skin. He hung back a minute to let his eyes adjust to the dark, and when they had, he scanned the interior.

If the boy was here, finding him wasn't going to be easy. Not in the dark. And not in the crowd bunched up against the tank.

Starting on one end, he slowly moved toward the other. Backs of heads, sides of faces. Short kids, tall kids. Kids on the ground, kids held in arms.

Then, at the very front of the farthest edge, a small, black head.

Nick's heart beat faster.

Could be.

If so, the boy was clever. He'd mashed himself in tightly, surrounded by as many people as possible.

Nick started toward him to get a closer look. As luck would have it, the boy turned his head. Greenish light from the glassed-in penguin case reflected off him, and once again Nick saw the black eyes and elfin face of Shelley's son.

In that instant of recognition, the boy also saw Nick.

Fear washed across Isaac's face.

He's as afraid of you as he is of Rennie or Frank or any of the others.

A pang of sadness went through Nick, but he hardened himself against it. The kid was right; he should be afraid.

As if Isaac had heard, he ducked down, disappearing into the crowd.

Nick darted right, then left. He was about to plunge into the crowd when the hard edge of a weapon stopped him.

"Slowly now," a voice whispered in his ear. "We don't want anyone to get hurt in here." The gun poked into Nick's back, pushing him toward the exit.

Clumps of people broke off from the crowd, also heading for the door. A few families, a strolling couple, an elderly man.

And in the midst of them, Isaac.

Nick stopped short. The man behind bumped into him. "What are you doing?" The gunman's voice was low and rough.

Nick whirled around. Not Sports Coat. Whoever he was, Nick didn't recognize him.

"Why don't you shoot me here, where it's dark." He smiled pleasantly. "Better chance of getting away."

The man shielded the gun from the crowd. "Are you crazy? I can't do it here—too many witnesses. Now move."

Nick thought it over, giving Isaac more time to get away. "Okay, but it's your funeral." He turned back around. Isaac was nowhere in sight. *Good boy.*

Just outside the building, Nick stopped again.

"What is it this time?" the man growled.

"Nothing much." The knife he'd hidden in his sleeve slid into his palm.

"Keep moving."

Nick took a step, then without warning, spun around. The knife flashed, slicing open the man's gun hand.

A yelp. The man dropped the gun and clutched his bleeding hand.

Nick put his foot on top of the fallen weapon. He smiled and waved away a passerby who slowed down to see what the commotion was about.

When the passerby had gone, Nick picked up the gun. It was a .44 Magnum Desert Eagle with a ten-inch barrel. Scoped, it would have been accurate to 100 yards. Lucky it wasn't scoped.

"What were you expecting," Nick said, "an army?"

The gunman glared, and Nick held the gun at his side, muzzle down, while he considered what to do.

"I told myself I wouldn't kill anyone I didn't have to, so don't make me shoot you." He motioned with his head, indicating the small space behind the penguin house. The man shuffled toward it. "On your knees."

"You bastard. You said you weren't going to use that."

"I said I wasn't going to shoot you." Nick brought the weapon down on the man's head. "I didn't say I wasn't going to use it."

Nick stashed the Magnum beneath his jacket and dragged the gunman beneath a bush. Taking off in a loping jog, Nick once more surveyed the area for a glimpse of the dark-haired boy.

Fifteen minutes later, Nick spotted him heading for a set of steps that led to a high viewing area. But the boy wasn't the only person Nick saw.

Rachel was right behind Isaac.

And they were both moving toward Frank.

Rachel lunged at Isaac's back, but the little boy had too much of a lead, and her fingers slashed empty air. Unable to reach him, she followed up the stairway and stood rooted to the steps as he ran right into Frank.

With a satisfied grunt, the man scooped him up. Isaac yelled and wiggled; Frank almost dropped him.

Horrified, she pushed her way forward. She'd been trying to formulate a plan ever since the boy ran away. Her position on the cafeteria patio had given her a clear view of the direction he'd taken, but she'd lost him in the crowd. When she spotted him again, he'd been one step ahead, close enough to see, never close enough to catch.

Now, she watched Isaac slap and kick at Frank. Her legs felt as though they moved in slow motion, anchored with lead weights. Would she ever reach him?

All of a sudden, Isaac buried his face against Frank's, as if embracing him. Frank let out a roar of pain and dropped the boy like a hot coal. A clear set of teeth marks embossed Frank's cheek.

Face twisted in fury, he lunged for the boy.

"No!" she cried out without thinking.

Frank looked up.

Oh, God. Was Frank one of the men who'd kidnapped her? Would he recognize her?

He glanced away, down to where Isaac had been. What had seemed an eternity was only a few seconds. Seconds Isaac had used to duck beneath Frank's legs and disappear into the crowd.

Frank cursed. He elbowed his way into the dense thicket of people.

"Hey, what d'you think you're doing?" Angry parents shoved him back, spitting him out almost at her feet.

Heart in her throat, Rachel pivoted and buried her nose in the tote, pretending to rummage around for something. Easing behind him, she gently squeezed her way into the crowd.

Laughter greeted her, and the excited sound of children's voices. She looked over to one side. Below, a carefully landscaped habitat of rock and water housed two polar bears.

"Excuse me." She maneuvered through the crowd. "My son is up ahead." She stepped on someone's foot. "Sorry—"

When at last she discovered him, Isaac was at the far end, edging away. She called to him, and his head lifted. He turned, hope flaring into his eyes.

"Mama?"

Eagerly, he moved toward her voice, but when he saw who knelt down, he stopped short.

"Hello, Isaac." She kept her voice soft and gentle. "My name is Rachel, and look what I have for you." She pulled his bear from her tote bag.

He stared longingly at the toy but made no move to take it. Emotion squeezed her chest. He was so little, and so scared.

"Here." She placed the bear in his arms. He buried his face in its fur, and Rachel pulled him toward her into the crowd. He stiffened the minute she touched him. "It's okay," she whispered. "I won't hurt you, I promise."

"Are you taking me back to the bad men?" His voice was small and fearful.

She stroked the hair away from his forehead. "No, honey, we're going to get you away from them."

"Are you taking me to my mommy?"

A wave of sadness rushed over her. "Oh, Isaac, I wish I could."

"Mama went away," he said unhappily.

"I know. But she sent me to find you. That's why I have your bear, see?" He watched her, unconvinced. "Look what else I have for you. Reach into my bag and see."

Isaac pulled out the T-shirt and ball cap she had hurriedly purchased at a souvenir stand.

"Let's see if they fit. Can you put it on yourself?" Rachel looked around. Kneeling, she was surrounded by a forest of legs. She prayed the thicket of limbs would provide the cover they needed. "Good job. You're a real big boy, aren't you?" The hat covered his dark hair, the bright turquoise T-shirt transformed the white one he'd been wearing. Not a great disguise, but it was the best she could do. "Ready?"

He nodded and Rachel picked him up. Still clinging to his bear, he put his arms around her neck. "That's right, hold on tight. The bad men are out there, and we may have to run. Can you hold on?" He nodded. "Good boy."

Searching in all directions, Rachel slowly stood, Isaac in her arms. Careful to keep her back to where Frank might be, she moved to the left. If he saw them at all, she hoped he would only see a woman with a small boy. A boy in a ball cap and a T-shirt who looked nothing like the boy he was looking for.

She laid Isaac's head on her shoulder. "Close your eyes, Isaac. Pretend you're sleeping. Can you do that?" He nodded against her neck. "Your mommy would be very proud of you."

Head burrowed against her, he held the bear so it covered half his face. She hoped the position would hide him enough. Forcing herself to move normally, she walked toward the steps.

The set of stairs was the longest Rachel had ever descended. With every step down, the bottom receded farther away. When her foot finally hit the last stair, she closed her eyes in relief.

Now they just had to get to the car.

"I see you're okay."

Rachel turned. Gasped. The man from the bench. The derelict.

He was coherent enough to stuff Martin into a body bag last night.

"Y-yes," she said. *Please earth, open up and swallow him.* "My son, though . . . I think he's had a rough evening."

The man laughed and started to reply. But instead of words, only a small grunt came out. As if her wish had been granted, he melted into a puddle at her feet. Amazed, she looked up and found herself facing Nick.

"Come on, let's go."

"What . . . what did you do?" She gazed in shock at the man on the ground.

"Never mind." Nick pulled her along. She saw him shove something farther up his sleeve as a crowd began to gather. "Just keep going. I'm right behind you."

They would have gotten clean away if Isaac hadn't opened his eyes and looked right at Nick.

The moment he did, the boy started screaming.

"What is it? What's the matter?" Rachel hugged him tight. "It's all right, I've got you. No one's going to hurt you."

Her words were swallowed by his screeching. Wailing in terror, he kicked and struggled, so out of control she couldn't hold him.

Nick took the child, shoving him roughly against his chest. "Shut your mouth," he growled, "or I'll shut it for you."

Holding Isaac tight, he began to run.

Chapter 14

Rachel ran from the zoo, following Nick east to the car. Her mouth dried up, her chest heaved. *Will I ever catch my breath?*

Isaac kicked and yowled; nothing soothed him. The hysteria created a beacon pinpointing their location. Soon several of Rennie's men lined up behind them.

Faster. Run faster.

But she was going as fast as she could.

Nick dodged a zigzag path down the street. For a few hundred yards, he lost their pursuers, but Isaac's howling led the men right back to them. After a while, she stopped hearing the screams. Her own huffing filled her ears.

Down side streets, around people, between speeding cars.

Her lungs gave out; she couldn't take another step.

She took another step.

And finally, finally, thank you God, the crying stopped.

Nick slowed to a fast walk; glancing over his shoulder, she saw Isaac quivering in exhausted sleep.

"Poor baby." She stroked Isaac's tired, sweaty face.

"Poor baby, my ass."

Scurrying low and ducking behind cars, they crossed a street and entered the garage. Once again, the attendant's booth was empty, but it didn't matter, as Nick had kept the car keys. Turning away from the vacant stall, Rachel rounded a corner and spotted the VW, its faded red hump a welcome sight. They tramped up the short ramp and headed for it.

Without warning, a viselike arm around Rachel's throat snapped her backward.

"Nick!"

She screamed again, but the arm choked off the sound, crushing her against a hard chest. Nick whipped around.

"Put down the boy," a male voice said. The cool, metallic circle of a gun barrel bit into her temple.

Rachel's blood froze.

"Let her go." Nick's stare drilled into the man behind her.

"Don't fuck with me! Put the boy down, or I'll blow her face off."

"You can have the kid, and you can have me. But you have to let her go, or you get nothing. Kill her, and you'll have to kill me. And you can't do that without killing the boy." Nick nodded down to the sleeping child in his arms. "And Rennie isn't going to like that."

Rachel couldn't see the man, but she sensed his indecision. Trembling, she focused on Nick's severe, implacable face. He never once looked at her, but she clung to his hard expression the way a rock climber clings to a sheer wall of granite.

As if it were the only thing keeping her alive.

She sweated out the silence. The next second might be the last she'd ever have. Or the next. Or the next. Pictures swam in her head. A pool of blood, black as night. Sightless eyes. Her mother's dead fingers, twitching.

Suddenly the hold around her throat loosened. The man flung her away.

Never taking his eyes off the man behind her, Nick said, "Come over here, Rachel."

Could she move? She was shaking so much. Somehow she found herself next to Nick. She faced her attacker.

The man in the sports coat, the one who had been at the zoo entrance, reading the paper.

"Put the kid down."

"I can't put him down," Nick said, "he's sleeping. You'll have to carry him."

"I can't carry—" But Nick was already unloading the boy into the man's arms.

The gunman struggled to hold the dead weight of the sleeping child and still keep his weapon trained on Nick. "Back off."

"I can't back off until you take him. Watch it, he's going to fall—"

Automatically, the man reached down to support Isaac's weight. For a second his gun hand was occupied with the boy.

In that instant, something flashed in Nick's palm. He moved fast. A hard, vicious upward thrust.

The man staggered, dropped the boy. Isaac hit the pavement, screaming. Shots thudded into the ground, their sound dulled as though by a silencer, and Rachel threw herself over the boy as more shots popped faintly behind her.

It lasted forever, but was over in seconds.

"Let's go," Nick said.

Go?

She couldn't go. She could only sit on the concrete, feeling sick.

Nick hauled her to her feet. Behind him, a body lay crumpled and still.

Mama?

Nick stepped into her line of sight, blocking her view.

No, not Mama.

"Get the boy in the car. Go on." He gave her a little push.

She lurched to the car on wobbly legs. Isaac clung to her, hiccuping with sobs, eyes blank and wide. *I know. I understand. I'm here.*

She put him in the backseat and looked toward Nick before getting in herself. He pulled something out of the body, and when he straightened, she saw the knife. Calmly, he used the man's sports coat to wipe it clean. Another wave of nausea passed through her, but she climbed into the back next to Isaac.

Nick dragged the dead man to a parked car, wedging him out of sight between the front bumper and the garage wall. It was a miracle the attendant hadn't shown up yet, but Nick suspected he was retrieving a car parked at the far end of the garage and had heard nothing. But blood splattered the ground where Rennie's man had fallen; someone would find him soon enough.

Nick checked himself. Red splotches on his hands, on his thighs, and just above the waistband of his pants.

God.

His legs weakened, and he braced his back against a concrete support, filled with self-loathing. A wail roared in his head. He wanted to shout, to howl like a wolf.

But he'd known this was coming. Ever since he'd laid eyes on Rennie again, Nick knew he'd end up stained with someone's blood.

He pounded the rough beam. *Don't think about it. Find a bathroom, wash your hands. Send Rachel for some clothes.* He had to keep going if he wanted to get them away.

Forcing himself to move, he stumbled to the VW and slipped behind the steering wheel, hands shaking, mouth so dry he would have given his life for a shot of whiskey.

Removing the Magnum from underneath his shirt, he stowed it in the glove compartment. The gun he'd taken from the dead man still had most of a clip left, and he laid it on the seat next to him, along with the knife. If he'd known he was going to confiscate an arsenal, he wouldn't have bothered with his last request to Danny Walsh that afternoon. In fact, his suddenly ample stockpile would be laughable if it weren't so sick.

Swallowing the nausea that threatened to erupt out his throat, he turned the key. In seconds they had pulled away.

He headed uptown, keeping to side streets as much as possible and constantly checking the rearview mirror for a tail. After fifteen minutes the sweat had dried, and he began to breathe a little easier. Now all he had to do was get out of the city.

He drove west, cutting through Central Park, his thoughts on his visit with Danny Walsh. The Irishman had been busy, but he'd showed up as promised at the deserted dockside warehouse where Nick had arranged to meet him.

They'd shaken hands. "What can I do for you, Nicky?"

Nick plunged right in. "I need a safe house. Something near enough to the city to make accessibility to Manhattan easy, but far enough away to be safe. And if it's in an area where's there's enough stuff to keep a kid happy, all the better."

"A kid?"

"A six-year-old."

Only the barest of pauses gave away Danny's surprise. "How long will you be needing it?"

"I don't know. A week, maybe two. A month at the outside. And I'm not asking. I'm telling. Can you help?"

"Possibly. Depends on what you've got."

"I've got your arms shipment for the Liberation Council."

Danny laughed. "Don't joke with me now." Then he took another look at Nick's face, and the laughter died. "You're serious."

"I don't know what port it's bound for, but I do know it had some kind of breakdown and had to stop at Malta for repairs. It probably left there yesterday or the day before."

Silence. Nick imagined the enormity of what he'd just said took a few moments to absorb.

"All right," Danny said at last. "But I'll need a few hours to check it out."

He canceled the rest of his appointments, and they retreated to a hole-in-the-wall apartment that was empty of everything but a computer, phone, and fax machine. Nick spent most of the afternoon there, waiting with Danny for confirmation. By four, the British had the ship in their sights, and Danny had given Nick directions to the safe house, a cabin on the Jersey shore.

He'd laughed at Nick's surprise. "The Irish have friends all over the world, Nicky. I had the refrigerator stocked for breakfast. What else can I do for you?"

Nick told him, and Danny said he would take care of it. Nick wrote down the directions to the cabin on a scrap of paper. After he'd left, he'd memorized them, then thrown the paper down the sewer.

Now he turned onto Columbus Avenue and then over to the West Side Highway. Luck was with them; traffic was slight. It didn't take him long to get to the Lincoln Tunnel.

Isaac whimpered when the car entered the darkness, but in the rearview mirror Nick saw Rachel gather the boy in her arms, and soon he was quiet again.

Ensconced in the backseat, Rachel tried to stop her teeth chattering. She was alive. They were all alive. That fact was so miraculous it brought tears to her eyes. But she quickly blinked them away so she wouldn't scare Isaac. He was huddled against her, a dark little thing with a gamin face and serious eyes the same color as Nick's.

She shuddered involuntarily, the feel of the gun against her head still imprinted on her memory. Leaning back, she closed her eyes, trying to shake off the terror. She had to tell Nick about the switched printout. He had to know they had a hold over Spier. But she couldn't do it now, not with Isaac here. She'd have to wait until she and Nick were alone. In the meantime, this mournful boy needed her attention.

Putting her own fears aside, she rummaged around in the tote bag at her feet. Through all the tumult, she had somehow managed to hang on to it, and to Isaac's bear, which was stuffed inside.

"Look, Isaac. Look who's here." She put the bear in his lap. "Do you think your bear was scared when the bad men were chasing us?"

Isaac didn't answer. He was staring at the back of Nick's head.

Nick's gaze flicked at her in the rearview mirror. "He's probably not sure he's escaped them. Martin told him I was one of the bad guys."

She turned to Isaac. "Is that right? Are you afraid of Nick?"

The boy didn't answer.

"He won't hurt you," Rachel said softly, "I promise. Look, he found your knapsack." She showed him the bag resting on the floor. "And he got you away from the men at the zoo, didn't he?"

Isaac still didn't respond. An air of isolation enveloped him, as if he were his own desert island and would brook no intruders. She'd seen that look a hundred times on Nick's face when he worked at the preschool.

Rachel ruffled his hair. "It's okay. You don't have to say anything now. But if you want to, I'm right here. No one's going to hurt you anymore. Not me, and not Nick."

Later she took out the paper and crayons she'd packed. Isaac stared at them for a while without touching them.

Rachel prodded him gently. "Do you like to draw? What kind of pictures can you make?"

But he didn't pick up a crayon. Instead, he spoke for the first time since they'd got in the car. "Am I going to the hospital?"

Rachel met Nick's gaze in the rearview mirror. "Is there someone in the hospital you want to visit?"

"The aunt who took care of him for Shelley was probably in the hospital before she died," Nick said.

"Do you want to visit your aunt, Isaac?"

"Auntie Mary went to the hospital, and then she went away."

Rachel swallowed the lump at the back of her throat. "A lot of people have gone away, haven't they? Well, we're not going away, honey. We're staying right here with you. But I don't think we'll go the hospital. Not today."

His little body relaxed against her. Without another word, he picked up a crayon and began to draw.

The car was steady but not fast; the trip took hours. Every twenty minutes or so Nick took a stray exit off the parkway to see if they were being followed. He never spotted anybody, but it didn't appear to ease his anxiety. And it made the trip interminable.

In the back, Isaac drew pictures that broke Rachel's

heart. Dark, angry blotches of color, he explained them to her in a matter-of-fact voice.

"These are the dead people." He pointed them out. "See the blood?"

At dusk, they stopped at a strip mall with a clothing store and a burger joint. Nick sent Rachel to look for clean clothes while he waited in the car. She brought back a pair of jeans and a white T-shirt. Nick changed in the restaurant's men's room, where he scrubbed the blood off his hands and changed into the new clothes, stifling any thoughts about what he was doing or why.

When he came out, he found Isaac and Rachel at a table, a hamburger and fries in front of the boy. It would have been better to take the food and go, but Nick didn't have the heart to say so.

The restaurant had a promotion for kids, and Nick bought a small plastic truck to replace the one they'd left at the zoo. He gave it to Isaac, and the boy played with zeal but little joy. He zoomed the truck over his hamburger and made engine noises, his face sober and intent.

Nick slid into the seat next to Isaac and watched, absorbed. Maybe it would be all right. Maybe they could work it out. For the first time, he allowed himself to acknowledge the one thing he hardly wanted to face.

He is mine. My son. My own.

Across the table, Rachel grinned at Nick and moved a drink out of Isaac's reach.

"How about eating a little of that hamburger," Nick said. Isaac slid the toy over a french-fry hill, and a couple of ketchup packets fell on the floor. Nick picked them up. "Why don't you eat before you spill something?" The engine noises grew louder. "Eat up." Gently, Nick took the toy away. "You can play with this later."

Quickly and deliberately, Isaac knocked over the drink, soaking Nick.

"Goddamn it!" Nick sprang to his feet.

Isaac stared straight ahead, his lips clamped shut. Rachel picked him up; his body was stiff and unyielding as she carried him out.

Hours later, they crossed the causeway onto Long Beach Island. They'd long ago given up talking. Isaac was asleep in the back, Rachel numb with fatigue in the front. Next to her, Nick retreated further and further into his own separate darkness. As the moon rose and the car zoomed over the miles, Rachel felt him freeze up beside her. Her own icy wall grew thicker with every foot of blacktop they traveled.

She didn't begin to relax until they drove over the low-slung bridge that separated the island from the mainland. Traversing the causeway was like crossing into another world. Security washed over her like a fresh, green wave, as if the bridge were the last link to danger, and once they were on the other side, no one could touch them. A fantasy maybe, but one she eagerly embraced.

On the other side of the bridge, neon lights and motels greeted them. They passed grocery stores and movie theaters, water parks and miniature golf courses. It looked so safe. So easy to hide among all these people.

Nick stopped to fill the car with gas. Rachel glanced back at the sleeping child and said, "Maybe we should find some place to stay and worry about the car in the morning."

"We may need to get away in a hurry."

Even that didn't jar her. She looked around at the gas station, at the rows of chips and cookies she saw through the window, at the signs hawking fishing gear and boat rentals.

Normal. It was all so normal.

After the fill-up, Nick drove on, scanning motels and residential streets. They rode for a long time; it turned out that Danny's rickety, weather-beaten cabin was located at the far end of the island.

Nick examined the place from the car, cataloging its advantages. For a start, it was off the road, almost on the beach, so they'd have few prying eyes. The path leading to it was well lit. Even in the dark, the streetlights provided a good view of the road.

He got out of the car along with Rachel. She stretched, raising her arms so her breasts were tautly outlined against her shirt.

Don't do that. He looked away, found a rock to stare at. Leaning into the backseat, he scooped up the sleeping child. Isaac stirred but didn't wake.

Nick took a minute to reconnoiter around the cabin, noting with satisfaction that a bent screen and wooden door were the only way inside. If unexpected visitors dropped by, they'd have plenty of warning.

Danny had chosen well.

Inside, the place was as tiny as the basement apartment Nick had left behind. Only a kitchenette, bathroom, a single bedroom. *Good.* The small cabin would be easier to defend than a multistoried beach house with levels of hiding places and a variety of entrances.

He carried the child into the bedroom, gently placing

him on the bed. Rachel brought his knapsack inside and laid it next to the bed. She stood beside Nick as he gazed down at the boy.

"He'll be okay," she said.

Nick nodded, not at all sure, and returned to the other room. Opening the refrigerator, he saw that Danny had been true to his word. A carton of milk stood square in the center of the upper shelf, along with orange juice, English muffins, butter, jam, and a cantaloupe.

Rachel wandered out of the bedroom. Nick glanced at her pale, tired face. She looked drained.

He was tempted to go to her, hold her. Tell her everything would be all right. He tore his gaze away. *Don't be an idiot.* He couldn't afford to start thinking about holding her, comforting her.

"Keep the cabin doors closed," he said. "The screen and the wood one. If someone wants in, let him work for it." He found the phone and pulled it out of the wall, stuffing it into an empty cabinet. "And no phone calls."

"Are more bad men coming?" Isaac stood just outside the bedroom, watchful eyes on Rachel.

"No, honey, we're safe here." She took his hand and walked him back inside. Nick followed, stopping in the doorway.

The boy looked down at the bed. He picked at the coverlet. "Will you . . . will you stay with me?" His voice came out small and pinched.

"As long as you want me to." She hugged him, and though he didn't resist, he didn't hug her back either.

She helped him take off his clothes, then pulled down the covers for him.

"Don't close the door." He crawled into the bed.

"I won't." She spoke with complete understanding, and Nick wondered if she was remembering her own nightly ritual after her mother had been killed.

Sitting on the bed next to the boy, she smiled. "Would you like me to sing to you before you go to sleep, or read a story? I brought in your knapsack, and I think there's a book inside."

"Where's my bear?"

"Here." Nick picked it up off the lumpy sofa and entered the bedroom, holding out the toy.

Isaac looked at the bear and then at the man. He hadn't said a word to Nick since he'd spilled the drink on him.

A nod from Rachel gave Nick the courage to take a step closer. He dropped the bear in the boy's lap. Isaac grabbed it and slid farther down in the covers. Nick stood a moment longer, looking at him.

Say something. Do something. "I'll be outside," he said at last.

Rachel grabbed his hand, keeping him a moment longer. Gently, she said to Isaac, "Why don't you say good-night to Nick?"

But the boy only stared at the ceiling.

Nick absorbed the rejection in silence, then left Rachel to sit with the boy.

Back in the kitchenette, Nick opened the long, slender broom closet Danny had described. A metal pail with a dried-up mop sat inside. Underneath the mop, Danny had hidden the Uzi Nick had requisitioned.

He took it out, relearning the feel of it. He could have requested a standard size, but this little mini would be easier to conceal. It was a good weapon; Nick had brokered thousands of them. He felt around inside the closet for the ammunition and stopped in mid-reach.

A lullaby floated into the room.

The back of his throat sealed up as Rachel's voice reached him, pure and sweet. He looked down at the weapon in his hand, staring at it as if it were some living, breathing thing, an extension of his arm. His soul.

Killer. The word whispered inside his head, an accusation voiced by a thousand tongues. That's what he was, what he'd always be.

Closing his eyes, he leaned his head against the edge of the closet and blotted out the haunting melody. Erased the picture in his mind of the gentle woman and the troubled boy. Bit by bit, he iced himself up, obliterating tenderness and regret, toughening himself until he could stand straight. Until he was ready to do what he had to do. Then he walked out the cabin door, firmly holding the Uzi.

Chapter 15

By the time Isaac fell asleep, the deepest part of the night was upon them. Rachel walked through the darkened cabin and out the front door, listening to the lazy rhythm of the water. The moon polished the ocean, turning the white tops of the waves into iridescent slivers. She took a deep breath, smelled the salt and the seaweed. Soon she was going to have to tell Nick what she'd done with Spier's document. But not now. Now all she wanted was a little peace and some space to breathe.

Behind the cabin, an old picnic table leaned into the sand. Nick sat on a bench, holding something between his knees. Rachel's heart stopped.

Sports Coat's gun.

"I'm leaving this for you." He put the weapon on the table. It lay between them, its blue-black barrel glinting in the moonlight, an unspoken message of what was still to come.

"It's a Ruger. Mark II model. Designed to be used at

very close range." He put a finger to his head and mimed a gun. "But it's lighter than the Magnum, so you'll be able to handle it easily."

She nodded wordlessly. The thought of holding a gun, let alone shooting someone, was so far removed from her experience she hardly knew what to say.

He rose. "I'll be back tomorrow or the day after. If not, I left a number inside you can call."

If not? Her heart thudded. "But . . . what about Isaac? I promised him you wouldn't go away."

"You'll be here."

"I'm not his father," she said. "You can't abandon him, Nick. Not now. He's lost so much already."

He threw her a pointed look. "He's not you, Rachel. And I'm not David Goodman." He started toward the car, and she chased after him.

"Could've fooled me. You're leaving, aren't you?"

"I have to. Rennie—"

"Forget Rennie." She ran ahead to block his way. "Someone else needs you now."

He raked fingers through his hair. "I'm the last thing that kid needs. You saw what happened today. What kind of father do you think I'd make? Instead of teaching him how to hit a baseball, I could teach him how to hit a target."

She spoke quietly. "You can teach him what you know, Nick. Teach him about the goodness that's inside you."

"Goodness?" He swore and sidestepped her, rugged face furrowed in scorn.

"It's there, Nick," she called to his retreating back. "I've seen it."

"You've seen it?" He whirled and descended on her. "You've seen me kill a man, but then, that's what I'm 'good' at."

"I've seen you risk your own life to protect mine. And only a good man moves heaven and earth to save a child."

He stopped as if she'd punched him, and despite the shock on his face, she plunged on. "You did those things. You saved my life today. And Isaac's."

"You don't know what you're talking about." He was rigid, his hands white-knuckled into fists. "You don't know the first thing about me."

"Yes, I do."

He grabbed her shoulders and shook her, nearly shouting. "How many 'good' men trade guns for cocaine? Or sell missiles on the black market? Do you know how many times I've intimidated, coerced, even hurt people? And not just grown men, but—" He clamped his jaw down and shoved her away. "You think I'm 'good'? Christ, you don't know the half of it." He wheeled and strode off again.

She found him leaning his head against the top of the car's open hood, staring hard at the engine.

"Go back to the cabin."

She ignored his curt command. "You say I don't know you, but you're wrong. I know what you did for Spier, but your life is different now. You're different."

He straightened and met her gaze. Beneath the night sky, his face was shadowed, the black brows a harsh line across his forehead. "No, Rachel, I'm exactly the same."

"Nick . . ."

"I can't be anyone's father!" He slammed down the

hood, then braced his two hands against it, visibly fighting for control. "I can't be Isaac's father. There's things about me . . . things I've done."

"What things? What have you done?"

"I can't . . . I can't tell you." He shuddered, and she rubbed his back softly, gently, soothing him.

"Yes, you can. You can, Nick. You can tell me anything."

She understood his fear. For years, darkness had wrapped around her soul like a twisted vine, invading her heart, choking her breath. But the darkness had been familiar, hers. Trusting someone else with it was the hardest thing she'd ever done. She'd been fifteen when she finally told Chris about her mother's murder, and he'd held her and cherished her, and helped her take her first real steps toward healing.

"You're safe. Whatever you say, I promise, you're safe."

Nick stared into the night and swallowed the boulder caught in his throat. He swore he'd never tell her, but it was the only way for her to see. The only way to make her understand why he couldn't stay with the boy.

He wiped his mouth with the back of his hand. "I . . . I brokered this deal—" A wave of nausea went through him, and he stopped to battle it, then started over. "Six years ago, I brokered an illegal buy for Libya—" Unable to face her, he stared at the car, trying to keep his voice flat. Trying to pretend the words were about someone else. "Spier bankrolled the deal in Panama, but our contact got cold feet at the last minute, so Rennie sent me and Marty to take care of the trouble. We ended up in this alley. I had the gun out, I was all set to finish him.

Only suddenly . . ." His voice wobbled, but he cleared it and pushed through. "Suddenly something moved in the shadows. A kid. A boy. Skinny little thing, dark hair, big eyes. He was living in a cardboard box." Sweat trickled down his back.

"Marty thought I'd gone nuts. I stood there forever, eyeballing that kid in the darkness. My gun is out. Marty is croaking, 'Do it, do it,' like some bullfrog in heat. And me, I'm still as a statue, staring at that kid."

He lifted his head and gazed into the night, but instead of the battered car or the moonlit beach or the woman he cared about more than life itself, he saw a boy whose eyes hoped for nothing. "God, it was like staring at myself . . ."

He didn't move, his gaze fixed on the shadowy Panamanian alley and a dark-haired boy. "Marty took out his knife, pushed me aside, and—" He stabbed the air, twisting the imaginary knife. "He gutted our man, right there in the alley. Jesus, I never saw so much blood. Neither had the kid. He stared at me, at Marty, the dead guy . . ." He uncurled his fist and dropped his hand. "No witnesses, it's Rennie's first rule. Marty didn't even clean the knife off, it was still so . . . bloody." He gave a shaky laugh. "I don't know why that always bothers me so much. What difference does it make whether you die from a clean knife or a dirty one? Dead is dead, isn't it?"

Something wet dribbled down his cheek. Not sweat this time.

"I tried to stop Marty, I swear I shouted at him." His throat tightened. "I should have shot him. I should have done whatever I needed to stop him. But I didn't." He clenched his jaw, forcing the words out. "I didn't . . . and he slit the kid's throat."

Silence stretched. Was it shock or repulsion that kept her from speaking? He didn't know. He didn't want to know. He only wanted to get the hell out of there, before he had to look at her again.

"So you see now." He scoured the moisture off his face with the heel of his hand. "You see why I can't stay." He turned and walked away.

"Nick, wait!"

Christ, leave me alone. Just let me get out of here.

Afraid to face her, he plodded to the picnic table like a man carrying a dead weight. He retrieved the Uzi and the ammo, then the Magnum.

"What are you doing?" She ran up behind him.

He imagined her eyes cold as mirrors, the warmth gone from them forever. He kept his back to her.

"Don't you understand yet? People die for Rennie. Not just bad people. Kids die, wives die, even sons. I'm not letting it happen anymore."

He checked the clip on the .44 and rammed it home. Picking up the Uzi, he started toward the car.

She ran after him. "Wait, you can't go now. I want to talk to you."

"There's nothing to talk about."

"There is Nick, you're wrong."

He threw the guns into the VW. "Put the Ruger some-where safe, where the kid can't get hold of it. If I'm not back in a few—"

"I don't care," she burst out. "I don't care what you did."

Slowly, he turned around and looked at her. She stood

in the moonlight, her face pale and tearstained, her chin jutting defiance.

"I don't care, Nick."

And that hurt almost more than anything. "Ah, Rachel. You should care. You should care very much."

"The past is past, Nick. It's over. Now is all that counts. And now, it only matters that you're here. If you failed one boy then, you didn't fail this boy now. Because we're here, aren't we? We're together. We're safe. And it's because of you, because of what you did today. Please, Nick. Please don't go."

Her loose hair blew in the breeze, and more than anything he wanted to touch it one last time. "I have to. It's the only way to keep you both safe."

"But what about you? What about keeping you safe?" Her voice caught.

"God, Rachel, don't."

"You can't leave us here alone." He could tell from the way she said it that she wasn't worried for herself. It was only an excuse to keep him there.

"You'll be fine. You have the Ruger."

"For God's sake, Nick, I don't know the first thing about guns. I don't know how to load it or aim it. I don't even know where the damn safety is or how to take it off."

"It's easy, Rachel. It's the easiest thing in the world."

He took her back to the table and put the gun in her hand. He showed her the clip and how to load and unload it. He put her finger on the trigger and explained it all to her. But she shook her head.

"I can't—"

"Yes, you can," he said patiently.

"Please, Nick. Don't go. Give us a day. Just one day."
She put her hands on his chest and looked up at him with
wide, pleading eyes. His throat was suddenly dry. She
was close, oh so close.

"It's better if I go now." But he didn't move.

She touched him then, her beautiful fingers tracing his
mouth. Her breath was in his face, her hands in his hair.
She drew him down, closer and closer still.

"Stay, Nick. Please. I want you to," she whispered.

Suddenly he knew that of all the things on earth, she
had found the only one that would keep him there.

And then her mouth was on his.

He sank into her kiss like a doomed man, as if falling
from a great height. Unable to control himself, he
wrapped his arms around her, lifting her off her feet, and
all his hunger burst through. He kissed her eyes and her
mouth and her chin, he buried his face in her hair. He
smelled her—God, she smelled so clean—he couldn't
get enough, would never get enough. He felt the skin on
her back and the warmth of her breast, and it was like
sweet absolution.

They fell to the ground, barely waiting to undo snaps
and zippers. Everything was fierce and furious, as if they
were each afraid the other would vanish into smoke if
they didn't hurry. It was finished in minutes, each one
panting from the pace and the ferocity.

And when it was over, she lay in his arms and kissed
him, and it began again, slow this time, a gentle waltz on
the sand. They spread out their clothes and lay on top of
them. Her body was silk, like velvet under his hand. He
stroked her belly and her breast, and she stretched, meeting the plane of his palms.

And when she moved on top of him and let him slip inside her, it was smooth and easy. Every stroke was heat, every movement a slow, slick flame.

She enveloped him in a haze of pure feeling, an ecstasy so thick he felt he might die from it. He lay on his back, his arms outstretched to take in more, more, he only wanted more. Above him, she moved like an ocean.

Wave after wave of forgiveness washed over him.

Rennie Spier stared blindly at the bank of TV screens in his office. From every set a CNN reporter stood on a Belfast street. He'd turned off the sound, but it was easy to guess what the story was about.

The British had found Martin's ship, and its capture dominated the news.

File footage of Northern Ireland replaced the reporter, and Rennie turned way. He had to stop thinking about Nicky. They would find him soon enough. This constant, angry burn would fade, and things would return to normal.

But now, visions of blood occupied him. Visions of Nicky naked and spread-eagled beneath the knife, sexless for all time.

Rennie's hand began to shake, and he gripped the curved edge of the desk. He had loved Nicky, had truly loved him. Rennie pictured the boy he'd brought into his home twenty years ago. The luxuries given him over the years, the money spent, the trust bestowed. But the pictures melted into one of his pretty, young, faithless wife. For six years he'd been patient. He'd made friends with suspicion, been partner to doubt. Now he knew. Nicky had proven himself a viper. And proven himself guilty once and for all.

Why else take the boy? If Isaac had truly been Rennie's, Nick would never have stolen him.

Besides, they'd all seen the child. He looked like his God-cursed mother, but his eyes were Nick's. No one had said so out loud, but Rennie had endured endless sidelong glances.

Did they think he was blind? Did they think he couldn't see the sly perception in their eyes as they looked from the boy's face to his and back again?

I'll take your balls, Nicky, and bury you screaming. The heat of fury burned Rennie's eyes. But first he'd take Nicky's woman. In front of him, so he could see what it was like. Spier shook with anger.

Ah, Nicky, Nicky. I gave you everything.

Just then the phone rang. It was Frank. "We have a problem."

"Fix it."

"I think you better see something."

"Then why do you bother me with useless phone calls?"

When Frank came in, Rennie didn't hide his irritation. "I don't want to be harassed with idiocies."

Frank laid a set of rumpled, curling papers in front of him. "Nicky traded the kid for this. Take a look at it."

Rennie turned the pages to one in the middle and glanced at it. He turned to the next page, and the next. He looked up at Frank, rage boiling through his veins. "What is this?"

Frank shook his head. "Looks to me like a double-cross."

Chapter 16

Nick woke with the sun on the beach and Rachel in his arms. He listened to the lap of water, knowing he should untangle himself and go; he still had unfinished business with Rennie. Instead he stroked Rachel's face, watching her eyes light up as she woke and saw him. He kissed her, slowly, deeply. As her mouth softened under his and her body melted against him, he knew nothing he had experienced in the past, and nothing he might experience in the future, would ever be as sweet and as full as this moment. He promised himself a day of it. One sunny oasis in all the darkness that lay ahead.

So they ate English muffins and marmalade for breakfast, and though she might have been curious, Rachel didn't ask where the food had come from, and Nick didn't volunteer the information. Isaac was quiet, too, as if he sensed this new thing between them.

After breakfast, Nick drove the car onto the beach behind the house so it couldn't be seen from the road.

They stuck close to the cabin that first morning. Wariness lingered, and he was reluctant to let them be seen. But Isaac grew restless and cranky in the afternoon, and Nick took them onto the shore. They had no bathing suits, but he didn't want them in the water where he couldn't protect them anyway. So they sat on towels, Isaac stiff and cautious, only occasionally dragging fingers through the sand. Nick brought the Uzi under a blanket and kept a firm grip on the gun.

He had a lot more trouble keeping a firm grip on his concentration. As the afternoon wore on, his eyes strayed inexorably to Rachel's, and what he saw there, the knowledge of what had happened between them, the heat and the light it created in the center of his being, made maintaining his vigilance increasingly more difficult. He should have been watching the horizon, but all he wanted to do was watch Rachel.

No, not all. He wanted to feel her skin beneath his hand again, feel her body beneath his own. He pushed the thoughts away. He was leaving. He'd stay until the sun went down, then he'd have to go.

But when evening finally arrived, he found himself on the beach with Rachel, telling himself he'd stay until morning. The moon rose, and the miracle happened all over again as she took his body into hers.

The next day, he could hardly look at himself in the bathroom mirror. His face was too real, too much a reminder of all the reasons why he didn't deserve to feel so . . . so—what?

Happy.

The realization exploded over him like a Roman candle. He was happy.

A stupid grin spread over his face; he lifted his head for an instant and caught a glimpse of himself.

Shit. You look like a fool. His grin widened.

At breakfast, he thought about leaving, then Rachel ran her hands over his back as she passed behind his chair, and he decided to stay one more day.

That afternoon he escorted Rachel and Isaac into town. The trip was crazy, but they needed supplies and a change of clothes. He could have gone by himself, but Isaac was stir-crazy, and though she didn't say so, he knew Rachel needed a break from the cramped cabin. So he ignored his misgivings and walked them down to the main road and the shops. Isaac held Rachel's hand, and though he wouldn't hold Nick's, he walked between them.

As they strolled around a corner toward the grocery store, they were stopped by a colorful sight. Bicycle after bicycle spilled out from a rental shop and littered the sidewalk. Tricycles and tandems, ten-speeds with racing stripes, no-speeds with woven wood baskets attached. They had to pick their way around them.

Isaac stared at the huge collection of spokes and wheels and handlebars, his eyes wide. He watched two children riding in circles on the side road next to the shop.

Nick looked from the bikes to the boy. "Which one do you like?"

Isaac didn't answer, and Rachel opened her mouth to speak to him. But Nick shook his head and knelt beside the boy.

"You don't have to talk if you don't want to," he said softly. "You don't have to say a single word. But if I don't know which bike you want, I might pick out a blue one when you want black, or red when you want silver."

"Who's the rider in this group?" An elderly man in a Dutch cap smiled down at them.

"Don't know if we've got one." Nick looked from the man back to the boy.

"Not got one? Why, this fella here looks like a rider to me." He winked at Nick. "Let's see . . ."

He moved among the vehicles as if they were familiar members of his family. One by one, he lifted out bikes and carried them to Isaac. When he finished, five bikes were spread in front of him.

"Which one you want?" Nick asked. Somber and thoughtful, the boy examined the selection as if it were the most important decision in his life. "Just point to the one you want, and it's yours for the duration." Slowly, Isaac walked over to a bright blue bike with streamers on the handlebars. The man in the cap smiled at Nick.

"Thanks." Nick smiled back. "Thanks a lot."

"Just part of the service. After all these years I've gotten pretty good at matching boy to bike. Now, do you need training wheels for him? I can—"

"No," Isaac piped up.

Everyone laughed. "I guess that answers that," said the man.

Nick nodded. God, how much he didn't know about the boy. Would he ever catch up?

"And what about you two? I can fix you up with something real nice. Flat as a pancake on the island, real easy ride."

Nick started to shake his head, but caught the look in

Rachel's eyes. Soon two more bicycles stood next to Isaac's.

The next day, Nick reluctantly let himself be persuaded to a bike ride up and down the length of the island. Isaac insisted on bringing his bear, and Rachel rode with it sitting primly inside her handlebar basket. She dressed Isaac in a newly purchased bathing suit, and later they stopped at the beach.

Nick scanned the sunny view of families scattered over the sand. Children ran and screamed with laughter, splashing in the surf, and Rachel smiled at him as if to say, *See, we're just like them.* He put an arm around her, wanting to believe, and the three of them melted into the crowd.

Rachel spread out a blanket, and Isaac sat on the edge, his feet in the sand. He wouldn't leave her side at first, but she propped up the bear so he could see it, and gradually he grew braver. By the end of the day he was playing at the shoreline while Nick and Rachel sat in the sand nearby.

"Look at this." She smiled fondly as she poked a finger into the bear's side. A seam had come undone. "Loved to death, like the Velveteen Rabbit."

"The who?" Nick looked up at her. He was lying on his side, braced on one elbow.

"The Velveteen Rabbit." She looked down her nose at him. "Don't tell me you never heard of the Velveteen Rabbit? Well, you certainly had a deprived childhood." *If you only knew.* "We'll have to remedy that." A mischievous gleam lit her eyes, and laughing, Nick pulled her on top of him.

"Bedtime stories?" He grinned up at her, and she kissed him lightly.

"Mmm. If you're good."

She sat up again, and he turned back to the boy, watching Isaac scoop wet sand into a plastic pail. Did he know about the Velveteen Rabbit?

"When are you going to tell him?" Rachel asked. Nick felt her gaze on him, warm with sympathy.

Laughing lightly, he shrugged off the sudden wave of emotion that swamped him. "What—about the Velveteen Rabbit?"

"That you're his father."

His stomach jolted. God, he couldn't bear thinking about it. To want something so much, something that seemed so impossible.

"I don't know."

"He's young, Nick, and kids are so resilient. He just needs time and love. And a chance to get to know you. Look, he's better already. He hasn't checked on us for almost half an hour."

Nick looked toward the shore. As always, Isaac was sober and intent. In sharp contrast, a little yellow-haired girl played nearby. She dumped a pail full of sand over her father's arm, laughing delightedly at his expression of mock anger.

"Go ahead," Rachel urged.

Slowly, he got to his feet. When he knelt down beside Isaac, the boy stopped patting the sand pile he had just made. He sat back on his heels and looked at Nick cautiously, a field mouse judging the dangers of an open meadow.

*What can I say to you, Isaac? My child. My son. How
can I help you trust me? Love me?*

Nick said nothing; he hadn't been too successful with
words anyway. Instead, he hunkered down on the sand
and began to dig a wide, circular moat around Isaac's
sand tower.

Wordlessly, Isaac watched him work.

After a while, the boy filled his pail again and upended it inside the moat, next to the other pile.

Immediately, he pulled back to watch Nick's reaction.

Nick was careful not to look at him. "We need four
towers to make a castle." He shaped the sand around the
moat into the semblance of a wall. Isaac filled his pail
again, dumping the packed sand inside the moat.

They played that way for the rest of the day, silent but
together. By the time they left, a little fissure of hope had
opened up inside Nick.

But that night, Isaac woke screaming for the first
time. Nick raced into the bedroom as the boy's terrified
shrieks split the world.

"It's all right, little man." He held him tight. "It's a
dream, just a bad dream. You're safe."

But nothing Nick did soothed the boy, and in the end
Rachel held Isaac until he fell asleep.

When she finally tiptoed out an hour later, Rachel
found Nick on the couch, staring at his hands and looking desolate. She knelt in front of him and gently tilted
his head up. "It's not your fault, Nick. It's to be expected.
Nightmares and worse, maybe."

"I know." He took her hands, and the feel of her skin
seemed to comfort him.

"I didn't sleep through the night for years after my

mother was killed. I still have an occasional nightmare about it." She leaned toward him, and he met her in the middle, foreheads touching.

"We're quite a bunch." His mouth curved in a regretful smile. "Haunted as well as hunted."

She cupped his cheek with her hand. "He'll be all right, Nick. It just takes time."

He closed his eyes, and without his saying it, she knew what he was thinking. Time was the only thing he didn't have. He had to go. Now, soon, or he'd never do it at all. She moved into the circle of his arms, pleading with him silently.

Not yet. Please. One more day.

She pictured Spier's documents sitting on the supply-closet shelf.

Tell him.

But he held her so close. The feel of him drew heat and the sweet ache for him inside her.

Tomorrow is soon enough. I'll tell him tomorrow.

But tomorrow never came. Three days stretched into four and four into five, and still Nick never left, and Rachel never confessed.

During the day, they surrounded themselves with crowds of doting parents. At the water slide, the amusement park, the pizza place. It wasn't hard to slip into the role themselves. And if the ice of fear touched her, it melted at night, drowned in the heat of their bodies.

In the morning, when the air was fresh and cool, they took long walks along the beach behind the cabin. Nick's face plainly said it was stupid. An entire beach with no place to hide.

But it was also irresistible.

Arms entwined, she and Nick strolled while Isaac picked up shells and broken crab legs. By the fifth day, Nick even had to tell him not to get too far ahead. They saw a family up early, too, young children in tow. The couple laughed together easily, and the father swept his son high in the air as if it were the most natural thing in the world. Rachel glanced over at Nick and saw a keen stab of envy shoot across his face.

That night, Nick and Rachel lay naked in the sand behind the cabin, side by side on an old blanket. Exposed to the night, Rachel shamelessly luxuriated in the feel of the sea air on her skin. Nick's hand feathered down her chest, over the mound of her breast and the plane of her belly.

"You're the most beautiful thing I've ever seen," he said, stroking her reverently.

She laughed and smiled mischievously. "Have you looked in the mirror lately?"

He gave her a mock jab on the chin and lay back, pulling her arm across his chest. His fingers encircled hers, the hard strength of his arm entwined with her own.

Looking up at the starry sky, she recalled the frozen man he'd been a few months ago. The man who swept the halls of the preschool, who emptied the trash and changed the lightbulbs with tense and secret silence.

So different now.

Joy bloomed inside her, and she closed her eyes against the emotion, taking a deep, steadying breath.

"You okay?" He turned his head toward her in concern.

"Mmm. You?"

"I feel like a firecracker ready to go off."

She laughed and rolled over. Bracing herself on one elbow, she looked down at him. The eyes that used to gaze dully past her now filled with light. As she bent to kiss him, the knowledge that she'd put the glow in his face filled her with fierce pride.

Maybe it was the dark velvet of night, or the liquid music of the tide. Maybe it was just relief and the glory of being alive one more day. But as her body joined with Nick's, the stars themselves exploded inside her. Her skin melted, her bones disappeared. All that remained was an arching splendor. Nick's mouth, her hands. Where did she stop and he begin?

They held each other and took each other, each glad of the taking. The flow of fingers, the wash of tongues, the stroke and pull of bodies moving in harmony. It happened over and over that night. Sleep a little, then wake, then the hot, tender dance began all over again.

At last they lay lazy and full, and when Rachel stood up, she was also a little sore. A small private lilt slanted inside her as she realized why, and she looked up at the moon with happy, dreamy eyes.

From his prone position, Nick wrapped a hand around her ankle. "Where are you going?"

She pulled on his T-shirt and smiled down at him. "I don't know. For a walk."

She was leaning against the car, looking out over the ocean when he found her. He came toward her on bare feet, wearing only jeans. The moon washed his naked chest with silver, highlighting his muscular smoothness. Struck dumb, she shivered at the sight.

If Nick noticed, he didn't say. He crossed his arms, surveying her and the car with critical eyes. She could only imagine what she looked like. Half naked, hair in a wild tangle, mouth swollen from his.

"Where did you get this heap anyway?"

"It was my father's." She made room for him as he settled beside her. "He left it to me when he died." She sighed. "I once let all the air out of the tires, hoping that would keep him home."

"Did it?"

"You don't become a legend in your own time by staying home and having tea parties with your daughter."

He slung an arm around her. "So that's why you don't want to help with the book."

"What do you mean?"

He shrugged. "You're still mad at him. For the tea parties . . . and everything else he missed."

"I'm not mad—" She stopped. She *was* mad. Not only for her father's abandonment of her, but because he died before she could forgive him.

She blinked into the darkness as sudden tears threatened. God, not now. Not when everything had been so beautiful. She didn't want to think about her father tonight.

Nick hugged her tight and kissed the top of her head. The comfort helped ease the swift rush of emotion that had surged out of nowhere. With a deep breath, she snuggled deeper into the safety of his embrace.

"It's funny, how we cling to each other," he said in a soft, distant voice. "No matter how he betrays you, no matter how many wrongs he does, your father is still that—your father. You can hate him, but even hate is just the twisted side of love."

Was he talking about her or himself? David Goodman or Rennie Spier?

As if he'd heard her thoughts, he said, "He was a dream, like God reaching down and plucking me up to heaven."

"Who was?"

"Rennie." He was gazing out over the horizon, lost in thought. "I was, I don't know, thirteen maybe. I'd been in and out of foster homes, group homes, every kind of home but the real thing. Somehow, I always found myself back on the street." He paused. "The thing I remember most is being hungry all the time. That last year was the worst. I'd grown a foot. Just shot up out of nowhere. When you're little, cadging for money and food is a breeze. But when you're edging up near six feet, it's a whole other story. I got caught shoplifting twice. The first time I talked the owner out of calling the police. The second time I ran. Scared the shit out of me. I'd been in juvie before, and it was worse than starving to death on the street."

"What did you do?"

He fell silent again, and she sensed he was wondering how much to reveal, how much to hold back.

"You don't have to tell me anything, Nick."

He gazed at her, a self-deprecating expression on his face. "You already know the worst, what difference could a few more sins make?"

"No difference at all."

He smiled and unwound his arm from around her. Tracing the line of her cheek, he gave the end of her nose a light tap. "Where do you come from, Rachel Goodman? Are you some fairy sprite sent from another world?"

"I'm as real as you are."

"No." His mouth quirked into a sad smile. "Not nearly as real. At least I hope not. So—" He swooped down and picked up a piece of driftwood. "Want to know what I did to keep myself from starving?"

"Only if you want to tell me."

He turned the piece of wood over in his hand. "I stood watch for drug dealers, pimps, loan sharks. I had a nice racket stealing car radios, CD players, cell phones. Anything I could get my hands on."

"Oh, Nick . . ."

He took a step away from her and with a tight, cruel toss, flung the driftwood back toward the shore. "Christ, it's been a long time since I thought about any of this."

"Nick, you don't have to—"

"It's okay. Like I said, it was a long time ago. It doesn't even matter anymore."

"It does matter." A quick bolt of anger darted through her. "Where were social services in all this? How could they just let you fend for yourself like that?"

"Kids slip through the cracks all the time."

Yes. Like Carla and all the other kids she'd never be able to rescue.

"Let's see." He braced an elbow against the car while he marshaled his memories. "I guess that's when I met Marty. He told me about a car ring that specialized in high-end imports, stuff like that. We offered our services, but we were just two dumb kids, and they laughed us out of the place. But the next day—" He smiled at some memory and shook his head. "The very next day,

we spotted this incredible Porsche. Flaming yellow,
bright as the sun. If we could steal that, I told Marty,
those dickheads would take us seriously."

"And did you?"

He laughed. "Not exactly. Frank caught us red-
handed. I thought he was going to kill us both."

"But he didn't."

"No," he said quietly, "he didn't."

"How come?"

"I don't know. Rennie took a shine to me." He
shrugged. "One of life's little mysteries."

"What about your parents?"

"Another black hole. I have only one clear memory,
and to this day I'm not sure what it is." He squinted into
the dark as if he was watching the scene unfold. "It's
night. Very cold. I'm five, maybe six, hunkered over a
street grate that spews steam from the subways. Someone tells me to stay there while they find something,
food maybe, or a place to sleep. I don't even know if it
was a man or a woman. When I try to focus on a face,
the scene . . . floats apart. Like mist. All I remember is
how cold I was, and then suddenly this billow of warmth
puffs up from the street, and I wanted to stay there forever."

He paused, then continued in a subdued voice. "You
know, there was a minute in the alley in Panama . . .
when I saw that kid . . . It was like looking at myself
staring back at me."

The sound of waves filled the silence. Then he blew
out a deep whoosh of breath. "Shit." Turning away, he
put both hands on the little car and leaned in at arm's

length. Head down, he squeezed his eyes shut, fighting for control.

Gently, Rachel laid a hand on his bare back.

"I should have stopped Marty," he said. "I should have just fucking stopped him." He turned back around, and in the moonlight she saw the agony on his face. "I shouldn't have even been there. I hated that kind of stuff. I was no good at it. Everyone knew it."

"Why did they send you, then?"

"I don't know." He shook his head. "But I didn't question it. I was a good soldier. I did what I was told. Besides, I wanted to go. Shelley had just given me my walking papers, and I was so messed up, I couldn't think straight. Killing someone sounded like a good idea."

"You cared about her that much?" Would she always have to contend with Shelley's ghost?

"Cared about her?" He appeared struck by that idea. "God, who knows. I cared about having her, I know that. It was like having a piece of Rennie."

"Do you mean it was like having something that belonged to him? Like . . . like stealing from him?"

He bent down, running his hand over tufts of dune grass. Rachel knelt beside him while the ocean rumbled behind.

"She was Rennie's wife, Nick. Sleeping with her was not only dangerous, it was a terrible betrayal of the man who'd literally rescued you from the gutter."

He rose and looked down at her, an acrid curve to his mouth. "I'm a nasty piece of work. I've told you that from the beginning."

"That's a matter of opinion," she snapped. "But whatever you are, you're not stupid. I can see you taking the risk if you loved her, but if you didn't—"

"Maybe I did love her." Irritation edged his voice. "I don't know. She was like a fever. Like some virus infecting me."

"So you couldn't help yourself?"

"I didn't want to help myself."

"Why?"

"She was the best fuck I'd ever had, that's why!" His eyes blazed at her. "All right? Satisfied?" He went to the blanket and started jerking up their clothes. "What difference does it make why I started sleeping with her? I'm not proud of it, but I did it. I'll tell you one thing. The nightmares stopped when I started sleeping with her. I loved her for that, if for nothing else."

Nightmares? "You had nightmares?"

He looked at her, then away. "I . . . I sometimes woke up crying. For a couple of years before Shelley and I—" With a sharp movement, he bundled the clothes together, then collected the four sneakers scattered about, all the while avoiding her eyes.

"Did you tell anyone?" she asked.

"Are you kidding? I barely acknowledged it to myself."

"What did you do?"

He sat back on his haunches and looked at her. "I started drinking, that's what I did. And I stopped reading the papers, I avoided the radio and TV."

"Whoa—" Rachel laughed. "You stop watching TV because you had nightmares? If TV gave people nightmares, half the country would be afflicted."

"Half the country doesn't see the things they pander shredding people to bits."

The smile died on her lips. "Oh, Nick." She looked down at her hands so he wouldn't see the pity in her eyes. "If you felt that way, why didn't you just leave?"

"Rennie wouldn't have let me. Not then. I was still too useful to him. It was only when I became completely dysfunctional that he let me go."

She looked over at him. His dark eyes were two pieces of night, deep with self-contempt. Suddenly, she understood. "So you arranged it."

"Arranged what?"

"To become dysfunctional."

He frowned. "That's ridiculous."

"Is it? At great risk and personal dishonor you sleep with a woman you don't even love. Why?"

"I told you, she was like a drug, like—"

Rachel shook her head. "I don't buy that. Oh, I'm sure the sex was great." She smiled at him. "Then again, sex with you would have to be great."

"Thank you, Dr. Ruth."

She ignored his sarcasm. "But there's more to it than just sex."

"Or should I say, Dr. Freud?"

"You were having nightmares, you wanted out, but you were trapped. So if you couldn't leave, what could you do?"

Arms crossed, he looked at her with glacial eyes.

Come on, Nick. Listen. Think. "What could you do?"

"I could get even."

Yes. "You could take a piece of Rennie. Steal his most

precious, most intimate possession. What did Rennie do to people who stole from him?"

"You know what he did."

"Yes, and that's one way out, isn't it?" Nick stared at her, and she plunged on. "You ever hear of death by cop? Some guys want to die so badly, they force the police into a situation where they have to shoot to kill."

"So this is death by Spier?"

"Why not?"

"Because it's crazy."

She shrugged. "Desperate people do desperate things."

"I wasn't that desperate." But something in his voice belied his words. "Besides, I'm still here." He spread his arms, indicating his obvious presence in the world.

"That's because Shelley ended your affair. Rennie won again. And then, they sent you to Panama."

He scowled at her. "One thing has nothing to do with the other."

"Would you have gone if you weren't so upset about Shelley?"

"I did what Rennie told me to do."

"And what happened?"

"You know what happened."

"No, I mean afterward. What happened to you?"

"What happened to me?" He gave a curt laugh. "I fell apart."

"You self-destructed. Don't you see? You couldn't get Rennie to do it, so you did it yourself. You destroyed the tool, Nick, so if nothing else, Rennie couldn't use it. Except that tool was you."

Nick didn't reply. Snapping up the rest of the clothes, he stalked into the cabin.

"Nick! Wait!" She'd skimmed too close, dug too deep. But how else to clean an infected wound?

Scrambling inside, she found him facing the closed door to Isaac's bedroom. "Nick—" Tentatively, she touched his back.

"I don't want you to have anything to do with that—that muck." His voice was low and fierce. "I want to keep you away from it, from Rennie, and Shelley, and—"

"And you?"

Slowly, he turned to face her. "Yeah, from me, too." He threw her a wan smile. "But I'm a selfish son of a bitch."

"No, you're not. There's goodness in you, Nick. I can see it, why can't you?"

His mouth twisted. "You'd see goodness in the guy who marched you to your grave."

"I'm not a fool."

"No. You're just good, so you assume the rest of us are, too. Well, we're not. I'm not. If I were, I'd be a million miles away from here. There are things I should be doing, things I know won't keep. But it's like my legs are lead and my brain is mush. And I don't care." He ran the back of his hand over her cheek. "I'm happy, Rachel. For the first time in my whole shitty little life, I'm actually happy. Call it goodness if you want, but to me it's just plain old-fashioned selfishness."

She slipped her arms around him, laying her head against his chest. She loved the feel of him like this, the smooth muscles of his back under her hands, his chest beneath her cheek, hard and strong. "Didn't Shelley make you happy, Nick, even a little bit?"

He sighed into her hair. "Maybe. I look back on it now, and she just seems like an obsession, a curse. Whereas you—" He kissed her throat, then her jaw. "God, you, Rachel—" He covered her mouth once, then again. And in between, he breathed, "You're like a prayer."

They met the morning coiled around each other, back outside on the blanket. Sleepy and a little sheepish at his own indulgence, Nick stumbled into the cabin, his arms entwined with Rachel's. A cheerful urge to share the sunrise with Isaac had overtaken them, and they'd rushed inside to wake the boy.

But when they opened the door to the bedroom, Isaac was gone. The bed was rumpled, but no little boy lay on top.

Panic slashed through Nick. He raced into the kitchen, flung open the broom closet, and grabbed the Uzi.

"Stay here!" But she was already out of the cabin.

Breathless and terrified, he raced after her—and found Isaac happily digging in the sand at the water's edge.

"He wanted to sleep outside, too," Rachel explained, and relief was so overwhelming, Nick swept Isaac up, hugging him tightly.

And like that, everything changed. With a curt command, Nick ordered Rachel to wait outside with Isaac while he restowed the Uzi. When he allowed them back in the cabin, she found him in the middle of the kitchen, staring at the closet where he'd hidden the guns.

Rachel recognized that bleak stare; Nick was thinking about leaving. He was thinking about going after Rennie, and she couldn't bear to watch.

"Get your suit on," she said to Isaac, "and we'll take a walk on the beach."

"No." The hardness was back in Nick's face.

"I want to go out." The boy's brows drew down in a black frown, a small replica of his father's.

"You've already been out. Now you're staying in." He sat the boy in a chair at the rickety kitchen table.

Rachel eyed Nick, a pulse pounding in her head. She had to tell him about the printout. If he knew she had Spier's papers, he wouldn't have to leave. He could put Rennie Spier away without killing him or dying in the process.

But Isaac's lips were trembling; they couldn't discuss it now. "We'll go for a walk later," she soothed.

"I don't think so." Nick's gaze skimmed the kitchen, lit on the closet where the guns waited, and flitted away again. The pulse in her head beat harder. *Tell him. Now.*

"Nick, we . . . we have to talk about something."

"Later. I need to think." His eyes drifted to the cabinet again.

"This can't wait. Why don't we take Isaac for a walk, and you and I can—"

"No."

The word was a treatise in implacability, and she bit her lip, trying to hold onto her panic. "You can't keep us trapped in here forever."

"Better here than the morgue."

"That's crazy." She put a hand on his arm, but he shrugged it off.

"No."

"Nick—"

"I said no!"

A plate crashed against the kitchen floor. Her head turned in time with Nick's. Isaac was pushing a glass toward the edge of the table.

Nick snatched the tumbler out of his hand.

"What are you doing?" Isaac stared hard at the tabletop, but said nothing. *"What are you doing?"*

"He's telling you he doesn't like it when you yell."

The boy pushed another plate off.

"Don't do that!"

A glass went over.

"You little—" Nick lifted him off the seat. Isaac kicked and pummeled him.

"Give him to me." Rachel said. *"Give him to me!"* She took the struggling boy. His small body trembled against her. Without another word, she rushed out of the cabin.

Nick stared after her, hating himself.

It was over. The whole sweet, wonderful charade was over. He slumped into the chair Isaac had vacated and raked a hand through his hair. God, he didn't want to go.

But Isaac's disappearance, harmless as it turned out, had punctured the dreamy bubble Nick had been living in for the past five days. He'd been negligent, stupid, a careless fool. Did he think Rennie would just go away? He was still out there. And Nick had no doubt the ruthless man was hunting for them.

He left the cabin and walked to the beach. The morning tide had left behind pebbles and shards of seashells that his bare feet pushed farther into the wet sand. Among the debris he spied a small conch shell, whole and untouched by the sea's violence. He picked it up and turned it over in his hand, anticipating the look on Isaac's face when he showed it to him. If the kid ever spoke to him again.

He closed his fingers around the shell, wishing he could stay and make things right with Isaac. Suddenly that seemed more important than revenge or justice. Nick didn't want to kill Rennie. He didn't want to kill anyone. He just wanted to live like any other ordinary man. Love his woman and raise his son.

He looked out over the sea, watching the perpetual motion of the waves. Rennie was like those waves, powerful and endless.

And like the sea, there was no bargaining with him.

Chapter 17

From a table outside an ice cream shop, Rachel sat next to Isaac and fought the compulsion to rub the skin off her wrists. In front of her, vacationers strolled up and down the street. Cars full of rowdy sunbathers zoomed past, bike riders in bathing suits cycled by. All blissfully unaware of danger.

She closed her eyes against the wave of panic and envy that washed over her. They'd been here over five days. If Spier were going to strike, wouldn't he have already tried?

She shivered in the heat. Five days or fifty, he was still a threat. And the only way to neutralize him was the printout.

She gazed down at the boy beside her. He ate his ice cream cone with sober concentration. He was so serious. Would he ever laugh? Would he ever squirm and jabber like other kids?

"Here, turn it around. That's right. So you won't drip."

God, how could she sound so tranquil? Nick was getting ready to kill Rennie Spier, and she was teaching a six-year-old how to eat ice cream.

She pictured Spier's documents lying calmly in the cramped supply closet at the school, and an idea began to form. Heart thrumming, she looked around for a phone but didn't see one nearby.

Giving Isaac a napkin, she helped him wipe his face. "Ready to go?" She held out her hand, but he didn't take it. He clutched the napkin tightly, twisting it between his fingers. Gently, she said, "What's wrong?"

"He's mad." His child's voice was so small she barely heard him.

"Who's mad? Nick?"

"He shouted."

She sighed and lifted him off his chair onto her lap. Her plan would have to wait a few more minutes. She put her arms around his rigid body.

"He's just worried. He wants you to be safe."

Isaac's voice grew even smaller. "Is he . . . is he going away?"

A rush of sadness sped through her. He had lost so much! "Not if I can help it. Come on."

Taking his hand, she walked him toward the pay phone in front of the grocery store. Once inside, she lifted him up so he could press all the buttons of her uncle's work number. As she waited for the receptionist to put her uncle on the line, she wondered how he felt about blackmail. Not too good, she'd guess. But blackmail was the perfect way to deal with Rennie Spier. And as long as the three of them were safe and alive, she'd turn over one page of the printout to Spier every six months. Otherwise, she'd arrange to have it sent to the authorities. Elliot could handle it, lawyer to lawyer, with whomever Spier wanted to appoint. No one would have to meet Spier or talk to him. Best of all, no one would have to kill him. Almost giddy with relief at the solution she'd devised, she waited impatiently for her uncle to come on the line.

"Rachel, my God, is that really you?" Elliot's voice was strained and upset.

"Of course it's me, who else—"

He cut in. "Where are you?"

His rudeness surprised her; Elliot was rarely rude. "Why, what's the matter?"

"Are you all right?"

"I'm fine, Uncle Elliot." But suddenly her heart began to drum again. "Has something happened? What's wrong?"

Nick dug his feet into the sand and stared at the waves, trying to figure out how the hell he would find the words to tell Rachel he was going, how he would even manage to make himself go.

"Nick!"

He turned, and there she stood, holding Isaac's hand, poised at the top of the rise leading down toward the shore. It seemed as if she'd sprung whole and beautiful from his thoughts. He forgot about their fight the minute he saw her, forgot that the time had come to leave. Happiness sparked as she dropped the boy's hand and flew down to Nick. Just the sight of her sent a surge of joy through him.

Then he got a good look at her face.

She was pale and shaken, eyes wide with horror.

"What is it?" He grabbed her by the shoulders. "Did something happen?" He shook her, but she couldn't get any words out. Tears spilled over her cheeks, yet she didn't make a sound, just stood frozen, staring at him like a statue in torment.

Then he saw what she was holding: one of the New York newspapers, clutched so tightly, he had to pry it out of her hand. The minute he got it away from her, she sank into the sand. She sobbed as if her soul were breaking up. He glanced down at the headline and felt the blood drain from his own heart: PRESCHOOL FIRE DAMAGES CHURCH, LEAVES TEACHER DEAD.

He gazed at the words until the letters blurred, but the name of the dead teacher burned clear in his mind. *Felice.*

Rennie had destroyed Rachel's school and killed Felice.

A weight of guilt descended, heavy as a load of cement blocks. He should have dealt with Rennie days ago. Instead Nick had stayed here, clutching at a dream until it was too late, and now someone else was dead. He pictured Felice's rotund form, remembered her sassiness, and the bright colors of the loose dresses she always wore burst into flames before his eyes.

Blame bowed his shoulders and weakened his knees until he wanted to drop into the sand beside Rachel, but he couldn't let himself fall; she was already down, and she needed him. He tried to coax her back to the house, but she wouldn't budge. He was prepared to carry her in, but she fought him with such wild savagery that in the end he left her by the water.

She cried on and off all afternoon. He and Isaac spent the time together. Whether he sensed Nick's neediness, or needed the comfort himself, Isaac didn't stray.

Once every hour, they checked on Rachel. Nick went alone the first time, but Isaac followed him the next, dragging his bear in one hand and slipping the other into Nick's. His heart constricted at the touch of those small fingers, but he said nothing. Hand in hand, they walked together until they'd gone far enough to spot Rachel without her seeing them. Sometimes she was meandering like a forlorn bird at the water's edge; other times she sat in the sand, staring at the indifferent and measureless breadth of the sea.

"Are the bad men coming?" Isaac asked once.

"No," Nick lied. "We're safe. No one's going to hurt you."

"Or Rachel?"

Nick swallowed hard, knowing that whatever was still to come, the damage had already been done. "Or Rachel," he said.

She came back to them in the evening, while Nick was slathering bread with peanut butter and jelly for Isaac. One minute the two of them were alone, and the next she stood in the doorway.

Face pale, she stooped to give Isaac a hug as he ran toward her. "It's okay," she told him. "I'm all right."

Nick made sandwiches, and they sat outside at the picnic table to eat. It was a quiet meal. Rachel barely touched her plate.

After dinner, Nick showed Isaac the conch shell he'd found earlier.

The boy turned it over in his hand, examining it carefully. "Where'd you find it?"

"On the beach," Nick told him. "Would you . . . would you like to see where?"

Isaac nodded, and a tiny flare of happiness kindled behind Rachel's eyes as the boy reached for Nick's hand. He kissed her then, a small, warm touch of his mouth to her cheek, and though the sadness didn't leave her face, she leaned against him briefly, and he felt that he'd comforted her.

That night, Nick put Isaac to bed for the first time. When he tucked Isaac in and handed him his bear, the boy looked at him earnestly. "Don't let her be sad anymore."

Nick took his son's hand, squeezed it. "I won't." The words felt like a vow, a promise between them.

Outside the bedroom, Rachel sank into a corner of the couch and waited for Nick. When at last the bedroom light clicked off and the door closed, he sat down beside her.

She shrank away, unworthy of comfort. "I should have been there, Nick. It should have been me, not Felice."

"That's crazy."

"It's my fault." Her voice cracked, and a tear plopped onto her hand.

"Oh, Rachel, honey, how can it possibly be your fault?" He rubbed her back, and she felt the warmth of his hand like an undeserved blessing. "You're as blameless in this as Felice was."

"You don't know." Her voice thickened with tears. "You don't know what I did."

"What?" Amusement gentled his voice, as if she couldn't possibly do anyone harm. "What did you do?"

They say confession is good for the soul, but Rachel wouldn't know. She could hardly get the words out. "I . . . I switched the printouts."

The comforting motion of his hand on her back slowed to a stop. "What do you mean?"

She couldn't look at him, so she stared blindly at the room instead. "I left Rennie a few . . . a few pages of his original and substituted the rest with used computer paper from school."

Stunned silence filled the room. For long minutes, Nick said nothing, no word of blame or censure. How could he? He couldn't get his mind around the words she'd just spoken. She'd switched the printout? Is that what she'd said? His brain moved like mud. He'd traded Isaac for . . . for used computer paper?

Suddenly, he couldn't breathe. Jackknifing to his feet, he sped to the door and wrenched it open, inhaling the cool, ocean night.

She'd switched the printout. Jesus Christ.

His hand fisted against the doorjamb. "I told you—"

"He would not let this go, Nick." Face pale, she rose, her voice wobbly but resolute. "You know it, I know it. With the printout we had some leverage, something to hold over him. A safety net."

"I told you not to worry about that. I was going to take care of it."

"Yeah, right." Her mouth thinned. "You think I don't know how you were going to 'take care of it'? That's why I did it, why I had to do it. Isaac would be safe from Spier, and you wouldn't have to . . . you wouldn't have to . . ." She clamped a shaky hand over her mouth and looked at him with dawning horror. He saw the realization come, saw the pain magnify in her face.

"I wouldn't have to kill him." He said it quietly, flatly. A statement of fact that twisted his gut and wrenched his heart. Because, of course, he had to kill Spier anyway.

She nodded, the full impact of the words finally hitting home. "Oh, God." She sank down on the couch, tears welling, her face stark with pain.

The sight of her anguish was almost more than he could bear. She'd done this for him, to keep him from doing what he should have done all along. Sweet God in heaven, he wished he could slit his throat where he stood.

Steeling himself against the agony in her face, he strode to the broom closet. To the Uzi.

"What are you doing?"

"I have to go. I have to stop him." He flung open the closet door, but before he could pick up the weapon, she wrapped herself around him, pinning his arms down.

"Don't, Nick. Please."

Christ. Just the touch of her sent heat spiraling through him, making him weak, making him want to give in and do what he'd been doing the last five days. Stay here with her.

He clamped his jaw down, forcing the emotions away. "Let go of me."

"You can't leave. I won't let you."

He pried her grip loose and picked up the gun.

"If you go, what I did will be for nothing. Please."

He checked the load, deliberately not looking at her. "I'm not sitting around waiting for Rennie to make his next move."

"God, it's all my fault. If I hadn't switched the printout, Felice would still be alive, and you wouldn't have to go after Rennie."

He swore softly, knowing the truth was anything but. "Switching the damn printout has nothing to do with it."

"But—"

"For God's sake, can't you get it through your head?" He pounded a fist on the closet. "Rennie could have burned down the place anyway—to draw me out. He used you once, why not again?" He grabbed the ammo box and yanked it open. "I'm the one who knew what he was capable of. I'm the one who knew what had to be done." He dumped the bullets into his pockets with an angry shake. "And I'm the one who put it off day after goddamn day."

He pushed past her to the cabinet where he'd stashed the Magnum. Checking the clip, he slammed it home, and she jumped at the sound. He saw her start, knew it meant she was sick with fear for him. Knew, too, that he had to ignore it, or he'd never leave. And leaving was the best thing he could do for her.

"You stayed because of me. Because of Isaac. And Nick, God, I wanted you to. I never even called to find out how the Parish Council meeting went. I was too busy—" She stopped, a stricken look on her face.

"With me."

She nodded, a hand over her mouth.

He understood that sick feeling, because he'd forgotten everything, too. Rennie, the world beyond this cabin.

Enmeshed in each other, they'd ignored it all, and now he had to make amends.

He shoved the .44 into the front of his jeans, slung the Uzi over his shoulder, and headed for the door. She sped ahead of him, barring the way, her face desperate.

"We can run. There has to be some place he can't find us."

"You know that's not true."

The knowledge was there in her eyes, but she balked anyway, pale and wretched.

He hardened his voice. "Get out of the way."

"Please, Nick."

"Get away from the goddamn door! Jesus, don't make me force you."

"Go ahead, force me. You think I'm going to make this easy for you?" Her eyes blazed with the sheen of tears. "You want me to beg, I'll beg. I'll do whatever it takes to keep you from walking out this door."

Christ, he wished he were made of stone. Without another word, he grabbed her arm, jerked her away from the door, opened it, and plunged through.

Rachel gasped when he shoved her aside so easily. A sob broke free, and then she ran out the door after him. "Wait! Nick, please. Oh God, wait!"

But he ignored her, tramping into the moonlit night. She darted after him, running over the rough ground and crying so hard she stumbled, lost her footing, and went sprawling face first in the sand. God, she was pathetic. It was just like then, just like all the times she ran after her father, begging him, pleading with him to stay. He never did. Now Nick was going, and she couldn't bear it. She scrambled to her feet, but by then, he was almost at the

VW. Panting, sobbing, she flew ahead, catching up just as he opened the door and threw the guns inside. She didn't waste a minute but flung herself at him, holding onto him with every ounce she had. "Please, Nick, please. I love you. Don't go."

For a moment, he stopped breathing. Then, as if she hadn't spoken, he reached up and untwined her arms from around his neck.

"Did you hear me? I said I love you."

Freed, he turned away, staring over the top of her father's car. "I love you, too." His voice sounded sad, sadder than anything she'd ever heard. "I've loved you from the minute I saw you standing in the yard at St. Anthony's."

She knew that. She'd known that all along. She sniffed and wiped her face with the back of her hand. "So you'll stay?"

He turned and looked at her, his eyes soft, dark pieces of night. "No."

Oh, God. Tears ran freely again, hot and thick. She swiped at them, but they kept coming. "T-take me with you, then."

He smiled, and for the first time since she'd told him about the printout, he touched her with gentleness, his hand cupping her cheek sweetly. "I need you to stay here, with Isaac."

Isaac. His son. She uttered a broken sound, half sob, half protest, and slowly he pulled her toward him until she was enveloped in his arms. "Will you do that for me? Will you stay with him and make sure he's okay?"

Her head lay against his chest. She could feel the hard

thump of his heart. *Not without you.* She closed her eyes and nodded.

His hand stroked the back of her head. "Thanks."

"Promise me you'll come back," she whispered.

He hesitated and she clenched her hands into fists, hitting his back with desperate fierceness. "Promise me."

"I . . . I promise."

"Not like my father."

Instead of answering, he kissed her forehead, her cheek, and her mouth. She bit back a sob at the touch of his lips. One last look, and he slid behind the wheel. The car door slammed shut, the sound echoing through all the years of her childhood. She sank to her knees, sobbing. Once again she watched as taillights disappeared into the darkness.

Chapter 18

Rachel didn't know how long she stayed outside. Long enough to hear the endless sound of waves overtake the noise of the car engine that took Nick away.

Stiff and exhausted, she dragged herself to her feet, eyes swollen and gritty from crying, and trudged back to the cabin. Without Nick, the room seemed bigger, emptier.

Like her life.

He'd left a cabinet door open, and she reached up to close it, but her hand stopped in mid-task. Inside lay a gun he'd left behind.

She stared at the thing. What had he called it?

It's a Ruger, she heard his voice say so many days ago. *Mark II model.*

A Ruger.

This was what had taken him away. This lethal piece of steel. A tear trickled down her cheek and she swiped at it angrily. Damn you, Nick Raine. Damn you and Rennie Spier and your whole sick, violent world.

She closed the door on the weapon.

Just then, Isaac whimpered in his sleep. Turning her back on the cabinet and its deadly contents, she slipped into his room. He'd kicked off his covers and lay on top of the sheets, a dark little angel in a too-big bed. She covered him up, retucking his bear beside him.

Sleep, baby. Sleep hard and long, and maybe by the time you wake up, your daddy will be back.

But even as she thought it, she knew Nick wasn't coming back. Not to Isaac, and not to her.

She sank onto the bed, wanting desperately to believe in Nick's promise. But even if he did come back, he would never be the same. If he killed again, it would haunt him forever.

She lay down beside Isaac, needing the comfort of his warmth, the closeness of his presence. Somehow, it seemed to bring her nearer to everything that mattered. Especially to Nick. She curled up around the boy and, shutting her eyes, let darkness take her.

She awoke with a start, and for a minute thought Nick was beside her. Then she realized the body beside her was too small. She was inside the cabin, not out on the beach, and Nick was gone.

Gone. The word held endless heartache.

She thought of the child sleeping next to her. How could she tell him that one more person had "gone away"? She sat up. At least he had a few more hours of peace. He wouldn't have to know his father had left him for a while yet. She slid off the bed and tiptoed to the door.

Closing it behind her, she stared at the beat-up couch and tiny kitchenette that had become her world. A world where all she could do was wait.

How long had she been sleeping?

Nick had taken his watch, and they had no clock, so she had no idea how much time had passed. She opened the cabin door, hoping to get some sense of the time by looking at the height of the rising sun or the color of the sky.

The first thing she saw was the car.

A car she'd never seen. Where no car had ever been before.

Oh, God.

A rapid step back, and she slammed both the screen and wooden doors behind her. She leaned heavily against them, as if her weight could somehow block out the vehicle's existence. What did it mean?

Nothing. It meant nothing. Just some early-morning tourist, stopping to gaze at the picturesque sight of the lonely cabin.

But almost as quickly as that explanation flitted through, another sank inside her with the heaviness of stone.

Rennie had found them.

Slumping against the door in a sudden wash of fatigue, she blinked away tears. She could not, she just could not deal with any more.

Then don't. She was making herself crazy anyway. It was only a car, for God's sake. Nothing more sinister than that.

But still, she locked the front door. And just to make sure, she pushed and pulled the sofa until it was tight

against the door. Then she clambered up on the kitchenette counter and peeked out the window high up in the
wall.

The car still sat there, waiting like a vulture.

Who was it? Who the hell was out there?

Should she wake Isaac and try to leave? But the only
exit was through the front door. And that would lead
right into the path of the car and whoever was in it.

She closed her eyes and leaned her head against the
wall, her options crumbling. No choice. She had no
choice. Jumping down, she faced the cabinets. With a
deep, deep breath, she opened the one that hid the Ruger.

You don't have to use it. The car was probably nothing anyway. But just in case, she picked up the gun with
a trembling hand and turned it over in her palm. Was this
the safety? She was still trying to remember what Nick
had shown her when the knock came.

She started, and the gun flew out of her hand, landing
with a metallic crash on the floor. *Oh, God.*

"Nick! Nick Raine!"

Shuddering uncontrollably, she scrambled to retrieve
the weapon.

Whoever was out there rattled the doorknob. "Are
you in there, Nicky?" He tried pulling the door. "Let me
in! Open the door!" He started pounding, such fierce,
deafening blows they should have awakened the dead.

A heavy weight slammed against the door.

Once.

Twice.

And a third time.

Rachel's hands shook like an earthquake. Slowly, she
raised the gun.

God, please keep Isaac asleep.

Please let this be the safety.

Please . . .

A loud splintering cracked the stillness. Clutching the Ruger tighter, she faced the door and dug her feet in.

The man burst through. She squeezed the trigger.

Nick sped over the causeway separating the island from the mainland. Slung low, the road hovered over the ocean, water gleaming black and fathomless on either side. If he hadn't had things to do, he would have run the car right over the edge, drowning himself and the last reminder of David Goodman.

Christ. As long as he lived, he would never forget the look on Rachel's face when he got into her father's battered old Beetle and drove away.

His hands tensed on the steering wheel. *She loves you.*

Fat lot of good it's done her.

His throat tightened, and for a minute he let his guard down, let himself think about the miracle of her love, the secret light in his heart of darkness.

But it only made him want to turn around and head back to her. So he gripped the wheel and toughened himself, remembering only that his love had brought her suffering, and staying would bring her more. Gaze fixed on the road, he headed north, sure of what he had to do. Rachel and Isaac would never be safe otherwise. And keeping them safe was all that mattered.

The sun was just starting to rise by the time he arrived at Gramercy Park and the refurbished warehouse that harbored Rennie's empire. Nick knew the four-square block around the park intimately. He had seen it in the shadow of dawn, as now, and in the bright light of day. When he was younger, he would walk around each street, counting doors and wondering whether the people behind them could possibly lead lives as fantastic and amazing as his own.

He could barely believe he'd been so naive.

As he drove past, he stared through the park's wrought-iron bars to the neat bushes and well-groomed paths. He remembered Rennie opening the gate with his owner's key, the two of them sitting on one of those benches to feed the pigeons. He saw the ghost of himself, thirteen or fourteen, so jazzed up with new clothes and hundred-dollar sneakers that sitting like an old lump on a bench and tossing stale bread to a bunch of birds was the last thing he wanted to do. But he'd returned with Rennie again and again, and after a while it began to seem less like the price Rennie exacted for whatever he had bought Nick that day. Until finally, weeks later— God, was it only weeks?—Nick had looked forward to the park, to the smell of grass and the sound of the birds fluttering at his feet.

And the sound of Rennie's deep, strangely accented voice.

Nick saw them then, two whispering forms on the bench. Fagin and his Artful Dodger. It seemed as if the mesmerizing sound of Rennie's voice floated over the iron fence like snake charmer's music. *If you are smart, if you pay attention and concentrate, you will see the world . . . places you have not even dreamed about yet. And you will be rich, richer than anything you could ever imagine.*

Nick stopped the car. He closed his eyes, the picture

of his younger self burned in his brain. Rennie should have killed him that first day in the kitchen. He should have let Frank pull the trigger on that old Luger when he'd had the chance twenty years ago.

But Rennie had chosen life, and Nick had thrived. He'd fed on excitement and drunk in power. Every promise Rennie ever made had come true.

And now it was time to pay him back.

Nick eyed the front of the building, steeling himself for what lay ahead. Part of him, the part that remembered the street kid he'd been before Rennie found him, that part wanted to walk away and forget all about Rennie Spier.

But that would leave Isaac and Rachel unprotected.

Leaning his head against the back of the seat, he drew the Uzi up to his chest. His fingers drifted over the shape of the weapon, its form hard and unyielding and as familiar as his own: stock, grip, trigger, magazine, barrel, sight, muzzle. He knew every detail; at 1,300 rounds per minute, it would take only two seconds to empty a 32-round magazine.

Slowly, Nick loosened his grip on the gun. He'd been holding it so tightly, his fingers had cramped up. He opened and closed his hand to get the blood flowing again, thinking about Rachel and Isaac, and the brief dream he'd had of them together. She would take the boy. If he could keep them alive, if he could make one last deal, she would shelter his son and keep him safe.

He watched the sun make its slow, bright journey up. How many men did Rennie have inside?

Enough to cut him down before he drew a last breath.

No, he couldn't go in shooting. He'd have to go in

clean, and hope he stayed alive long enough to lure Rennie out.

Stashing the submachine gun underneath the seat and the Magnum in the glove compartment, Nick opened the door and walked toward the brownstone. Rising light glinted off something on one of the rooftops. The sun striking a corner of a building, or the gleam of a rifle scope?

Just in case, he came forward slowly, letting them get a nice, long look. Carefully, he raised his arms and placed both hands on top of his head. At the door, he turned around, so they could see he had no weapons at his back either.

The elevator was waiting for him. He stepped inside and watched the descent, hands pressed tight against the glass.

Frank stood at the bottom with a 9mm Glock clenched in his fist. Face tight, he shoved Nick ahead of him, through the courtyard and into a corridor. Every few feet, a gauntlet of armed men silently guarded the way. Nick stopped counting after twenty.

Expecting Frank to lead him to the SATCO elevator, he was mildly surprised when they passed it by, leaving the armada behind.

"Where are we going?"

"You'll see." The Glock jabbed Nick in the back, pushing him forward.

Bastard. He whipped around. "Why don't you give me a hint?"

Frank drove the gun into the side of Nick's mouth. "You always were a real wise guy with a smartass mouth. I should have wiped it off your face years ago, when I first found out you were screwing that little tramp."

Nick went cold. So Frank *had* known. "You didn't tell Rennie."

"And break his heart? I don't think so. Besides, he wouldn't have believed me anyway. His golden boy a traitor? If I hadn't seen the two of you with my own eyes, I wouldn't have believed it myself."

"You saw us?"

"Why else do you think I told Rennie to send you to Panama? I had to get you out of the house before the whole thing with Shelley blew up in our faces." He leaned in closer. "But it blew up anyway, didn't it, Nicky? Didn't it?" He rammed the gun tight against Nick's jaw.

Needles of panic shot through Nick's chest, but he fought them back. "You going to shoot me, and rob Rennie of the pleasure?"

Frank loosed his grip. "He loved you like a son."

"No. He just used me."

"And you paid him back, didn't you?" Frank gave him another brutal shove. "I hope you get everything you deserve."

Nick stumbled down the corridor, giving himself time to think. The wasteland of the last six years, the death toll that kept rising—it hadn't started in Panama, as he used to think. It all started with Shelley and his uncontrollable desire for her. If he hadn't slept with her, if he hadn't chosen faithlessness over fidelity, none of the rest would have happened. Call it suicide or revenge, as Rachel and Frank had, or call it lust, the name Nick gave to it, the end was the same. From the man in Panama and the nameless boy in the alley to Shelley, Martin, and now Felice, the deaths unfurled like a red carpet that ended at his feet.

Frank was right. Nick deserved everything he had coming.

They turned a corner, and now he knew where they were heading. The kitchen. Frank was taking him to the kitchen. He laughed to himself. His life with Rennie had begun in the kitchen. Fitting it should end there.

Rennie stood alone at the center of the gleaming room. Impeccably dressed in a dark suit, he looked as strong and potent as ever. His thick white hair slanted fiercely back from his forehead, and his eyes had a chilly blue clarity to them. Even the lines on his face, the slight sag of his chin—these signs of experience and age—added to the aura.

One look, and Nick was breathing faster, but he met Rennie's gaze with a level one of his own. All Nick had to do was stay alive long enough.

"No helpers today?" He didn't bother hiding his sarcasm.

"Some things are best handled personally," Rennie said.

"It's been a long time since you got involved so intimately."

"I assure you, my skills are as sharp as ever."

Their gazes locked, a moment of acknowledgment. Before this was over, one of them would die.

Then Rennie gave Nick a thin smile, and gestured him forward. Frank prodded him with the gun until Nick stood beside a stainless steel prep table, a few feet from Rennie. Frank shoved him into a chair and jerked his arms backward over the table, tying his hands to a chair on the other side. The cold of the steel bit into him, the tabletop hard and unforgiving.

Rennie watched dispassionately. "When I was younger, I was caught running guns into Algeria. This is a trick the French taught me. They call it the Little Rack."

Taut and imprisoned, Nick's arms and shoulders stretched backward at an excruciating angle. Rennie leaned a hip against the table edge and stroked a hand down Nick's head, gently at first, then firmer until he gripped the back of his neck. Rennie exerted just the slightest pressure, but the move pushed Nick's body forward and tightened the pull between his already aching shoulders and arms. A gasp of pain hissed from between his teeth.

Rennie smiled. "You should not have used those phony papers from the school and put so many innocent people at risk. I was surprised, it isn't like you."

Nick's jaw tightened, but he said nothing, accepting the blame to avoid exposing Rachel.

Rennie looked amused. "Are you angry, Nick?"

Angry didn't begin to cover it.

Rennie backhanded him across the mouth. "Are you angry?"

"Yeah." He tasted the metallic wash of blood. "Yeah, I'm angry."

Rennie spread his hands in a gesture of disbelief. "But what do you have to be angry about? Has someone you trusted betrayed you? Has someone you gave the world to thrown it back in your face and tried to ruin you?" He didn't wait for an answer, but moved closer, leaning in.

His voice hardened. "Now that I've discovered your little deception, where are the rest of my documents?"

Nick remained silent, calculating how long he could hold the older man at bay.

"Where are they?" Rennie pushed Nick's shoulders forward, and he screamed in pain. "The papers, Nick. And Miss Goodman and the boy. Where have you hidden them?"

"I'm not going to tell you that, and you know it."

Rennie moved faster than Nick thought humanly possible. He didn't even see where the knife came from. One minute he was whole, the next Rennie's stiletto sliced through Nick's cheek close to his ear.

Another scream ripped through him, and Rennie smashed him hard across the mouth again. "Where are they?"

Jesus. Nick couldn't move without creating more agony for himself. "I'm not going to tell you, Rennie." His voice sounded hoarse and papery, but he managed to keep it steady. "If that's what you're after, you might as well kill me now and get it over with."

"Ah, I see." Rennie's smile was ghastly. "A noble sacrifice. How very like you. But no, I do not think we will kill you so fast. We have hours of enjoyment ahead of us. Isn't that right, Frank?"

"We know they're on the Jersey shore," Frank said from somewhere behind Nick. "Your girlfriend called her uncle yesterday, and we traced it to a phone booth on Long Beach Island. I got men out there now. They'll find her and the kid eventually. Why not spare yourself all this mess and tell us where they are?"

Panic overrode the pain. Rachel hadn't said a thing

about a phone call. Christ. If they found Rachel and Isaac before he could . . . No, stick to the plan. Just stick to the plan. "I can't do that, Frank."

Rennie sighed and signaled Frank to push Nick's head forward. Frank complied with a shove that almost separated Nick's arms from his shoulders. He screamed in agony, and Rennie clamped his hand around Nick's throat, forcing his head up. The stiletto was now an inch closer to Nick's eye; if he wanted to, he could have seen the blurred outline of the thin, sharp tip. Sweat poured down his back and his muscles tensed, but Rennie only traced a line down the side of Nick's face with the flat of his blade.

"Do you believe in love, Nicky?" He trailed back up Nick's cheek, the knife moving closer to his eye. "They say love comes from Cupid's bow, but I think love is more like a knife than an arrow. Love is a weapon you hold in your hand. One that stabs and wounds. Close. Intimate." The knife reached the corner of his eye and stopped. "You're a bigger fool than I thought if you are doing this for love."

Nick met Rennie's gaze, treacherous as deep water. "Fuck off."

The older man slashed downward, cutting through Nick's brow and slicing off a piece of his ear.

They played with him like that for what seemed like an eternity, and Nick held out long enough to make it real, but not so long that they had time to find Rachel and Isaac.

Unless they already had.

He pushed that thought away, concentrating on staying alive another few minutes.

"So. Are you ready to tell us what we want to know?" Rennie pushed him forward again, stretching his arms to the point of breaking.

He groaned. "I'll . . . make you a deal."

"No more deals, Nicky."

"The papers are gone. Burned in the fire. But I found another copy of the books. Let Rachel and the boy go and you can have it."

Rennie laughed. "You think I am an idiot? You have nothing. Just time enough for us to find your girl. For me to do to you what you did to me. Only I'll make you watch."

Nick struggled to keep his voice from shaking. "No, you'll let her go, and the boy. You don't want to take the risk."

Rennie looked at him sadly. "You could have been the best there is, Nicky. I would have given you everything. But you took from me. From *me*." Anguish and outrage warred in Rennie's voice before it became deadly again. "And now I'm going to take from you."

Nick gathered the last vestiges of his strength. "You want to take from me, you take from me, old man. Not them. Me. You want to cut me up a piece at a time, cut off my balls, my head, I'll let you do whatever sick little thing you want. I'll crawl for you, Rennie, and maybe even deserve it, but first you have to let them go."

"Let me shoot him right now and put an end to this," Frank said.

"Go ahead." Nick's voice was weary. "You think I care? Christ, it would be a relief." He looked at Rennie, keeping himself from passing out by sheer force of will. "So . . . do we have a deal?"

Rennie studied him. It was all Nick could do to return the other man's stare.

"All right," Rennie said at last. "Tell me about this"— he waved a disbelieving hand in front of Nick's face— "this copy you say you have."

A tiny bud of hope flowered. "It was in the kid's knapsack. Your men didn't find the kid's things when they searched the fish plant, did they?"

Rennie looked at him skeptically and squeezed the mangled mess of Nick's ear.

He grit his teeth, hissing through the pain. "A hidden pocket . . . concealed a computer disk. It goes to . . . the *New York Times* in twenty-four hours. Twenty hours—" he amended, checking the clock above one of the stainless steel sinks. It was nine-fifteen. God, he'd been here almost five hours. He only hoped it was long enough.

"Where is it?"

Nick shook his head. "I'll take you to it. You'd kill me right now if I told you."

He felt rather than saw the wordless conference between Frank and Rennie. Closing his eyes, he leaned as far back over the steel table as he could, searching for an infinitesimal moment of relief that the tiniest shift in position would give his tortured shoulders.

He heard Frank speak. "We can always finish him off later."

Chapter 19

Rachel fired the gun again. The intruder dove behind the couch.

"For the love of God, don't shoot!"

Rachel ignored him and squeezed off another round. Like the other two, the bullet went wide, this time smashing into the wall to the right of the ruined door.

Then the bedroom door opened, and Isaac stumbled out. "Rachel!"

"Get back in the bedroom, Isaac! Don't come out, do you hear me?"

But the distraction was all the man needed. Without even knowing how he did it, Rachel found herself thrown to the floor, a knee in her back, her gun hand wrenched behind her, and the weapon yanked out of her hand.

That's when Isaac began to scream—high, earsplitting sounds so full of unhinged terror, they sent shivers down Rachel's spine. They worked on the man, too, because almost immediately, he released his hold.

"Go!" he yelled over the awful shrieks. "Go to him."

She rushed to the doorway, where Isaac stood frozen, his eyes closed and his mouth open in rigid horror. The minute she touched him, he fought like a demon, and impossibly, his screams intensified.

"Hush, baby, it's me. It's all right. I'm all right."

But he didn't hear or even notice her.

"Oh Isaac, please. Please open your eyes. It's me, everything is all right." She managed to contain his flailing arms and began to croon, rocking him tightly against her breast. His terrible sounds drowned out her voice, but slowly, gradually, she made headway. In a few minutes the screaming lessened in intensity. A few more, and Isaac opened his eyes.

When he saw the man, his voice started to rise again, but Rachel quickly took him into the bedroom and closed the door. The stranger made no protest, but that didn't stop her heart from pounding. As she rocked and gentled Isaac, all she could think about was the man in the next room, who was now armed with her gun.

"Hush, baby, shh. It's all right. I'm right here, I've got you. I won't let you go."

She held him until he fell asleep in her arms, but when she put him back to bed, he awoke and clung desperately to her.

"It's okay, I won't leave you. Shh, close your eyes now. That's right." She held him against her until he was sound asleep; then, holding him in her arms, she opened the door a crack and peeked through.

The man had pushed the couch away from the door

and was sitting on it, elbows on his knees, head down. Lean and wiry, he looked to be in his late forties, dressed casually in khakis and a windbreaker. Not exactly the Rennie Spier uniform. Then again, maybe he was a hired hand—a day man, Nick had called it.

She bit her lip, wishing there was a window, a secret door, anything that would make escape possible. But unless she wanted to stay in the bedroom for the rest of her life, she had no choice but to go out there. Heart pounding, she opened the door a little wider and stepped out.

The man jumped up, "Here, sit down. The boy must be heavy."

Keeping a vigilant eye on the stranger, she settled into one corner of the couch while he sat on the opposite arm. She began to notice other things about him, like the intelligence in his green eyes and the Irish lilt in his voice.

"Didn't mean to scare you," he said with an apologetic smile. "Just didn't see how we could talk if you kept on shooting at me."

She saw the amusement in his eyes and ignored it, looking at him darkly, suspicion rife in her mind. "Did Rennie Spier send you?"

The man's brows rose in surprise. "No. My name is Danny Walsh. I'm a friend of Nicky's."

"A f-friend of Nick's." She heard the uneasy quiver in her voice.

"I arranged for the house." He waved an arm, gesturing around the room. "Not exactly up to Nicky's usual, but suitable. I trust it's been useful."

"*You* arranged this house?"

"Nick met me about a week ago and said he needed a safe house. He mentioned a child."

Rachel thought back. The day she and Nick left the preschool to get Isaac, Nick had said he'd seen a friend. Had it been this man?

He looked down at the boy sleeping in her arms, and she followed his gaze. Isaac's face was tearstained and hot. Strands of black hair stuck to his forehead. Danny lifted his eyes and met Rachel's. He seemed to ask for an explanation, but she offered none. Instead, she said bluntly, "Who are you, Mr. Walsh?"

"Like I said, an old friend of Nick's." He looked around the room. "Where is he? I've got to talk to him. Been trying the phone for days, but no one answered."

"We unplugged it."

He nodded thoughtfully. "You unplug the phone, you greet callers with a gun." Danny gave her a long, serious look. "What kind of trouble are you in? Does it have anything to do with the shipment?"

"What shipment?"

Danny sighed and stood, pacing the small room. "Look, Miss—"

Rachel hesitated, not sure if even giving her name might be dangerous. But if Rennie Spier had sent this man, surely he would have known who she was. Suddenly relief washed through her that was so profound, tears came to her eyes. She quickly blinked them away. This man was Nick's friend, not Rennie's.

"Goodman. Rachel Goodman. Please, call me Rachel."

He pursed his lips. "Rachel . . . Isaac. Quite a biblical collection you've got here. We Irish always have our nose out for the hand of God." He winked at her, and she could see he was trying to put her at ease.

"You're Irish?"

"Used to buy little sundries for the IRA, which is how I met Nicky. I'm working for the peace now. When Nick asked me to help him find a safe place, I'm guessing for you and the boy, he traded some information about an arms shipment to the Irish Liberation Council. Maybe you've seen the news reports."

Rachel nodded. In spite of their isolation, she would have had to be deaf as well as blind not to know about the spectacular capture of that floating munitions dump. Nick had been responsible for that?

"The ship was very important to a broad coalition of Irish terror groups who're against the peace in Northern Ireland. Those arms would've blasted the provisional government into smithereens and set us back years. But the people who paid for them, well, this has been a great blow." He sat back down and steepled his hands. "These people don't take kindly to traitors. There's already talk about blaming the loss of the arms on the shipper."

Her mind was whirling. "The . . . the shipper?"

He spoke quietly, as if he thought it best to break this next bit of information to her slowly. "That information could only have come to us through someone on the inside."

"I see." She began to tremble all over again.

"Of course, they can't know exactly who it was. I've never used Nick's name. But it isn't hard to figure out it must be someone in Spier's organization. Somehow, somewhere, they'll take revenge on Rennie Spier. We're already hearing the rumors. Nick and I—well, I've known the lad since he was seventeen, bright and shiny as a new penny. I'd like to warn him."

Rachel looked blindly into the room. When was it going to end? When would their lives become normal again?

God, she couldn't breathe. Isaac's hot, sweaty body and the tiny, windowless cabin were smothering her. Gently she disengaged herself from the boy, and though he snuffled in sleep, he didn't wake.

She crossed to the door and, as she opened it, saw the bullet holes she'd put there. Her hand began to shake, and she quickly stepped outside where the day was bright and clear. The cool morning air tingled on her face. She closed her eyes, inhaling the sharp scent of the ocean.

"Are you all right, girl?" Danny put a gentle hand on her shoulder, and she gave him a shaky laugh.

"If terrified and scared to death qualify as all right, I guess I am."

"If I can get to Nicky, I can help."

She looked down the dirt path to the car at the end. Her earlier fear of it seemed silly now.

"He took the car, so Isaac and I are stranded. If I tell you where he is, will you take us with you?"

"Of course," Danny Walsh said. "Anywhere you want to go."

So once again Rachel found herself huddled against Isaac in the backseat of a car. The drive was shorter this time. Danny wasn't worried about being tailed and took the most direct route. Even so, the trip seemed to take an eternity. For a little while he tried to amuse them with stories of Nick, but all the tales inevitably ended in drunken carousing, which was inappropriate for a six-year-old.

Eventually they drifted into silence. Isaac fell asleep, but Rachel woke him when he began to jerk and whimper. He didn't ask about Nick, only observing once that he had gone away.

"Yes," Rachel said, "but he'll be back. We'll see him in a little while."

Isaac didn't respond, and she knew he didn't believe her. She couldn't blame him; she hardly believed it herself.

The clock on Danny's dashboard read nine-thirty by the time they reached Spier's headquarters. She'd spent half the ride scraping at her wrists, the other half with her hands gripped into such tight fists, her nails had gouged out half-moon craters in her palms.

"Oh, God, there's the car." She pointed across the park to the familiar shape of the VW. "The old-fashioned Beetle. It's mine. Nick took it last night."

"Good. He's here, then."

Danny insisted she stay in the car while he went in, and if it hadn't been for Isaac, she would have ignored him. But she couldn't leave the sleeping child alone. Torn between protecting the boy and her own intense desire to see Nick alive with his soul intact and no more deaths on his conscience, she stared out the car's windshield until her eyes burned. Danny jogged toward a building whose entrance in the middle of the block was the only one on that street.

Frank's gun was a pitiless escort at the back of Nick's neck. He stumbled through the underground tunnel to the garage where the limousine was parked, his hands still tied behind his back. Beside him, Spier marched in silence. No one said a word. No one had to.

When they arrived at the limousine, Frank opened the passenger door and pushed Nick toward it. "Get in."

But Nick shook his head and turned to face Rennie. "I do the driving."

Spier eyed him with suspicion. "What difference does it make who drives?"

Nick clamped down on the throbbing pain in his shoulder and the burn of the gashes in his face, neck, and chest. "You want the disk, I drive. Otherwise, kill me now and see what the press does with the information."

Rennie's jaw clenched. His gaze flicked to Frank, who shrugged, and then back to Nick. Doubt turned to certainty in the older man's eyes.

"No. This is some kind of trick. I know you, Nicky."

A hot dart of panic stabbed Nick at the truth of Rennie's words. *You know me too well, old man.* But he schooled his face to show nothing. "And I know you. I let Frank drive, he could take me anywhere and put a bullet in my brain. No thanks. This is my deal. I'm in control. I drive."

Rennie scowled. Nick could see he was only half convinced. Despair almost pulled Nick under. His arms were weak and shaky, his brain fuzzed with the effort of staying upright. *Focus. Clear your goddamn head.* He had to get control of the car. Everything was wasted otherwise.

An eternity passed while Rennie's gaze bored into Nick. Then the stiletto was under Nick's chin again, pushing back his head and drawing blood. "All right. But travel under the speed limit. And Frank sits in front, his gun on you every minute."

"He can bring a cannon for all I care."

"You make any kind of crazy move, and Frank will grab the wheel. You'll be dead before you can blink."

"I'll keep that in mind."

Rennie released him and sliced through the thongs binding Nick's hands. Massaging the places where sweat had rubbed his wrists raw, he let out the breath he'd been holding.

Frank grumbled, but eased around the front and settled into the passenger seat while Rennie got in the back. Nick slid into the driver's seat, and as his hands touched the steering wheel, a great calm settled over him. Down the long, dim drive to the exit Nick kept his mind on the low bridge connecting the mainland to Long Beach Island. The causeway skimmed the surface of the water. All he had to do was gun the engine and spin the wheel. The limo would crash through the railing and plunge into the water.

Too well. You know me too well.

Frank was a problem, but Nick could handle him. He had to. Everyone depended on him, and this time he'd get it right. He pictured Rachel's face laughing in the moonlight. He remembered the feel of Isaac's small hand.

Keep them safe.

The only way to do that was to see Rennie dead. And if that meant Nick died too, well, he'd protect those he loved and clear his own debt at the same time.

At the garage entrance, he waited calmly for traffic to clear, then pulled into the street. Rachel had said she saw the good in him; for the first time he felt a glimmer of it.

*   *   *

Through the windshield, Rachel watched Danny Walsh climb the steps of the building that housed Rennie Spier's empire. A converted warehouse, Danny had told her, it was surrounded by streets filled with gentle brownstones, elegant wrought-iron railings, and graceful urns filled with ivy and pink geraniums. A pot of flowers added a splash of red to Spier's exterior too, making it blend well with the mannerly neighborhood. But she shivered at what the building hid inside.

Tense with anticipation, she clutched her wrist in a death grip as Danny reached the door. Just as he put his hand on the knob, a limousine turned the corner.

The car curved around in slow, stately progression, and Rachel had plenty of time to recognize it from the preschool. The driver's side was closest to her, and the window was down. She caught a glimpse of a dark head behind the wheel, someone else beside him. Was that Nick driving? Hope made her heart leap.

The black beast of a car halted halfway into its turn as if the driver had caught sight of something. Danny, perhaps? Unable to stop herself, Rachel bounded out of Danny's car and ran toward the limousine.

"Nick!"

The head turned toward her. It *was* Nick. And he'd seen her. Happiness swelled into her chest. He was alive. Alive!

"Rachel! Stay in the car," Danny called to her from the entrance.

For an instant, she looked away from the limo toward Danny.

Her mouth opened; she intended to reply.

But before she could, the world exploded into flames.

*　　　*　　　*

Rachel remembered very little of the blast. Not the sting of flying glass, the fiery heat, the deafening roar. She didn't remember the impact flinging her backward or Danny dragging her away when she tried to hurtle toward the burning limo with some desperate thought of saving Nick. All this she found out later, when she woke in the motel with Isaac. The cuts on her face, the smell of flames on her clothes, the bruise on her shoulder from the force of the blast that knocked her down—these were the only proof that Nick was dead.

She stared at Danny dully as he repeated the words hours later in the motel room.

"No. It's not true."

"You saw it with your own eyes."

Inside her head, the car blew up in achingly slow motion. She quashed the pictures, refusing to believe them. "I don't care."

"Rachel—"

"I want to see his body."

"You can't. The people who did this are still out there. It's not safe."

"I don't care!" She rushed headlong to the door, but Danny pulled her back. "You can't just be thinking of yourself, Rachel. There's the boy, too." He glanced over to the corner where Isaac's small dark form huddled into a chair. But she barely noticed the child.

"I won't let you keep me here," she said, her voice rising wildly.

"I'm sorry."

She whirled away from him and collapsed into a chair, sobbing again. Beneath the gulping, soul-sickened noise she was making, she heard the sound of Danny's voice on the phone again.

He'd been on the goddamn phone ever since he'd whisked her away from . . . from . . . She closed her eyes. God, she couldn't even *think* the words, let alone say them aloud.

A small hand slipped into hers. Looking up, she saw the dark, heart-shaped face of Nick's son. Panic filled his eyes; a worried frown creased his brow. She had forgotten all about him. If Danny hadn't stopped her, she would have left Isaac behind, and broken her promise to Nick.

"I'm sorry," she said in a broken voice. "I didn't mean to scare you." She swept him into her lap, brushing the hair away from his face. He wrapped his arms around her neck, and she held him tight.

They spent the night in the motel, and the next day Danny drove them to another, this one near Atlantic City. Two days later, he sent a car with "Francie's Flowers" painted on the side to take them to a run-down apartment building outside Philadelphia.

For the next few months Danny shuffled them up and down the East Coast. Gradually, Rachel stopped asking where they were going. She stopped caring.

She slept a lot. Sometimes whole days passed in sleep. When she woke, the TV was always blaring in the background, and Isaac was always watching her. With his dark eyes so similar to Nick's, it hurt to look at him. As her father had, she wanted to turn her back on every reminder. But unlike her father, she couldn't palm Isaac off on relatives. She was all he had left, and she wouldn't desert him. She helped him dress, packed their meager belongings, and trudged into the next vehicle, the next motel room—all the while hemorrhaging on the inside.

One evening, a knock sounded on the motel door. *Don't answer it. If you answer it, you'll have to wake up.*

The knock came again, and Isaac called, "Who is it?"

"Someone order a pizza?" A voice through the door.

Pizza. Her stomach turned over. She could hardly remember what real food tasted like. Only greasy hamburgers. And pizza.

She raised heavy eyelids and saw Isaac drag a chair over to the door, climb up, and peek through the peephole, like she'd taught him.

"Just a minute," he said through the closed door.

She watched from a distance, as if she were the audience and the child a movie. He found her purse, opened it, and took out some money. He didn't ask if he had enough; he seemed to know the correct amount. No surprise, given the number of pizzas they'd ordered and the way he observed her every move. He forced the bills through the slit under the door.

"Leave it outside," he said.

"Are you all right, kid?" The deliveryman's voice sounded uneasy, even through the door. "Is your . . . is someone with you? A grown-up?"

"My mom is resting," Isaac said. "Just leave the pizza and go."

He watched through the peephole, then climbed down off the chair, opened the door, and retrieved the box. It was bigger than he was. Balancing it carefully, he laid it at the foot of the bed and struggled with the hot pie inside. Finally, he freed up a slice and offered it to Rachel.

Her heart squeezed. She should be taking care of him, not the other way around.

She sat up. Isaac put the pizza in her hand and turned to get his own dinner. He sat down beside her and saw she hadn't taken a bite.

"Aren't you hungry?"

Emotion closed her throat so she couldn't speak.

He looked down at his lap. "Don't be sad anymore. It doesn't help. Everyone goes away anyway."

He was right. Everyone she'd ever loved had abandoned her. Her mother, her father, Nick. Whether they had a choice about it or not, the result was the same. She was alone.

Isaac leaned against her arm, and she looked down at him. Not quite alone. Not this time.

She slipped her arm around him. "You told that man I was your mom."

He looked up at her with Nick's dark intensity. "Will you be? Until . . . until you go away?"

God, she couldn't even look at him without hurting. But she couldn't refuse him, either. He needed her. And maybe she needed him.

Isaac wasn't the only thing that pulled her toward life again. Her own body was making demands, demands she tried hard to ignore. But by Halloween she was sure.

They were somewhere in Delaware, just north of Wilmington, when the inevitable move came. Rachel refused to go. She sat next to the pumpkin outside the motel office and pulled Isaac into her lap, telling the driver she wouldn't budge until he called Danny Walsh and arranged a meeting with him.

Danny was there the next day, and he was furious.

"What's this, Rachel? I canceled some very important meetings to come down here, only to find that you're fine, the little lad is fine, everyone's fine."

"I want to go home."

He turned away, throwing up his hands in exasperation. "Mother of God, she wants to go home," he muttered. Then turning back to her he shouted, "Do you think this is a vacation? You can't just cancel your reservations and walk away."

"We can't stay like this forever! If I eat one more french fry I'll turn into one. We live like roaches in the dark, scurrying from one motel room to another. Isaac should start school. He needs to be around other children."

"We've been through this, Rachel. You agreed to let me protect you."

"Not for the rest of my life. It's been three months. Surely by now everything is all right. And if it isn't . . . I'm just going to have to take that risk."

"You don't have to be taking chances. Just a few more weeks, and I'm sure we'll have things under control."

"I'm sorry, but no. We can't do this anymore. If you won't help me, I'll leave by myself."

Danny sighed and ran a hand through his thinning hair. "This is crazy, and you know it. Get your things and I'll take you to the next—"

"I'm pregnant."

"You're what?" He looked at her as if she'd grown another head.

"I'm not having Nick's baby in some mangy hotel room. I'm going home. With or without your help."

He sank down on the lumpy bed. Propping an elbow

on the scarred bedside table, he lowered his head into his hand.

"Oh, one more thing," she added. "Isaac, where's your bear?"

The boy had been sitting in a chair, quietly watching the scene unfold. At Rachel's question, he jumped up and ran to a corner of the room where he'd stashed his bear atop a small chest of drawers. He came back and handed the stuffed animal to her.

"At first I thought it was torn," she said. "Someone had sewn up the seam using the wrong color thread, and the stitches were coming apart. But it wasn't a tear. The entire seam had been carefully cut and sewn back together. Whoever did it, Shelley probably, but maybe Martin, used a contrasting color so they could find the seam easily."

Danny looked at her, puzzled and irritated. "What're you jabbering about?"

"This." She reached inside the bear and pulled out a computer disk.

Chapter 20

The moment her cousin parked the car, Rachel climbed out and stood on the curb, gazing at the small wood-frame house. A threadbare lawn adorned the front, along with a few scraggly bushes that looked pitifully under-nourished in the winter light. Not exactly a palace, but it had the requisite three bedrooms, and best of all, a large maple, whose thick branches would be perfect for a wooden swing. Set in the middle of a quiet, working-class neighborhood, the house would be safe and warm, a good shelter for Nick's family. Beneath her coat, she caressed the small mound of her belly and whispered, "What do you think, baby? Does it feel like home to you?"

The car door opened, and Isaac slid out to come stand beside her.

"Is it ours?" After weeks of living in other people's houses, including camping out in her one-bedroom apartment and numerous overnights at her aunt and uncle's, the thought of his own place obviously over-whelmed him.

She slipped her hand around his, her son now, thanks to family court. "It's ours."

"And I have my own room?"

"You have your own room."

"And we won't have to move again?"

She squeezed his hand. She'd been answering the same questions for days. "We won't have to move."

Chris came around from the driver's side. "You all right?" He put an arm around her shoulder.

She leaned her head against him and sighed. "I'm fine."

"Does it really have a sandbox in the back?" Isaac looked up at her, a spark of excitement behind the serious expression in his eyes.

She smiled. "Would I lie? Go ahead. Check it out." He stared at the house and then back at her.

She tousled his hair. He still had trouble leaving her. "All right, Uncle Chris and I will come, too." She lumbered over the lawn, her six months of pregnancy swelling the loose dress she wore below the coat.

Like the patch of grass in front of the house, the back-yard was small, the scrap of lawn made smaller by a rusted laundry rack and the promised sandbox. Isaac ran to the edge and dug in.

Chris looked around. He didn't say much, but then, he didn't have to. She could see the worry behind his eyes.

She put a hand on his arm. "It's fine, Chris."

"It's so . . . small."

"It's got everything we need. And it was affordable."

He shook his head. "I wish you would have let my parents help you out more."

"They did help. I wouldn't have been able to buy this without their help."

But even with her aunt and uncle's support, it had taken longer than she expected to find the right place at the right price. January was almost gone now. A few more months, and the baby would be here.

Nick's baby.

Familiar pain pinched her chest.

"Hello? Anyone home?" Aunt Julia waved as she tiptoed over the grass in her heels, holding onto a Toys "R" Us bag.

Rachel repressed the tiny irritation at her aunt's approach. If anyone asked, Rachel was quick to admit that Julia and Elliot had been wonderful. They'd offered to help in any way they could, in spite of the fact that Rachel hadn't been able to answer many of their questions. But just as it had been that first day back, Julia's overbright smile couldn't hide the bead of worry in her eyes.

She put her arm around Rachel's shoulder and squeezed. "How are you feeling?"

"I'm fine." As fine as anyone can be with a hole in her soul.

Her aunt stepped over to the sandbox and knelt beside Isaac. "And how are you doing, young man? Have you seen your room yet?"

He shook his head, eyeing the colorfully wrapped box she held out.

"Did you know that everyone who moves into a new house gets a housewarming gift? It's a rule."

Rachel clucked with mock disapproval. Every time Julia saw Isaac, she bought him something. "You're going to spoil him."

Isaac tore off the paper and pulled out a dump truck.

"For the sandbox," Julia said.

The gift brought a shy smile of pleasure to the boy's face, and with a pang, Rachel saw Nick looking out at her from his black eyes.

But if Julia saw the resemblance, she didn't say. She merely looked at Isaac critically. "Do you think I'm spoiling you?"

He shook his head vigorously, and they all laughed.

"Me neither," she confided. Rising, she turned to Rachel. "And if I am, I thought I'd make a party of it. I brought dinner, too. First night in your new home, you certainly don't want to cook. And there's something else."

Rachel rolled her eyes. "No more, please. You've been too generous already." This was true enough, as every month they sent Rachel a check so she didn't have to face going back to work yet. And her uncle's many legal contacts had made Isaac's adoption a smooth, easy process.

Ignoring Rachel's protest, Julia handed Chris her car keys. "It's in the trunk. Would you bring it in the house?"

While Chris went around to the front, Rachel unlocked the back door for the first time since the movers had left.

Inside, boxes littered the floor. Julia and Rachel took off their coats and laid them over the kitchen counter, then navigated through the mess into the front of the house, where Rachel opened the door for her cousin.

He came through it, swamped by a large, wooden something in his arms. He set the thing down in the middle of the living room, and Rachel saw that it was a cradle.

"I thought it was time I brought a gift for the baby," Julia said quietly. "Your grandmother gave it to me when Chris was born, and your mother used it for you. I . . . I hope you don't mind. Some women prefer new things for their children instead of hand-me-downs."

"Mind?" Rachel's heart squeezed. She ran her hand over the intricately carved wood, her throat tightening with emotion. Like a link in a chain, the cradle connected her to people she had loved and lost. She gripped the beautiful wooden headboard, swallowing hard. When she finally found her voice all she could manage to say was, "I'm honored. Thank you."

Her aunt smiled, tears in her eyes.

She loves me.

How could Rachel have missed that all these years?

She put her arms around Julia and hugged her. "Thank you, Aunt Julia. For everything."

After dinner, Julia and Chris helped unpack some of the boxes. They made a small dent in the task, staying until Isaac was asleep and Rachel yawned with fatigue.

"Time to go," Chris said, collecting his mother's purse and helping her on with her coat.

"I'll call you tomorrow," Julia said at the door.

Rachel squeezed her aunt's hand. "I'd like that."

Chris paused, looking as though he had something to say, but wasn't sure how to say it. "Look, Rachel—"

"What's up?" She hoped it wasn't another lecture on accepting help or taking care of herself.

He sighed. "I don't want to upset you, but that writer—Dana Gershon, the one who wanted to do a book on your father—well, she's been calling me. She still wants to talk to you. I've been stalling, but I can't stall forever. I have a feeling she'll find you eventually, with or without my help."

Rachel remembered Dana's offer to donate part of the profits from her book to the school at St. Anthony's. A rush of sorrow ran through her. She hadn't thought about her school or her bigger dreams for a long time. Too many other losses to think about.

"What do you want me to do?" Chris asked.

For some reason the thought of exploring her father's world wasn't as distasteful as it had been. After all, David Goodman was as much a part of her baby's legacy as the Bradshaw cradle. "I don't know. Let me think about it."

The next day, she drove out to Long Island and collected the boxes of her father's correspondence from the Bradshaws' attic.

There were five in all, and that night after Isaac was in bed, she opened the first box. Inside, she found a jumble of papers, notebooks, and manila envelopes. One letter snagged her attention immediately. It was addressed to Julia and written in her father's familiar loopy hand.

Thank you for the picture Rachel drew of the pond and the trees. I have it in a place of honor in my office, so I can look at it whenever I miss her.

He'd missed her? Rachel looked up, staring out over the mess of papers strewn over the living room floor. She remembered that picture. She'd asked her aunt to send it to him, but he never mentioned it. She thought Julia hadn't mailed it. Or if she had, that he didn't give a damn.

Heart racing, she read the letter again, and then once more. Had her father cared about her all this time? She set the letter in a separate pile, too afraid to hope, and picked up another letter with trembling hands.

Stomach in a knot, she scanned the page and came to another warm, loving reference to herself. It was the same with the one after that.

Tears welled, and she blinked them away so she could see. Barely pausing, she went through all five boxes and read countless letters to her aunt and uncle, countless times that her father had asked about her. By the time she finished the last box, her shoulders ached, her eyes were gritty, and it was time to wake Isaac for school. Smiling and weepy, she went to his room, hugging the knowledge of those letters to herself. Even if she hadn't been with her father, she had always been in his thoughts.

As Nick was always in hers. Staring down at the sleeping boy, she couldn't help but recall the man who'd fathered him. Isaac had slept through the night, a feat Nick would have been glad about. *He loved you, Isaac.* She'd never let him doubt it.

She drove Isaac to school and watched him stroll into the building, a miniature Nick walking away from her.

Normally she headed home after dropping him off, but this time she drove into the city. She hadn't wanted to know what had happened to Nick that awful day of the bombing, but now she waited hours at the precinct house until the detective in charge of Nick's case could see her. But when he finally appeared, stoop-shouldered and weary-eyed, he wasn't much help.

"Our investigation is still pending. I can't talk about it."

"You must have some ideas. It's been months now. Why were they in the car? Where were they going?"

He shuffled his feet and avoided looking at the small, round swell of her belly. "I wish I could help you, but we're still trying to put the pieces together."

Frustrated, she left the police and drove to the local office of the FBI, who were also investigating. This time, the agent in charge saw her right away. Crisp and professional in his dark suit and tie, he was equally unforthcoming.

"I understand your concern, but there's nothing I can tell you about Mr. Raine. My advice is to go home, have your baby, and try to forget all this. If anything should come up, someone will be in touch."

Someone was in touch. The next day, Danny Walsh rapped on her door. He'd barely stepped over the threshold when he grabbed her elbow and steered her onto the nearest seat.

Wagging a finger, he paced in front of her, his green eyes gleaming. "You must stop asking questions, Rachel. The only people who can answer them are dead."

She raised her chin, refusing to be bullied. "I have to know what happened. Why was Nick driving the car? Where was he going?"

He rubbed a hand through his thinning hair and didn't answer her questions either. "It isn't safe for you to chase after this. You can't be drawing attention to yourself. Do you think Nicky would want this? Putting yourself and the child in danger? I want your word now. No more talking to the police or FBI."

She made no guarantees, but after he was gone, she walked into the kitchen and, resting her hands on the growing mound of her baby, gazed through the window at the small backyard. It was a gray, dreary day. Outside, the branches on the maple stuck out stark and bare. The gloom outside echoed the emptiness inside her.

Once again, she heard Nick's voice. *I want to keep you away from that muck.*

And he had. She was safe now. Safe in her little house, safe from him. And now it was her turn to make sure his children were safe—even if it meant never really knowing what had happened to their father.

She leaned her head against the window. "You win," she whispered to Nick's ghost. "No more questions I can't answer."

But it felt like losing him all over again.

Two nights later, Danny Walsh watched a figure slip out the back of the military hospital and limp toward the car. Like a ghost, the man was between worlds—no longer what he used to be and not quite ready for what he would become. *Ghost* suited him, and that's the code name he'd been given by everyone who dealt with him. Even Danny had taken to calling him that, at least in his head.

Besides the moon, little brightness lit up the back of the building, but even in the dim light it was clear that the Ghost leaned heavily on a cane. Slowly he hobbled closer, and Danny saw the sheen of sweat filming his face. Danny leaned across the front seat and swung open the passenger door.

The Ghost settled in heavily, with a groan that sounded pain-filled, for all it was half repressed.

Danny sighed. "You didn't take your medicine again." A statement of the obvious rather than a question.

"That stuff turns my head into a cotton ball."

Danny turned on the ignition and began backing out. "I don't know another soul who's harder on himself."

A mixture of grit and amusement tilted the corners of the man's mouth. "Someone else I know once said the same thing."

Danny pulled around to the front of the building, then onto the road leaning toward the checkpoint that was the only exit. He kept the speed low, maneuvering the car carefully so he would jostle his passenger as little as possible.

"Your escape is beyond crazy, you know, and puts me in a touchy position. Your doctors will never forgive me, let alone your government. You could wreck the whole deal."

"I don't give a damn about the deal."

Danny couldn't keep the aggrieved tone out of his voice. "Well, it wasn't you who called in every favor on the books, was it now?"

"I'll try to make it up to you," the Ghost replied dryly.

Danny pursed his lips and raised a sandy eyebrow. "For someone who claims he's gotten over his death wish, you can be a damn reckless pain in the ass."

"Enough. I've heard the lectures already." He winced as the car went over a speed bump.

"She'll still be there in a month or two. By then you'll have finished testifying, your injuries will be better, and—"

"You should have told her."

Danny grumbled a curse below his breath. "You weren't there, boy-o. You didn't see how out of control she was. She insisted on seeing you. Loudly insisted, just like she's doing now. And that could've alerted certain parties and put your life—what little was left of it at the time, I grant you—and hers in danger. And I'm not telling you anything you don't already know, am I now?"

The passenger gave a curt headshake, indicating that he wasn't. "Still, you should have told her. You don't know what this will mean to her. I do."

Danny shook his head. What he should have done was kept his damn mouth shut this morning and let his friend go on believing that everyone knew about his survival.

Ahead of him, the gates loomed. Inside the guardhouse the soldier reached for a clipboard as the car lights swung toward him. Danny looked over at his passenger. His dark hair had been cropped short to allow the surgeons to get at the head wound. He sat unevenly, a result of the metal still embedded in his back, and his right leg stuck out at an agonizingly awkward angle.

Danny slowed the car to a stop. "One last chance to change your mind. It's a long drive to the island, and it may take a day or two to get her there. Sure you want to do this?"

Lines of pain etched the rugged face, now almost gaunt from its battle with death. "I'm sure."

"Your keepers will be mad as hell when they find out you escaped. Twelve hours was barely enough time to get the papers prepared, let alone cover your tracks. No guarantees I can keep them away."

"If I run into trouble, I'll handle it and leave your name out. Just get me there. And her."

He had one final card to play. "You're still taking a chance, you know."

The Ghost turned his head and shot Danny a disgusted look. "Nice try. You told me yourself there's been no buzz about me for weeks. And no doubts about my untimely demise. I'm doing this, Danny. Quit talking and go. The longer we sit here, the worse my damn leg's going to feel."

Another deep sigh escaped the Irishman. He started the car again and pulled up to the checkpoint. Muttering curses for all fools in love, he committed himself irrevocably by handing the guard the two sets of forged papers, his own and his passenger's.

The papers were perfect, so he didn't expect trouble, but still he tensed while the guard examined them. Then the soldier flashed a light inside the car, illuminating the empty backseat and the two men in front. It lingered on the man in the passenger seat, and for once, Danny wished the Ghost could live up to his code name and disappear. But he was real enough, and the guard's hard gaze swept over him, taking in every detail. Danny's hands began to sweat.

"Something wrong?" Outwardly calm, he grinned at the guard.

It seemed to take forever before the soldier responded. "Better buckle up," he said.

"Of course," Danny said quickly, sliding on his seat belt and helping his passenger do the same. The guard handed back the papers, checked something off on the clipboard, and stepped inside the guardhouse to activate the switch that lifted the barrier blocking the road.

Danny put the car in gear and drove off, breathing out relief. If the man beside him was equally relieved, he didn't say. He sat still, watching the road fly by in the darkness, an air of expectancy about him, as if holding his breath and waiting for his life to begin again. The thought troubled Danny, but when he glanced over, the Ghost's face looked more serene than it had in months.

"You're sure about the baby?"

Danny's brows shot up. It was the first time the Ghost had mentioned the baby since Danny had told the truth that morning. "Oh aye, I'm very sure."

The Ghost nodded, his taut face thoughtful. Then he leaned his head against the head rest, closed his eyes, and smiled.

When Danny called, Rachel was rereading her father's correspondence and trying to ignore the resurgence of grief created by giving up her search for information about Nick. But the minute she heard Danny mention the cabin, a lump of ice settled in her stomach. The last thing she wanted was to face those memories.

"It's hours away. I'll never get back in time to pick up Isaac."

"See if your aunt can pick him up."

"But why—"

"You said you wanted answers. I'll bring them to the cabin."

Her heart began to race. "What do you mean? Do you know why Nick was driving the limousine?"

"I'll tell you when you arrive."

"But—"

"At the cabin." He hung up.

She growled in frustration, but called Julia and made arrangements for her to pick up Isaac at school. Then she packed up the car and headed for the Jersey shore.

It was raining, a gray, drenching winter day. She drove carefully through the downpour, trying not to think about what waited at the end of the journey. In spite of the months that had elapsed since she'd traveled this road, the trip brought back every memory with gut-wrenching vividness. Every glance, every smile, every line in Nick's dark face was suddenly in the forefront of her mind.

God, she didn't want to remember.

But she did.

She remembered the open, hungry way he used to look at her. And later, the way his dark eyes lit when he kissed her. She remembered the feel of his body next to her. Inside her.

And the slow, hesitant approach to his son, how much he wanted Isaac to trust him, love him.

The road blurred ahead, and she pulled the car over, jabbing at her watery eyes. It was cruel of Danny to suggest this. Agony to face what she could never have again.

Just then the baby kicked. Rachel took in a sharp little breath, surprised by the wondrous, fluttery sensation.

Oh, Nick. She smiled, stroking the place where the baby poked her. Loving him may have brought pain, but it also brought joy, the greatest of which was right here beneath her fingers. Nick would have been proud of this baby. Proud of both his children. They were his family now, she and Isaac and the new baby. His story was their story, and she owed them all the truth, no matter how many painful memories she had to endure to get it. She turned the wheel and got back on the road.

When she arrived at the cabin, no car sat in front, and she assumed she'd arrived before Danny. She hoped the cabin had heat; it was even colder by the sea than at home. She got out of the car and, wrapping her coat around her, ran through the chilly rain to the door.

It wasn't locked, so she pushed it open and tumbled inside, shivering as she inhaled the familiar smell of ocean and mildew. At least it was warm; one of Danny's mysterious men must have already turned up the thermostat. Taking off her coat, she shook water from her hair, looking down while she dusted the drops from her braid.

Finished, she straightened and jumped when she saw the man in the bedroom doorway. "My God, you scared—"

And froze in her tracks.

Chapter 21

Nick watched Rachel come into the cabin. Every nerve ending was on fire; his shoulder, his leg, even his head throbbed, and that hadn't bothered him for weeks. He'd been here a day and a half and didn't know how much time he had before the Feds found him, but right now none of that mattered. Nothing mattered, not his hands, which were a sweaty mess, nor his heart, which drummed so hard he wouldn't have been surprised to see it erupt out of his chest.

Nothing mattered but the fact that she was here.

He couldn't speak. All he could do was drink in the sight of her. Her honey-brown hair, wrapped in the sweet, familiar braid, her penny-bright eyes. And God, that swell beneath the dress. *The baby.* His heart twisted. He had barely believed Danny about the baby. Now, he wanted to touch it, feel his child growing under her heart. But he tightened his hold on the cane, letting her absorb the sight of him. Just seeing him would be shock enough, let alone the changes.

"My God, oh my God." She breathed the words on a whisper.

Slowly, she floated across the room, her face a kaleidoscope of emotion. Terror, amazement, hope.

She raised her arm. Touched him.

A ripple of heat shuddered through him even though her hand shook and the feel of it on his face was a mixture of caution and fear, as if she wasn't sure he was real, but desperately wanted him to be.

"Is it you? Is it really you?"

His throat tightened. Softly he said, "It's me, Rachel." *What's left of me.*

Then with a cry, she was in his arms, laughing and crying and clinging to him. He wrapped himself around her, not caring that he had to give up the cane to do it, causing a hot stab of torment to shoot up his leg. He held her as if he'd never let her go, felt her tremble, felt the baby between them, laughed and half cried himself.

He found her mouth, sank into her kiss as though it were the breath of life itself. He held her face in his hands, felt the warmth of her lips, her tongue, ran his hands down her back and over the soft curve of her rear, pressing her in, feeling that body, so different now, yet so the same, against his.

And for an instant he felt as though he'd come home, as if he'd been adrift in a hurricane and found safe harbor at last. And he was so full, so grateful for this one sweet moment of happiness that he could hardly believe he had once wanted to die.

"I knew it! God, I knew you were alive!" She kissed

his eyes, his cheeks, his jaw, giggling through tears while she did it.

And then, as if she'd only just heard her own words, she stiffened in his arms. Slowly, she pulled back. The joy in her face seeped away, dissolving into something else. Something he'd been steeling himself for ever since Danny had told him the truth two days ago.

She slapped him.

"You goddamn bastard."

Then she burst into tears again.

He absorbed the slap, ignoring the fear that flashed up his spine and ended in his aching shoulder. *Get a grip. Concentrate.* No matter what she thought or said, no matter what she did, he wasn't going to let anything come between them again. But he didn't have much time.

He reached for her. "Rachel—"

"No, don't touch me. Oh, God. I mean, it's just—" She gulped, her voice quivery with tears. "All this time, all this time when I felt like my heart had been ripped out of me, all this goddamn time . . ."

After months of lying down, the strain of standing was suddenly taking its toll. Sweat slithered down his back, and he picked up the cane, bracing himself against the doorjamb to take some of the weight off his damaged leg.

"I'm sorry. If I'd known, believe me I would have spared you that. But I only found out the day before yesterday that you didn't know I'd survived."

She stared at him as if his words were so outrageous she couldn't comprehend them. "You didn't know . . ." Slowly, she retreated until the backs of her knees hit the couch and she collapsed into the sofa. "I don't understand. I don't understand any of this. You're here, alive . . ." She shook her head, tears welling again. "How? Why?"

A sharp wave of dizziness hit him, but he clutched the cane, his fingers biting into the rubber-coated handle to steady himself. "I promised, didn't I?"

He met her copper gaze, now as shiny with tears as it had been that night so many months ago. And he knew she was remembering the last time they'd seen each other, the last words they'd spoken.

He hadn't intended to keep that promise. He'd intended to die, but somehow he'd screwed that up. He leaned into the wall, trying to shore up his trembling body. Someone up there had a wicked sense of humor. Someone he'd be grateful to for the rest of his life.

"I wanted you to know . . ." Across the room, her face shimmered, and he blinked the sweat out of his eyes. What was it he wanted her to know? "I wanted . . ." He felt himself waver and gripped the cane so hard his knuckles turned white. "Didn't break . . ."

"Nick?" Her voice echoed, coming from a great distance.

Minute. Give me a minute.

He saw her stand, or thought he did. Heard another sound. His name? No, Nick wasn't his name anymore. *Don't fold.* He took a breath. He didn't seem to have any air in his lungs, but he tried to get the words out anyway. "Didn't break . . ." No good. He felt himself slipping, heard the words he'd been looking for in his head. *My promise.*

"Nick!"

Rachel rushed to the doorway and got there in time to prevent him from smashing his head on the way down. *Oh, God.*

Kneeling beside him, she saw him plainly for the first time, and not through a fog of shock or joy or anger. She traced the gash that cut through one black brow and eyed the mangled mess of his left ear. And his leg. She ran a hand down his thigh, remembering the beauty of it.

Oh, God, what had they done to him?

She eased his head onto her lap and glanced around the cabin, feeling helpless. He was big, and moving him would be hard, but she could do it if only she knew it wouldn't hurt him more.

Just as she was debating it, he groaned.

"Hush, Nick, hush." She brushed his forehead and the dark stubble of his hair. A ridge on the right side, just above his ear, indicated another scar. Her chest tightened as she realized why his hair had been buzzed off.

Another groan, and this time his eyes fluttered open. They seemed to focus and glaze and refocus on her. Then his hand moved, and she felt it on her face, wiping up the tears she hadn't even known were there.

"No more crying," he said softly.

She breathed out an ocean of air and nodded.

"Help me up."

She did the best she could, but he was so big and heavy. Twice he had to put weight on the injured leg. His jaw tightened but he said nothing, and she cringed, knowing the agony was there whether he admitted to it or not.

By the time she got him to the bed, dark circles stained his shirt under the arms and on his back. She propped him up against the pillows, then sat on the edge of the bed beside him, still trembling from the ordeal.

A bottle of pills lay on the nightstand. Painkillers. She picked them up. "When did you take the last one?"

Breathing heavily, he closed his eyes briefly, clearly exhausted. "I don't know. Day before yesterday, day before that."

Stupid man. "Let me get you some water."

She stood, and he grabbed her wrist, faster and stronger than she would have expected of a man in his condition. "No. I can't take them. Not yet." He tried to sit up higher in the bed, and the blood drained from his face as he swallowed another jolt of pain. "Not until we finish."

Worry sharpened her voice, and she snapped at him. "Why aren't you in a hospital?"

He sighed, shifted, and grimaced with the effort. "I was, up until a couple of days ago."

Astonishment mixed with the anger. "Your doctor released you like this?"

"Not exactly."

It was like pulling teeth. "Well, what did happen?"

"I left."

"Left?"

"Escaped."

She gave him a short disbelieving laugh. "Escaped? Where were you, in prison?"

"Sort of. I was being held in some kind of military facility near Washington. I don't even know which one."

His answer wiped the laugh off her face, and she stared at him. "What's going on, Nick? What happened to you?"

"Look, I don't have a lot of time. There's probably a bunch of guys in uniform trying to find me, and even if they don't, I don't know how much longer I'll be able to hold up. I can go through all this later. Right now I want to—"

"No. Tell me now."

For a moment, he looked at her, clearly eager to talk about something else. But she held his gaze, determined not to be put off. She had to know. Everything.

Then he sighed. "Danny made a deal with the Feds, and I broke it by coming here."

Danny. She'd forgotten about Danny. She was supposed to meet him . . .

She stiffened as the puzzle fell into place.

"He knew. My God, Danny knew you were alive." The enormity of the betrayal was so unbelievable, it forced her to her feet. "Why didn't he tell me? Why the hell—"

"He was trying to keep you safe, Rachel. You and Isaac. And me. The more noise you made about seeing me, the more dangerous things got. He figured if you thought I was dead, so would everyone else."

"I'll wring his neck."

"I hope not. He saved my life." And slowly, he told her how Danny Walsh had talked the government of the United States into letting Nicky Raine die.

"I was half dead already." He looked down at his leg. "My leg was crushed, my skull fractured. I was in a coma for longer than I want to think about, and then mostly flat on my back until two days ago. But somehow he talked them into keeping me under wraps in exchange for everything I knew about Rennie's operation and the black-market arms trade."

My God. "Okay, so maybe I won't wring his neck. Maybe I'll just break his legs."

His mouth twisted in a wry smile. "Maybe I'll help."

She smiled back at him, and for a minute it felt as though none of this had happened, not the bomb, the separation, the grief. Though the lines of his rugged face had deepened, his black eyes were sharp and hungry, and their expression sent a shaft of heat tearing through her. Tears pricked her eyes. He was alive. My God. Alive. She could hardly believe it.

"But how did you . . ." She shook her head, unable to find the words. "I saw the car . . . the bomb . . . how did you . . ."

"Survive?" He gave her a small, tight smile. "The Liberation Council wanted revenge for the loss of their arms shipment, and that meant hurting someone high up in Rennie's organization. So they designed the bomb to blow up the back of the car, where the important people usually sit. I was in front, driving, so the full force of it missed me."

She shuddered. He'd come so close. "I saw two people in the front."

"The other one was Frank. I'm told he survived the bomb, but never made it out of surgery."

"But . . . why were you driving? Why were you even in the car?"

Briefly he told her of his plan to lure Rennie out of his compound with a phony story about a copy of his printout.

"But you didn't know about the disk then."

"No." He shot her a rueful smile. "But it made sense that Martin would have a backup somewhere. Rennie would have had one. And he hadn't found Isaac's things. I told him it was hidden in his knapsack."

"And he believed you?"

"Not at first. But I stuck to my story. I knew he would check it out. He wouldn't take the risk."

"But once you got him in the car, where were you planning to take him if the disk didn't exist? And what were you going to do when you got there?"

He looked away, his expression remote. Something in his face told her this was the heart of the story, the hardest part to tell.

Squeezing his hand, she said gently, "It's all right, Nick, you know you can tell me anything."

His gaze swung to hers, his dark eyes bleak. "Not anything. Not this."

"Anything," she reassured him. "Where were you taking Rennie?"

"Nowhere." His jaw tightened, as if he were steeling himself for battle. "I was planning to drive the limo into the ocean."

"You were . . ." A shiver ran through her. "You were going to kill yourself?"

He threw her an acrid smile. "Well, I didn't think about it like that. I only knew I had to keep you and Isaac safe. The only way to do that was to see Rennie dead. I thought I'd better go along to make sure he stayed dead."

She stood abruptly, suddenly desperate to get away.

He snatched her arm again. "Where you going?"

Looking around blindly, she grasped at the first

excuse she could think of. "Into the kitchen to get you some water."

"I don't need water. Wait—dammit!"

Behind her, she heard him cursing and groaning, but she paid no attention. All she could think about was the fact that he'd been right. That was the one thing she didn't want to know.

Because he'd lied. He hadn't kept his promise at all. He had never intended to come back.

She found herself at the sink and turned on the faucet. The sound of the water drowned out the sound of whatever he was doing. She stared at the heavy stream splashing into the sink and relived that moment six months ago when he'd promised to return. A sick feeling clawed at her stomach, and she grabbed herself to keep from doubling over.

She didn't hear him loom up to her. It was only when he reached around and cut off the water that she realized he'd gotten out of bed and followed her.

She glowered at him. "Are you crazy? You shouldn't be up." He was sweating again, the moisture dampening the rim of his hair. "You should be in bed, in a hospital."

"I didn't have a choice," he said quietly, and she knew he wasn't referring to bed rest. "Nothing would have stopped Rennie short of hell. You know that."

She did know, but it didn't change anything. She had to get out of there. If she stayed, he'd only break her heart again.

She tried to step away, but he used the cane to block her path. "Where are you going?"

"Home. Isaac will be finished with school. I have to pick him up."

"Your aunt is picking him up."

She glared at him through angry tears. How did he know that? Oh, yes, Danny. His compatriot in conspiracy. She swiped at her traitorous eyes and slipped around his cane. "I have to go."

Somehow, he hobbled in front of her. One part of her knew that move must have hurt. The other part refused to care.

"You can go later. After we talk. Then if you want, I'll let you go anywhere. But first you have to listen to me."

His battered body stood in her way. He was thin, too thin. She could easily have evaded him but had the feeling he'd kill himself following her. And much as he wanted to die, she declined to be the cause again.

"What is there to say, Nick? We needed protecting, and you were willing to die to do it. I know that should make me eternally grateful, and it does." She smiled at him, the wave of pain that washed over her turning it into a rictus. "God, Nick, it does. It makes my heart turn over with love for you. But the thing is"—she swallowed, fighting through tears—"the thing is, I don't want a dead hero. Dying is easy, Nick. It's the living that's hard."

"I'm here, aren't I?"

"Yes, you are, and you know what's funny?" She laughed, sour and sharp. "If the car hadn't blown up, you wouldn't be. The only reason you're standing here is that car bomb. I guess we should send the Irish Liberation Council a thank-you, because if it had been up to you—"

"I did what I had to."

"I know. That's the kicker, isn't it?" She ran a hand

over the top of her head, trying to stop the sick rush of certainty that he'd had no choice. "And who knows, maybe you're right. Maybe choice is an illusion, and we're all backed into corners, doing what we have to do. I'm sure my father would have said the same thing. But if that's true, how do I know you won't make the same choice next week or next year?"

"Rachel—"

She shook her head, hugging herself. "I can't go through that again. I can't sit home day after day wondering when you'll come back or if you'll come back. I spent my childhood like that, I won't spend the rest of my life that way. And I couldn't take another loss." She rubbed her arms, chilled despite the cabin's stuffiness. "You don't know . . . you don't know what it was like. I thought . . . I thought I'd died myself."

"But you didn't." His face was fierce, his black eyes dark with intensity. "You're alive, and by some crazy miracle and Danny's help, so am I. And I love you." He pulled her roughly toward him, enveloping her in his embrace. "I love you, Rachel. I'm not going anywhere. I want to spend the rest of my life with you. With our children."

Stiff within the circle of his arms, she tried to stay numb to his words. It was the first time he'd mentioned Isaac or the baby, and her heart almost melted. She felt the child stir inside her as if saying, *Listen to him, trust him.* But what did an unborn child know about trust? Or about sticking when it was so much easier to bolt?

"I'm sorry. I just . . . can't do this." She untangled herself and headed for the door.

"Dammit, don't go!" He started after her, but his leg

gave way and he fell, clutching the counter at the last minute to keep himself from hitting the floor.

Her heart dropped to her toes, and she ran back to support him. "For God's sake, Nick."

He grit his teeth, cursing, and with massive effort, pulled himself upright.

"You should be in bed."

"Only . . . if you . . . come with me." He grinned, but she could see what it cost him.

She couldn't bear it. She couldn't stand watching the pain flit across his face while he tried to ignore it. "I'll come if you take one of your pills."

He shook his head, a sad smile on his face. "Can't. It'll put me to sleep . . . and how do I know you'll still . . . be here when I wake up?"

Slinging one of his arms around her shoulder, she helped him back to the bedroom. "You'll just have to trust me."

He snorted. "Then you'll . . . have to . . . do the same. Trust me."

She eased him onto the bed, a hard feat to accomplish without hurting him. But eventually he was propped against the pillows again. She went back to the kitchen and returned with a glass of water. Uncapping the medicine bottle, she shook out the pills and handed him one. She closed the bottle and saw the name printed on the label.

"Who's Adam Newman?"

His hand fisted around the tablet but he didn't bring it to his mouth. "Me."

"I don't understand."

He shut his eyes. His face looked gray. "It was part of

Danny's deal. He figured I'd always be a target unless the bomb did what it was supposed to do. So Nicky Raine died, and Adam Newman was born."

She stared at him, the endless complications of his life closing in on her like a trap. And like a hunted animal, she could see the trap in all its danger but was oddly fascinated by it. She rolled the name around in her head, trying it out. *Adam Newman.* Adam, the first man. And Newman. The significance of the name wasn't lost on her. A new man. New start. New life.

He latched onto her hand, tugging her down beside him. "I am a new man, Rachel."

But it was risky to believe; she removed her hand from his. "Take your pill."

"I told you, I'm expecting visitors."

"A few hours' sleep won't kill you." She glared until he put the medicine in his mouth. "Swallow." She tipped the glass against his mouth and forced him to gulp. He coughed and growled at her.

"Jesus Christ. You're worse than the nurses in the hospital."

"Someone ought to give them a lesson, then."

He sank back against the pillow, clearly irritated. "Look, these things go off like rockets. I only have a few minutes, and I don't want to spend them arguing." He patted the bed beside him. "Come here."

She backed away. "Not on your life."

He laughed, dry and mirthless. "I could lie and say I don't give a damn about your body, but the truth is, I couldn't do anything about it anyway. I'll be out cold in a few minutes. I'm not interested in you. Not yet." He watched her from the bed, his eyes as hard and ruthless as she'd ever seen them. "Don't make me get up and drag you here. I could do it, but it'd hurt like hell."

From the look on his face she didn't doubt it. She wished to hell she didn't care if he killed himself, but the bitter truth was, she did.

"I'll stay until you fall asleep," she said begrudgingly.

"Fine."

Keeping a cautious eye on him, she walked to the far side of the bed and lay down.

"Roll away any farther, and you'll fall off," he said drily.

"You wanted me here. I'm here."

"Christ." He shifted a bit closer, and she closed her eyes against the wince of pain the movement caused. "You make it goddamn hard for a father to be near his kid." And then to her utter amazement, he put a hand on the baby.

Her gaze flew to his, and instinctively she covered his hand with her own.

His mouth curved in amusement. "I told you I didn't want to jump your bones." He smiled softly. "But I'm dying of curiosity about this."

He pressed his fingers against her belly, and emotion tightened the back of her throat. She couldn't speak, couldn't move. She felt the heat of his hand beneath hers, their fingers intertwined above their growing child. It was the moment she'd craved, the moment she'd wanted ever since she realized she was carrying his child. A moment she thought she'd never have.

"When Danny told me about the baby . . . I don't know, I thought he was kidding. A great big joke on the dead man." He stroked the circumference of her abdomen, slow and gentle, as if needing to experience every inch of her. "But he wasn't joking." His voice blew soft, reverent. "God, you're so beautiful. Are you all right? Is the baby all right?"

She had to clear her throat before she could talk. "We're fine. Healthy. Perfectly fine."

"You have everything you need? Doctors, medicines, whatever? I've got money. A lot of money. I'll give you anything you want."

"I don't need anything." *Except you.*

He closed his eyes. She could see him drifting, but he kept his hand on her. "You can leave if you want, you can try to cut me out of your life, but I swear I'll find you. I'm not letting another kid of mine grow up without me."

A tear leaked quietly, but thank God, he wasn't looking.

His voice grew softer, dreamy. "Danny and the Feds, they called me the Ghost. It was my code name. Big secret. Wasn't supposed to know." His breathing slowed more, grew deeper and even. His words started to slur. "But I'm not . . . a ghost . . . not anymore. I'm Adam . . . the first man . . . new man. Adam . . . Newman."

Silence. She stared up at the ceiling, tears falling sideways down her face onto the bed. God, what should she do? She couldn't think with his hand on her like that, claiming her, his heat warming them both, her and the child. She had to get up, get away.

She rose, thinking he'd fallen asleep, but he murmured something, something so soft and low she had to lean over to hear it. "Could have . . . stayed away. You'd . . . never . . . known the difference."

She stilled, her heart racing.

Looking down at him, she suddenly saw what she hadn't seen before. Not Nick, not her dark, doomed love who had chosen death and gotten his wish, but Adam, the man who had crawled out of a hospital bed and escaped an army to come back to her. The man who could have kept Danny's secret and stayed away forever. The man who'd come back, wounded and half dead.

She slipped out of bed. He was sleeping deeply now, and she ran a hand gently over his shorn head.

He'd come back. When he didn't have to. He'd come back.

Running outside to the car, she found her cell phone and punched in the emergency number Danny had given her long ago.

It took the Irishman five hours to get an ambulance there. Nick was just waking up when the medics arrived. Groggy, he eyed the government agent, who stood overseeing the two soldiers assembling a portable gurney. "Someone call in the marines?"

One of the medics nodded over to Rachel, who stood at the foot of the bed. "Your girlfriend."

Nick absorbed that information without flinching, but turned hard eyes on her. "So much for trust."

She flushed. "You need to be in a hospital, Nick."

He nodded, his face a sardonic mask. "And you're the girl who's gonna put me there."

The other medic intervened. "Not until we put you on this gurney."

He moved toward the bed, but Nick fought him off. It wasn't much of a fight, not against two large, healthy soldiers.

"What are you doing? Don't hurt him." Rachel pushed herself between Nick and his adversaries, who quickly had him restrained and groaning in pain. "Leave him alone. Get away." She shoved at them, and they backed off, holding up hands in surrender; no one wanted to battle a pregnant woman.

But seeing Nick's truculent attitude, the agent pulled out a gun and a pair of handcuffs.

"No!" Rachel faced him, shielding Nick's body with her own. "No guns. And I was promised he wouldn't be cuffed. He's going back voluntarily, on his own."

"The hell I am."

The two men glared at each other while the medics stood with powerful arms crossed, waiting.

"Five minutes," she asked the Suit. "Give me five minutes alone with him."

A reluctant nod, and the three men left, closing the door behind them.

Nick turned on her, his face a brewing storm. "I told you, I'm not going anywhere. My kids aren't growing up without me."

"You have obligations, Nick. To yourself and to some very important people who want to hear what you have to say."

"I don't care about any damn—"

"I do." She put his hand on the mound of the baby. "I want you strong and healthy so you can help our baby come into the world. I want you free to prove I wasn't wrong to believe in you. You need to go back to the hospital. You need to get well."

"And then what—you disappear over the horizon?"

"I'll be waiting. Anywhere you want me to be."

He watched her out of narrowed eyes. "Why should I believe you?"

"Because you trust me. And because I'm trusting you. I love you. You came back when you didn't have to, so I'm gambling on that love." She drilled him with a look. "But if you wind up dead again, all bets are off. So—" She stuck out her hand. "Do we have a deal?"

He studied her closely, thinking it over. Then a slow grin spread over his face, and he slipped his hand into hers. "Deal," he said, and tightened his grip before she could pull away. "I know I said I wasn't up to jumping you, but I don't see why in hell you can't jump me." And the next thing she knew, he'd tugged her on top of him till she straddled him. "I've been dreaming about this for months." And he kissed her.

It was deep and long, and full of promise. She shivered at the touch of his lips, lost in sensations she never thought she'd feel again. His mouth mesmerized her, seduced her, made her forget. She opened herself to him and he came inside, his tongue soft and warm, possessing her lips and every other part of her. His wild hands combed her hair, skated over her back, under her dress, and rubbed hot, so hot on her belly. Beneath her, the ridge of his erection seared through her panties. The feel of his hard, remembered length spiraled her higher and higher, so she arced and sizzled with every electric touch.

"Rachel. God, I love you."

Everything was wet. Mouth, tongue, her dress where he washed the nipples on her breast right through the material. She groaned against his mouth and rubbed herself over him. His hands on her hips held her steady while she clung to him, desperate to reclaim everything they had lost. He kissed her and rocked her and she felt him beneath her, through their clothes, every move an exquisite agony. And the feeling blossomed and grew, billowing out and enveloping her with heat and power until she couldn't stop it, and with a cry that he swallowed with his mouth, she shattered.

And then she collapsed, sobbing against him.

"Shh." He held her, stroking her. "It's all right. Everything's going to be all right now."

"I thought I'd never . . . God, never feel you again . . ." She wrapped her arms around him, holding onto him like precious cargo.

"I know. Shh." He kissed her cheeks and her forehead. "Don't think about it. It's over."

A rap on the door interrupted them. "What's going on in there?"

He kissed her softly. "Should we tell him?"

She gave him a don't-you-dare look, wiping her eyes with the heels of her hand. "Just a minute!"

Hastily, she straightened her clothes and ran to open the door. Her face heated as the agent, looking suspicious, checked the room. His eyes lingered on Nick, and Rachel only hoped her face didn't give too much away.

"He's . . . he's ready now."

With a snap of his wrist, the agent signaled to the medics, who transferred Nick to the gurney. In ten seconds, he was out the door, Rachel running after them.

"Wait! Wait a fucking minute! She's pregnant, for crissakes." He reached up and grabbed one of the medics by the front of his shirt to slow him down.

The soldier pulled the material out of Nick's hand.

"Relax, pal. We'll let you say good-bye." They stopped at the open doors of the van, and Rachel caught up.

She grabbed his hand, holding on to him with everything she had. "I don't want you to go."

He kissed the back of her hand. "It's all right. We have a deal, remember? And don't forget our date in a couple of months." He rubbed her belly.

She smiled, laughing through tears that seemed to come all too easily, whether she was miserable or happy. God, pregnant women were a messy lot. "Three months. You have three months, and then I'm afraid I'll have to go without you."

"You do, and I'll hunt you down." He pulled her toward him and kissed her hard.

Then the medics swung him into the ambulance and closed the doors. She heard the slam, as final as any she'd heard her whole life. Another car taking away another man she loved.

But as she watched the taillights fade into the distance, she knew this time was different.

Because this man would be coming back.

Adam

Rachel stood on the Carolina shore and let the November breeze caress her face. She thought she'd never be able to face the tide again, but now that the government had relocated them nearby, she found its rhythms peaceful. Funny what time could do. How it dulled the edge of pain.

Isaac squealed as the waves chased him back, and she smiled at him. His small dark face, so like Nick in coloring, blazed with excitement as he ran toward the ocean again, daring it to catch him.

He'd adjusted well to their new home. And to the new last name and the new relationships in his life. Father, sister. So many changes for a little boy to absorb.

So many changes for her as well. The new bond with her aunt and uncle remained strong, and she'd spent the last three months of her pregnancy helping Dana Gershon with her book on David Goodman. The work had brought Rachel close to her father at a time when she needed all her family around her. Now the first draft was almost done; preliminary chapters had sent the publisher into paroxysms of praise. They'd predicted a big hit, which meant money for her institute.

She strolled along the water's edge, inhaling the sharp, fresh scent. She was almost ready to start thinking about that money. And her work.

Although it was nearly winter, the day was surprisingly warm. The sun shone bright in a pale blue sky, and she raised her face, closing her eyes to absorb the heat. When she opened them again, Isaac was waving to someone in the distance. She turned away from the hypnotic spell of the sea to watch the figure who stood on the deck overlooking the beach.

Adam Newman waved back. His stiff leg ached, and he massaged it, leaning against the railing to take some of the weight off. As he braced his forearm against the wood, the dull sheen of a wedding band stared back at him from the third finger of his left hand.

At his feet, Nicole sat in her carrier, kicking and babbling up to the sun. As always, disbelief coursed through him when he looked at her. That new life could spring out of all that death . . . It was nothing short of a miracle, a rainbow after a terrible storm.

He heard a distant shout and turned back to the water. His wife and son danced in and out of the tide. Warmth blossomed inside as he watched them, grateful beyond words for the new life they shared.

As for the rest, he was learning to live with it. Though he remembered nothing of the explosion, the nameless boy from the alley in Panama still haunted him. But now when he bolted awake at night, sweating and icy cold with fear, knowing bone-deep that nothing he did could entirely atone for the past, Rachel's warm body comforted him.

Isaac still dreamed, too. But when he screamed into the darkness, Adam huddled with him. Night after night they came together, the dreams a terrible bond, but a bond nonetheless. And while they waited together for the light, or for sleep, to claim them once more, the boy grew to trust him.

Him. Adam.

The bomb had burned away his old self, leaving the rest bare and stark, but pure. Strong. He felt the goodness inside him now—a small spark, but burning brighter every day. He could never compensate for what he'd done; nothing could bring back the dead. But he could do his part to ease the suffering of the living.

He watched Rachel sweep up Isaac's hand and felt the safety-deposit-box key inside his pocket. For the first time since he'd put it away seven years ago, he was thankful for all that money. Not for himself, but for all the nameless kids in all the alleys who ever needed help. Someday soon, Rachel would want her school back, and he was going to give it to her. She didn't know it yet, but he'd already established an endowment to get it started.

Now he watched Isaac run toward him, while Rachel tried in vain to catch up. They had all lost a lot. But they had much, so very much, to be grateful for.

Isaac and Rachel pounded up the steps, stopping breathless in front of him.

"I won!" Isaac cried.

"You didn't have to carry this." Rachel handed him a pail full of driftwood and broken shells.

"I would have won anyway," Isaac insisted, "wouldn't I?" He turned to his father for support.

Adam smiled. "Yeah, Ike, I think you would have."

"Well, the prize for winning is dinner." Rachel laughed, and stooped down to smile at Nicole. "I'll bet you're hungry, too!" She lifted the baby out of her seat and clucked at her in that high, silly voice adults always use with infants.

"Hey," Isaac cried, "she smiled!" And everyone had to have a turn trying to make her smile again.

As Rachel played with the baby, Adam watched the wind play with her braid. Short wisps of honey-brown hair danced around her face. He brushed them back, thankful to the center of his being for her love. And her trust.

Now she leaned into his hand, rubbing against him like a cat. "If you want to eat this Thanksgiving, we'd better go in. The turkey's done, but there's still potatoes to mash."

Isaac raced ahead, leaving the pail just outside the door. Rachel waited for Adam to take up his cane, matching her steps to his slow, uneven gait.

A newspaper sat on a chair just inside the door. He threw it onto the couch, barely glancing at it. For months now, he'd been watching the papers for some sign that his information had started an in-depth investigation of the arms trade. He'd been bled dry by every bureaucrat and Pentagon flunky in Washington; Rennie's organization and the whole black-market arms industry had been picked clean. The disk Rachel had given Danny had been a big help, too.

A lot of what he'd divulged had been potentially

explosive, but the powerful protect their own. So far, nothing had come of any of it.

Only one news item had caught his attention in the year since Nick Raine had died—a small story on the second page of the local section that Rachel had saved for Isaac in case he ever wanted to know what had happened to his mother. She'd shown it to Adam over the summer, and with the sound of children playing in the background, he'd sat on the wooden swing he'd built for the backyard maple tree and read about the arrest of one Harris Mape for the vehicular homicide of Shelley Spier. An alcoholic with seventy-eight DUIs to his name, Mape had been driving without a license, blind drunk, the night he ran down Shelley.

So Rennie hadn't killed his wife after all.

But of course, he had. Shelley wouldn't have been caught in the path of a drunken madman if she hadn't been running from Rennie.

All during that long July afternoon, Adam had sat in the swing, staring off into the distance, trying to come to terms with the truth, and his own responsibility for it. Toward evening, Rachel had come outside to stand behind him. He could still feel the comforting weight of her hand on his shoulder, as if her touch could absorb his lingering guilt over not helping Shelley.

"You're helping her now," Rachel had said. "Isaac is safe from Rennie, and that's what she wanted."

A burst of laughter brought him back to the present. He saw that Isaac had gone into the bathroom, and under cover of washing his hands and face was making an unholy mess.

"Someone better get in there and supervise," Rachel

said, with a pointed look that clearly said that "someone" was him.

She handed him the baby and went into the kitchen while he hobbled into the bathroom.

"Hey, Ike, what are you doing in here?" He gave his son a mock frown.

"Cleaning up." Isaac grinned, and the sight made Adam's throat tighten. The smiles came more easily now; still, every one was a precious gift.

"Looks like you're doing a better job making a mess than cleaning up."

The boy giggled. "I know."

He helped Isaac dry his hands, and in the process Adam caught a glimpse of his face in the mirror over the sink. For the thousandth time, he wondered why Rachel wanted to tie herself to a stiff-legged, scarred-up hulk.

It doesn't matter why. It only matters that she does.

While the gravy simmered and the potatoes bubbled on top of the stove, Rachel set the table. It stood in front of the big bay window of the beach house they'd rented for the weekend. She laid out the plates and the silverware and watched the ocean moving ceaselessly over the shore. Over and over the tide took away the land, then gave it back.

She had lost Nick and found him again. Been loved and abandoned and loved again. Would she ever understand why? Would she ever truly understand the miracle that had kept them all alive, and in the end given Nick back to them?

No more than she could understand the tide. She could only trust that it would continue. That whatever love she lost would be returned. Reshaped into something unexpected, perhaps, reformed and renamed, but returned nevertheless.

When everything was ready, they put the baby in her high chair. Adam and Isaac sat down, and Rachel brought out the turkey on a big platter. Isaac's eyes bulged at the size of it, and Rachel laughed at his expression as she set the plate down.

Adam smiled at Isaac, too, but it was an odd smile, tinged with awe.

Rachel understood that look. It was an expression of surprise and profound gratitude, as if every tiny moment of happiness was an unexpected blessing.

Sitting down, she found her husband's hand and slipped her other around her son's. In turn, Isaac reached over and held onto Nicole. Adam put a finger into his daughter's other hand, and as always, she curled her own around it.

For a few brief moments they sat quietly, all four of them holding hands as if in prayer, framed by the window and the silver gray sea.

Then Adam picked up the knife Rachel had laid at his plate and began to carve the bird.

About the Author

A native New Yorker, Annie Solomon has been dreaming up stories since she was ten. After a twelve-year career in advertising, where she rose to Vice President and Head Writer at a mid-size agency, she abandoned the air conditioners, furnaces, and heat pumps of her professional life for her first love—romance. An avid knitter, she now lives in Nashville with her husband and daughter.

More

Annie Solomon!

❧

Please turn this page

for a preview of

DEAD RINGER

available soon.

1

"Baby, oh baby, oh baby."

Like a hot breeze, a hoot of laughter drifted across the night-lit airfield as Finn Carver descended from the charter plane.

The man with the laugh crossed his arms and leaned against the car parked on the edge of the Memphis tarmac. The runway lights illuminated his linebacker frame, marine buzz-cut, and habitual boyish grin. "My, my, my, don't you look good."

But Finn was in no mood for teasing. "Cut the crap, Jack." He pitched his briefcase and overnight bag to Jack Saunders and tried to ignore the gleam in the younger man's eyes as he snagged the luggage while making a big production out of admiring Finn's tuxedo.

"Yessir." Jack gave a long, low wolf whistle. "The storm troopers have definitely arrived."

Finn eyed Jack's baggy Hawaiian shirt, worn untucked over a pair of rumpled khakis. "I wouldn't talk. You could take a few fashion lessons yourself."

Jack shrugged off the criticism the way he always did. "Yeah, but then I'd lose the thing that makes me so . . . so me."

Behind them, the pilot hurried into the hangar, leaving Finn and Jack alone on the empty tarmac. It was past midnight, and the heavy delta air crawled beneath the collar of Finn's white dress shirt. But heat wasn't the only thing making him sweat.

He scowled, crushing that thought. Nothing on earth would put him on the run, least of all a woman. But he wrenched off his black jacket anyway and tossed it in the back of the car before folding himself into the passenger seat.

"Come on, Jack," Finn called to the other man out of the still open car door. "It's not like the bad guys are going to wait while you get your rocks off ragging me."

Jack slammed the door shut and stowed Finn's bag and briefcase in the trunk. Moments later, he slid behind the wheel. "I gather you want to skip the 'how are you's?"

"Just brief me."

Jack shook his head and started the car. "Someday you're going to learn to slow down and say hello."

"Jack—"

"Just trying to save your life here, buddy. You saved mine."

"I didn't—"

"You gotta learn to loosen up. You don't want to keel over from a heart attack before you're forty, do you?"

"Jack . . ." He could give the younger man a heart attack himself and his voice clearly said so.

Jack only grinned at the threatening tone.

Jesus, the guy was worse than a puppy. Nothing you did put him off.

But Jack finally held up his hands in surrender. "Okay, I get it. Work, work, work. So here's the deal." Suddenly he was all business. "I drop you off, then take your stuff to the motel. Pick up your key at the desk. Here's the address." He fished a business card from his shirt pocket and handed it to Finn. "I stashed a cop at the house to keep an eye on things. I'll leave the car there and catch a ride back with him." He reached into the glove compartment. "Here," he said. "Credit cards, driver's license, social security card. Welcome back, Agent Carver."

Finn shuffled through the identification, saw his own name printed on everything, and replaced the cards he'd been carrying in his wallet for the past six days. He let out a tense breath and leaned back against the headrest. It was good to be clean for once. Twelve hours ago he'd been unshaven, scouring dockside bars and lowlife coffee shops for even the slightest hint of where the package he'd been hunting might land. All he'd unearthed were the same rumors they'd been hearing for weeks. Something big, powerful, and nuclear was going on the market but no one knew where or when.

Then Roper had contacted him. They'd found the girl.

Finn had grabbed a fast haircut, a tux, and boarded the charter almost before he'd had time to breathe. And now here he was, about to resurrect a ghost.

"You're sure this is her?" Finn asked.

"People told me you had a problem with trust," Jack said in a mock mournful voice, "but I didn't want to believe it." He reached for a manila envelope imprisoned by the visor in front of him, flipped it into Finn's lap, and started the engine.

As the car pulled away from the hangar, Finn slipped out the surveillance pictures inside and swore softly.

"What'd I tell you?" Jack said. "It's her."

"Now this is hard to believe."

"The eyes don't lie."

Finn nodded thoughtfully. No, they didn't, but pictures did. He'd have to see for himself. "Where is she?"

"At Beamer's digs. Partying. Hence the party clothes." Jack nodded toward Finn and the tuxedo he wore.

"I thought Beamer just died."

"A week ago." Jack gave a cynical snort. "But everyone handles grief in their own special way."

Finn slipped into silence, thinking about the woman in the pictures. He didn't know much about her, but what he knew was keeping his palms slick, even in the air-conditioned car. His record was piss-poor when it came to working with women, especially this kind. Third-rate "actress," second-rate country singer, first-rate gold digger.

Everyone had their talents. And clearly men were hers. Old men. With lots of money. Lucky for him that was exactly the skill he needed right now.

Yeah, real lucky.

"Beamer was what," Finn said, scanning the report enclosed in the envelope, "soulmate number four?"

"And counting," Jack replied. "She chews 'em up and spits 'em out. Can't help but admire her, though. At least she's well paid."

"Those extra bucks are going to come in handy since Uncle Sam doesn't pay top dollar."

"That's assuming she'll do it."

"Oh, she'll do it. She's been hunting her momma for years. And with Beamer out of the picture, her free ride's gone."

"She's vulnerable," Jack said, egging him on. "Probably lonely, afraid—"

"Exactly. Just ripe for the picking."

Jack shook his head. "Jesus, you're a cold bastard."

Not cold enough, if his sweaty hands were proof. "It's a cold world, Jack, and we're the ones keeping it from getting colder. I do what it takes to get the job done."

Twenty minutes later Jack headed up a long winding drive that led to a large estate overlooking the Mississippi River. The house was old and dignified, or it had been. Right now lights blazed out the windows like cut-rate diamonds, and raunchy, bass-heavy music pounded so loudly through the front door Finn could hear it outside.

His pulse notched up, pushed by a big fat slice of déjà vu. Scanning the grounds, he checked the perimeter and picked out Jack's cop, who was dressed as a uniformed valet.

At a nod, he came to the driver's side. Jack rolled down the window and murmured softly, "Everything okay?"

The cop knelt to window level. "Party's still going

strong. The other valet tells me it'll rage for hours yet." He eyed Finn curiously. "This him?"

Before Jack could reply, Finn got out of the car. "Thanks for keeping an eye on things. We'll take it from here."

"No problem," the cop said as he rose. "Anytime you need a little extra coverage on the lady, I'm your man."

"Why's that?" Coolly, Finn regarded the other man over the car roof; he didn't like the blasé attitude. "Easy night?"

The other man laughed. "Shit, no. Boring as hell, but oh so easy on the eyes." He came toward Finn on a slow lope. "You ever see her?"

Finn got his jacket out of the back and put it on. "Just pictures."

The cop gave Finn another measuring look. "Heard a rumor they were sending in some hotshot under-cover guy. If it's you, you're in for a real treat, pal. But I got some advice." He leaned in close, grinned, and stabbed Finn with a finger. "Make sure you hold on to your zipper."

Angelina Mercer stood in a corner of Arthur Beamer's large, luxurious living room and watched the party swirl around her. Because of the June heat and the crush of people, the air-conditioning was set at arctic, and she was cold.

Don't blame it on the air, party girl.

She shivered. Truth was she'd been cold for a week. Ever since she found Arthur Beamer, crumpled on the floor, dead from a massive stroke. Tears pricked her eyes but she blinked them away. God, she missed the old man.

She looked around at the drunken bodies crowded into Beamer's house. The party was exactly as he'd specified; loud, crowded, and full of booze. He would have loved the send-off.

Too bad it wasn't doing much for her. She looked down at the vodka in her hand. She should be drunk; she needed to be drunk.

Trouble was, she didn't feel like drinking tonight.

Darling girl, she heard Beamer's crusty voice say in her head. *Life is too short for the mopes.*

The familiar phrase sent the corners of her mouth upward. It was the first time in a week she'd had the urge to smile.

Suddenly she felt the old man frowning down on her from wherever the hell he was now. More than anything, she wanted to wipe away that frown and put the mischievous smile back on his eighty-year-old face.

The hell with the mopes.

The hell with death and loss and moving on. This party was for Beamer, and she'd be damned if she'd disappoint him. She raised her glass heavenward.

Here's to you, old man. She tossed back half her drink and plunged into the crowd.

Finn stepped inside the house and grimaced at the full force of the sound. Trash music. Trashy as the woman throwing this wake.

Tuxedos and gowns swarmed over the plush interior. He pushed his way past the laughing group gathered under the hallway's vaulted ceiling. Screaming to be heard over the noise, the party-goers paid no attention to him. Balloons and streamers lay in disarray. He stepped over them, pushed some away. That peculiar been-here-done-that feeling grew stronger as a cold wind swirled around him. Someone handed him a drink, but he set it down. He needed a clear head tonight.

The crowd thickened as he moved inward. Black satin over white brocade. Well-fed men standing in clusters around marble sculptures. Wraith-thin women draped over expensive furniture. A few turned his way with an interested eye, but he ignored them. He knew all about those women.

Just as he knew all about the other glassy-eyed faces he maneuvered past. Faces with too much liquor and too much money. Recognizable, though he didn't know a single one.

A burst of laughter came at him from the sidelines, sharp as a gunshot. Oh, yeah, he'd been here before. Somewhere someone was coking up, dropping ecstasy or whatever designer drug was the trend of the hour. There was sex here, too. In the coatroom, the closet, in furtive corners, people mating like rats in a dark alley. And somewhere there was betrayal. Not his own this time, but it was here, he could smell it. The knowledge rose up like a sickness, the haze of booze and smoke sliding over his shoulders like a coat he hadn't worn in a long while.

And then he saw her.

A banner that read BYE-BYE BEAMER spanned the living-room entrance. Inside the room, the furniture had been pushed back, a baby grand stuffed into a corner to make room for the horde. Suddenly, the crowd parted and there she was, the hair looser, the clothes outrageous, the face younger. But the resemblance was unmistakable.

A shaft of something almost like fear pierced him quick and sharp. Deep down he'd been hoping the pictures had been deceptive, that Roper and Jack and everyone else had gotten it wrong.

But, they hadn't.

She held a drink in one hand, and her lithe body undulated in an impromptu belly dance while a ring of men clapped and cheered her on. Thick blond hair fell in voluptuous waves around her face and shoulders. A clingy white skirt, shimmery with silver thread, hugged the curve of her hips and exposed the top of her navel. Although it reached her ankles and the knife-sharp heels she wore, the skirt was slashed open to the top of her shapely thigh. Encased in a skimpy, sequined halter, her full breasts shone white and shiny as her skirt. Between the two, bare skin gleamed tan and supple, and exquisitely tempting.

Your mouth's watering, Carver.

No, it isn't.

He leaned into the living room's arched entrance and watched Angelina Mercer work the room. Her long, tanned leg swung sinuously in and out of the opening in her skirt. Her smooth arms wove above her head, her hips gyrated, her eyes glittered with the challenge, *come get me if you dare.* He'd bet that every male in the room felt something move in his shorts.

Including him.

The cop's parting words echoed in Finn's head, but he dismissed them.

Get a grip. You know what she is.

Yeah, only too well.

A final guitar chord screamed, and she upended her drink, downing every drop. "Here's to Beamer!"

Her crowd of admirers cheered. "To Beamer!"

Ample breasts rising and falling in breathlessness, she headed out of the male circle, skin glistening with exertion.

"More!" The crowd took up the cry, stamping their feet in time with the chant. "More, more, more!"

"You know what they say about too much of a good thing," she shouted over the blare of the next song. With a laugh, she threw herself at one of the men and gave him a loud smooch on the mouth. "Get drunk everyone!"

And she whooshed out of the circle toward Finn.

He lounged against the arch, making no overt move to catch her attention. She'd notice him soon enough. Much as he didn't want to, he'd make sure of it.

Then the man she'd just kissed pulled her roughly back into his arms, and the problem of meeting her took care of itself.

She laughed and tried to squirm away, but the drunk had her fast. "Come on, baby, let's have a little more of that."

"Let go of me." Rising panic edged her voice and Finn pushed himself off the entry. He strolled toward the struggling couple and casually placed an arm around the drunk, looking for all the world like his best friend. Except Finn tightened his grip, squeezing so hard, the drunk gasped in pain and dropped his hold on Angelina.

Finn smiled. "You may want more, but the lady's had enough." Before the guy could react, Finn spun him around until the drunk staggered dizzily and faced the center of the room. "Back to the party, pal."

He gave the man a gentle shove, and he disappeared into the crowd.

Then Finn turned to the woman, who raised an amused eyebrow at him. "Well, well, Sir Galahad. Nicely done."

A cool one. Good. For what he wanted she would need to be cool. He could almost admire her if she hadn't also teetered toward him, the liquor showing.

"Thank you." She extended her hand in a graceful arc, as though he should kiss it. Something on her left shoulder caught his attention—an odd-shaped beauty mark or tattoo—but before he could examine it, she levered herself closer and he found himself staring into a pair of ice-green eyes.

That's right, Angelina. Come to papa. "Not Galahad," he said.

"Robin Hood?" She poked him playfully in the chest with one long, slim, manicured finger. "Whoever you are, I don't know you." Her breasts brushed his arm, her perfume coiled around him, and the blood went straight to his groin.

Silently, he cursed his own weakness and winked at her. "Sure you do."

"Friend of Beamer's?"

"I knew him, yeah."

She appraised him, a shrewd expression on her face. "No. I don't think you did."

He smiled. "Friend of a friend."

She grinned back; she had his number now. "*You* are a party crasher."

He didn't deny it. "What's a party without a few uninvited . . . friends?"

She dropped an arm lazily over his shoulder and

looked up at him. Her hip grazed his. Unwanted heat seared him. Everything he'd been afraid of since Roper told him about her came screaming back, but he forced himself to stand still and ignore the sweat starting at the back of his neck where her arm lay like a cool steel trap.

She smiled, her lips promising worlds. "Do you have a name . . . friend?"

A moment ago, he would have sworn her eyes looked bright, but up close the green was tinged with sadness. Weary eyes. Old eyes.

Where had he seen eyes like that before?

He said, "Finn."

"Fin?" She threw him the "that's weird" look he always got when he introduced himself.

"Yeah, Finn. Like in shark."

She laughed, throwing her head back. "Well, *Fin*," she said, giving his name mock emphasis, "sharks like to swim around in the cool and the wet, and you're all dry." She held up her empty glass, swirling the ice. "Me, too."

She told him what she was drinking and he went to find her a refill.

When he returned, she was gone.

Figures.

But chasing her was part of the game.

He found her outside on the deck where thick summer air drenched him in the overripe smell of damp soil and honeysuckle. A wooden railing surrounded the space on three sides and she was standing on it, leaning against the home's outer wall. Hands behind her back, face to the stars, she'd closed her eyes as if absorbing the moonlight.

Thirty feet below, the Mississippi River lay shrouded in woods and darkness, and the only thing separating her from the abyss was six inches of railing.

"Why don't you come down and join me?" All he needed was to have her break her cheap, beautiful neck.

"Where's my drink?"

He handed the glass to her, and she swallowed a third of the contents, laughing as some spilled down the side of her mouth. A ripple of distaste ran through him, but he kept it off his face while she wiped her chin with the back of her wrist and gazed down at him with excited eyes. "Why don't *you* join *me*, Mr. Sharkman?"

"Because someone needs to catch you when you fall."

"I won't fall." To prove it, she stepped away from the wall and began to pace the railing like a tightrope walker.

Jesus Christ.

Honed to stilettos, her four-inch heels barely found purchase. "See? Graceful as a cat." She giggled and almost lost her balance.

"Watch out!" He jumped toward her, but she righted herself, laughing.

"Nervous? Didn't know sharks had nerves."

Eyes fixed on her, he paced the length of the railing, following her high-wire dance.

When she reached the middle, she raised her arms wide and cried out to the night. "Halloo, Beamer!" She cocked her head, but no answer came. "Do you think he's out there, doing the rumba in heaven? God, but that old man loved to dance."

"Did he?" He watched closely. Was she wobbling?

"Poor Beamer." Her voice caught. *Tears?* He would have thought her incapable of it.

To prove his point, she laughed again, shouting into the chasm below. "Did you hear that, Beamer, you old coot? Poor you!" She giggled and wavered again. "Whoops." Her arms pinwheeled.

Fear spiked; he'd had enough. Fastening one hand on the back of her halter, he pulled her toward him. Her drink went flying and she landed with a thump in his arms.

"Hey . . . what' d you do that for?"

"You want to kill yourself, do it on someone else's watch."

She twined her arms around his neck and smiled lazily up at him. "You're the only one who would have missed me."

"What about all your 'friends' in there?" He nodded back toward the party inside.

"All party crashers. Like you, Sharkman." She snuggled up against him.

He tensed, trying not to like the feel of her bare midriff beneath his fingers. Or the curve of her hip or the view down the front of her tiny halter. She wiggled, settling in.

"Mmm, I like sharks." Her eyes closed, then opened again. "Big, black-haired sharks . . ." Her head drifted onto his shoulder. ". . . with ocean eyes, and sharp, cruel mouths."

He looked down; she was asleep. And suddenly he knew why the party smelled familiar and where he'd seen that sick-and-tired look he'd observed in her eyes.

His wife.